CAROLYN STEEDMAN was born in 1947 and grew up in South London. She studied history at the University of Sussex and Newnham College, Cambridge from 1965–72 and, after leaving university, became a primary school teacher, a job she did for eight years. She is also a social historian, and her book *Policing the Victorian Community* will be published in 1983. In 1982 she began working on a language project at the Institute of Education in London, and also developed her interest in the relation-ship between mothers and daughters in working-class households. She divides her time between Leamington Spa and London, and is working in her spare time on a biography of Rachel and Margaret Macmillan.

Three eight-year-old working class girls write a story, about the house they will live in one day, the streets of their decaying urban estate, about love and motherhood and the pattern of life they expect to inherit one day. In *The Tidy House*, the author analyses this fascinating document, and looks too at the history of children's writing, children's relationships with adults, as well as literature, theories of education and linguistics to come to her highly original and controversial conclusions on how children confront the way things are and the way they might be.

THE
TIDY HOUSE

LITTLE GIRLS WRITING

CAROLYN STEEDMAN

Virago

Published in Great Britain by VIRAGO PRESS Limited,
Ely House, 37 Dover Street, London W1X 4HS.

Designed by Geoff Green

British Library Cataloguing in Publication Data
Steedman, Carolyn
  The tidy house.
  1. Girls—Socioeconomic status
  I. Title
  305.2′34   HQ792.G7
  ISBN 0-86068-321-4
  ISBN 0-86068-326-5 Pbk

Typeset by Colset Pty Ltd and printed in Great Britain by
The Anchor Press, Tiptree, Essex

CONTENTS

ACKNOWLEDGEMENTS

I would like to thank the Humanities Research Center of the University of Texas at Austin, and Mrs A.H.B. Coleridge for permission to quote from the journals of Mary Elizabeth Coleridge, Florence Lind Coleridge and Sara Coleridge; the Houghton Library for Rare Manuscripts of Harvard University for permission to quote from the Alcott family papers; the Armstrong Browning Library of Baylor University, Waco, Texas, for permission to quote from the papers of Elizabeth Barrett Browning; the Henry W. and Albert A. Berg Collection of the New York Public Library, Astor, Lenox and Tilden Foundation for permission to quote from the Moulton Barrett family papers. I am grateful to the archivists of the Cheshire Record Office and Lord Stanley of Alderney, Nottinghamshire Record Office, and the Archive Repositories of the West Sussex Council and Lord Egremont for their permission to quote from the Journal of Catherine Stanley, the Journal of Mary Georgiana Wilkinson, and the Diary of Constance Primrose, respectively.

The Harland Howard song 'No Charge' which is quoted on p. 127 was recorded by J.J. Barrie in 1976 on the Chopper label, © EMI Music Publishing Ltd, 1976, and is reproduced with their kind permission. A great many people have talked to me about 'The Tidy House' – the children's story, and my manuscript – and I am grateful for the insights and information they have provided. I would like to thank Henrietta Dombey, Christine McCarney, John Churcher, Karen Clarke, the Women's Studies Seminar of the University of Texas at Austin, the Humanities Research Center staff and Elizabeth Warnock Fernea, Sabre Weber, Standish Meacham, also of UT at Austin, and Simon Frith. Some of the material in this book appeared in *Feminist Review* and *Screen Education*; I am grateful for the help and advice of their editorial collectives. To those who read *The Tidy House* as well as talking to me about it – Cathy Urwin, Ursula Owen and Mark Steedman – my especial thanks.

This book is for Carla, Lindie and Melissa, and all the children in their class.

She had been playing houses . . . and tiring of it was walking rather aimlessly . . . when it suddenly flashed into her
mind that she was *she*

> [Richard Hughes, *A High Wind*
> *in Jamaica*]

Mrs Wix gave a sidelong look. She still had room for
wonder at what Maisie knew.

> [Henry James, *What Maisie*
> *Knew*]

INTRODUCTION

In the summer of 1976, three working-class eight-year-old girls, Melissa, Carla and Lindie, wrote a story about romantic love, marriage and sexual relations, the desire of mothers for children and their resentment of them, and the means by which those children are brought up to inhabit a social world.

This book, which takes its title from the children's narrative, offers an account of their story, and suggests what interpretations we, as adults, can make of it. Their story, which is structured around two opposing views of child-care held by their two central female characters, served the children as investigation of the ideas and beliefs by which they themselves were being brought up, and their text can serve us too in this way.

The children wrote their story during one July week of a summer term and the draft they made during that week was kept, as were the typed and edited versions that were bound and displayed at the time for classroom use.[1] On the Wednesday of the week in which the children wrote, a tape recorder ran almost continuously on their table[2] and there exists some four hours of recorded conversation which illuminates the process of the children's collaboration, but which also, as largely undirected, spontaneous talk between three working-class little girls, is important in its own right, as evidence of their beliefs about love, sex, marriage, birth, motherhood and the process of their own socialisation. Indeed, these topics of their conversation are the major themes of 'The Tidy House'; their discussion of them provides both a commentary on their written narrative and one means of interpreting it.[3]

Those who read this book may find in it an unaccountable absence. It describes, and is a commentary on, an extended, collaborative story written by three little girls in a primary school classroom. But schools and

1

classrooms are rarely mentioned in the following pages – though the classroom is undeniably *there*, in the day-long noise of twenty-two eight- and nine-year-olds that forms the graphically unrepresented background to the transcribed tape recordings of Appendix 1. This introduction, then, is for explaining briefly those points that are not dealt with in the book as a whole: 'The Tidy House' was written in a school and I was the teacher of the children who wrote it.

What follows at the end of this introduction is an account of the children's social environment and a description of the particular pedagogy of the particular classroom in which they found themselves; but in spite of this description I do not really think it is possible to write about primary schools and being a teacher within them. I feel that even in the relatively plain account below the voice will be misheard, and that I will mis-leadingly appear to move as confidently as the science teacher at the beginning of Margaret Drabble's *Jerusalem the Golden*, among the arcane yet domestic tools of my noble craft.[4] It is in any case difficult to explain to outsiders what an unfamiliar job of work is like, but teaching occupies a special position when it comes to such descriptions, for it is at once concerned with what everyone has experience of – childhood – and what to many is an <u>unfamiliar category of human being</u> – children. People who work behind bars and nurses have this same access to the daily comedy, life's tragedy, because, like teachers, they work in a situation where human emotion, need, and conflict must be adjusted to the ordered pattern of a job of work. There is a common assumption that those who do such work have the casual public right to talk about what people – children – are *really* like and what *really* motivates them. To people unfamiliar with children (or in some cases, because of familiarity), primary school teaching seems a job at once menial and awe-inspiring, and teachers are allowed to present their view of life, the human comedy, as a true and neutral description of the way things really are.[5] Secondary schools, on the other hand, belong to the general structure of social and political analysis. Their intentions and purposes are linked with the labour market and with institutions of higher education, by virtue of the exam system they operate, by the education of the teachers within them and by the age of their pupils.

Quite simply, most reasonably well-informed people do not know what happens in primary schools, or, if they do, do not know what political and social theories uphold practice within them. This absence of a general understanding of the primary school is a kind of reflexive analogy of the history of education, which operates outside general historical inquiry, and of pedagogy, which is strangely divorced from the psychology, linguistics and sociology on which it is based.

Within a vast educational literature there is a substantial number of treatises that deal with the failure of the primary school to make connections with the lives of working-class children, its failure to teach them even halfway adequately, its success in deferring hope, breaking promises, spoiling lives and making children stupid. Sustained and passionate attacks on this destruction of young children's lives like *Death at an Early Age* and *The Way It Spozed To Be*[6] arise out of a set of historical circumstances in the USA that are not directly mirrored in our own, here on the other side of the Atlantic. These books, and many others like them, are generally concerned with the fate of black children in the American school system. There is a common vocabulary of social analysis in the USA which admits of racism as a structuring factor of social life. But in Britain there is no similar, everyday, laconic understanding that here it is class attitudes (within which racism finds its expression) that shape the quiet, genteel and sentimental oppression of working-class children in many of our primary schools.[7] It is possible that what propels the discrete repression of ability in working-class children in some primary schools is the class background of their teachers[8] – and their gender. This point is raised again in this introduction. We need to know a great deal more than we do at present about the ramifications of class and gender in primary schools and what the implications for children within them are.

Attendance at a primary school and the common pattern of life within them measure out a vast communality of social experience. It is probable that more children experience primary schooling than they do being mothered by a natural parent or growing up in a nuclear family; yet our conventional methods of psychological and social analysis do not really take this into account. Because of this absence of primary schooling from general social analysis, it is difficult to assess what it is that happens to working-class girls during their early school years and difficult to make sense of the contradiction implied in their superior early academic performance when compared with that of little boys.[9]

Primary school classrooms ask from children attention, the capacity to listen, a large degree of patience, and a sensitivity to human needs. Girls between four and eleven have usually had these virtues inculcated with a greater degree of firmness than have little boys and their experience is superficially confirmed in the classroom in a way denied their brothers. To say this is not to deny the deleterious effect of little girls eternally being told to sit down and be quiet, their obedience counted on as the linchpin of classroom discipline and organisation, of always being the ones who wash the paintbrushes and stay behind to help clear up and who never get asked to move the desks and who can't play football (though boys are taught to sew), of always, always, being praised for being good, kind, thoughtful little girls. The primary school celebrates the qualities that bind women; but this celebration does not put little girls at an *educational* disadvantage. In fact, as any confirmation of the known self-will, it actually aids the learning process.[10]

It is possible to argue that some little girls' situation of primary emergency, as far as their schooling is concerned, is due to the fact that they are working class, not that they are female, and that the situation of emergency is one that they share to some extent with working-class little boys. This distinction between situations of primary and secondary emergency is Andrea Dworkin's, and she explains it in *Woman Hating* by offering the example of a Jewish woman on her way to a concentration camp, whose fate may be made more hideous than it already is by the fact of being female, but who is going to die because she is Jewish. In this case, her being a woman is her situation of secondary emergency.[11] The example appears extravagant only because it is English primary school children who are under discussion here. The distinction itself is an extremely useful one and by keeping it in mind a great many issues in the education of girls can be clarified; for the children who wrote 'The Tidy House' were poor and working class and were thus the subjects of a particular educational history and of a current climate of educational theory and assumption.

A deep and hopeless sentimentality about the educability of working-class children has been fostered among teachers during the last decade, by reactions to the falsely rumoured failure of Headstart in the USA,[12] to the end of the compensatory education boom in this country, and by the dissemination of shabby theories of social, linguistic and cultural deprivation. All these factors have occasionally served to couch in liberal and publicly acceptable terms the idea that many working-class children can be made happy and kept occupied in school, but that only on rare occasions can their performance be improved.

This sentimentality runs deep and has a longer history than the last ten years. Teachers are the particular professional inheritors of a history of psychology that tells them that intelligence is largely innate and that education can do little more than keep children moving in their allotted ranks. Many teachers, of course, have refused to accept such an inheritance; but to mention it is to indicate the vague and undocumented place where academic and scientific ideas become translated into the prosaic assumptions of a job of work. The developments that have taken place over the last century in teachers' ideas and beliefs about the abilities of working-class children measure out the unwritten underside of the history of intelligence testing, its links with medical surveying and its propulsion by the tenets of evolutionary biology. The history of intelligence testing in this country has recently been written in full.[13] What is far less explored is the effect that this history has had on children in primary classrooms and on their teachers. It is almost impossible for a teacher to look at a room full of children and not to see them in some way as being stretched out along some curve of ability, some measuring up to and exceeding the average, some falling behind. This is the historical inheritance we operate with, whether we do so consciously or not, and it has become a matter of 'common sense' and common observation rather than a matter of theory to know as a teacher that children of class IV and V parents are going to perform relatively badly compared with children of higher socio-economic groups. It is difficult to discuss these matters in primary schools because the word 'class' is somehow felt to be rude, and to call children 'working class' somehow insulting.

Arguments about inheritance and environment, about innate general intelligence and about assessment, undergo a sea-change as they enter the place they are meant to describe, that is, a classroom full of children. The essential point is that they cease to be arguments at all, and become rather a tool of the trade, a dimension of the job, a way of seeing. Teaching is an example of a work situation that preserves in its organisational hierarchy the division between those who evolve theories and map out schemata for operation and those who do the work, but who are also expected to be minor and admiring partners in the theoretical process. Other examples of this kind of work are nursing and policing, where the passive absorption of large-scale theoretical constructs (those of medicine and the law) is deemed to be necessary for operation on the ward and on the street.

The tradition of assessment and testing in schools provides, as has been suggested, an accessible and convenient way of seeing large groups of children and understanding the differences between them. Psychometric testing was inspired by evolutionary biology and within that tradition was designed to show the mental differences between individuals, rather than the actual capacities of individual children.[14] Its concern with the inheritance of characteristics and the innateness of abilities dictated that the differences between male and female were, and are, considered less important than the differences between mixed populations of children, their status defined by performance, not by sex.[15] Within our school system psychometric testing came to be used in the early part of the century to predict the educational performance of large groups of children. What teachers know as a result of this history, and as a matter of 'common sense', is that, in general, ability groupings turn out in practice to make rough and comprehensible matches with social class divisions.

In the everyday working world of the primary school, there is another tradition within educational psychology that seems to confirm the class differences that the history of mental testing underlines. The tradition of child study and of analytic child psychology diverged from the psychometric approach quite early in this century. The split can be seen in almost allegorical terms, with Piaget sitting down in Binet's Parisian laboratory in 1921 to standardise Burt's reasoning tests for French-speaking children and coming to the conclusion that the thought that lay behind the particular errors that children made on these tests outlined a more fruitful field of operation than did placing them on a scale according to the sheer number of mistakes they made.[16] Individual child study has always played a role in the psychological training of teachers, but the two traditions rest in uneasy alliance in schools, the uneasiness compounded by the implications of the classic works of child study, which suggest that once the watching is over and the child's behaviour or thought assimilated into a general theoretical scheme, there is little left for a teacher to actually *do*.[17] The common-sense solution to the contradictions between these two theoretical approaches arrived at by many teachers of working-class children who are not learning very well is to conclude that although the errors of the middle-class children, who are the traditional subjects of child study, are interesting and revelatory of the learning process, nevertheless, for 'our lot', here in a Social Priority school, labelling the disability is more appropriate.

The educational and social vulnerability experienced by many working-class children during their schooling is also one dimension of an adult job of work. It is, quite simply, depressing to teach and to produce so little change in the educational performance of many children. As a context to this sense of personal ineffectiveness is a set of extremely common social attitudes that bestows the qualities of martyrdom and stupidity on women who, like nurses and teachers, earn money by taking what are seen as natural skills into the market-place.[18] Teachers in primary schools frequently feel hard done by, and rightly so, for the primary school day means hard work, and salaries and promotional opportunities are smaller and fewer than in secondary schools. They frequently feel stupid too, for the hierarchical structure of our system of higher education certainly lets them know that they are themselves in possession of an inferior education.

There is a substantial literature that documents the reaction of teachers to the depression of hope – theirs and the children's – that is frequently the result of teaching in working-class areas. The American documents of radical anger mentioned at the beginning of this introduction were written, without exception, by men. I have thought of this as I have wept in the ladies' lavatory and *not said anything* in the staffroom, and as I have lain awake at night contemplating all the mild and genteel methods by which working-class children are led to see – out of what kind and painful necessity it is done! – that, really, they aren't very clever, really, can never be like their teachers' own children at home or the celestial children who occupy the suburban schools on the other side of the river. I have thought about the men who wrote those books, rehearsed their denunciations, as I have wondered how to deal with the fact that the perpetrators of our mild English horrors are mainly women, like me.

For women, however, there is the possibility of the romantic solution. Primary school classrooms are usually private places, rows of tidy houses strung along a corridor and a terrible intimacy grows there, six hours a day, eleven months a year. The clatter of the children may retreat, the room becomes a momentarily silent place, as if in a tank of water all the little fishes are strangely looking in from outside and there flashes the sudden, quick perception of oneself as a lonely, misunderstood martyr. The literature provides for this feminine romance,[19] and school systems rarely discourage the eccentric, convinced, hard-working saint and martyr, for her labour comes cheap and lack of promotion is really what she expects. But it is clearly not a feasible solution for anyone who belongs to a trade union, has taken industrial action or talked to other workers about the difficulties of the job. It places, as well, enormous burdens on the children who have to share their room with a lonely saint.

As teachers, then, we may either consciously or unconsciously operate with, or try to deny, the theories of intelligence and average attainment that are our inheritance; and our inheritance may become a chosen field of battle. But these theories and beliefs are not restricted to schools. It seems that they have entered into the general consciousness and that, as pervasive and largely undiscussed social mythology, they are a most effective method of social policing. But we do not know how the idea of innate intelligence was arrived at as a popularly accepted social theory. More particularly, we do not know how so many working-class parents have been made to concur in the extraordinary belief that schools cannot be expected to do as much for their children as those of the middle class.[20]

The question of the primary school lies at the very base of our culture and our politics and, until political and historical theories admit both the experience of childhood and the experience of schooling, then I do not think it is possible to write about primary schools without being misunderstood. The important thing is to take the school and childhood out of the empty wastes of the history of education and enter them into history, to explore the social beliefs that support schools not from their vantage point, nor from that of education, but as artefacts of our culture. This, then, is not a book about schools. It is about little girls and their mediation and manipulation of a culture in written words. However, in the absence of any common description of the school and the experience of all our children within them, a contradiction will remain: it was a school system that made Carla, Melissa and Lindie (however inadequately) literate. Their story, the subject of this book, was written in a school and no other institution in our society could have brought about the communality of its making, nor the insight into the operation of our culture that its words help us perceive.

The school in which Melissa, Carla and Lindie wrote 'The Tidy House' was a Social Priority school, one of those legacies of the Educational Priority Area boom of the 1960s where, according to the position of a catchment area on a checklist of multiple deprivation (parents unemployed, number of unsupported parents, state of local housing, number of physically and mentally handicapped children etc.), schools receive an increased capitation allowance for each child and teachers are paid a small allowance which is added to their salary.[21] At the beginning of 1980 there were some 21,000 maintained primary and secondary schools in England. Just over 3,000 of these were designated Social Priority schools.[22]

By many external indices, then, the children who wrote the story that is the subject of this book came from a background of material deprivation. They had, like all the children in their class and many thousands of others, to deal with the tension, conflict and anxiety that are the attendants of poverty. It has been observed many times before that children in such circumstances have to deal with problems that would floor many twice their age and that attempts on their part to cope with these difficulties do not merely mirror the complexities of the adult life that surrounds them, but are rather a measure of the way in which the exigencies of general social life become their own and a dominant factor in the growth of their sense of self.[23]

I do not know to what extent a more specific account of their environment may be useful for an interpretation of their story. The setting of their school and their story was a 1930s' housing estate on the outskirts of a town. Like many such estates round the country it was built then as part of a programme of slum clearance.[24] Under varying policies of local government the estate had been used from time to time as a dump for 'problem families' from a very wide geographical area. As such estates go, it is a relatively stable and homogeneous community and repeats in some streets the patterns of neighbourhood that were removed from closely packed lanes of Victorian cottages fifty years ago.[25] However, the estate did not enjoy a good reputation in the town, and the local press frequently reported cases of disorderly conduct, drunkenness, fraud, vandalism and family violence by its inhabitants. An essential and important feature of life on this estate was that the majority of dwellings was composed of houses, not bungalows or flats. The tidy house was a real representation of the children's homes.

In the last weeks of a summer term there is frequently a specific concern added to the general anxiety of many children in working-class primary schools: they do not know what is going to happen to them in September. It is the policy in some schools not to tell the children which class they will be in next year, nor which teacher will be theirs, until the last day of term. This evasion is meant to prevent trouble with parents and children objecting to the choice made for them. So when Lindie asked me which class the three of them were going to be in next year (TH tapes: p. 170) and I replied, 'I really don't know,' I was, quite simply, lying. There was, then, within the school and in this particular classroom, a sense of dislocation, of change, a feeling that things were coming to an end. The children knew as well that I was to leave permanently in a couple of weeks' time, to move to another part of the country.

By July 1976 the children and I had been together six hours a day for eleven months. The timetable under which we operated meant that the children were only absent from the classroom when some of them went swimming and when the whole class had a music lesson. The class was a small one (one of the benefits of attending and working in a Social Priority school) and though it started off with twenty-seven in it, the numbers had dropped to twenty-two by the beginning of the spring term.

Many English primary schools offer their teachers a generous and liberal freedom to do what they will within the confines of their own classroom (occasionally and cynically presented as 'Shut the door, keep them quiet and you can do pretty much what you like') and, as the story 'The Tidy House' was the product of a particular place and time, it is probably worth describing the pedagogy that may have had some influence on its formal structure, that is, on its use of dialogue, its presentation of character and the construction of its plot. I think that the means by which the children came to work collaboratively ought to be indicated, for it was not just a matter of choice and free association, but was quite deliberately designed by me (though I never anticipated the production of 'The Tidy House').

In the children's classroom I operated what is in the jargon called the 'modified integrated day':[26] each week or ten days I prepared a programme of work for each child in the class, which was designed to help them with individual difficulties, to extend and elaborate work presented in class and group lessons and to prepare for the introduction of new topics and themes. Each child's programme was written up on a large piece of squared paper; when children had completed pieces of work, returned the workcard, science equipment, paints, tape recorder, or whatever they had needed to their place, they coloured in the appropriate square opposite their name.

In the particular jargon of this particular classroom, this was called 'your own work' ('Go and wash that paint palette, Sharon, and then you can do a bit of your own work'), and it occupied the children for perhaps two and a half hours each day. It was not a method of instruction, but a means of preparation, consolidation, revision and practice. It was a way of engineering the space available and the activity of the children, a way of getting things done. It was possible to group children together to work and to direct them by this means to any activity. In the second week of July two of Melissa's and Carla's squares read 'Write a story', and an arrow linked this message to 'Paint a picture'.

It was a method of organisation that also allowed for flexibility (I

10

was able to accommodate a researcher with a tape recorder for a whole day and let 'your own work' extend beyond a couple of hours). However, far more important than this was the fact that this arrangement allowed the children to be in charge of the small physical world of the classroom. They knew where things were kept, could get out and put away equipment, did not have to ask for a rubber, a piece of lined paper, some ultramarine powder paint, a B2 pencil, a hand-lens, a headphone set. Such a method of classroom organisation enables children to rely not only on their teacher, but on each other for advice, support, information and comment.[27]

The children were read to a great deal: 'The Tidy House' was the end product of a long exposure to a particular type of literature and to the idea of authorship. Though I read a wide variety of material to the children the most common type was probably the folk-fairy-tale. I used Jacobs's *English Fairy Tales*, but, far more frequently than that volume, Amabel Williams Ellis's *Fairy Tales from the British Isles*.[28] The feature of this collection is its presentation of conversation as the dynamic point of human relationships. Fairy-tales do in any case promote the perception of the magic word, the act that makes things happen; but the Williams Ellis collection is unusual in that the settings are prosaic, the people ordinary (not often princesses and queens, but 'girls', 'stepmothers', little old men and little old women), and that what they say to each other changes the world. I think that not only the structure of the folk-fairy-tale, but more importantly the narrative technique of this collection, had a certain effect on all the writing produced by this class. Its influence is discussed again in Chapters 4 and 6.

The children were familiar with the idea of authorship and the production of books. In a cupboard there were pieces of paper, wallpaper cut to the correct size to make covers, needles and thread and a long-arm stapler. The children knew how to make a book out of these materials, design a title page, make a list of contents. By the end of the year they had produced many. (All the examples of contemporary children's writing in the following pages are taken from the corpus produced by this class.) Often, though not always, I typed out their stories and non-fiction books and made their volumes for them. I emphasised that there was a difference between the content of writing and its formal presentation; or, rather, I often said that in a first draft they did not need to worry about spelling, or capital letters and full stops. All that could be dealt with later, when the final copy was made.

All this is, I think, useful background information for an interpretation of 'The Tidy House', though very little of it is mentioned again in the main body of this book. It is important, though, to make one clear statement that is echoed throughout the following pages. The children who wrote 'The Tidy House' and the rest of their class were in no way exceptional children – how could they be? The circumstances of their social life had worked against the comfort and confidence that can help provide good school performance. There was time spent in care, child guidance for enuresis, notes in the files about battering, to measure out the lives of sad depressed little girls, violent aggressive little boys: they were, many of them, poor readers, bad spellers. The writing they produced, though vastly revealing to us of child development under conditions of poverty, is only extraordinary in what it demonstrates of children's involvement in the process of their own socialisation.

It is extremely important not to confuse our appreciation and understanding of their text with their consciousness and motivation. The three girls wrote the story because they were expected to and because they enjoyed doing it. They did not *set out* to reveal what we may come to see as the message of 'The Tidy House'. In this adult sense, they were *not* motivated to convey something to an audience by use of the written word. We can, I think, with perfect propriety, set the children to one side and examine their text for evidence of the huge mythologies of love and sex that inform our culture and of the way in which working-class girls become working-class women, just as we might watch children's play and find it revelatory. But it would be a grave mistake to *involve* children in our discoveries and theories and to impute to them the desire to please us in this way.

This book is divided into three parts. The first part includes a long introductory essay which precedes a transcript of the children's story. They together form the first part of this book. Chapter 1, 'At the Door of the Tidy House', is itself divided into four sections. The first describes the narrative of 'The Tidy House' and the children's composition of it. The second outlines ways of reading the children's story in the light of current theories about child language. The third section indicates some of the uses that can be made of the children's story in an investigation of childhood socialisation and working-class culture. The last part of this chapter deals with the use the children made of their own writing.

In Part Two of this book, the reader is asked to leave the tidy house and to consider the history of the publication of children's writing, theories of language development and the strange absence of writing from such theories and the history of working-class girlhood. Chapters 3, 4 and 5 are in this way an elaboration of the themes introduced in Chapter 1. After a considerable absence, Part Three returns the reader, with new insights and new information, to the children who wrote 'The Tidy House', and in particular to the child Carla, whose particular narrative it was in the first place.

The appendices are composed of the tape recordings that accompanied one day of the children's composition and a facsimile of 'The Tidy House' (which also appears in transcript at the end of Part One).

The children's story – both the transcription and the facsimile – and the taped conversation of Appendix 1 are reproduced in this book as the pieces of primary evidence on which its argument rest. This means in fact that they do not have to be read in the chronological order of their presentation – do not in fact, have to be read at all, only referred to, as is constantly done throughout these pages. However, some readers may prefer to read the transcribed tape recordings when they have finished reading Part One.

PART ONE

Because . . . children's stories deal in the main part with the normative conflicts that are part and parcel of socialisation within this culture, they are also primitive statements of the prevailing mythologies of this culture. According to some authorities, this is where mythologies are born. They develop out of narrative. We like to think therefore, that in collecting children's stories, we are dealing with the underbelly of living mythology.

[Brian Sutton-Smith, 'The Importance of the Story Taker', *Urban Review*, 8:2 (Summer 1975), pp. 85–95]

1

AT THE
DOOR OF THE TIDY HOUSE

THE NARRATIVE

It was a very hot summer, the summer of 1976. The doors and windows of the classroom stood open to the acres of stained cement houses stretching to the parched hills up behind the rubbish tip. The clatter of the girls' platform soles measured out the time as they moved about the classroom; the heavy air divided us, as it heightened sudden sounds and movements. It is sound and movement that form memories of that week, as well as the pieces of paper, the drawings, the words that trickle like sand from the tape recorder now. I have carried evidence from that week around, preserved it, as if it bore the seeds of a new life, a way of explaining, a means of understanding. Yet the story that Lindie, Melissa and Carla produced during that hot July week, 'The Tidy House', is difficult material to interpret, partly because it is so totally without guile. There are no dragons for translation here, no princess sits weeping in her high tower, enchantment is not employed. The tidy house is the house that the three children will live in one day; their characters walk to the shops and the nursery school through the streets of the children's own decaying urban housing estate. The children that Carla, Lindie and Melissa created in 'The Tidy House' (a uniformly irritating, maddening crew) are at once the children they know they will have and how their own parents think them to be. The dialogue of the story, out of which the narrative is mainly constructed, acts as a cold and assessing eye cast upon a set of emotional and social circumstances. In 'The Tidy House' no one is forgiven.

The story was written in collaboration. The children listened to each other's reading of portions of the text, adjusted their own contributions in that light and produced a story written by three people and not just a collection of linked narratives. Different versions of the same scene were produced on three occasions. This does not necessarily demonstrate a lack of control over their narrative structure, but rather their deep interest in the subject matter of these scenes.[1] A great deal of their planning is recorded in the transcribed tapes of Appendix 1, but much more must have gone on at playtime and dinner-time and whilst walking to and from school. That evidence is not available to us here. A fourth child, who had been excluded from their project because of a quarrel, joined Carla, Lindie and Melissa on Thursday and wrote one section of the story (TH facsimile: pp. 212–13/TH transcript: p. 54/TH tapes: p. 182). The relationship of this and other aspects of the children's current reality to 'The Tidy House' is dealt with in the third part of this book. An interest in the structure and arrangement of written language is common among literate children of this age and Melissa, Lindie and Carla (and, on Thursday, Lisa) divided their story into three parts, variously called episodes, volumes and books.[2]

Though the writing of 'The Tidy House' was a collaborative effort, the first part was written by Carla some time during the Monday of the week in question and handed to me just before the close of afternoon school. Her extraordinarily accurate ear for conversation was now, a week before her ninth birthday, being directly employed. The confidence and verve of her opening passage arrested me when it was first put into my hands, and still has that power after several years and many readings:

> One day a girl and boy said,
> Is it springtime?
> Yes, I think so. Why?
> Because we've got visitors.
> Who?
> Jamie and Jason. Here they come.
>
> Hello, our Toby! I haven't seen you
> for a long time.
> Polkadot's outside
> and the sunflowers are bigger than us.

facsimile: pp. 184–5/TH transcript: p. 42

Two married couples meet here in the back garden of a council house and they are the central characters of the story. Jo and Mark, whose tidy house it is, are childless. The visitors, Jamie and Jason, have a small son called Carl who is just coming up to his fourth birthday when the story

18

opens.[3] The plot is simple: it is concerned with the getting and regretting of children. Jo, the childless wife, indulges her best friend's little boy with 10p pieces and ice creams, is criticised by his mother Jamie for spoiling him, and gets a child to prove that she does know how to bring up children (TH transcript: p. 50/ tapes: p. 175). 'She's up in competition, see?' said Carla by way of explanation (TH tapes: p. 176). With grim satisfaction the three writers had Jo produce boy twins, Simon and Scott. They called the last part of 'The Tidy House' 'The Tidy House That is No More a Tidy House' (TH facsimile: p. 209/TH transcript: p. 53/ TH tapes: p. 175), and dourly catalogued the strain and tension involved in bringing up noisy, demanding little boys whose role in the story is to untidy the tidy house.

The fictional Jamie, Carl's mother, produces another boy during the course of the story and he, as he grows up, fights continually with his brother Carl. All the child characters created by the three girls were, in fact, boys. The fictional Jamie, though, longs for a girl: 'She wanted a girl because she had thought up a name, the name was Jeannie. Jamie adored that name, she thought it was lovely' (Melissa: TH facsimile: p. 214/TH transcript: p. 54). The girl child is never born, but so strong was Melissa's desire to create a fictional female child that she brought her character Jamie to the very point of parturition before abruptly having her produce another boy. The direction taken by the other children dictated this aspect of the plot (TH facsimile: pp. 209–17/TH transcript: pp. 53–55).

'The Tidy House' is unusual among stories written by children, in that much of the narrative is conveyed by means of dialogue. The children frequently abandoned the use of the simple past tense, which is the habitual tense of young children when writing, being characteristic of diary writing and necessary in most narratives that begin with 'Once upon a time'. Much of 'The Tidy House', by contrast, was written in the timeless present of dialogue. The extraordinary dark nights of whispering and fumbling in the getting of children, overheard by an eight-year-old child through the thin walls of her 1930s' council house bedroom, were recorded thus:

What time is it?
11 o'clock at night.
Oh no! Let's get to bed.
OK.
Night, sweetheart. See you in the morning.

Turn the light off, Mark.
I'm going to. Sorry.
All right.
I want to get asleep.
Don't worry, you'll get to sleep in time.
Don't let us, really, this time of the night.

[Carla: TH facsimile: pp. 186–88/TH
transcript: p. 43]

The other two girls, who became co-authors of '*The Tidy House*' some
time on the Tuesday of the week in question, always sought to make
concrete the scenes that Carla constructed entirely by the use of conversation. They made a collage picture of the tidy house and described it so that
it became clear that the Toby of the opening passage is a dog ('He is black
with a white chest'), that Polkadot was a rabbit and that each room in the
house displays different curtains and that roses and sunflowers grow in
the garden (TH facsimile: p. 189/TH transcript: p. 44).

In the same way, Melissa tried to make visible the bedroom scene that
Carla wrote. She drew a picture for the cover of the second book, which
depicted the most private and secret recess of the tidy house, the bedroom
of the childless couple, Jo and Mark (TH tapes: p. 170). There are hearts
everywhere. They make the shape of the lamps, the outline of flowers in a
vase. On the floor of the bedroom is what appears to be a circular rug,
covered with a pattern of hearts. Carla was scathing about this visual
interpretation of night's desires:

Carla:	. . . Miss, never seen heart flowers.
Teacher:	That's the rug, is it?
Melissa:	No, that's a nest of babies.
Teacher:	Oh. A nest of babies. Of course! In every bedroom a nest of babies.
Lindie:	Yes, of course there is. (Quotes) 'What is the mother without them?'[4]
All:	Mmm.

[TH tapes: p. 178]

Particularly important, since the story was written by three little girls,
is the symbolism of the house, the nest and the baby. For all three
children, the writing of 'The Tidy House' was a way of trying to understand life's mysteries. The children knew how babies were conceived and
born and knew that I knew they did. The nest of babies was a serious
physical metaphor and also a serious statement of their own feelings about

what lay behind the closed bedroom door, in the parental and private place. The children's use of this apparently ready-made symbolic system, and the way in which they appear to use it to examine their feelings about reproduction is dealt with in Chapter 6. In fact a careful reading of the children's text demonstrates that they took nothing, not even their pattern of symbols, as it came, but rather reworked them in order to understand the social life they represented. The doctor's advice to Jo (childless wife at the beginning of the story) to 'try harder' in order to conceive a child, was dealt with in a scene both furtive and ribald that Carla and Lindie, who both made attempts at it, knew was dirty enough to necessitate the literary euphemism of the dash to replace the unsayable, unwritable word (TH facsimile: p. 208/TH transcript: p. 53).[5] The children were deeply interested in such matters, but the structure of their plot and their intensive use of dialogue must lead us, as adult readers, far beyond simple interpretations of the house as the female body, the invasion of childbirth both courted and regretted and the boy babies as the symbolic achievement of that which little girls lack. For the characters in their created world *were* the little girls who wrote and the children writing were at once tired and despairing mothers and irritating, noisy little boys. Forced to distance themselves from the untidiness, noise and lack of consideration that are socially disapproved of in little girls, they bestowed these attributes upon the small boys of their story and, as they did so, wrote not precisely of themselves, but rather of how they knew they were often perceived by their parents.

The child character Carl, caught in an irritating and depressing relationship with his mother, was drawn from life. Only one of the three writers actually had a younger brother, but in the extended families to which they belonged the girls did not need little boys in the house to know exactly what they were like. Six months before 'The Tidy House' was started, Carla wrote:

> On Saturday my aunt and uncle and my cousin Carl come up my house. On Sunday all of us had some ice cream, but Carl would not eat it. After my mum cleared up, Carl wanted some ice cream, but there was none left, and he started to cry. He was after biscuits the whole time. He ate a whole tin of biscuits.
>
> [Carla, diary entry, January 1976]

From that plain account developed her acute observation of the emotional politics of family and social life: the having of babies out of rivalry, the persuasion and cajoling of children into life, the passive pressure on men by women to become fathers, the conflict over differing theories of child-rearing and the disintegration of those theories when a child cries or the chimes of the ice-cream van are heard in the street outside the tidy house.

The child Carl cries a good deal. A thin, persistent whine fills the pages of 'The Tidy House'. On his fourth birthday, after three crying bouts, his mother Jamie remarks, in heartfelt voice, 'Tomorrow he goes to school, thank God' (TH facsimile: p. 201/TH transcript: p. 48).[6] The three writers were almost entirely without sympathy for their character, as their recorded commentary reveals: 'He's babyish isn't he . . . His dad pampered him . . . He's spoiled. By his nan and grandad' (TH tapes: p. 167). They softened towards their creation on only one occasion, when Carl receives a small car as a birthday present. He fell 'in love with it. He was playing every day with it' (TH facsimile: p. 204/ TH transcript: p. 51). They watch his appealing and childish antics with an indulgent but wary eye:

> they sang happy birthday to him.
> He got all shy
> and covered his eyes up
> and hid behind the chair
> and when it was over
> Jo put a candle on Carl's bit of cake
> and he blew the candle out
> and they had a good time up Jo's house
> [Melissa/TH facsimile: p. 203/TH
> transcript: p. 51]

It is with such looks and glances that our bondage is bought. Carla, Lindie and Melissa kept their distance from such pretty tricks partly because they knew what treachery lay in the relationship forged by them. Two of the children were the eldest in their family and had at one time felt the displacement suffered by older children when a new and charming baby enters a household. Yet it was Lindie, the youngest in her family, who dealt with this question when she described Darren, the baby that the writers had Jamie bear in part three of the story, instead of the longed-for girl. Lindie wrote:

The baby was called Darren
and he was lovely.

When he was four
he and Carl were always fighting
but Darren never got the blame
and Carl always got sent to bed.
Carl hated him
and —— because he was not spoiled anymore
and neither was Darren.
Darren was lucky,
'Though I'm not,' thought Carl.

[TH facsimile: pp. 209–11/TH transcript: p. 53]

But their distance was also kept for another, more dimly perceived reason. They understood the desire for babies, their pretty talk, their funny ways, but they knew at the same time their mothers' deep ambivalence about their presence. The irritation of Carl's presence was a representation of the difficulties they knew they presented to their own mothers.

At the end of Carl's first day at school, in part two of 'The Tidy House', he refused to go home (having earlier refused to go into the building) and his mother has to carry him screaming out of the classroom (TH facsimile: p. 201/TH transcript: p. 51). 'Big lump,' remarked Lindie dispassionately; but Carla swiftly reached the heart of the matter, the point of having constructed the scene under discussion: 'My mum would love us if we didn't want to come home. From school.' Carla remembered quite clearly how glad her mother had been, four years before to 'Get [her] off to school . . . get rid of [her]'. What she understood of this memory was her mother's aching desire that her children be no longer there, her dream of freedom, the vision of her suddenly mobile, driving around in a car she didn't possess and didn't know how to operate. We asked Carla how many of her little sisters were still under school age:

Teacher:	Who's still at home?
Carla:	Jeannie.
Teacher:	How old's she?
Carla:	Three.
Teacher:	What will your mum do when she's off to school?
Carla:	Go out I suppose . . . Go out and get rid of us. That's what she says she's gonna do. And she's not going to come back and she's going to leave my dad, do all the work and he's got to go up and down to school. And she said and if she does come back she's going to come back on on one condition, my dad's got to buy her a new car.

[TH tapes: p. 166]

The Tidy House

Later, when two of the girls were asked why one of their characters, Mark, husband of the childless Jo, didn't want children, Carla suggested, 'Probably hates kids,' and Lindie immediately continued with, 'I think all mums do, don't they?' (TH tapes: p. 176). It is mothers who matter, whose bed is the nest of babies, who make decisions and negotiate children into life:

Carla:	[Jo] met Mark. And they decided to get married. And she wanted a baby from the beginning—
Lindie:	But he wouldn't let her—
Carla:	And then he sort of liked the idea.

[TH tapes: p. 176]

It is the very ambivalence of their mothers' regard that defines their power, which is to decide between life and their children's not existing, between their being loved and their being unwanted.

All three children, through a discussion of their own narrative, remembered their first day at school, the admonition that they hand on to their own characters: 'Don't cry; if you cry you get bad luck' (TH tapes: p. 173). Later they moved on to discuss their family life. Divorces were listed, half-brothers and sisters counted, the number of children in a family compared through the generations (TH tapes: pp. 176, 178–9). Fathers were dismissed in a curt list of variations. They could be flirted with, made an ally against a brother (TH tapes: p. 179). They were absences – 'comes in at eleven, goes out again' (TH tapes: p. 179) – and their sudden and violent anger at the spending of money was related to the daily mystery of their absence and the unknown process that gets a living and brings wages home (TH tapes: p. 180). The children saw their parents' approval of them expressed most clearly in the spending of those wages on them and, in this way, Lindie was felt to be the most favoured child:

Carla:	. . . Her mum and dad spoils her when it's her birthday.
Lindie:	Yeah, I know. I get, I get . . .
Carla:	She gets gold chain necklaces.
Lindie:	Last Easter . . . me and my brother got two whole bags of Easter eggs.

[TH tapes: p. 177]

Lindie was the youngest of a very large family with several older half-brothers and -sisters already going out to work. Her parents did have more to spend on her than those of Carla and Melissa whose children were all under nine and who were therefore at quite a different stage of the domestic economy cycle.

What informed the writing of 'The Tidy House' was the tension that lay at the roots of the writers' existence. They knew that their parents' situation was one of poverty and that the presence of children only increased it. 'If you never had no children,' said Carla towards the end of Wednesday morning, 'you'd be well off, wouldn't you. You'd have plenty of money' (TH tapes: p. 168).[7] They knew that children were longed for, materially desired, but that their presence meant irritation, regret and resentment. Their knowledge of the reproductive process gave them, as it must all children who do not understand their existence to be a mysterious, unquestionable accident, the clear image of the possibility that they need not necessarily have been born. Carla knew that conception could be prevented, that women didn't get pregnant as long as they remembered to take their pills. But that wasn't the point: 'they can't help it [having babies], can they?' (TH tapes: p. 175). 'The Tidy House' is about this sort of compulsion and necessity. The children's task was urgent: they needed to understand what set of social beliefs had brought them into being. They used the act of writing in order to take part in the process of their own socialisation. Keeping the distinction between adults' use of children's writing and children's use of it firmly in mind, the next section suggests ways of reading the children's text.

READING THE NARRATIVE

The children's story was a spontaneous production, or at least as spontaneous as anything produced in classroom ever is. They were not asked to write a piece of realistic fiction based on neighbourhood life, it was never suggested that they explore the relationship between mothers and children, nor the contrast between the desire for children and the reality of their presence. Writing a romance of family life was never proposed to them and there were no literary models for 'The Tidy House' that the children had access to, at least not in school, during the year 1975–6.[8] The only external motive for producing such a story was the oblique instruction 'Write a story' on a work chart (Introduction, p. 10) and that instruction had been given many times before. The children were not interviewed about their story in a formal way after it was written, and the presence in the classroom of another adult with a tape recorder on the Wednesday of the week of writing had long been arranged and was merely coincidental.

Our decision to devote recording time to the dialogue of Carla, Lindie and Melissa was deliberately taken (TH tapes: p. 159), but the recordings themselves are fortuitous. We did question the children about their story as they wrote it, but we were constrained in many ways: by not having read the text properly, by the needs of the other children, by the proprieties of a classroom relationship. It was a day like any other. If it hadn't been, we might have asked more informed and penetrating questions than the ones that are recorded in Appendix 1.

Given these circumstances then, it makes most sense to read 'The Tidy House' as a kind of historical document, a fragment of a life that cannot now be resurrected, whose authors cannot be appealed to for explication or verification, which is open to interpretation by what we know from other sources about childhood, working-class life and female social-isation. A view of the children's text as a kind of historical fragment is, however, more than a metaphor. 'The Tidy House' and its authors' discussion of it provides brief and shadowy access to a continuing historical process about which we know very little. The *experience* of childhood, particularly of working-class childhood, has not yet entered into our general accounts of social history. We know a good deal about the external dimensions of working-class childhood in history, about death rates, about infanticide and abandonment, about child labour and child health in the nineteenth and twentieth centuries and there is work of vital importance showing adults making use of their memories and under-standing of their childhood.[9] But this is evidence of a different order to that presented in the transcription of a child's words. To use the latter is to allow a current and felt experience to be reckoned. It is argued in this book (later in this chapter, more particularly in Chapter 5) that we need the outline of a history of working-class little girlhood, constructed out of children's felt experiences, if we are to interpret 'The Tidy House', just as 'The Tidy House', being the direct evidence of working-class children, can itself illuminate the recent historical experience of working-class childhood.

One benefit of a careful reading of 'The Tidy House' for the historical study of childhood is an increased sensitivity to the organisation of the texts by which children's *spoken* evidence from the past has been preserved. This point will be raised again when the transcribed words of little girls from the 1850s and 1860s are considered in Chapter 5. But it is in fact questions arising from the nature of *written* language that raise the most extensive difficulties in dealing with 'The Tidy House'. How does a reader set about understanding such a story? There are two sets of problems to consider when we as adults come to read the writings of children. The first concerns the obvious difficulties that children, as yet imperfectly in command of written language, encounter. Our reaction to spelling mistakes, to errors in syntax, to distortions in imagery that arise from a child's incomplete comprehension of the world, is often expressed as a sentimental delight in their misapprehension. A minor but flourishing field of publishing since the 1850s has been the reproduction of children's writing – nearly always that of little girls. The charming childish error, the pretty, entertaining mistake, have enthralled little girls' editors now for 130 years, but this adult desire to be entertained and bewitched by feminine transgression is about as relevant to an understanding of children's writing as a delight in a little girls' pretty lisping is to an understanding of her development of spoken language. This publishing history, and its relationship to the domestic education that propelled it, is discussed in Chapter 3.

The second set of problems is concerned with the *use* that young children make of language, both spoken and written, and the part it plays in their growth and development. It is concerned with real distinctions between the intentions of adults and children when they come to write (or paint, or draw). The children who wrote 'The Tidy House' did not set out to inform an audience of something when they wrote; they did not intend to move us, or to change our minds or opinions. The warmth and delight that we often feel at witnessing the trial and error involved in children's writing should not be confused with the children's own motivations and can in fact trivialise an important means of growth. Concentration on pretty deficiencies when children's writing has been edited in the past rose out of a desire to make the writing interesting in adult terms. But as it is created out of quite different motives from that of adults, the writing of children cannot be interesting or absorbing in the way that fiction written for adults (or children) by adults is. It is most helpful, in fact, to anticipate dullness when reading children's literary productions.

The obvious and superficial differences between child and adult writing – the spelling errors, the handwriting – are distracting to the reader, partly because they promote the indulgent smile, and partly because they deflect attention from interpreting the text. For this reason, 'The Tidy House' is reproduced here in both facsimile and transcription.

Because the transcription is easier to read and less graphically distracting, it alone will be used for reference from now on, except when comparisons between the two need to be made.

Children may be hampered by poor writing skills and by an inability to spell, though, in the history of child writing, not many have been hindered in this way, except where adult strictures upon handwriting and spelling have made their task impossible. In fact, children with extremely limited reading and writing skills can use written language in a deliberate and highly structured way. It is language caught in the pencil marks on the page and made permanent and objective that is of obvious importance here, but whilst we know a good deal about the impact of literacy on primitive societies and about the psychological changes wrought in adults by the acquisition of writing skills, there is very little known about the profound changes that the discovery and acquisition of a writing system bring about in the life of a child.[10] In Chapter 4 some suggestions are advanced about why writing has been relatively neglected in the study of child language.

The act of writing in childhood bears an obvious relation to the imaginative play of children – which we do know a good deal about – and its role in enabling them to see a situation from differing perspectives.[11] But writing, unlike play, lets children watch and act from two perspectives simultaneously, to be, as Lindie, Carla and Melissa were when they wrote 'The Tidy House', both irritated mothers and desired and resented babies. To use written words like this, as a way of abstracting meaning from the contradictory events of the real world, children need to be operating at a minimal level of literary competence. They need some understanding of conventional orthography and its relationship to the sound and meaning of language; but all that means in fact is that the child needs to know what it means to write, and that what she has written can be read. She needs to be able to read and write only well enough to be able to operate independently. Because children can manipulate the symbols of their social circumstances with these minimal tools, they do in fact need editors when their writing is to be read by adults or by other children. In both cases an editor needs acquaintance with the categories of verbal and written error common to children of that age and some knowledge of local dialect. When children's writing is edited in school, corrections are made so that other children can use it as reading material and so that conventional orthography and syntactic structure can be emphasised.[12] But the editor who corrects surface errors in children's writing for an adult audience (and editing here emphatically does *not* mean cutting, or altering the child's grammatical arrangement) must perform far more of a translator's role. Ideally, adult readers should have access to both the child's unedited text, and to a sympathetic and revealing edition of it.

To make the edition revealing, children do often have to be consulted over what they meant by their writing. I typed the final version of Part One of 'The Tidy House' from Carla's draft (TH facsimile: p. 185/TH transcript: p. 42) and spent some whimsical moments interpreting 'pockadots' (which Carla had told me before the end of school was 'polkadots') as some version of sunspots dancing in the garden around the burgeoning sunflowers. (It has to be admitted that in the tedious routine of typing out children's writing for classroom use not all of it gets read very carefully.) I was told next morning that Polkadot was a rabbit and perhaps Melissa was prompted to write her strictly factual guide to the tidy house (TH transcript: p. 44) as a prophylactic against such romanticism. But a child's opinion cannot always be sought. It was an editoral decision to put the conversation between Carla's characters on the page without quotation marks, because she used what they were saying to each other to control and structure events in a way that Lindie and Melissa didn't (though they came to practice this technique more towards the end of the story). At the beginning of 'The Tidy House' Lindie and Melissa used 'he said', 'she said' in a way that Carla never did. In some sense, Carla deliberately omitted quotation marks, for she knew what they were and could employ them to some extent. There is meaning here in this omission that is more useful to adults in interpreting this child's perceptions of the world than there was for the child who wrote the words.

Carla had a fine ear for conversation: developed, encouraged, well taught, she could later in life come to write very well indeed. Her success and effectiveness in writing did not depend on a fast and legible joined hand, nor on a mastery of our spelling system, nor on an ability to maintain continuity over involved linguistic structures. What the manipulation of the words on the page enabled her to do was to gain some sort of access to the meaning of her life. The means by which Melissa and Lindie gained a similar understanding are less narratively striking than those of Carla, yet all three children made the discovery that written language allowed them to do something that spoken language does not allow, that is, to move beyond the constraints of an audience and the demands of that audience that subject matter be made clear, actors named and that the process of events described be sequentially consistent. By using dialogue to construct much of 'The Tidy House', the children achieved a kind of abstract manipulation of beliefs, theories and ideas about their social world.

But if we interpret this manipulation of the meaning of a social world as the child's deliberate intention, then we miss the point. Children's writing (and child art in general) cannot be *equated* with adult writing and art. As long as we do not see children's writing as the same sort of production as that of adults, then we are free to use it as a window on to child development, free to know that it is not significant that some pieces of work are more appealing, seem better than others. Writing is a means of growth available to all children, producing artefacts wrought by their own internal rules, just as a child's first spoken sentences have a structure and validity in their own right and are not simply some imperfect version of adult production.

From this standpoint it is irrelevant that Carla's narrative is more striking than that of Lindie and Melissa: 'A work of art must be born of conscious intention and striving: and the spectator . . . must be able to infer this. A child paints simply to grow up . . . The adult paints in order to add to and . . . alter life.'[13] John Berger's distinction is of vital importance, but there are difficulties involved in using it. He deals here with children's paintings and drawings, not with their writing, and it is easier for adults to see a purpose and intention in a child's story that is not discernible in a drawing. Fictional writing deals with change through time and usually presents a contrast between action and background. It is much easier to see a child's painting as 'an almost natural object', as being 'like a flower',[14] the intention behind it unimportant. Drawing does not allow for the elaborated *process* and sequence of understanding that a piece of extended writing provides for a child and that we can see at work as we read the child's writing. What is more, if we see in child art only the *absence* of the intention that informs adult art, then it becomes impossible to explain what children are actually up to when they manipulate their world in written words (or drawings). In order to discover what it was that Carla, Melissa and Lindie were doing when they wrote 'The Tidy House' we need some understanding of the boundaries of the writing system they used, a knowledge of their social world and a description of their synthesis of the two. These three factors outline the contents of Chapters 4, 5, 6, and 7.

This section of Chapter 1 has been concerned with an adult reading of children's texts and has suggested that reactions to such writing in the past has been part of a wider set of attitudes towards female children. In general our reaction to children's writing is propelled by an oblique recognition of the tension within it: we know that children grown up, that the symbolic representation manifested in writing is of its very nature transitory, that the errors disappear, just as in the end nearly all of us stop saying that 'Goldilocks woked up and runned away.' A child who arranges the pieces of her life not with a doll, nor a skipping game, nor a smashed tower of bricks, but with written *words*, arranges them in a highly deliberate way. Using those words we can, through the glass of distance and forgetfulness, half remembering our own lost childhood, ask at last what understanding of social circumstances it was that prompted the writing of 'The Tidy House'.

AN ADULT USE OF THE NARRATIVE

In their story, the children described the pattern of a social life, and the narrative served them as an exploration of the social theories by which they were being brought up. It is valuable to adult readers precisely because it is an account of socialisation from underneath – from the children's vantage point. One of the difficulties with the notion of socialisation is the opaqueness of what exactly it is that is being conveyed to children and what are the value and beliefs that they assimilate in the process.[15] There are large-scale theoretical constructs that describe the possible mechanisms of this process[16] and several detailed descriptions of what parents believe they are doing in bringing up their children.[17] But evidence from the subjects of this process is rare. Treated in this way, as evidence of socialisation in working-class, mid-twentieth-century Britain, it becomes clear that 'The Tidy House' was used by the children who wrote it in two central ways: their episodic drama of family life articulated certain values and norms for the children; but, more than this, the text served as a way of questioning those values and of questioning the future that they saw lay before them. It was in this sense a deliberate attempt to take hold of the confusions and contradictions with which they were being presented and to synthesise them. In short, 'The Tidy House' is valuable evidence of the fact that children are not the passive subjects of their socialisation, but active, thoughtful and frequently resentful participants in the process. It is in fact because the children were

31

manipulating real beliefs and theories that were an actual feature of their daily life and because their attempt to understand them was serious and purposeful that their description of life on a large council estate, of child-rearing and sexual relations, can be relied upon as being generally accurate.

The central mechanism of their story's plot is an argument about two theories of child-rearing. The characters Jo and Jamie represent different positions on the question of 'pampering' and 'spoiling' children[18] (TH transcript: p. 50/TH tapes: p. 175). In their voices the opposing theories are clearly expressed and Jo gets pregnant in order to justify the indulgence she has been accused of showing her friend's little boy. Carla, Lindie and Melissa were convinced that their character Carl's crying and tempers had been created by this easy availability of material goods – 10p pieces and ice cream (TH tapes: p. 168).

We meet Carl, the central child character of the story, just before his fourth birthday, at exactly the time that the mothers of 700 Nottingham four-year-olds were interviewed in the mid-1960s. Their evidence makes up most of the Newson's *Four Years Old in an Urban Community* and it is instructive to look at the fictional Carl in its light. Our first extensive view of Carl is on his birthday. He is not a self-reliant child and his only independent actions in the story are following his mother to her friend's house and going alone to buy ice cream from the mobile van that tours the estate (TH transcript: pp. 46, 48).[19] The chimes of this van are as dominant in the background of 'The Tidy House' as they were in the housing estate interviews in the Newson inquiry. Carl's usual response to disappointment or frustration is tears (TH transcript: pp. 46, 47, 48). One major temper tantrum is reported in the story and on two separate occasions his parents have to remove him bodily from the scene (TH transcript: pp. 55, 47, 51).[20] 'The Tidy House' describes jealousy between siblings: when Jamie and Jason have their second child, Darren, his brother's incomprehension of financial circumstances and the new reins on spending promotes anger and resentment on Carl's part (TH transcript: pp. 53, 55). By way of contrast with their created character, Carla, Lindie and Melissa were deeply aware of the extent to which economic circumstances dictate styles of child-rearing, as their recorded commentary often revealed (TH tapes: pp. 166, 168, 177, 180).[21] Carl, in a manner typical of four-year-olds, is deeply attached to a special toy (the little car given to him on his fourth birthday) and his creators were aware that his choice of plaything was dictated by economic necessity as much as by parental attitude (TH transcript: pp. 50, 51/TH tapes: p. 174).[22] In 'The Tidy House', Jason, Carl's father, is shown caring for his child; but his role is really as limited and as dependent on the novelty of his presence as the literature suggests it is in a majority of working-class families (TH transcripts: pp. 46, 47).[23]

All this is interesting confirmation of much sociological investigation. Particularly striking is the children's sense of human growth and their overt presentation of the difference in capacity and understanding between four years and nine. But what Carla, Melissa and Lindie wrote was a story, not a description of a four-year-old, and their character Carl is both emblem of their plot and a symbol of the inevitability of women's lives. The child is presented through his mother's eyes and it is in fact impossible to see him except in this way. To Jamie, Carl is a nuisance: she clearly holds to the opinion that a good child is a quiet one.[24] He gets on her nerves by talking (his general noisiness is resented), by following her about, and by refusing to leave his play when asked to get ready for school (TH transcript: pp. 46, 49, 50, 51).[25] Like three-quarters of all mothers, Jamie probably smacks her child at least once a week.[26] There are five scenes in 'The Tidy House' that display Carl's behaviour and he is smacked in two of them (TH transcript: pp. 46, 48, 49, 50, 55), once for showing his mother up in public.[27] In the story his conversation and activity is twice curtailed with a curt 'Shut up' (TH transcript: pp. 46, 54), though Jamie does often attempt to reason with her son, especially when she is trying to stop him from crying (TH transcript: pp. 48, 49, 50, 54).[28] The technique she uses on these occasions looks on the face of it like 'bamboozlement', which has been described as the use of a threat which has little basis in reality, but which carries some conviction for the child, and which is used by adults to promote short-term compliance with their wishes.[29] Jamie tells Carl that if he cries on his birthday he 'will get bad luck' (TH transcript: p. 50). This is far closer to the expression of a general superstition held by adults and conveyed to children. In the story its use is presented as a means by which Jamie attempts to get her little boy to behave in an appropriately masculine way, whilst Carla, Melissa and Lindie were personally exercised by the implications of this common saying and were trying to decide whether or not to believe their own mothers on this point (TH tapes: p. 173).

Carl and his mother Jamie are realistic figures. But in an important way Carl is not just an accurately described four-year-old, for his role in the plot is that of *child in general*, and some of his behaviour is representative of someone much younger than four. When the three girls were questioned about what exactly Carl had done to provoke his mother's anger in one episode of their story, they searched around for a piece of punishable behaviour, and came up with 'he probably kept pulling all the things down at home' (TH tapes: p. 172). In the Newson inquiry at least, this was reported by mothers as more typical of one-year-olds than of four-year-olds.[30] It was a general perception of children as those who 'untidy the tidy house'[31] that enabled the writers to encompass nine years of development in one character. At the age of nine Carl serves the same purpose in the plot that he did at four (and as the other much younger children in the story do from birth onwards): he makes demands on his mother that she cannot meet.

To call Carl a symbol of children in general is not to suggest that Melissa, Carla and Lindie had unrealistic ideas about child development: the concerns of nine-year-old Carl, friendless and ganged-up on in the school playground, were their concerns as they turned nine and the language and ability in rational argument that Lisa had Carl use in her contribution to 'The Tidy House' (TH transcript: p. 54) is the language of a child of nine, just as the other writers' descriptions of Carl's verbal interactions with Jamie at four years were descriptively accurate. He is told at nine to go out and fight his own battles,[32] and to shut up when his demands on his mother continue, just as he was at four. Used as a symbol of a child, Carl acted as a representative of his creators. They perceived an ambivalence about their presence in the adults who surrounded them, and in order to cope with it, they at once agreed that children were indeed a nuisance and at the same time deflected the *personal* accusation by making all the children in their story boys.

One theme that we as adults can extract from 'The Tidy House' is that of the ambivalence of motherhood. This ambivalence, and children's relationship to it, has scarcely yet entered into psychological or historical accounts of childhood, though it has been noted by sociologists and recently explored by Ann Oakley.[33] History is mentioned here because accounts of working-class childhood have so often been written to encompass the myth of 'our mam'. This myth has been elaborated in many autobiographical and fictional accounts of working-class boyhood, where 'the best woman who ever lived' walks silently through the pages, strong-armed, martyred, utterly devoted to her children.[34] Male accounts of working-class childhood are seriously challenged when little girls, the

At the Door of the Tidy House

daughters of such mothers, create different figures, their love ambiguous, their strength difficult to interpret. In this way, the perceptions that 'The Tidy House' allows can be used to re-interpret the words of other little girls that re-tell the story of working-class motherhood.

It is important to note here that in their text the children presented relationships between men and women, and types of marriage, that contradict their brief descriptions of their own fathers (TH transcript: pp. 45–47/TH tapes: p. 179). Jason and Mark, the husbands of the tidy houses, are not central to the plot, but their early relationships with Jamie and Jo are ones of friendship and co-operation. The decision to have children is taken by women – they switch out the light, make the sexual advances and consult the doctor when they fail to conceive. They make the moves to accomplish their end – it is an end of loneliness, frustration and certainly an end to the social life, the going out, the visiting that occupies the early pages of 'The Tidy House'. But this curtailed social life is not the central image or restriction in the story. The most overt expression of the frustration that children represent to mothers is rather in the picture of the tidy house made untidy.[35]

We have learned a great deal in recent years about the cultural and political forces that shape little girls into women and, as childhood socialisation has been increasingly subject to investigation from a feminist perspective, it has become a common and useful practice to make cross-cultural comparisons of growth and development in childhood.[36] Perspectives like these are of great importance and it is necessary to make again and again the point that elsewhere things are different and that women are not necessarily and biologically bound to be the way our society expects them to be. But there are problems connected with stopping the anthropological machine and plucking one aspect of an exotic culture for comparative purposes. In many cases we simply do not know enough about the culture in question to estimate exactly what kind of comparison is being made. Comparisons are also often made without relating the particular aspect of the foreign culture to change and development in the society in question: we do not discover to what extent a child-rearing practice is subject to discussion, what ambivalence may attach to its use, nor what tension might be involved in its application. It is not of course always interesting or necessary to find out how things got to be the way they are; but, as the investigation of female socialisation is concerned with that precise question, it would seem helpful to use comparisons that allow for the notion of development in child-rearing practices.

35

In many instances a comparison with a recent period of our own history can tell us something more precise about the development of working-class eight- and nine-year-old girls in the late 1970s than can examples drawn from simple, small-scale societies that operate under a quite different economic organisation from the one that is our legacy from the nineteenth century. By virtue of living in an altered and developed version of mid-nineteenth-century Britain we do in fact have a great deal of intuitive understanding of the Victorian working-class girls whose evidence is used in Chapter 5. We have a language in common with them and a visual sense of their environment, which, though it has been subject to great alteration since the 1860s, was still much like our own. The social and class relationships that we experience are evolved and altered versions of those the children knew and out of which their sense of self was forged. Knowing the occupations of those long-dead children's parents, we can place them accurately on the socio-economic index: we know in fact what place they occupied in their society and what they had to say about it is accessible in a way that the perceptions of an eight-year-old Balinese child cannot be accessible.

We could add to these points many other factors where our common-sense, intuitive understanding of those children's lives makes their experience relevant to a contemporary situation. We know the pattern of housing in urban conurbations and the difficulties and dangers of city streets; we understand a pattern of seasons and weather and the kind of clothing it necessitates; we can recognise their games and know why they possessed the few toys they did; we need no recipes for the food they ate and their experiences of being mothered and the arrangements of family life they knew speak to our own. Above all, we understand the basic economic organisation of the society they inhabited, for we inhabit it still.

Information on all of these points is available from the transcribed words of a few working-class children. The social relations experienced by working children in the 1850s and 1860s, and their account of the emotional and economic alliances with their households, form part of the history of what was explored in 'The Tidy House'. However, Melissa, Lindie and Carla were able to question – albeit falteringly – received ideas about motherhood, the desirability of having children, relationships between the sexes and between women and children, where the Victorian working-class girls could not. We need a history if we are to understand why this was the case.

Using historical material in this way also carries with it the advantages of a particular theory of social history. Conventional historical narrative largely ignores the experience of those caught up in large-scale development, or at best treats the felt and articulated experience of its victims as mere comment on the narrative itself. But people's history – history written from underneath, from the viewpoint of the poor and unimportant – holds that such felt experience constitutes evidence of what really happened.[37] It is assumed here that the words of the Victorian working children used in Chapter 5 constitute important evidence of nineteenth-century childhood, are not just a comment on an established history of childhood but have the power to alter the historical narrative itself.

Of course, theoretical frameworks and the practice of history are very different matters and it is only by a deal of effort on the part of feminist historians that the experience of being a woman has been allowed a foot in the door of historical analysis. The absence of childhood measures out a much larger and emptier space, for whilst all people start out by being children, the felt experience of being a child is rarely reckoned within social history.[38] No material is transparent and the attitudes and beliefs of the middle-class gentlemen who interviewed little girls in the mid-nineteenth century of course influenced their responses. But their words were transcribed, and this is of immense value, for it means that a modern understanding of child language can be used to gain some access to their experience and the meanings they expressed in spoken words. Helpful though these revealed meanings are for an interpretation of 'The Tidy House', it is important to bear in mind the fact that they are to some extent without a context, for working-class childhood does not yet have a history.

THE CHILDREN'S USE OF THEIR NARRATIVE

'The Tidy House' is unlike much of the writing that children produce in order to think about their condition. There is nothing here represented as dragon or giant and no dreadful possibility clothes itself as a black witch. It does not follow the conventional three-part pattern of the fairy-tale – assault on a given situation, striving, resolution – that many children use as a model for their story writing. Nor does it use the journal form. (British primary school children are as familiar with the public affirmation of daily life in the open, pedagogical diary as any female inhabitant of

37

a nineteenth-century upper-middle-class nursery was.) But 'The Tidy House' does not proceed step by step through the simple past-tense narration of real events that is the feature of the public diary. By their use of dialogue to direct the narrative, the children brought the story into a kind of timeless present. It is not so much that their characters – talking, shouting, quarrelling, smacking, crying – provide an allegory of what they saw their life would be, but rather as if they stand as constant, formless, insistent commentators on what already *is*. The characters are never described; we know nothing of what they wear, nor the colour of their hair, nor what they hand over to each other as anniversary gifts (TH transcript: p. 46). What the children chose to make visually substantial was the tidy house itself and the rooms within it (TH transcript: pp. 44, 45).

To an adult audience, the timeless quality of the children's prose and the visual insubstantiality of its setting communicates a kind of inevitability. There is some support for this critical reaction to be found in the children's recorded commentary on their story. Their discussion of 'The Tidy House', even when it centred on aspects of the story not yet written, was couched in the present and past tenses:

Teacher:	What did she [Jo] do before she got married?
Carla:	Dunno.
Lindie:	She's a typist . . . My aunt used to be a typist.

[TH tapes: p. 176]

Melissa:	And we thought, um, that, er, Jamie would have a boy, and Carl and the boy, the little boy, always used to have fights. And then, and then . . .
Teacher:	Why do all these people have these babies?
Melissa:	And then Carl won't be pampered, will he?

[TH tapes: p. 175]

The children seemed to imply that their story was not a means of talking about the future, for there was none. Their lives had already been lived. The imagery seems dull and stark, a fantasy constructed out of the workaday, the dull, the uneventful. We reacted to Carla's animated face as she spoke of clothes, the unbearableness of flat-heeled sandals (in a summer of platform soles), the appropriate garb for a funeral, in much the same way as one of those nineteenth-century social investigators of working-class childhood, Henry Mayhew, did, when he listened to one of the little girls he interviewed describe how she kept herself clothed. In a way, perhaps, we found the listening harder than he did, for we no longer operate by a theory of social interaction which holds that the contemplation of the results of poverty is spiritually good for us:[39]

Carla: She [Carla's mother] had to go [to a funeral] all in blue, she never
              had no black shoes. Don't wear black anyway, do you?
Second   No; I went to a funeral the other day and
Teacher: there was nobody in black.
Carla: Dark blue's next to black, because my mum bought a dark blue
              top and a dark blue skirt and it came to twenty quid. And my dad
              went mad – just over a funeral.

[TH tapes: p. 180][40]

All my money I puts into a club and draws it out to buy clothes with. It's
better than spending it on sweet stuff for them that has a living to earn.

[Watercress seller, eight years, 1850 (?)][41]

We expect more than this from children now. They confound us when they speak, as the watercress seller did and as the writers of 'The Tidy House' do, not about childhood, nor about adulthood, but about some serious preparation for the latter, of some ideas and beliefs wrought out of material so threadbare and poverty-stricken that it seems no more able to keep a soul warm than did the watercress seller's shawl her body. The text of 'The Tidy House' seems to offer us permission to take part in that long and hallowed reaction of exquisite sadness felt at the contemplation of warped lives, cramped hopes, opportunity lost. The little watercress seller quoted above, moves heavily in the dusk of her Clerkenwell court, playing a game with her friends, her baby sister on her hip,[42] and suddenly, movingly, we can see Carla in her place:

> My sister is the youngest
> I am the eldest.
> My mum works in town
> With all my family
> And leaves my little sister
> In the arm of me.

[Carla, poem, April 1976]

But all we have in 'The Tidy House' are some children's words and we need some way of interpreting them that is both helpful and uncondescending. When there are no dragons, no frogs to kiss as metaphors, then we must look at the words and the linguistic and social structures that support them. As they wrote, the children perceived the contradictions of the life that faced them and writing enabled them to briefly hold those contradictions together and to examine them. So, by putting the words on the page, the children halted the inexorable processes of their life and, at the same time, by writing, performed that 'imaginative' trans-formation of reality which is in no way passive'.[43] Their ability to specu-late and reflect was rooted in the very restrictions that prompted the writing of 'The Tidy House'. The long hours in their mothers' company, the dreary walks to the shops, up and down to the nursery school with recalcitrant toddlers in tow, the visits, the cups of tea, all that talk – 'stand still and shut up' – gave the children access to a symbolic form of this life that they could manipulate and change in written words.

It is in the symbol of the baby, and the transformation of the figure of the small child in their story, that this active reworking of experience is most clearly to be seen. The children watched their creation Carl with a wary eye, refused to be seduced by his prattle, his playful antics, his hiding behind the sofa, his big breath to blow out the candles on his cake. He was more than a baby: they had made him a symbol of what might happen to them and, briefly, in one week of writing, understood that they resented the implications of that future.

By Thursday, too, they were resenting the inevitability of their chosen narrative. Already on Wednesday afternoon, they had seen that there was no end to what they had started:

Teacher: What's going to happen to all these people?
Melissa: We're going to have another book.
            We're going to have four books.
Teacher: Four books?
Lindie: We're gonna try four books.

[TH tapes: p. 174]

Melissa: We got another book to do, and in the fifth book . . . the fourth book's going to be the longest out of the lot . . .

[TH tapes: p. 176]

Seeing no way out of the episodic, repetitive narrative they had con-structed for themselves, the children simply shut the door of the tidy house and abandoned their story.

2

'THE TIDY HOUSE':
A TRANSCRIPTION OF THE STORY

'The Tidy House', a four-part collaborative story of just over 2,000 words, was written by Carla, Melissa and Lindie (with a fourth child, Lisa, joining them towards the end) during one week of July 1976. It occupied the children for several hours of Monday, Tuesday, Wednesday and Thursday, though by the end of the week their interest in the project was waning. The most concentrated writing took place on Wednesday, the day represented by the transcribed tape recordings of Appendix 1. The part of the story between pages 48 and 51 of the transcript that immediately follows was written on that Wednesday.

As the children gave me each day's composition at the end of school, it was typed out and given back to them in book form to read the following morning. This was usual practice with much of the writing produced by children in this class, and, in the normal course of classroom events, part of the children's original draft was destroyed. In particular, the whole of the section that was bound into the second volume (the same pages as those mentioned above) is missing. There is, however, a full record of this writing – the children read these pages over to each other, I read the material back to them – in the tape transcripts as well as in the typed transcript of 1976, here reproduced. The transcript then constitutes a full record of their story in a way that the facsimile of Appendix 2 does not.

In the transcript the name of the child who wrote a particular section is indicated; and shifts in time within individual narrations, as well as changes of narrator, are indicated with an asterisk.

The Tidy House

Characters

Jamie	A young wife. Mother of Carl and later of Darren.
Jason	Husband of Jamie. Father of Carl and Darren.
Jo	Wife of the tidy house. Becomes mother of Simon and Scott in the course of the story.
Mark	Husband of Jo and of the tidy house.
Susan	A friend of Jo's (makes no appearance in the story).
Carl	Small son of Jamie and Jason. Brother of Darren.
Mum	Mother of Jason. Grandmother of Carl.
Jane	Possibly the sister of Jason (makes no appearance in the story).
A doctor	
Darren	Second son of Jamie and Jason. Brother of Carl.
Jeannie	A girl child desired by Jamie. The child is never born.
Simon Scott	Twin brothers. Sons of Jo and Mark and of the tidy house.
Toby	A dog.
Polkadot	A rabbit.

A Transcription of the Story

Part One [Carla]

One day a girl and a boy said,
Is it springtime?
Yes, I think so. Why?
Because we've got visitors.
Who?
Jamie and Jason. Here they come.

Hello, our Toby! I haven't seen you
for a long time.

Polkadot's outside
and the sunflowers are bigger than us.

Mark, let's go and see.
OK.

[TH facsimile: pp. 184–5]

42

Look, Polkadot's had babies.
Can Jamie and Jason have one, Jo?
Yes, Mark, if they want.

Jason, let's have Ginger.
Jamie's made a name up for him already.

*

It was a lovely tea. Thank you.
Come again, please.
Give my love to Mum and Dad.
We will.
Bye.
See you soon.

*

What time is it?
Eleven o'clock at night.
Oh no! Let's get to bed.
OK.
'Night, sweetheart. See you in the morning.
Turn the light off, Mark.
I'm going to.
Sorry.
All right.
I want to get asleep.
Don't worry, you'll get to sleep in time.
Don't let us, really, this time of the night.
Shall I wait till the morning?
Oh stop it.

*

Morning
Don't speak.
No, you.
No.

[TH facsimile: pp. 185–8]

Why don't you?
Look, it's all over.
Thank you, Mark.

Mark kissed Jo, Jo kissed Mark.

End of Part One

*

Part Two [Melissa]

In the back garden
there is lots of sunflowers.
They're bigger than Jo and Mark.
They also have rose bushes.
They've got a dog called Toby.
He is black with a white chest
and they've got a rabbit named Polkadot,
it is white and black.

Now, outside their house
it is brown on the walls
and has blue curtains on the right side
and brown cord on the left
and on the top right-hand
is fancy coloured curtains
and on the top left-hand corner
is brown cord.

The street Jo and Mark live in
is called Hertford
and their number is 60.

Jo has no friends
so her friends from college come up.

Down Jo's street
is a big boy called Fred.
He made fun of Jo,
he called her big head,
but Jo got her own back.

[TH facsimile: pp. 188–90]

She called out,
'Big bully,
big nut,
and big bum.'

When she got in
she used to tell Mark
and Mark had a good go at him.
He did not want to see
his wife unhappy.

One day Mark said,
'I'll go shopping for you.'
'Ah, thank you.
I'm so pleased.
Anyway, I've got quite a bad headache.
I'll tell you what,' said Jo,
'I'll go up Susan's
and ask her if she's got
some tablets for headaches.'

'All right. I'll go shopping now.'
'Bye.'

So Mark went shopping
and Jo went up Susan's for a tablet.

Now Susan lived in a different house.
She lived in a bungalow
and Jo lived in a house,
and they had their bedroom upstairs
not downstairs like Susan's bedroom
which had a bedroom downstairs.

Jo got the tablet
and Mark got the shopping
and they had tea and went to bed.
Then all of a sudden
there was a knock on the door.

[TH facsimile: pp. 190–3]

45

Jo answered it.
'Mark, it's Jason.'
'All right, I'll come down, Jo.'
'Let's all have a cup of tea.'
'Do you want a cake?'
'Yes please. Thank you.'
'Bye. I've got to go.'

The end of Part Two

*

Part Three [Carla]
Jamie came over to Jo's house.

Hello. Happy anniversary.
Oh, you silly thing – hang on,
the door bell is ringing.

A boy said,
Is my mummy here?
Yes. Jamie, here is Carl.
Go home. I won't be a minute.
No, I want to stay here.
All right. Stand still and shut up.

Jamie smacked Carl.
Carl started to cry.

Then Mark and Jason came home.
Jason said,
What's all this then?

Carl ran up
and Jason picked him up
and stopped him from crying.
He gave Carl 10p
to get an ice cream

[TH facsimile: pp. 193–6]

when the ice-cream man came round.
Thank you, Daddy.

Carl was three and a half years old.

Jo said,
Let's have some tea.
Carl said,
Can I have a cup of tea? Please.
Please, Aunty Jo.
No.
So Carl started to cry.
Shut up.

Jason took Carl over his nan's.
He said,
Mum, will you look after Carl
while me and Jamie goes over
to Mark and Jo's house, please?
Yes, dear. Go and enjoy yourself.
Thanks, Mum.
See you later, Jason. Oh and, Jason, my –
Write a letter to Jane please, Mum.

This is what she said in the letter:

Dear Jane,
Are you still loving a man that you know? –
Is there still no charge? –
– Dor, dor, dor, dor –

Do you love Jason and Jo
and Mum and Dad
do you come back to me?
From Mum, Dad and kids. X

No charge.

*

[TH facsimile: pp. 196–8]

One day on a Monday, August 21,
it was Carl's birthday.
Jamie was quite pleased
to get him off to school.
She went up to Jo's house.
Jo gave Carl a card.
He wanted a present,
so he started to cry.
Stop it now!
Boys don't cry on their birthday, do they?

That minute the ice-cream man came round.
Jo gave Carl 15p to get an ice cream.
Jamie said,
Don't spend too much.
Give me the 10p, that's a good boy.
So he got a 5p ice cream.

[original missing]

While Carl was getting his ice cream
Jamie said to Jo
Tonight me and Jason are taking Carl out.
Mark and you can come too.
Thank you. I've got a present upstairs for Carl.
Carl came in with no ice cream
and he was crying.
What's the matter, Carl?
He dropped his ice cream.
Never mind, Carl,
Aunty's got you a present – look!
He started to laugh
and said thank you.
Tomorrow he goes to school,
thank God for that.

Carl's present
was three pounds, a shirt
and a colouring book
and pencils and shapes.

[TH facsimile: pp. 199–201]

The Tidy House

That's nice, Jo, said Jamie.
Do you want one?
Ha ha, very funny.
Tell me if you are glad
Carl is going to school.

*

[original missing]

Part Three [Lindie]

At School

At school Carl cried all the time.
When Jamie left the school
Carl was a bit better.
He stopped crying
and played with the other children.
He played with the sand
and the cars
and when Jamie came
Carl didn't want to go home
and he cried.
Jamie had to say,
'Big boys don't cry
and not on their birthdays, do they?'
'No, Mummy,' he said.
'You can come back tomorrow, say goodbye.'
He said goodbye
and they said, 'Goodbye, see you tomorrow.'

'Where are we going, Mummy?'
'To go and see Mark and Jo.'
'Oh,' he said
and carried on walking.

[original missing]

When they came to Jo's house
he ran in the gate and in the house

49

and hugged her.
'Hello, Jo,' he said.
'Hello, Jo,' said Jamie. 'How are you?'
'Oh fine,' said Jo. 'How are you?'
'All right,' said Jamie,
'but Carl is getting on my nerves.
I am really fed up with him.'
And Jo said, 'Don't be mean.'
'I'm not. It's because he's so spoilt.
I don't like children being spoilt.'

[original missing]

*

Part Three [Melissa]

It was a special day today
because it was Carl's birthday.
He opened his cards.
He got a card from Jamie and Jason
and one from Jo and Mark
and he got one from his nan and grandad,
he got 10p with that.
He got one from the USA.
His aunt sent it with a dollar
and a little car.
He thought it was a neat little car.
He was playing with it
till it was schooltime.
He got so used to playing with his car
that when Jamie called him for school
he started to cry because he didn't want to go.
But Jamie said,
'Don't cry on your birthday,
you get bad luck, don't you?'
'Yes, mummy.'
So he stopped crying
and got ready.
Then he went.

[original missing]

Carl had a good time at school
and when it was time to come home
he didn't want to go home.
He started to cry
so Jamie had to carry him out
until he got to the gates.
Then he got down and walked home
and when he got home
he played with his car until it was dinner-time.
After dinner
they went up Jo and Mark's house
and had a cup of tea up there
and a sandwich and a bit of cake
and they sang happy birthday to him.
He got all shy
and covered his eyes up
and hid behind the chair
and when it was over
Jo put a candle on Carl's bit of cake
and he blew the candle out
and they had a good time up Jo's house.
Then when they had to go
Jo gave him a present.
It was a big car,
it was as big as a toy dog.

Carl was overjoyed,
he fell in love with it
he was playing every day with it.
Jamie had trouble
getting him to school
because he would not go
so she had to let him
take it with him.

*

[TH facsimile: pp. 202–4]

Part Three [Lindie]

At night
Jamie and Jason went to bed.
Jamie said,
'Do it, darling, do it.'
In the morning
Jamie took Carl to school
and went to see the doctor.
When it was her turn
the doctor had a look at her stomach
and he said,
'Come back tomorrow
and I will tell you tomorrow
what's going to happen.'

That night in bed
Jamie said,
'I don't know if I'm pregnant.
I have to see the doctor again tomorrow.
Good night.'
They both went to sleep.
In the morning
Jamie took Carl to school
and went back to the doctor
and he said,
'You're pregnant.'

*

Episode Three [Carla]

At the night
Jo and Mark wanted a baby.
Mark agreed at this.
They sat up all night kissing,
kissing Jo all night.
Jo said,
I love you.
Mark said,

[TH facsimile: pp. 205–8]

52

The Tidy House

I love you too.
They went asleep happy.

In the morning
Jo went to the doctor's.
He said,
I think if you tried harder
you will have twins.
What, do the —— harder?
Yes, dear.
Thank you, doctor. Bye.
See you soon.
I'll come up tomorrow.

*

Part Four [Lindie]

The Tidy House That Is No More a Tidy House.

Jamie was soon pregnant
and soon she was in the hospital
and soon had a baby
another boy it was.
'What can we call it, Jason?'
'I don't know, dear. What about Darren?'
'All right.'
The baby was called Darren
and he was lovely.

When he was four
he and Carl were always fighting
but Darren never got the blame
and Carl always got sent to bed.
Carl hated him
and because he was not spoilt anymore
and neither was Darren
Darren was lucky
'Though I'm not,' thought Carl.

*

[TH facsimile: pp. 208–11]

The Tidy House

Part Four [Lisa]

When Carl was nine
he was in the middle school.
He only had two friends
and one day his two friends
broke friends with him.
He did not have no friends to play with.
Now, the boys who was his friends
got boys and started to fight him
When Carl went home
he told Jamie,
but Jamie said,
'You stick up for yourself.'
'But I –'
'But what?'
'I can't because they are bigger than me.'
'You can get Jason on the ground.'
'Yes I know,
but you get the blame when it is not you.'
'Oh, shut up.'

*

Part Four [Melissa]

Jamie wanted a baby.
She wanted a girl
because she had thought up a name.
The name was Jeannie.
Jamie adored that name
she thought it was lovely
and Jo thought it was a good idea
to have a girl and call it Jeannie
and Mark agreed.
So when Jamie had her
Carl's brother was called Darren
and they did not have so much money as before
which got Carl into tempers
and went in his bedroom and cried

[TH facsimile: pp. 212–15]

54

so he was quite naughty.
One day, when Jamie
was down the town
Jamie bought Darren a little bottle of lemon
and only got Carl a cake
and that made Carl get into a temper
and he started shouting
and Jamie gave him a hard smack
which made Carl cry all the way home.
When they got home
they gave Darren a bit of bread
and Carl
and then they went up Jo's and Mark's.
They saw Simon and Scott.
They were one and a half
but Darren kept on
pushing the twins over
and making them cry
so Jamie had to sit him on her lap
until it was time
for the twins to go to bed.
Then she would put him down.
So it went on like that.

Soon they went home
and had tea
and went to bed
and

[TH facsimile: pp. 215–18]

PART TWO

I ain't a child, and I shan't be a woman till I'm twenty, but I'm past eight, I am. I don't know nothing about what I earns in a year, I only knows how many pennies goes to a shilling, and two ha'pence goes to a penny, and four fardens goes to a penny. I know too how many fardens goes to tuppence – eight.

[Eight-year-old street
trader, 1850]

A NOTE ON QUOTATIONS

All the children's writing quoted in Part Two (and Part Three) of this book is, apart from historical material, taken from work produced by children in Lindie, Melissa and Carla's class during the year 1975–6. These quotations have been edited, that is, in transcribing the children's written words punctuation and spelling have been corrected. The historical material, however, is presented in unedited transcription, and an oblique stroke indicates original line endings.

The reader is now asked to leave the tidy house for most of the second part of this book. In the next three chapters a history of attitudes to little girls as writers, an account of writing as language development, and a history of working-class little girlhood is presented. That the reader is asked to make this excursion is a reflection of the difficulties that the writer was placed in by 'The Tidy House'. The problem is simple: there is no ready-made interpretive device with which to approach the children's story. It was necessary to construct one, drawing on a wide variety of sources. It was the children's story itself that demanded this mapping out of a history of attitude and feeling, for in 'The Tidy House' they manipulated a culture and a set of psychological relationships that are not often described within the official interpretive devices of the history of childhood, or of child development. In Part Three the reader is returned to the tidy house and should then be able to see more clearly how the story served the children who wrote it and how it may serve us, as readers of it.

3

DOMESTIC EDUCATION AND THE READING PUBLIC: THE HISTORICAL USES OF CHILDREN'S WRITING

The publication of children's writing has a history which spans about a century and a half and an examination of this history reveals two central adult purposes. The first was interpretative and had to do with the tradition of child study that seeks in children's play, words, and dreams a revelation of their unconscious beliefs and convictions. The second and older motive for the publication of children's writing was the adult search for delight and gratification in watching the sweet pathos of childhood innocence unfold itself. As the camera allowed the sustained contemplation of the limpid eyes and fragile flesh of childhood,[1] so did a minor verbal version of it, published facsimiles and transcripts of children's writing, allow some adults to believe that they had penetrated the very heart of childhood, in order to live 'child-life' anew.

The history of this publication then, reveals motives and reactions that are at once respectable and dubious. There are two reasons for surveying this history, both of which aid an interpretation of 'The Tidy House'. The story written by Melissa, Lindie and Carla is the artefact of children who were active participants in the process of their upbringing. The text served them as a kind of theoretical construct of social life and social relations, of information about reproduction, their observations of mothering and the feelings of individuals in the face of perceived social necessity. In the simplest of terms, 'The Tidy House' was a way of thinking about the social system that they were in the process of learning and, for us to assess the manner and content of that learning, we need a knowledge of the society they lived in. Whatever and whenever children write, and no matter what exotic metaphors they may employ, they write out of their own social circumstances and a study of the texts of nineteenth-century children, even though they were written out of very

The Tidy House

different circumstances, most of them in the space of the upper-middle-class schoolroom, none of them in a crowded classroom, show little girls engaged in the same process as Lindie, Melissa and Carla. All of them struggled to turn their meanings into adult meanings.[2] Their written words provided the means for their reflection on the restrictions and expectations of womanhood and meditation on their own theories of romantic love. As in 'The Tidy House', it is the words on the page, the shifts in topic, the symbols employed and the tenses used that make the evidence for us to interpret.

What is more, all children who write are forced into some kind of premeditated choice in their presentation of ideas. Writing demands deliberation and reflection and what is presented by the child has the value of the contracted,[3] of that which has been worked upon and manipulated. To the convictions about the world that children reveal in spoken language[4] can be added the *deliberated* convictions that are revealed in some children's writing. This kind of conviction can be extracted from historical material as well as from contemporary texts.

The dubious motives that underlay some nineteenth- and early twentieth-century publication of children's writing are of equal importance to the ones outlined above. They played a minor but important role in the development of the cult of the child. The mid-nineteenth-century establishment of the child as a literary figure representing both immortality and the transient nature of earthly life has been well documented.[5] But concurrent with this literary development was the growth of a much wider social assumption that children might be used as soothing, artless and innocent figures of relaxation and spiritual refreshment by adults.

What an examination of the facsimiles and transcriptions of children's writing that figured in this development can serve to demonstrate is that the cult of the child was really the cult of the little girl.[6] It was almost without exception the writing of little girls that was published. This is by way of striking contrast with scientific child study, the subjects of which have usually been boys. This distinction, and particularly the evidential basis of child psychology, in discussed in Chapter 4, but it is important to note here that the interest in 'child-life' that prompted the publication of little girls' writing was the frivolous, entertaining and relaxing underside to the serious study of childhood and child psychology.[7]

This verbal celebration of infantile femininity is part of the historical legacy that little girls in modern society have to operate under. Such publication played a part as well in defining the ways in which we see and understand little girls, so it is important in its own right and not just for the insights it provides into the interaction between child and audience when children come to write. With a few exceptions, the published writing of nineteenth- and early twentieth-century children was in diary form. To a large extent this form represents the predilections of the adults who used children's writing as part of their teaching method. But the desire to get close the children, to touch their experience without the interference of a story, is a factor in the adult attraction towards little girlhood that is demonstrated in the editing of some of this published writing. In the middle-class domestic interiors, which were the source of much of this writing, there existed a maternal and domestic pedagogy that set girls, not boys, the task of composition.[8] Most published texts of children's writing came out of this common domestic practice and many unpublished journals kept by children turn up in archive collections of family papers and demonstrate the same adult purposes and the same uses by children that the published ones do.

There were three major waves in the publication of children's writing. The first, beginning in the 1850s, was a serious component in the delineation of the romantic, Wordsworthian child, and was one of the foundations of the cult of 'child-life'. The general dissemination of this romance had one effect of developing a general consciousness of the particularity of childhood, and, in its turn, the cult of the child was an important component of scientific child study which, prompted by evolutionary biology and anthropological inquiry, evolved towards the end of the nineteenth century. Some children's writing was published in order to further the scientific exploration of the child mind.[9] The psychologist Sully told parents and teachers in training in 1894 that whilst individual child study would act as 'a lamp on to racial intelligence', an essential qualification for undertaking it was 'a keen, loving interest in children'.[10] The trained psychological observer and the seeker after 'the pure springs of nature for spiritual refreshment'[11] operated in tandem at the end of the nineteenth century. When one of Freud's earliest disciples, Hermine Hug-Hellmuth, reshuffled her childhood memories in order to produce an account of female adolescent sexuality that was psychoanalytically correct,[12] Freud greeted *A Young Girl's Diary* with a scientific enthusiasm that had taken its vocabulary from the romantic study of child-life:

This diary is a gem. Never before I believe has anything been written enabling us to see so clearly into the soul of a young girl . . . We are shown the dawn of love . . . how the mystery of the sexual life first presses itself on the attention and then takes entire possession of the growing intelligence, so that the child suffers under the load of secret knowledge, but gradually becomes enabled to shoulder the burden . . . a description at once so charming, so serious and so artless that it cannot fail to be of supreme interest to educationalists and psychologists.[13]

The third period of publication of children's writing, producing by far the largest number of volumes, took place between the two world wars. Psychological investigation and a search for the experience of innocence still prompted editors and publishers, but the significant difference between this last group of volumes and the earlier two is that many of these last were written expressly for publication. Indeed in some of them the adult desire to be pleased and amused by the prattle of children is so readily pandered to that they seem to have been designed for the purpose.

Throughout the history outlined above, dates of publication did not always represent the time of production and many texts were first published decades after they were written. Many of the published diaries were written by girls who had died young and a public taste for being edified by the recounting of death at an early age meant that some editors could point out to their readers the perfection of brief flowering of child-life.[14] A child's writing was more likely to be preserved as memorabilia if she died and families who many years later handed over to an editor her extant writing often saw their act as one of remembrance, the making of a memorial.[15]

Bearing this chronology of publication in mind, it is important to isolate the varied uses that adults made of children's texts. Adults wanted children to write and, for different reasons, wanted to read their writing. There was a pedagogical motive, which will be discussed later in this chapter, but much more overt on some occasions was the establishment by adults of a set of theories about childhood, its isolation as an area of human experience and the creation of a literature and a history of this experience. The major publications of children's writings in the 1850s and 1860s were quite explicit about their purpose. The four editions of Marjory Fleming's *Journal* between 1858 and 1863 not only established quite deliberately a cult for this long-dead child (and took a great many liberties with her character and her text in the process) but also outlined a new literary approach to 'child-life'.[16] When the Vicar of Taunton introduced *Little Charlie's Life* (a facsimile of an autobiography written by a child between his sixth and eighth year, and one of the few such publications of a male child's writing) in 1863 he made quite plain his appreciation of childhood as a marriage between innocence and eternity:

> His whole individuality bore out very strikingly Wordsworth's analysis of childhood and its impression of immortality, for there never was a time when he had not a sense of things unseen, a realisation of God's presence . . . Blessed childhood! let us cherish it, reverence it, learn from it. The little child 'set in the midst' is still given to us by the Divine Teacher . . .[17]

As the romantic, Wordsworthian child was established in literary parlance, another motive on the part of editors and audience emerged, that of seeking the adult in the child, of both creating and watching through the mirror of her words the feminine sexuality of the little girl, just as the camera enabled Victorian gentlemen to watch her large eyes and dimpled cheeks through the lens.[18] The vastly increased production of children's published texts in the early part of this century exemplifies this kind of motivation.

The boom in the publication of children's writing in this country and in the USA in the 1920s and 1930s followed on the success of Opal Whiteley, whose adolescent recasting of the scraps of her childhood diary in *The Story of Opal: The Journal of an Understanding Heart* was very widely read and promoted on both sides of the Atlantic.[19] Despite the self-conscious sentimentality of the work, it still makes ripples and is quoted and reproduced in collections of children's writings.[20] What was market-able in 1920 as a picture of childhood still has an appeal for some audiences today. The central features of its almost plotless panegyric to nature are pretty spelling errors, a naivety about adult intention and behaviour that borders on an arch knowingness and an affinity on the child's part with all growing things, particularly babies, flowers and fluffy animals.[21] *The Journal of an Understanding Heart* achieved its great success at a time when child psychology was emphasising ideas about innate intelligence and the importance of heredity in development. The accessibility of such ideas may have had something to do with the ready acceptance of Opal's story, for much of the *Journal* was designed to show that the author was the natural child of the house of Bourbon-Orléans and not the daughter of the Oregon lumberjack who raised her.[22] Contained within the anthropo-morphic nature study, the coy conversations with animals, plants and rivers that makes up most of the *Journal*, is a powerful retelling of Freud's 'family romance', the common childhood fantasy of really being the child of parents richer, nobler and more glamorous than one's own.[23] As the adolescent author of this myth of childhood, Opal Whiteley had to present her own infant consciousness as finer and more sensitive than that of the family in which she grew up. The response of readers at the time (and of some of her later editors) was to find in the *Journal* the affirmation of a poetic consciousness that could be plucked directly from the garden of childhood. Indeed, so strong is the impulse to find in little girlhood an area of experience and consciousness that can be used by adults that as late as 1965 it was possible for the latest in a long line of Whiteley editors to become affected by her prose style and to compose this hymn to eternal feminine childhood:

> the tumbling dancing sparkling outpourings of one of the most joyous minds to express itself at any age . . . (*The Story of Opal*) was one long haunting love song of a lover of the earth in rhythms no singer had ever used before, a token of return for the love of every fern and flower, every velvety little thing that scurried through the woods . . .[24]

When Opal Whiteley's words are used today it is in order to evoke a type of special and revelatory girlhood and a feminine poetic. Two recent examples of this search for the pre-formed woman in the child are *Heart Songs: Intimate Diaries of Young Girls* (title and collophon excavated from *The Story of Opal*), and the publication of Anaïs Nin's earliest diary in *Lintotte*.[25] These publications usually deal with the writings of adolescent girls and should not be confused with the productions of younger children which are being dealt with here. The feature of adolescent writing is the author's consciousness of what she is up to:

> How I came to be writing a diary is easy to explain; it's because I am enthusiastic about everything new, and I have decided now to carry this through so that in later years I can better remember the days of my youth

wrote the twelve-year-old Karen Horey in 1897.[26] By way of contrast with these stated motives for writing, younger children usually do so because some adult expects them to.

Some of the books of children's writing that followed on the success of Opal Whiteley were either ghosted or written by children at the suggestion of parents who had an eye to the children's book market.[27] A Hollywood child star kept a journal that was published and the daughters of two contemporary writers of children's fiction had stories and diaries published.[28] For some established writers of stories for girls, tracing the growth of child into woman by presentation of an original biography was a useful literary device.[29] Many of the diaries were heavily didactic, enjoining their audience to clean their teeth and love their mothers even when they seemed mean.[30]

The presentation of the child's text to the public followed a distinct pattern. There was usually an introduction by a disinterested adult who pleaded the authenticity of the document.[31] Were the document historical, then the story of its discovery (hidden in a cupboard, in a box of dusty old papers, in a locked drawer opened on a rainy afternoon) was outlined.[32] Often, serious attention was paid to the physical appearance of the discovered text – a tightly compressed diary with a lock, 'a neat pile of little fat copy books' – as satisfying to hold as the little girl who wrote it.'[33] A photograph of the little authoress was often presented. Pleas for the child's ordinariness were tempered either by the suggestion of her child 'genius', or by a description of the *type* of childhood that she repre-sented. Especially favoured and often described by editors were isolated and mildly eccentric middle-class households, where the romance of bourgeois individualism was played out and highly intelligent children might 'dodge the governess and let the rest of the world go hang'.[34] The high spot of such descriptive introduction was probably reached in the editorial foreword to Mimsy Rhys's *Mr Hermit Crab: A Tale for Children by a Child*, which was found not only in 'a carved Jacobean chest', but also in the drawing-room of a Dorsetshire rectory.[35]

Editors were frank about the use of these texts to adults: 'Once in a long time an authentic bit of childhood is captured and held within the pages of a book so that other children in spirit, whether young or old, may enjoy it.'[36] These were documents for use in that long continuum of childhood that was seen to stretch into adult life, the ever-present area of feeling that needed only the slightest stimulus to be made immanent.[37] They were books by which to re-enter the secret garden – or, as one editor put it more prosaically in 1936, 'to be kept on a near-by shelf when life seems hurried and nerve-wracking'.[38]

Just like these editors of the 1920s and 1930s, modern compilers of children's texts are often quite explicit about what they want and need from children and have, in pursuit of a particular image of childhood, often denied the evidence of the text before them. Thus the stately and elegant prose of twelve-year-old Emily Shore, elaborated in the 1830s around her observations of wild life and the social and political reality of her upper-middle-class family's role in their Bedfordshire village,[39] has been rejected by her most recent editors as being 'too prolix and pedantic'.[40] The evidence of a girl ordering and realising her social self is ignored, as is much of the work of natural history of which her journal is largely composed. A changed and acceptable child, representative of a more favoured view of childhood is constructed by her editors around the story of a sick lark that Emily Shore fed and observed and whose dying she watched with a detached interest.[41] The reader is told that 'when she wrote about those dear to her, papa, mama, the little ones . . . especially the lark . . . the big words, the stilted showy sentences were forgotten – most of them – and the story welled up from a tender heart'.[42]

What such editors have valued is the 'charming' error, the 'inimitable humour of unconscious literature', and access to 'the secrets of child-hood'.[43] Still higher in their estimation has rested a vision of children as bearers of some profound message of innocence and insight brought to adults from somewhere beyond this vale of tears. 'Where a child got such insight and art is a question that baffles us,' wrote an astounded Dundee clergyman as he presented the work of eleven-year-old Helen Douglas Adam to the world in 1924. He recommended to readers the 'courage of [their] ignorance [to] simply believe that there are elect minds that can mediate between us and the Father of Light.'[44]

Tastes in profundity and sentiment change and it is difficult for modern readers to find *The Elfin Pedlar and Other Tales Told by Pixie Pool* anything but nauseating:

> Hush! the fairies are dancing
> Dancing in the dell
> The dickie birds are watching
> The fairies weave their spell[45]

But the impulse to find a message for adults in the words of children still motivates serious and considered work. R.D. Laing transcribed his *Conversations with Children* partly because it is 'useful for adults to be in touch with childhood . . . Our understanding of ourselves is enormously impoverished if we are out of touch with childhood.'[46] There is no doubt of the truth of this. But the context and setting for such conversations are often the modern equivalent of the desirable Dorsetshire rectory: it is a certain type and class of child whose words we are invited to peruse for our growth in self-awareness.

In the history of published children's writing, the bearer of the profound message was almost invariably a girl (though, as Little Charlie demonstrates, a very young 'solitary . . . mother-taught' boy might serve the purpose as long as he stayed within the domestic interior and was instructed by women[47]). As Victorian editors propounded the virtues of the Wordsworthian child they occasionally mentioned the valuable domestic history contained within her written words. Indeed, the *Diary of Anna Green Winslow*, written in the 1770s and published 120 years later, Harriet Spencer's writing from the same period, Marjory Fleming's *Journal* of 1810–11, Emily Shore's from the 1830s, the diaries of the Alcott sisters written in the 1840s, Ellen Buxton's account of domestic life in the 1860s,[48] and many other unpublished diaries offer rare insight into child-care and domestic education on both sides of the Atlantic, into relationships with servants and other primary care-takers in middle-class households, into the development of female friendship and the inculcation of ideas of romantic love in little girls, into the growth of class consciousness and the development in these children of the idea of the social self. These diaries offer such good evidence because their composition was designed to promote more or less overt reflection on some of these matters. But the stuff of the domestic day is dull and many children's accounts of their own education and socialisation remain unread in the archives, for they fail to touch those veins of humour and tenderness that have made famous the *Journal* of Marjory Fleming, and Daisy Ashford's *The Young Visiters (sic)*.[49] What editors of such work have done is, as we have seen, to confuse their own appreciation of the text with the child's intention. As long as editors search for adult motivation in children who write, they will reject what does not appeal in adult terms and apologise for finding children's writing 'in general, a horrible genre'.[50] When dullness has reached the public presses it is where a posthumous search for the roots of a woman's genius has been carried out, as for example in the case of Anaïs Nin's first journal, or of the juvenilia of Elizabeth Barrett Browning.[51]

In the middle-class Victorian schoolroom that generated much of this writing, the cultivation of a good hand and some practice in letter writing, the verbal cement of bourgeois relations, were rationales for the pedagogic device of child diary writing. In some educational arrangements made within extended families, daily journal entries served as a letter-book, a cumulative account of the child's absence from home.[52] Some little girls were encouraged to keep a journal for the duration of a holiday abroad[53] and when Mary Georgiana Wilkinson's mother was absent from home for a month in 1819 her daughter kept a diary as a kind of insurance on her mother's part that all educational activity would not cease whilst she was away.[54] Children's diary writing was used as a basis for spelling lessons, as is still the practice with much school diary writing today. However, several nineteenth-century manuscript diaries show the instructor's interest in underlining and correction waning after the first few entries.[55] This kind of journal writing arose out of domestic expediency as much as it did out of educational theory and, where an explicit pedagogy of journal keeping existed, supervision of a child's written words might be much more consistent.

Amos Bronson Alcott possessed such a pedagogy, and it was put into practice in various New England schools in the 1830s and 1840s.[56] His four daughters all kept journals and eight-year-old Anna Alcott knew that her writing depended on her father's presence: 'Father went to Plymouth and when he is gone I do not write in my Journal . . . I have not written in my journal for some days, father has been in Boston'.[57] Her father held that a child's diary offered 'a means of self-inspection and self-knowledge, – enabling the writers to give unity to their own being by bringing all outward facts into some relation with their individuality'.[58] Alcott's daughters wrote their journals on their slates and, later, after correction by their father, copied them into their diaries. This seems to have been a fairly common practice among nineteenth-century children who kept journals. The children were asked to produce highly finished and public pieces of work: 'Sometimes Father hears me read and spell what I write in my Journal after I have written it. This learns me to read and spell and write, Father says he learned to read and spell and write in this way'.[59]

When a child wrote directly in her diary without making a preliminary draft on a slate, the presence, absence and type of error indicates whether or not a published journal was worked over in later years in order to devise saleable and appealing mistakes for a reading public. It is necessary, though, to be very careful about the categories and meanings of a child's written errors. In 1921 the editors of the English translation of *A Young Girl's Diary* told their readers that mistakes in grammar and spelling were 'manifestations of affective trends . . . errors in functioning brought about by the influence of the Unconscious'.[60] Spelling errors certainly can be used to show how a child theorises about the relationship between sound and symbol in English. Very young children frequently invent a spelling system, drawing on their own observations of phonology and articulation.[61] But this theorising on the child's part demonstrates a quite different psychological mechanism at work from the manifestation of the unconscious mind.

By the time that children have become reasonably competent in reading and writing, as Carla, Lindie and Melissa were and as the nineteenth-century girls of seven to twelve whose writing is under discussion here were, a great many other influences have fed into an earlier invented spelling strategy.[62] By this age, children have usually been taught some method of spelling. They have been exposed to orthodox spelling in their reading and a visual memory of words operates with the remnants of the child's earlier, invented system. Writing with a pencil or pen on paper (instead of, for instance, building words with manipulable letters or alphabet blocks) emphasises to the child the shape and appearance of the word and demands that she attempt to recreate it in her mind's eye. Handwriting styles can also influence the kind of errors that a child makes. In the full copperplate used by nearly all the nineteeth-century children whose work is mentioned here, the curved and elaborate lines used to join letters apparently led all of them sometimes to believe that they had graphically represented sounds that they had not in fact represented.

We can see more clearly how some of these factors influence a child's strategy when she comes to spell what she wants to write, by briefly considering one spelling mistake from 'The Tidy House'. In Carla's spelling of 'what' in 'Jason said wate this then' (Jason said, 'What's this then?') (TH facsimile: p. 195) a description of her strategy might go something like this: 'I know/ wot/ has one extra letter – what do I know about stupid extra letters? – Ah yes, everyone's always going on about magic "e", and/ mat/ is spelt "mate" with an extra letter – so, it must be "wate".' Carla did in fact spell this word correctly several times, when her visual recall was more accurate, or her reasoning different. Because such mistakes actually reflect the way the language works, there is a particular usefulness in knowing what are the spelling errors that young writers, using English as their first language, are likely to make. 'New sance' for 'nuisance' in Opal Whiteley's 'the mama where I live says I am a new sance. I think it is something that grown-ups don't like to have around,' and Mary Paxon's 'Part Rige' for 'partridge' are not the sort of errors that children of that age commonly make. In fact it is highly unlikely that the first would ever be made. But they are cute and appealing and they do represent an adult idea of how children spell.[63]

Useful as these insights from modern research on children's spelling are for literary detective work, it is much more important to consider the content of children's writing. What many nineteenth-century little girls were asked to practise – and far more important for their future life than correct spelling – was the construction of a domestic narrative that solidified and re-affirmed the unfolding of the placid domestic day:

> This morning/ I went in/ the garden/ and then/ Annie came/out and we/ read the Round /Robin toget/ her till din/ ner time. In the after/ noon Papa/ went to catch /salmon and we were to/ have met him/ on our way/ to Waters/ meet and to have/ walked home with/ him but we/ did not meet/ him after all./ It was a love/ ly walk we/ saw and/ followed a lit/ tle girl with a pitcher and/ she filled it /at a dear lit /tle spring in/ the rock and/ gave us a dink [sic]/ out of it Then/ we bought/ some crack/ nell biscuits/ at a house/ and came/ home very/ tired.[64]

Seven-year-old Florence Lind Coleridge who made this entry in her diary in September 1874 wrote for an audience that would learn nothing new from their reading of her words. The sister, the aunt, the mother and the nursemaid Annie had accompanied the child through this day as they did through so many others that were similarly and dully recounted. The construction of this narrative was partly a preparation for relating such detail to more distant future audiences in the practice of letter writing. The child was shown how to weigh and place domestic detail in temporal sequence, to write a current chronology of respectable upper-middle-class life and, by recounting to people what those people already knew, how to mirror social life in her words and confirm its solid existence. A journal also provided an effective way for children not only to rehearse maxims, but to construct for themselves social attitudes and beliefs out of what they heard and observed in the adult world around them. Thus in 1856 when touring Italy with her family, ten-year-old Constance Primrose noted that the numerous beggar children who 'assailed' them on the road to Rome were 'all as fat as could be'.[65] The parroted observation became her own.

Florence Lind Coleridge kept her journal for two months in 1874; her sister Mary Elizabeth, older by two years, kept hers from the age of eight until she was well into her teens.[66] In all the written words the children produced, no conversation was ever reported. The significant figures of the children's world made their silent ponderous way through the domestic narrative. It was certainly the case that the children were not asked to practise the construction of dialogue when they wrote in their diaries, but even the indirect reporting of speech was absent from the sisters' writing (it is extremely rare in most children's journals from the nineteenth century). This absence may perhaps reflect a wider perception of the adults who directed their learning, of dialogue as undynamic. This point has some bearing on 'The Tidy House', where the children who wrote it demonstrate quite clearly their understanding that conversation might bring about an alteration of circumstances. The relationship of this understanding to their social environment is examined in the next chapter. But, by way of contrast with the written words of Melissa, Carla and Lindie, the Coleridge sisters' words confirmed the world both as it was, and as it was supposed to be, all interchange, all movement, all conflict impaled on the past tense listing of events.

The simple past tense listing of events is of course a feature of child diary writing: teachers in modern primary schools can be heard to complain that were the skies to fall some children would still write in their diaries the next day, 'Last night I went home had my tea and went to bed.' Every day for one month in 1819, Mary Wilkinson repeated a variation of this basic formula:

> Friday. up by seven worked till eight/ cleaned my birds till half past
> eight/ had my milk layed down finished/ my breakfast practised by half
> past/ ten lessons over by eleven made my/ letter out by one dined by half
> past/ one half hour by two play till half/ past two wrote my letter by six/
> had tea watered plants till half past/ seven in bed by eight[67]

Formulae like these fill up the pages and play a positive role as well in confirming a child's own experience. Eight-year-old Arethusa Cullam used the word 'beautiful' at least once on each page of the travel diary she kept during her tour of Italy with her parents in 1822–3.[68] Twenty years later another child diarist suggested a possible reason for such repetition: 'Beautiful is my favourite word,' wrote Anna Alcott at the age of twelve. 'If I like anything I always say it is beautiful. It is a beautiful word.'[69] It is a very satisfying word to say and any child who has mastered its treacherous combination of vowels might like to make as much use of it as possible.

But even though the simple narrative structure of diary writing and the repetition that this structure encourages are extremely confining, there is still room within it for a child to record and examine her feelings – though this is not of course consciously done, except where it is explicitly encouraged and taught, as it was by Bronson Alcott. In spite of the severe limitations of the style imposed on her, Mary Elizabeth

Coleridge was able to express both her concern for, and her irritation at, her younger sister: 'Florry had left her spade on the stones and when she went to look for it the waves had taken it'; 'Florry dashed her hoop stick against the wall and broke off a piece of it'; 'Today Mama made Marmalade & we helped to cut the chips. Florry had to have several pieces of orange peel as she often scraped them into holes.'[70]

The adults who read the accounts of the Coleridge sisters often reminded the children of significant details omitted by them in their narrative, sometimes tagging the detail on at the end of the child's account. Later, the children came to make this kind of revision for themselves, putting right the time sequence of their narrative.[71] The correct order of things was of great importance to the children and their mother. The chronology they constructed supplied a kind of embedded evaluation of their experience. This evaluation did not interrupt the chronological listing of events and provided for a more intense mirroring of their society in the children's words.

The evaluative technique of the polite letter writer was learned early – it was used by seven-year-old Florence in the extract on page 72: 'It was a lovely walk.' In the sisters' diaries it is found again and again in descriptions of the weather: 'A lovely day'; 'the rain was dreadful this morning'; 'dreadfully rainy again'. The device of evaluation marked moments of pleasure for the children: 'when I got in it [the sea] was very nice'. The moment of evaluation, the place where the chronology was briefly halted, particularly marked the places where the world was seen to offer an acceptable, amusing and pleasing picture to the beholder as in Florence's description of the working-class child fetching water, quoted above.[72]

The diary entries of Florence's nine-year-old sister, Mary Elizabeth, demonstrate similar uses of this device. The example below is particularly useful for showing how this Victorian upper-middle-class child came to assess information provided by the outside world in terms of the source of that information. In March 1871 the children, on holiday on the south coast, went with their aunt and some family friends to a local tourist spot:

> A little boy showed us/ the way to the Dripping/ Well . . . As we came/ up to the Lover's Seat/ the boy said would you/ like to 'ear the 'istory/ of the Lover's Seat and/ Aunty said yes/ The 'istory of it was this/There was once a young lady called Elizabeth/ something and a man/ whose name I cannot/ remember and they/ wanted to marry. But the parents of the/ woman did not want/ her to marry this man/ so they put her up at/

Fairlight that he might/ not come to visit her./ But one day as she was/ taking a walk along/ the rocks she saw the/ man and waved her/ handkerchief to show/ him she was there and/ for six nights they met/ on the Lover's Seat and/ then they married/ He went away to a Revenue Cutter and/ was drowned off the/ Isle of White. She was/ so broken hearted that/ she went to her par/ ents but they were/ so angry that they/ would have nothing/ to do with her and/ then she went to the/ rocks and said/ The shells of the ocean/ shall be my bed/ while the shrimps go waggling over my 'ead/ and she gave a great/ leap but a branch/ of a tree caught her/ and the Captain of the/ Revenue Cutter com/ ing up saved her and she was so greatful/ to him that she marri/ ed him and they lived/ 'appily and had a large family.[73]

In all their childhood diary keeping this was the first and last time that either of the sisters told a story. There was tension in this recounting. It is noticeable in the carefully outlined appreciation of the rustic burlesque (the child had learned from somewhere or someone how to express common speech with a dropped aspirate), and the narrative contrast between direct quotation of this comedy ('waggling over my 'ead') and the places where she found the story compelling and it briefly became her own. A developing knowledge of the correct way in which to perceive the social world and its inhabitants can be seen in the shift from 'lady' to 'woman', from the high-handed forgetting of names to the remembrance of great detail. The basis of this tension was the conflict perceived by the child between the arresting nature of this story of romantic love and the social position of the teller of it.

Mary Elizabeth Coleridge was not able to explore the possibilities of action with either her own use of the story form or her own use of dialogue. Looking back at her childhood many years later she recalled that she was 'such a numb unliving child that all that period of my life is vague and twilight, and I can recall scarcely anything except the sharp sensations of fear that broke the dull dream of my days'.[74] Whatever it was that frightened her, the structure and format of her childhood diary prevented even the oblique expression of fear. The style she practised was in fact a lesson in restraint, a method of turning all possibility into the historical past.

In using these children's texts, the task of the investigator must partly be to outline the way in which the general and pervasive ideas about social life that were presented to them mediated their writing. In this way, the destination of the child in adult life is unimportant; the task is not to look for the roots of uniqueness, nor the adult poet in the child. What the children's words represent is an example of their manipulating and re-ordering their social and emotional experiences in written language. What they produced is evidence of the way in which their biographical experiences came to be categorised in the terms of their particular social environment.[75] It is then possible to use their texts, in much the same way as children's spoken language has been used, to reconstruct the theories they evolved in order to become part of a particular society in a particular place and time.[76]

To do this, the reader needs to know about that social world, to understand the particularity of an upper-middle-class household in mid-Victorian England, to know where it stood in a network of political and class relations. To learn this was, after all, the primary unspoken task of the childhoods evidenced above. The task in reading the Coleridge sisters' texts, for example, is to keep separate what was learned from how that learning was done. What was learned is of real historical importance; but the way of learning it is relevant to an interpretation of 'The Tidy House' in demonstrating some of the means taken by children to learn an adult world. So, on the one hand, we must follow Florence and Mary Elizabeth as they ride their hired donkeys up and down Folkestone beach, through a privileged and statistically insignificant Victorian childhood, and, on the other hand, take from their dull recounting of it, insights into the ways in which, in other circumstances and at other times, little girls have used written language in order to become the women they were expected to be. For nearly all children perform this task; and all children, having been made minimally competent in the written language, perform this symbolic re-ordering of their experience.

It is only at a stage of development later than the one under consideration here that children become conscious of the meaning of their writing and evolve theories about its purpose. At the age of twelve or thirteen Elizabeth Moulton Barrett, in co-operation with her mother, carefully edited and transcribed many of the stories and journal entries she had written at the age of eight and nine.[77] Five years measures a period of rapid growth of spelling and handwriting ability, and the elegant appearance of the adolescent transcriptions, with their occasionally added maxims and epigrams show Elizabeth Barrett collecting her own archives for a later history of her childhood genius so that all her 'past days [might] appear as a bright star'.[78] There is an exceptional value in seeing this teenage girl come to an understanding of what function her childhood writing had served her: she knew that she had created herself in the act of writing – 'SELF LOVE may have prompted my not unwilling pen.'[79]

As the examples above have indicated, the journal keeping of many nineteenth-century girls served the pedagogical purposes of the adults who instructed them. 'I like to have you make observations about our conversations and your own thoughts,' wrote Abigail Alcott in her eleven-year-old daughter's journal in November 1843. 'It helps you to express them and to understand your little self. Remember dear girl, that a diary should be an epitome of your life'.[80] Louisa May Alcott had written much of pleasing her mother and her failures in the attempt during the previous year. The child's observations were written in an open book of socialisation, designed to be read by mother and child. The particular context of a diary was not however necessary for this written communication between child and instructor. Mary Moulton Barrett, for example, played publisher in her daughter's game of authorship (all the children in the Moulton Barrett family received massive encouragement to write).[81] 'Madame,' wrote eight-year-old Elizabeth Barrett to her mother in 1814, 'I request you to accept this little story for three shillings and to write copies to be sold to the public. I am Madame, Your Most obt. Humble servant, Elizabeth Barrett'.[82] Playful communication like this was rare, though it did fuel the production of domestic magazines produced by families of children.[83] In most child writing the purpose of communication between tutor and child was a means for the child to reflect on her errors and record lessons learned on the domestic battle front: 'I had a happy day today and felt happy after I went to bed. It was because I had been good'.[84]

'I have been a Naughty Girl. /I have been a Naughty Girl,' recorded seven-year-old Marjory Fleming in the summer of 1810. A few weeks later she detailed a similar falling from grace:

> I confess that I have been/ more like a little young/ Devil than a creature for/ when Isabella went up/ the stairs to reach me reli/ gion and my multi/ plication and to be good/ and all my other lessons/ I stamped with my feet/ and threw my new hat/ an was dreadfuly passionate/ but she never whiped me/ but gently said Marjory/ go into another room and/ think what a great crime/ you are committing/ letting your temper/ git the better of you/ but I went so sulkely that/ the Devil got the better of me/ but she never never whip me/ so that I think I would/ be the better of it and the next time that I behave/ ill I think she should do it/ for she never does it but she/ is very indulgent to me but/ I am very ungratefll to/ hir [85]

The protagonists here were not mother and daughter, but cousins, one of seven years, the other in her late teens. Marjory Fleming (1803–11), the daughter of a Kirkaldy accountant, spent most of the three years before her death living in the household of her maternal aunt at Ravelston and Braehead on the other side of the Firth of Forth. The arrangement was partly made for educational purposes and it suited both cousins, for Marjory dearly loved Isa Keith – 'my dear little mama'[86] – and Isa Keith was in her turn able to play a role she much enjoyed, that of the educating heroine.[87] At the suggestion of the older girl, Marjory kept a journal and in its pages the firm yet patient governess, the calm instructress, was able to see her own character unfold in the child's words: 'Isabella says when we pray we should/ pray fervently and not rattel over a praye'; 'she never whiped me/ but gently said Marjory/ go into another room and/ think what a great crime/ you are committing'; 'I wrote so ill that she took it/ away and locted it up/ in her desk where I/ stood trying to open/ it till she made me come/ and read my bible/ but I was in a bad honour/ and red it so Carelessly/ and ill that she took/ it from me and her/ blood ran cold but she/ never punished me/ she is as gental as a lamb'; 'Isabella gave me praise for checking my temper.'[88] Marjory's journal was read with delight by the adults in her family and, besides rehearsing lessons here, she was also playing to the gallery.

The journal also formed the basis of spelling lessons, of instruction in punctuation and sentence composition. It served as a record of the books the child read, as a copybook for adages and maxims, as a way of summarising sermons heard and, though not overtly so, as a record of an education in feeling and sentiment. Finally, as indicated above, it provided a means for Marjory Fleming to reflect on her progress through the landscape of self-control that Isa Keith had sketched out.

The journals were first published in the 1850s and have been through many editions and appeared in many anthologies of children's writing since then.[89] What seems to have ensured the huge posthumous success of Marjory Fleming's journals, letters and poems was the fact that they made an audience laugh at the same time as they brought tears of sadness to the eye as the insubstantiality of childhood was contemplated. The psychologist Sully caught this tone of exquisite sadness perfectly when in 1896 he described the value of child study (though he was not here discussing Marjory Fleming):

> We moderns are given to relieving the strained attitude of reverence and pity by momentary outbursts of humourous merriment. The child, whilst

appealing to our admiration and our pity, makes a loud and many-voiced appeal to our sense of laughter in things. It is indeed hard to say whether he is most amusing when setting at naught in his quiet lordly way, our most extolled views, our ideas of what is true or false, of the proper use of things, or when labouring in his perfectly self-conceived fashion to overtake us and to be as experienced and conventional as ourselves[90]

Even those who in the later part of the nineteenth century provided an astringent correction to the mawkishness surrounding the presentation of Marjory Fleming's work, saw in it a particular model for adult–child relationships. Mark Twain's appreciation for her *Journal* centred not only on her funniness and charm and the appeal of her passionate tempers, but on the usefulness to adults of the child's innocent yet revealing eye.[91] When he (and it is important to make it clear that Mark Twain was not at all sentimental about Marjory Fleming) discovered in the 1880s that his daughter Susy was writing his biography, he began to pose for the child's writing so that he might be revealed to himself in her prose. 'Whenever I think of Susy I think of Marjorie [sic]' he wrote many years later, and nearly a hundred pages of his own autobiography is taken up with his daughter's portrait of him.[92] The great chronicler of domestic comedy valued children's reflection of their social world, the way in which they mirrored the absurdities of adult behaviour in artless and hilarious prose.

'What is closest to her is, of course, what we want,' remarked Walter de la Mare of Marjory Fleming in 1935.[93] With him, and with generations of responsive readers across the years, we hold out our arms to this long-dead child with her 'continual propensity to laugh' – 'I like loud Mirement & laughter'[94] – the vigour with which she investigated the world and recounted what she saw there. Her journal is, as Isa Keith knew, 'a very amusing production indeed'.[95] To read it is to feel something of that tenderness and delight that we experience when we watch children dressing up, tottering in high heels, skirts trailing across the floor:

A Mirtal is a beautifull plant/ & so is a Geramem & nettel Geramem/ Climbing is a talent which the bear/ excels in and so does monkeys apes &/ baboons. I have been washing my dools cloths today & I like it very much/ people who have a good Conscience is alwa/ happy but those who have a bad one is al/ -ways unhappy and discontented/ There is a dog that yels continualy/ & I pity him to the bottom of my heart/ indeed I do./ Tales of fashionable life ar/ very good storys Isabella campels me/ to sit down & not to rise till this/ page is done but it is very near finished/ only one line to write

Love your/ enemy as your friend and not as/ your foe this is a very windy
stor/ my day and and looks as if it was/ going to snow or rain but it is/
only my opinion which/ is not always correct. – I am reading some
novletts and one call/ ed the Pidgeon is an excelent/ one and a charming
one – I think the price of a pineapple is yery dear for I here/ it is a whole
bright goulden/ geinie/ that might have sustained a/ poor family a whole
week and more/ [96]

It is significant that Frank Sidgwick, editing *The Complete Marjory
Fleming* in 1934, called her posthumous readers her 'lovers'.[97] What made
her a funny and pretty ornament to family life was part of that long tradition in our culture that, within domestic interiors, has looked to pretty
little girls for entertainment of the kind that a kitten or a puppy might
provide. Ellen Moers called this 'the warpage of gifted girls by an excess
of domestic admiration',[98] but it is clear that within recent history many
ordinary and unexceptional little girls have been watched with an attention and admiration that is not usually bestowed on little boys. So the
attentions paid to Marjory Fleming were not merely posthumous, but
were also an important part of her socialisation.

It is clear from the pages of her journal that Marjory Fleming's
relationship with her cousin was viewed by both of them as some
important preparation for the child's future role within the domain of
romantic love and domestic felicity. Although forbidden several times by
her cousin and tutor Isabella 'to speak about love', in 1810 and 1811 she
and Marjory made their way together through a long booklist of
romantic fiction.[99] The overt lesson to be learned was that 'heroick love
doth win disgrace';[100] yet the child recorded again and again the kisses she
received from middle-aged gentlemen visiting the house, who made play-
fully grave proposals of marriage to her, who walked hand in hand with
their 'loveress' through the grounds at Braehead.[101] 'In the love novels
all/ the heroins are very des/ perate,' wrote the eight-year-old girl;
'Isabella will not/ allow me to speak about lovers/ and heroins.' Isabella
Keith's rule about the improper discussion of men and romantic love was
several times recorded in her cousin's journal.[102] The rule was not strictly
enforced though, presumably because the Fleming and Keith families
found the child's observations as charming and funny as generations of
more distant readers have – and Marjory certainly knew her amusement
value:

A sailor called here to say/ farewell it must be dread/ full to leave his
native country/ where he might get a wife/ or perhaps me/ for I love/

> him very much & with/ all my heart but O I/ forgot Isabella forbid me
> to/ speak about love . . . a delightful/ young man beloved by all his
> friends and espacialy by/ me his loveress but I must not talk any longer
> about hin/ for Isa said it is not proper for to speak of gentalm.[103]

Carefully recorded strictures against the discussion of romance served
two purposes. They rounded out the character of Isabella Keith as
governess/heroine and allowed the child to contemplate the etiquette and
value of worldly love. The child's desire to enter the arena of adult sexuality was, in fact, tutored, and this tutoring was done out of a conflict that
the journal entries did to some extent resolve. Margery might record that
love was 'a very papithatick thing as well as troublesome',[104] but she was
encouraged to dwell on Isa Keith's virtues and the accomplishments that
gave her an advantage on the marriage market.[105] Margery learned the
lessons of female virtue by practising fond and romantic attachment to her
'lover Isa'.[106] The warm and affectionate tussles in bed over the possession
of the pillows, the wriggling child who kept her cousin awake at
night – 'Isabella says I disturbed her repose' – the long conversations,
the reading done in bed, all this was recorded, just as were Marjory's
furious outbursts of temper against Isa the tutor.[107] The child's feelings
towards her cousin were active and passionate and the journal was a
mirror in which Isabella Keith contemplated her tutelage in the child's
words and Marjory, out of active love, saw the woman she might
become.

In the examples above can be seen some of the ways in which writing
was used within theories of domestic pedagogy in the nineteenth-century
upper-middle-class household. Domestic experience was recorded and
objectified in the children's written words, and at the same time the
contstruction of their narrative helped them to reflect on their own
individual failings within the context of a deeply felt relationship with
an adult. Autobiographical domestic narration was confining, the possibilities for analysis, for rejecting the order of events and the inevitability
of chronology, severely limited. The construction of a story, on the other
hand, offered more scope for children to reject the dictates of chronology.

Yet the domestic pedagogy of the nineteenth century did not invite
story writing and the evidence is that where girls did practise the
construction of fiction they performed in isolation, often using materials
that did not guarantee the preservation of their work.[108] Adults were in
any case less likely to cherish fiction as memorabilia. Where a particular

domestic pedagogy did encourage story writing – as in the case of the Moulton Barrett household – production was often married to the learning of general moral precepts, another form of the instructive reflection that diary writing was understood to promote. During her ninth year Elizabeth Barrett wrote at least three stories, each structured around a lesson to be learned: on the importance of not getting lost; on the consequences of disobedience; on the punishment of vice by the worldly reversal of fortune.[109] To illustrate pieces of conventional wisdom in this way was still not to operate within so confining a structure as the diary. For, given the need to make something happen in order to forward the narrative, the writer was able to stand aside from it. In writing a story she was not part of its chronology, and was able by using this form to manipulate her own experiences – those of being lost, of being disobedient, of doing wrong – with greater freedom. Yet stories like these, which are plots built around moral precepts, have rarely, unless produced by a child who grew to be a famous woman, been published. Their relentless dullness could not serve the purpose of Daisy Ashford's *The Young Visiters*, which was to entertain adults without effort on their part. If children's writing in the past did not serve to amuse adults, then it was not published.

The publication of child writing outlines the uses that have been made of children's written language. It has been employed to reinforce general social theories about childhood: childhood as an area of innocence, or as a charming arena of budding adult sexuality, or of children as bearers of some important yet inarticulate message for adults. What has been especially valued by readers in the past is the flattering mirror of adult intention that some child writing seems to provide. For when children have shown a misunderstanding of adult motivation or adult rules and strictures in their writing, they rarely portray adults as unkind, or as purposefully misleading, merely as puzzling. Adults have been able to make the pleasant discovery of their failings through the 'unconscious humour' of children's words.

Children's writing is still published, and much of it is as mawkish as anything the 1920s produced. But two important developments have taken place of the last half-century and they have altered general expectations of children's literary productions. First of all, the map of early spoken language has been vastly extended and filled in. Knowing the general pattern and sequence in the acquisition of English as a first language we are better able to judge what is and what is not developmentally likely to be the form of young children's writing. Secondly, the results of investigating this first spoken language have been attached to more general theories of child development. It is in this expanded under-standing of childhood as development that we can see the greatest dif-ferences in reactions to children's writing between the 1920s and now. Of course, the study of child development already had a considerable history by 1920, but it was then still possible to see childhood as some undifferentiated state of mind still buried deep in all adults, rather than as a period in psychological growth. It is clear that those who responded with enthusiasm to such works as *The Story of Opal* and *The Elfin Pedlar* were not really interested in what they might tell them about child development or child language, were not even really very interested in whether or not they had truly been written by children, as long as they made some mystical statement about childhood and made the child in everyone accessible.[110] Work in child development over the last half-century insists on the idea of development, of a more or less orderly growth in capacity and performance in all aspects of the child's inter-action with the world. Even so, neither theories of child language nor accounts of children's socialisation within Western societies take into account the role that writing plays in the social and emotional develop-ment of young children.

The acquisition of literacy has been a task placed upon restricted groups of children in many societies in the past. But within the recent history of Western societies, learning the written code has been demanded of all children, regardless of their background or status.[111] Very little attention has been paid, in historical terms, to this enormous communality of experience. Neither social history nor theories of child language can tell us very much about what children do with writing, or what writing does for them. This chapter has drawn evidence from a recent period of our history when the acquisition of more than a minimal literacy was asked only of a limited number of children. Using a number of these nineteenth-century texts it becomes clear that it is possible to strip away the uses that adults made of them and see a function that writing performed for the little girls who wrote that was neither demanded nor anticipated by their instructors. It is particularly striking that the act of writing was on occasions a means by which children actively rejected and embraced the overtly expressed principles of their upbringing and in this way came to comprehend and absorb an adult world of meaning at their own level of understanding. The journals of the Alcott sisters, and especially that of

Marjory Fleming, show this process with a particular clarity.

Evidence of this process has so far been drawn from an extremely limited social milieu. It is important to go beyond this reservation and to understand that the whole edifice of Western developmental psychology rests on the testimony of a limited number of middle- and upper-class children who have been questioned and observed since the time of Rousseau. In order to read 'The Tidy House', we need a sense of the difference in individual psychologies that growing up in different classes of society imposes, and the writing of the middle-class Victorian children that has been used in this chapter suggests that it is possible to find such evidence for historical periods as well as for the present.

Chapter 4 considers the theories of child development and language development that might be expected to provide an interpretation of 'The Tidy House'. However, once the children's story is seen from the children's point of view, and the act of writing it regarded as serving their developmental and psychological needs, then it becomes clear that the absence of writing from developmental accounts of childhood diminishes the usefulness of these conventional interpretive devices. Like the development of spoken language, written language enables children to perform what would otherwise be an impossible task. The next chapter begins to outline the particular task that confronted Carla, Melissa and Lindie.

4

LEARNING THE SOCIAL WORLD: CHILDREN'S USE OF WRITING

There is a whole network of interpretative devices that leads to the very door of 'The Tidy House'; but the interpretative disciplines of child psychology, of developmental linguistics and of the history of childhood do not get us past its threshold and the general purpose of this chapter is to suggest why this is the case. Much of the previous argument has dwelt on the uses that adults have made of the idea of childhood and it is proposed here to outline briefly a history of child study and child psychology that is based on the particular experiences of particular children and which has implied that the schema thus constructed have universal application. Within this context, and using the insights provided by the study of child language, the function that the act of writing served for Carla, Melissa and Lindie is considered, as much as possible from the children's point of view. Both these questions serve as preliminaries to the next chapter, in which the history and experience of working-class little girlhood is considered in more detail.

Watching children is one of the pastimes of our civilisation and, within the recent history of our culture, the results of this observation have been recorded. Recounting the natural history of child development was the self-elected task of many upper-middle-class women in the nineteenth century. 'His hands and feet are large,' observed Sara Coleridge of her infant son in 1832:

> He is particularly merry early in the morning. He has not yet been vaccinated. He has dribbled for the last fortnight and now begins to use his hands and cuffs my hand whilst he is sucking and sometimes tries to pull away. He will be 11 weeks old next Thursday. God bless him! Little darling. I shall continue this account journal wise[1]

The detached observation of a natural phenomenon was the stylistic mark of such records. The scientific observation of children, in which a pattern of events was drawn together to describe a coherent development, had its roots in a practice earlier than that of the bourgeois nursery of the early nineteenth century, in the observation of the inhabitants of royal and aristocratic nurseries in the seventeenth and eighteenth centuries.[2] Between that rehearsal of the sayings of princes and the late nineteenth-century anthropological interest in child development as a key to evolutionary understanding lay the records of many middle-class women, who understood their diaries of child development to be types of natural history. Catherine Stanley of Alderly, Cheshire, prefaced her record, which she started keeping in 1812, with this quotation from the enlightenment philosopher Read:

> If we could obtain a distinct and full history of all that hath passed in the mind of a child from the beginning of life and sensation till it grows up . . . this would be a treasure of natural history which would probably give more light into the human faculties, than all the systems of philosophies about them from the beginning of the world.[3]

It was as a naturalist and a philosopher that she observed her son a few days later:

> He shewed a strong antipathy to a dead bird on touching it and afterwards to anything like fur or feathers, but by giving him a dog of fur to play with, he forgot it by degrees[4]

Within the long domestic history of child observation, many fathers too – the most noted being Charles Darwin – kept developmental diaries.[5] The impression that child observation was a male practice can only derive from the fact that more fathers' than mothers' journals were published; this is an entirely unsurprising reversal of the sex bias to be seen in the publication of *children's* writing, where what the reader sought was the relaxing and frivolous femininity of little girls' diaries. The late nineteenth-century child study movement spoke explicitly to fathers,[6] and many of them, with serious careers to further within the new discipline of psychology, reported on their own children's development.[7] But there are so many mothers' developmental journals in the archives that it is difficult to believe that it was not, predominantly and privately, a female exercise.[8]

There were many motives for women's recording. Started as a health record, Sara Coleridge's account of her son's ingestion and excretion became a metaphor for her own physical sickness and increasing depression. Yet through all the dark nights of motherhood that she recounted, the account of her child's growth remained clear and factual. Elizabeth Gaskell's account of her infant daughter's physical and linguistic progress became the outline of a spiritual and moral journey undertaken by mother and child. Yet the details of growth – the words acquired, the steps taken – were plainly and factually recorded.[9] The intimacy between mother and child, becoming, as in Sara Coleridge's case, the dark confusion of two bodies, two sets of desires, was seen as a violation of the principle of neutral observation and the tension and anguish of some nineteenth-century mothers' accounts was in part an acknowledgement that they were moving outside the objective principles of record keeping. Child-watching became commercially catered for in the middle of the century and in 1850 Isabella Stevenson was able to set down Robert Louis's childhood in one of the blank 'Baby Books' then available.[10]

As a method of child study, the domestic diary has never really fallen out of favour. As child psychology over the last thirty years has turned its attention more minutely towards children's development of spoken language, the domestic observation of small children has continued to provide the basis for most contemporary theories of syntactic and semantic development[11] and developmental linguists have continued to use the most convenient subjects to hand: their own small children and those of friends and acquaintances.[12]

Earlier in this century, it was on this foundation of the domestic study of the individual child that Freud and Piaget built.[13] The natural history of childhood was expanded by moving beyond the limits of the physical world and the family circle. But though the dreams, play and conversation of children were employed to lay bare their unconscious mind, the space of the bourgeois nursery still lay around: it was pointed out long ago that much of Piaget's early investigation was undertaken in a nursery school that was deliberately set up to promote the child's individual and self-directed activity and that minimised the opportunities for collaboration and contact.[14]

To present this brief outline is to point out that the foundations of child psychology and the general understanding of childhood that has been extracted from its classic texts are based on particular historical circumstances – on the growth and development of real children from particular class and cultural backgrounds. The idea of the child which the early twentieth-century psychologists had in mind during the course of their investigations was that which had been established by countless observations and recordings in the middle-class nurseries of a century past. This idea was frequently represented in the figures of their own children at home.

Much, though not of course all, of our understanding of child development is based on conversation with, and observation of, little boys over the past two hundred years, and nowhere (except perhaps in law) is the 'sex-neutral "he" '[15] better established than in the literature of child psychology. The casual identification of little boys with 'children' had its roots in the domestic practice outlined above, where common sense often seemed to indicate that the most reasonable way to discuss the development of girls was in comparison with their brothers.[16]

There is of course a substantial body of work on the development of little girls deriving from the psychoanalytic tradition and normative educational psychology puts an equal number of questions to girls as it does to boys. But the tradition of psychoanalysis itself prevents us from seeing girls' development except in comparison with that of boys, their behaviour *more* passive, their play *less* aggressive. Much of the theory of female infant sexuality falls away if there is not a little boy with a penis to compare the little girl with.[17] Classrooms usually contain roughly equal numbers of boys and girls, but nowhere in the literature is there to be found a calm statement like this: 'The method we have adopted is as follows. Two of us followed each a child (a girl) for about a month in the morning class'. When Piaget wrote that sentence in 1926 the word in parentheses was of course, 'boy'.[18] A girl will not do as a representative of all children.[19]

It is a legacy of the history of domestic observation as well as a reflection of the realities of biological development that the basic organising principle of child psychology attributes the most significant period of development to children's earliest years. Current theories of child language are for the main part organised around children's initial acquisition of their first language[20] and the only well-mapped developmental schema of child language that we so far possess concern children under the age of five. There has been investigation of the spoken language of children between the ages of five and twelve (and some of these investigations are discussed below), but there are two problems involved in using the results of this investigation in an interpretation of 'The Tidy House'. First of all, there does not seem to be a direct relationship between the difficulties encountered in spoken language by children of this age and the use they make of written language. Reading 'The Tidy House' in the light of the syntactic development of school-age children would make an interesting exercise, but it would not help us past the second and more fundamental problem, which is that no theory of language acquisition can deal with the matter and content of children's productions like 'The Tidy House'.

For instance, Carol Chomsky has shown that children of Carla, Lindie and Melissa's age have difficulty in understanding and using some pronouns.[21] The children did occasionally demonstrate a confused usage in their conversation (TH tapes: pp. 172, 173), and it is tempting to see their repetition of names instead of the appropriate pronoun in 'The Tidy House' as linked to this general difficulty in spoken language, as a way of avoiding misuse:

When she got in/ she used to tell Mark/ and Mark had a good go at him.

Jamie smacked Carl/ Carl started to cry

they had their bedroom upstairs/ not downstairs like Susan's bedroom/ which had a bedroom downstairs

[TH transcript: pp. 45, 46, 45]

Appealing though this explanation is (and appealing as the incantatory quality that this repetition bestows is), it is far more likely that because writing is slow, and for children of this age still a task that demands conscious control of a writing implement, that in the course of constructing a sentence they forget that they already have something 'in focus', and could use a pronoun.

The same argument applies to the children's use of tenses in their writing. Children of seven, eight and nine often get into difficulties in the construction of sentences involving conditional tenses:

we thought . . . that . . . Jamie would have a boy and that Carl and the boy, the little boy, always used to have fights.

I think she might have one, might she

[TH tapes: pp. 175, 168]

'The Tidy House' is striking in that it is a narrative constructed almost entirely in the present tense. But there is no necessary connection between the simple, timeless present of the children's story and certain difficulties they shared with their age group in verbal tense usage. The children used the simple present tense because they were interested in what people did to each other when they spoke about real happenings in the real world, and to pursue this interest conversation had necessarily to be presented in this way.

It is not the language system that they employed, nor the relationship in syntactic terms, of the written to the spoken, that is of essential interest in 'The Tidy House'. Writing, as far as the children were concerned, seemed to be viewed by them as the adequately wielded tool that allowed them to explore much broader and more important questions. The dialogue of which the story is largely composed may in fact tell us practically nothing about the relationship of speech to writing in children of five to twelve; it tells us rather about a social environment in which dialogue has a status and power that the children particularised, not because they could articulate that power, but because they had spent nine years observing its effects. Quite simply, their text offers evidence that people talking to each other, and the effects that this talking had, was the most important and powerful event that the children ever witnessed.

Given the background outlined above to a modern understanding of child langauge, 'The Tidy House' raises several awkward questions, for it was written in a classroom, by eight-year-old working-class girls, and was constructed in written language. If we approach the children's story in this tradition of inquiry we find that its authors are older than the majority of the subjects of child study. We find that the vision imposed by the tradition of psychometric testing makes it difficult to see productions of working-class children in their own right, rather than in comparison with the superior efforts of children from more comfortable circumstances. We find that the sociology of schooling recounts a long history of working-class children's failures in a school environment, and chronicles an apparent lag in their linguistic development, compared with middle-class children.[22] We find also, when we consider the content of 'The Tidy House', that only silence within literature, politics, history and sociology bears witness to the experiences of the children's mothers, which, in writing their story, Carla, Lindie and Melissa attempted to comprehend and assess.[23]

Writing viewed as a form of language acquisition is almost entirely missing from the canons of development linguistics. There is important work on young children's spelling errors, and on the evolution of scribble and drawing into the symbolic representation of speech in written language;[24] but the children who wrote 'The Tidy House' were much older than the subjects of these inquiries and were operating at a level of competence and ability not represented in this small body of literature. Educational theory has categorised the writing children produce in schools and the influences on children as writers have been outlined.[25] But these studies do not deal with the acquisition of the written code and, beyond outlining some affective uses of language, they do not tell us what writing does for the children who produce it.

There are two obvious and interconnected reasons for this absence. First of all, any account of socialisation within Western societies must take into account the recent experience of most of its children, which is to pass, at a relatively young age, from the family to the school, where knowledge is presented in a formal objective way, not assimilated through the children's identification with people who matter to them, as it is in the home, but rather through instruction and learning. In the literature this place of secondary socialisation, the school, is characterised as 'formal', the knowledge presented there as 'objective',[26] and this image bothers those who have investigated the language of children over five. Within anthropological studies of child language there is an understandable impulse to seek the least influenced and mediated of speech – the story told on the street corner, the verbal play overheard by the non-judgemental, almost absent adult.[27] Children's writing, on the other hand, is massively influenced by adults and is nearly always the result of some kind of adult intervention. Children clearly perceive writing as a *task*, by virtue of the physical activity involved as well as by their interpretation of adult intention and in performing it children try to please adults and to adopt models of narrative and ways of working that they divine will be praised and appreciated. When Carla was explaining to the other two girls who had just joined her how to go about writing 'The Tidy House', she fabricated a physical task for them that bore no relation to what was actually expected of her in that specific situation, but was a pretty revealing estimate of what she saw was generally acceptable and praiseworthy:

Lindie: Look, shall I carry on writing something?
Carla: Give something to Miss. Because, you see, got to have five
            pages of it. Each thing. Here you are. [Showing her contribu-
            tion.] Look.

[TH tapes: p. 164]

There are other ways in which children's writing is influenced. There are many ways of teaching children to read and the evidence is that reading methods influence the production of their first written sentences.[28] Radically different approaches to spelling are presented to children and these taught theories are mapped on to their own existing notions about the relationship of sound to symbol.[29] Often children are only given practice in a very limited range of written language forms and it is likely that differing narrative structures give children acquaintance with particular reconstructions of reality.[30]

Most of the writing produced by children in our society is produced in schools and schools *are* arenas of cultural mediation. All these factors add up to the uneasiness that investigators feel when they come to consider a taught form of language as opposed to one that is spontaneously and inevitably acquired. Second, and as part of a more general absence of developmental evidence from older children, is the fact that it is disturbing to the observer when the subject can offer opinion and reflection, instead of merely providing the phenomena of speech errors or gestures to be recorded. It is difficult for a methodology that is centred on naturalistic observation to cope with consciousness on the part of its subjects and writing does offer children a means by which they can consciously reflect on the form of linguistic production and evolve opinions about its contents.

As an extension and elaboration of the power of spoken language to make experience concrete and objective,[31] written language makes it both permanent and manipulable.[32] The delay and reflection involved in using an alphabetic writing system, which demands of most eight-year-olds pause for thought about the relationship of sound to symbol in spelling many words, the time and effort involved in putting the marks on the paper, both make the idea of permanence and manipulation available to children. Language is made visible and not only are they enabled to understand what it is to consider and reconsider an idea, but the ability to alter the form of that idea – to rub it out and do it again – introduces the more powerful notion of human beings having the power to bring about change:

Carla	[reading Melissa's portion of the text]: Lissa, what's it say?
Lindie:	Well, do you want to rub it out for Melissa?
Melissa:	No, I'll put it straight.
Carla:	Don't make sense.
. . .	
Melissa:	Do you think I should start again? . . . Shall I start again? . . . Oh, Miss . . . [The teacher is on the other side of the room.] I don't know if it's all right.

Carla: It's all got to be typed out. You're only doing it roughly anyway, aren't you?

Melissa: Shall I write 'a special day' . . .

[Long pause whilst the children write.]

            I writ so far: 'It was a special day today because it was Carl's birthday. He was four. He opened his cards, he got one –'

Carla: Shall I read what I've put, and you read what you've put? This is episode two of 'The Tidy House'. 'One day on a Monday August 21st it was Carl's birthday . . .'

[TH tapes: pp. 161–62]

The picture of the formal and objective knowledge acquired in the schoolroom retreats a little. This is not to deny that schools do provide a formal setting for the acquisition of of knowledge; but what we really do not know is whether or not the children within them see the knowledge to be acquired in that particular way. It may be that the acquisition of writing skills is not perceived by the child as an essay in assimilating impersonal schema, but simply as a new way of investigating interesting and personal questions.

Investigators of children's writing have, for a century now, seen a tension existing between its form and content.[33] Much of the criticism that Vygotsky directed in the 1920s at pedagogy's narrow conception of writing in the child's cultural development still holds good today.[34] There is still a vast – and entirely justifiable – enthusiasm for the inculcation of the technical skills that writing involves (the motor skills involved in putting pencil to paper), but many children in British primary schools are taught to write within the context of an educational theory that emphasises to both the children and their teachers that writing is speech written down and that children's most valuable possession in the process of becoming literate is their mastery of the spoken code.[35]

Vygotsky's early and seminal contribution to this debate was to outline the developmental history of written language in children and to show by what means they come to know that writing is *not* just speech written down, but that, like language itself, it is 'second order symbolism which gradually becomes direct symbolism'. What this means in effect is that

> written language consists of signs that designate the sounds and words of
> the spoken language, which, in turn are signs for real entities and
> relations. Gradually, this intermediate link, spoken language, disappears
> and written language is converted into a system of signs that directly
> symbolise the entities and relationships between them.[36]

Within Vygotsky's account there are perceptions of vital importance, though most of them concern children much younger than Carla, Lindie and Melissa. Most striking is the presentation of the enormity of the very young child's discovery that speech can be drawn, recorded and made visible. The discovery of the power of making something visible out of the aural is found in other case studies and from these we know of the time and effort that four- and five-year-olds are prepared to invest in their first spellings and how such efforts on their part can result in an abstract and theoretical spelling system, which, though wrong in adult terms, is the result of the child's own reflection on a language system.[37] The invented spellings of pre-school children investigated by Charles Read represent a stage in the development of written language in Vygotsky's account.[38]

But it was the quality of abstraction, the child's detachment from the situation in hand, that was seen by Vygotsky to mark the developmental importance of writing, as of the earlier acquisition of spoken language. To function even minimally the child must 'disengage himself from the sensory aspects of speech, and replace words by images of words'.[39] In this particular account abstraction is compounded by the fact that when writing children usually speak to no one, or imagine someone to speak to, whilst in conversation it is the moment by moment interaction with an interlocutor that determines the direction of speech and children do not have to think consciously about *how* to direct it, as they must do when writing.[40]

These psychological insights are powerful and important, but problems remain in employing them for an interpretation of 'The Tidy House'. Some difficulties are minor – one rests on the particularity of the circumstances of Vygotsky's study and his implication that school children usually work in isolation, writing about formal and abstract matters.[41] The process of composing 'The Tidy House' shows that these are not a necessary background to children writing. What is more, all writers, not just young children, must make a constant movement back and forth between the spoken and the written, in order to assess what it is that they have just put on the page.[42] If the real problem seems to be that there is as yet no psychological description of the means by which children come to directly represent the world in written language, as in Vygotsky's account, then this absence may be accounted for by our refusal to consider the *matter* of children's writing, to take it seriously as a theoretical construct of a social and sexual world. In the case of working-class children, we do not in fact take the world they represent in writing very seriously either.[43]

Carla, Melissa and Lindie knew quite well what writing was. They understood it as a system that they were still in the process of mastering, but the basic elements of which they had long ago learned. Their familiarity with its processes, the drafts needed, the revisions possible, is seen in their brisk discussion in the extract from the tapes quoted on page 92, as well as in Melissa's musings on her temporary inability to get started. They knew quite a lot about how they went about spelling words:

Melissa: That one's meant to be 'special', but I couldn't work it out, you see.

[TH tapes: p. 172]

They were in fact, much more articulate and confident in discussing the form and technicalities of their story than they were in talking about its meaning, where questions about the motivations of their characters were sometimes greeted with puzzlement (TH tapes: pp. 167, 172). It was the meaning of their culture that they were trying to learn. This task was a difficult one and it was those difficulties that engaged their attention.

As *part* of their inquiry, language and language use was of real interest to them. They were particularly fascinated by the particular styles of spoken language that they encountered. In the extract below, which is from Lindie's portion of the text, she shows attention to the speech of very young children, but more particularly to the tension that can under-lie polite conversation:

'Where are we going, Mummy?'
'To go and see Mark and Jo.'
'Oh,' he said
and carried on walking.
When they came to Jo's house
he ran in the gate and in the house
and hugged her.
'Hello, Jo,' he said.
'Hello, Jo,' said Jamie. 'How are you?'
'Oh fine,' said Jo. 'How are you?'
'All right,' said Jamie,
'but Carl is really getting on my nerves.
I am really fed up with him.'
And Jo said, 'Don't be mean.'

95

'I'm not. It's because he's so spoiled.
I don't like children being spoiled.'

[TH transcript: pp. 49–50]

The children knew that what would move their plot forward was this strained interchange between their characters Jo and Jamie:

Teacher:	Have you any idea of what's going to happen to these people in the end?
Lindie:	Oh yes, Miss. We was thinking that Jo and . . .
Melissa:	Jo and Mark have twins . . . and we thought, um, that Jamie would have a boy and Carl and the boy, the little boy, always used to have fights. And then, and then . . .
Teacher:	Why do all these people have these babies?
Melissa:	And then Carl won't be pampered, will he?
Carla:	They can't help it, can they?
Teacher:	Can't they?
Carla:	No.
Teacher:	But they've gone two years without having a baby; why haven't they had one so far?
Lindie:	Because if . . . you . . . read mine . . .
Carla:	She never forgot to take her pill.
. . .	
Lindie:	Yeah, well, did you read my end bit? Jamie had a little row with her, and she told her that they, that her and . . .
Teacher:	Oh. [Reading text] 'I don't like children being spoiled'?
. . .	
Lindie:	Jamie criticised the way Jo spoiled Carl.
Teacher:	And that made Jo think that she ought to have one to show that she could do it?
Carla:	And she has twins.
Melissa:	And she has twins.

[TH tapes: p. 175]

Two sets of interests are demonstrated by the children here: one is a concern with the way the world works, the way things actually happen; the other is a concern with the cadence, stress and patterning of dialogue. Work on children's speech play shows that seven- and eight-year-olds are still absorbed by the phonology of English long after they have mastered all its sounds.[44] The rhymes, catches and jokes of children in this age group show a determination to rehearse particular sequences of sounds; this interest in the patterning of sounds is much closer to an adult poetic interest in the possibilities of the language than it is to the baby's babbling, where it is possibly a simpler kind of practice that is going on.

Children of Carla's age do not need to practise the language in this way; what she was interested in doing was playing with it, exploring it. This concern was particularly evident in a series of 'songs' that Carla completed after 'The Tidy House' had been abandoned. These are discussed in the last chapter of this book, but one of them, 'Jack Got the Sack', shows Carla's investigatory concerns with the language that are also noticeable in the echoing dialogue of 'The Tidy House':

> Jack, Jack, got the sack
>
> 'Oh, Jack, go to work please
> to get some money for the children.'
> 'Oh all right.'
> 'Bye.'
>
> Jack came back soon, at half past two.
> Jack got the sack.
>
> 'Jack, you've got the sack.'
> 'I've got the sack.'
> 'What are we going to do now?'
> 'Don't ask me.'
>
> Jack went to every place he could think of.
> He got back home at five o'clock.
>
> 'I can't get a job now.'
>
> Jeannie his wife said,
> 'I don't care. Just get a job, Jack.
> We'll starve to death.'
>
> They had a row, and Jeannie left Jack.
> The girls came too.
>
> Oh how sad Jeannie was.
>
> She got a job as a barmaid.
> It was good money at twenty pounds a week.
> Jeannie bought Lindie a bike to ride
> and Melissa a doll and their friend Lisa a dog.
> They were happy for ever after.

[Carla, song, July 1976]

In their conversation the children showed a deep interest in adult language: they imitated adults, mimicked accents and the implications of one particularly striking overheard phrase ('I couldn't be bothered to take the price off') found its way into one of the pictures drawn to accompany 'The Tidy House' (TH tapes: pp. 170, 171). Their story was in itself an exegesis on adult roles. All these concerns can be found in the investigated speech play of children[45] and 'The Tidy House' had the form of an extension and elaboration of these concerns into written language.

The striving inherent in children's physical play can also be found in the writing presented here. In play, children operate at the edge of their competence – 'as if the child was trying to jump above the level of his behaviour' – preferring adult roles in imaginary games, showing the 'single wish . . . the desire to be big and grown up'.[46] The desire to reach out beyond the borders of ease and competence is even more evident in speech play: children struggle to practise adult social roles, laugh at jokes they don't quite understand, practise riddles the point of which just eludes them.[47]

Writing then would seem to have served Carla, Lindie and Melissa in two ways. It offered them the chance to play with the sound patterns of their first language and also to deal with the systems of social meanings that underlay the words they wrote. As adults we need interpretative devices for approaching this assimilation of meaning in children's writing, but we have as yet only inadequate tools to do it by. The heart of the difficulty lies in the fact that in the written production with which we are centrally concerned, it was a culture that the children attempted to make meaningful. To do this – to write 'The Tidy House' – they used a linguistic system that has for the main part been defined as operating outside culture and politics.[48] Neither does literary analysis help us very much, for the devices of literary criticism usually assume that we know something of the relationship between the word and its meaning, the sign and the signified. But children who write do not necessarily use adult meanings and in some cases are, by writing, actively involved in making their own. On the evidence of 'The Tidy House' and many other pieces of children's writing it would seem that it is not enough to distinguish between the events of a story (which may be real happenings in the real world) and the significance of those events (mapped out and held together in narrative), nor to analyse literary production in terms of the tension and exchange between an event and its meaning.[49] For Carla, Lindie and Melissa, the act of writing actually *produced* the meaning of the events that had caught their attention. For them it was the making that was important and the active process by which they came to understand the relationships between the underlying principles of desire, intention and event that formed their social world. Most theories of literary analysis are, in any case, concerned with the relationship between the writer and the text, and the text and the audience, whilst in children's writing we need to look for what the writing does for the writer, not what the writer does to it, nor what it does for us.

The text of 'The Tidy House' served the children in a particular way, because they chose, for the main part, to direct their narrative by means of dialogue. It was noted in the last chapter that the personal domestic narrative practised by nineteenth-century child writers rarely presented dialogue. Yet it is possible to use this device in written autobiographical narrative. In the following diary entry, written by Melissa five months before 'The Tidy House' was started, conversation is presented as the directional force in social life:

> On Saturday it snowed and I had to stop in. I played with my Tiny Tears
> and my pram. Then my brother came in to jump on his bed, so he did.
> Soon we came down and my mum went up to make the beds. When she
> came down she was angry. I asked her why and she said, You just wait
> till your father gets home and then you'll have something to jump about,
> and I said, What's wrong? And she said to me, Your brother has broken
> a leg off his bed. But she did not tell my dad.[50]

> [Melissa, diary entry, February 1976]

As a matter of fact, in most children's lives the words of adults *are* what move events forward, forbid and prevent action:

> Yesterday when I got home I asked my mum if Carla could come up, and
> my mum said yes. So I went to Carla's mum with her, and her mum said
> yes, so we went

> [Melissa, diary entry, December 1975]

As far as the children were concerned, their diaries, in contrast with the nineteenth-century ones described in Chapter 3, were designed to tell someone who did not already know what had happened. They were not merely for recording events but for explaining how those events came about. In this diary entry by Carla, the final explication is directed at the reader:

> On Saturday my dad won a silver cup and two second prizes, one third
> prize and fourth prize, and on Friday my dad wasn't so grumpy and on
> Saturday my dad bought chocolate pennies and chocolate Father

Christmases home. Mummy said we can eat it after dinner, Christmas
dinner that is. I have three sisters so my dad only bought four Father
Christmases home.

[Carla, diary entry, December 1975]

In their diary writing, the children were highly conscious of their
audience: they believed that their diaries were written in order to tell me
(and sometimes other children) something we didn't know. But in
writing 'The Tidy House' the notion of an audience, and the need to be
clear about what had happened, to *explain*, seemed to have pressed far less
upon them. They knew that their words would be read; but they
obviously did not feel it necessary to put themselves in the place of me (or
another reader) as they wrote. In developmental terms this could be seen
as a move back from their growth in objectivity and detachment, a regres-
sion in their developing ability to see the world from the vantage point of
others. But to interpret the narrative perspective of 'The Tidy House'
only in this way would be to ignore the particular psychological uses they
found they could make of it.

It was their use of the story form that enabled the children to use
conversation not just as an explanation of events in 'The Tidy House',
but as a way of structuring narrative. The simplest kind of narrative is a
sequence of clauses that is structured by memory of real events and
matched to the order of events being described, as in the examples
below.[51] The first two are examples of verbal narrative; the third and
fourth were written:

> I was once in a great crowd
> and getting crushed
> and there was a very tall soldier close by me
> and he lifted me, basket and all, right up to his shoulder
> and carried me clean out of the crowd.
> He had stripes on his arm.
> 'I shouldn't like you to be in such a trade',
> says he, 'if you were my child'.[52]
>
> [Street trader, nine years old, 1850(?)]

> When I was going to the shop
> to get Sally's birthday card
> that Suzanne Williams come
> and she started hitting me
> So I goes . . .
> Wait till you get up school,
> I'll soon get you.
>
> [Carla, TH tapes: p. 165]

Last night I played skipping.
Then some boys came up
and took Melissa's rope.

[Carla, diary entry, September 1975]

On Saturday I got up
and got dressed.
Then I walked all the way up Grange Rise
to see my nanny.
Then I had some chips
and got my hat and coat on
Then me and my auntie Janice
went down the town to see Jaws.

[Sharon, diary entry, February 1976]

In these examples, the clauses are ordered in temporal sequence and to alter the sequence would be to make a false representation of the events they describe. In the first, second and fourth example above, the children all halted their narratives in order to explain details to their listeners. But the explanations ('to get Sally's birthday card', 'to see my nanny') did not disturb the sequence of events and all of these children displayed a great concern for the proper order of things, the Victorian street trader, for example, detailing the soldier's stripes not as part of a general description of him ('a very tall soldier'), but at the point she noticed them in her temporally accurate recounting – when she was lifted to his shoulder.

When clauses in an autobiographical account refer to generalised events that may have occurred many times, they cannot be used to shape a narrative. Children can then present an arrangement of clauses that are clustered according to theme, each group of clauses conveying certain types of information:

When I was little
I was half good and half bad.
I would get my dad's ladder
and climb up my mum's washing line.
And when my mum was not looking
I would go to the bedrooms
and take all the blankets off the beds.
When my dad took me to the woods
and we was walking
I would run back to the car
when my dad was looking for me
my dad could not find me
so he went back to the car.

When he saw me in the car
he would smack me.
When I was good:
on my birthday when I got my birthday cake
my mum would cut it
and I would share it all out.
When my brother and sister was born
I would be nice to them
and they did the same things as I done.

[Donna, essay, March 1976]

Even within simple past tense narratives, children seek to group and organise events and thereby demonstrate some of the inadequacies of simple, temporarily accurate narrative in explaining the course of events:

On Saturday Melissa came up my house. It was three o'clock when she came up my house. She went home at five o'clock. I took her home, but before that I went to my mum's friend's house in Maypole Street. Melissa went home at last and so did I.

[Carla, diary entry, October 1975]

Within the confines of autobiographical narration, children seek to complicate and dramatise their accounts. In Carla's verbal description of the fight at the paper shop (p. 100 above) she used the device of compounding two actions by the use of the present participle, as in 'when I was going to the shop'. Not only did this orientate her audience, but it also set the tone for the whole narrative, in that it intensified the suddeness and injustice of the attack.[53]

Here, in another narrative from the recorded conversation of the three children, Carla presented her audience with a synopsis of the narrative before she started it, suspended it with an evaluation, and at the end returned the resolution to the initial summary. She was describing the loss of one of her father's racing pigeons:

He's got pigeons.
He lost . . . He had seventy-one.
He lost them.
One flew out the basket.
Ted, his partner, forgot to put the brick on it
and it was found in the shed
and he opened the door
and it flew away.
He had seventy.
He put them in a race
and now he won't send anymore for racing.[54]

[TH tapes: p. 179]

There are in fact two narratives here, one to do with the actual loss of the bird (this narrative would begin 'Ted his partner, forgot to put the brick on/ and one flew out the basket'), and another to do with how the loss of this pigeon (and possibly others) stopped her father from competing with them. The narratives are intertwined because the presence of an audience demanded explanation of the sequence of events. Carla made the decision to do this: her audience at that particular moment wasn't really very interested in what she was saying.

Children's verbal narration can demonstrate a manipulation and re-ordering of temporal sequence in order to satisfy the demands of an audience, or what, in some cases, the child divines to be the needs of an audience. Many verbal narratives have been collected from children under conditions where demonstration of a certain skill was deemed by both child and researcher to be a component of the situation. In the finely wrought, aggressively displayed accounts of adolescent boys on the streets of New York, in children invited to tell their jokes to interested adults, in cultures observed where story-telling is understood to be a transaction between adult and child, in the attentive researcher writing down the stories of nursery school children,[55] children are asked not to explain something, but to show what they are capable of. But in some other situations, where narration is not a matter of displaying, but a matter of telling, it seems that children do perceive that the extremely simple form of language of which narration consists is inadequate to their purposes. Particularly, its temporarily accurate structure contrasts with the complexity, the shifts in temporal scale, that are witnessed by children in dialogue. One of Carla's devices in her description of the fight at the paper shop was to resolve her account with a quotation from the interchange between the two protagonists: 'So I goes . . . "Wait till you get to school, I'll soon get you." ' The difference between the narration of display and the narration of explication rests on the child's judgement of what her audience does not yet know. When a narrative serves as an explanation of a current situation, then the introduction of dialogue can serve as a link between past and present events, as in this account, where a thirteen-year-old crossing sweeper explained her current situation to Henry Mayhew in 1850:

> Then I got right down to the Fountings in Trafalgar Square . . .
> There were a good many boys and girls on that crossing . . .
> so I went along with them.
> When I fust went

103

they said 'here's another fresh 'un.'
They come up to me and says
'Are you going to sweep here?'
and I says 'Yes'
and they says 'You mustn't come here; there's too many;'
and I says 'They're different ones every day,' – for they're not regular
there, but shift about
They didn't say another word to me,
and so I stopped.[56]

[Crossing sweeper, thirteen years old, 1850(?)]

The early practice of written autobiographical narrative, by abstracting in linear form principles of narration (say what happened in the order that it happened), actually intensifies them and, as has been seen, children frequently show a great concern for the correct order of things in their diary writing. Personal *verbal* narration is frequently suspended because the audience prompts evaluation; but in writing there is no demanding audience present. Often, when children try to engage an adult's attention in order to tell them something, they announce 'a piece of trouble', so that in a situation where they are the inferior participants they gain the right to speak.[57] It has been pointed out that one of the burdens on the verbal narrator is actually to recount something that is reportable, that will not elicit the response 'So what?' from an audience.[58] This kind of pressure of audience disappears to some extent when children write. Yet many of the constraints of verbal narration do transfer to written narrative. The child can, for instance, imagine an audience and respond to it; and the objectification of the 'I' on the page, and the tense that the child is bound to use, suggests to her that as a witness to the event she is describing she must tell the truth about it and must confirm it.

Written, first-person narration does in fact convey these two messages to the writer: that the events she describes really took place and that she was there, a witness to them. The only way to avoid saying what happened is not to mention it at all. But the narrative technique of story telling offers much greater scope for selection, abstraction and reversal of events. When stories are written down, the permanence offered by script means that children can abandon many of the restraints of recounting, that is, they can get by without saying who it is that is speaking and can forward action without necessarily placing it in time or space.

In the class where Carla, Melissa and Lindie spent the year 1975–6, the folk-fairy-tale was often used as a model for story writing. The eight-year-old girl who wrote the following story demonstrated conscious use of the model in her careful attention to incantatory repetition and the arbitrarily introduced shifts in narrative that are a feature of the genre:

> This story is called the Magic Cat.
> Once upon a time there was a little old man and a little old woman. One day the little old woman said that 'I would like a pet.' 'But what pet?' said the little old man. 'I think I would like a cat.' 'So would I,' said the little old man. So they saved up as much as they can. One day they saved up £3.80. That was how much the white cats were. So they bought a white cat and named it Whitebum. The little old man had a mat. The cat liked the mat so much that it would not lay on the other mats. One day the little old woman said, 'We must get the cat a mat the same.' They saved up as much as they can. Once more in a year they had saved up £2.99. That was how much a mat the same was. So they bought a mat the same and when the cat went out for its walk the little old man changed the mats. He put the new mat, they put the other mat in a box. The cat did not know the difference between the mats. One year later the cat died, so they saved up to buy another cat. One day they saved up as much as they can. In a year and a half they had saved up £2.90 so they bought another cat and it too was white with black ears so they called it Black Roses. But one day the little old man said, 'I would like to be rich,' and when the cat saw these words the cat sat on the mat and very still. He said, 'White Roses' and when the cat was off the mat the little old man and the little old woman and when they saw the money they both said, 'A.magic cat!' all at once. Now they could have what they wanted. One day a man said that he would like to buy the cat but the little old man said that 'You cannot have it for all the gold in the world.' The man came back to the house for a year. At last the man gave up, never came back again. The world was so angry that they killed every cat in the world, all for the magic cat. The magic cat they did not kill for if it was dead the magic would go somewhere else. In ten years the cat died and a year later the little old man died, and ten years later the old woman died.
> [Donna, story, April 1976]

As much of the child as the model of the folk-fairy-tale entered into this story. Particularly noticeable is her detailing of money saved and money spent, a real domestic preoccupation of all her peers. Some of the features of elaborated personal narration enter into the story as well: she was uncertain about whether to render dialogue directly, or whether to place it completely within the tense structure of the story. She had doubts on two occasions about how to maintain continuity of tense, as in 'they saved up as much as they can'. But what she was certain about was that the wishes and desires expressed in dialogue made things happen and the felicitous error of writing 'saw' for 'heard' in 'when the cat saw these words the cat sat on the mat and very still', seems to be an expression of her preoccupation with making words visible and powerful in the act of writing.

'The Tidy House' is not elaborated on a model as is 'The Magic Cat'. It bears far more relation to the very earliest stories told by children, which are fictional abstractions of the narrator's own experience. The famous example of this genre is in Harvey Sacks's account of a two-year-old girl's story: 'the baby cried, the mommy picked it up', a story built around the classic announcement of 'a piece of trouble'.[59] It contains as well many elements of personal biographical narration. The third person of Melissa's simple recounting of imaginary events could theoretically and easily be replaced by 'I' – Jamie's voice could become Melissa's, and she could talk of herself and the child Carl as 'we': 'After dinner/ we went up Jo and Mark's house'(TH transcript: p. 51).

But Carla, for most of her account, had no truck with this simple past tense narration, and we, as adult readers, cannot perform a similar trick upon her text.[60] Apart from announcing in her opening line that it was a boy and a girl who are speaking (which is in itself ambiguous for it is not apparent whether it is children or adults speaking) Carla left the reader to work out who was speaking and who was doing what to whom, even when entirely new characters were introduced into the story. Thus a large portion of Carla's contribution was couched in the timeless present of dialogue:

> What time is it?
> 11 o'clock at night.
> Oh no! Let's get to bed.
> . . .
> Do you want one?
> Ha ha, very funny.
> Tell me if you are glad Carl is going to school.
>
> [Carla, TH transcripts: pp. 43, 49]

In the absence of indicative pronouns, without specific references to the subjects of this passage, it is impossible to recast the present tense of this dialogue in the past. It is possible to interpret Carla's text as a denial of the circumstances she is describing, as a statement that they did *not* happen, that she was *not* there, *not* a witness. If this part of the story had been told verbally it would have had to have been structured in the simple past tense and the child would have had to present herself as some kind of witness to

the events she was describing.[61] The border here between an adult interpretation of the children's words and the children's awareness of how
their text served them is not as uncertain as it might appear. The children
knew they were writing a story – producing a fiction – and not describing real, witnessed events (TH tapes: pp. 167, 174, 175). Taken with
their general ambivalence towards their characters and the actions of their
characters, these particular portions of 'The Tidy House' become precisely *not* like play, nor the wish fulfilment of dreams: it is as if, projected
on to a screen, the events of the story take place *out there*, out of real time,
and the children briefly watch them, involved and fascinated, denying at
the same time that this will be their future, that they will have children
they don't want and spend their days in irritation and regret. This
manner of writing, then, was not only a most precise means of understanding the social meanings that confronted the children but was also a
way of evolving opinions about that meaning.

But of course not all of 'The Tidy House' employs this particular use of
dialogue, nor are all the events of the story conveyed through descriptions
of conversational acts. The most important sociological fact about the
writing of 'The Tidy House' was that the children worked together,
swiftly establishing the conventions of writing, so that very little preliminary discussion took place.[62] In the course of this collaborative writing
the children influenced each other (and of course they shared as well a life
and a friendship that is not evidenced here). In fact Carla came to abandon
the exclusive use of dialogue as the story progressed, just as Melissa,
Lindie and Lisa (who joined them towards the end) began to make more
use of dialogue.

When children write, they can see (literally, see) that they can alter and
manipulate the meaning of events. The evidence here is to do with the
image of dialogue in written form and the temporal changes that are
effected when it is used to any great extent, as for instance the way in
which 'The Tidy House' takes place in a continuous present because of
the tense that has to be employed when narrative is forwarded by
dialogue. None of this is to speak about the children's investment of the
symbols of their story – the house, the nest, the baby – with meaning;
this topic will be dealt with in Chapter 6. But it is to speak of children's
ability, when using written language, to delay, deny and defer the
implications of narrative by placing it quite out of time. Shifting rapidly
through the temporal changes of 'The Tidy House', the children saw
something of the interconnection of feeling, belief and action in the social

world. Thus in Lindie's pivotal scene (TH transcript: p. 50) she was able at once to demonstrate her own feelings about babies, and babies that were also little boys, observe an edgy interchange between her two adult characters and at the same time listen to her own parents' complaint about her: 'I don't like children being spoiled.'

A central development in the cognitive life of young children is the growth of their ability to see themselves as they are seen by others. In the classic texts of child psychology this is described as the child's growth away from egocentricity, and in language development this process is matched by an increasing ability in children to take on the perspective of the listener when they speak[63] In Vygotsky's account of this process, the egocentric speech of early childhood becomes 'inner speech' some time in the early school years, as children's ability to use language for rational, reflexive dialogue increases. Inner speech, on the other hand, is unvoiced, elliptical, 'to a large extent thinking in pure meanings'.[64]

Understood in this context, writing is an elaboration of the process of language development: as a writer, a child must make continual shifts in perspective between herself as composer, herself as her audience for her writing, herself and her created characters. In the immediate act of writing, the child needs to be both herself and other people. It is possible that writing like that produced in 'The Tidy House' plays a role comparable to the child's development of inner speech, which is most important in that it somehow enables children to become aware of the process itself, to understand that there is a distinction between the personal, elliptical, confused manipulation of meanings and the final production, offered to the world.[65] 'The Tidy House' is *not* a finished and final artefact, but is incomplete and contradictory and represents in this way the individual's notion of what needs to be done in the face of puzzling questions about an actual social reality.

The important feature of writing for children may be that it gives them a conscious understanding of some of the processes involved in the activity itself. Many comparisons have been made in this chapter between the function served by play and that served by writing for the children involved. But if seven-, eight- and nine-year-olds were to be asked what play is *for*, they would have difficulty in understanding the question, and would probably respond with a description of the activity itself. Yet not only is the question 'What's writing for?' comprehensible to literate children of this age,[66] but they are able to articulate the idea that it is for recording spoken language. That this is an inadequate and misleading description of the act of writing in psychological terms is not the point. The point is that writing may occupy a rare position in the life of children of this age, in that it is an activity that in itself demands an articulation of its purpose.

It has been noted before that what writing 'The Tidy House' provided Carla, Melissa and Lindie with was a powerful notion of change. The idea of change functioned in several ways, the simplest and most accessible being the children's understanding that as writers they could alter the words on the page, cross them out, start again. They were able to alter the sequence and effect of events witnessed in the real world by constructing a fiction. By writing, and particularly by making use of dialogue, they were able to analyse the way in which the words of adults altered events and to envision for themselves possible changes in circumstances. It is probable that children who are illiterate are quite unable to make these analyses or perform these transformations. This point is raised again in the next chapter.

Throughout this chapter it has been emphasised that what the children sought to make plain to themselves in writing 'The Tidy House' was the meaning of a social and cultural world. Their efforts having been outlined, we need to consider the content of their story. The girls who wrote 'The Tidy House' were working-class children and the next chapter is designed to outline a history that brought them to the point of writing and that at the same time helps to reveal the purpose and meaning of their story. What binds the evidence of Lindie, Melissa and Carla together with the fragmentary words of other working-class girls who lived over a century ago is a continuity of historical experience that, for the main part, lies outside our official records of childhood socialisation. The material conditions of a childhood of poverty have, of course, altered considerably since the 1850s and 1860s (the period from which the majority of evidence used in the next chapter is drawn); but the words of little girls from that time – match makers, street sellers, glovers, lace makers – can, in many cases, lead to a deeper understanding of modern working-class girlhood than can the normative accounts of development that make up classic child psychology, which was constructed in the manner described at the beginning of this chapter.

This chapter, was completed before the appearance of Gunther Kress's *Learning to Write*, which provides a psychological and linguistic description of writing in children.[67]

5

SELF AND SOCIALISATION: THE LOST HISTORY OF WORKING-CLASS CHILDHOOD

The experience of a vast number of working-class children who have lived through our recent history has not been assimilated into the theories of childhood that form the basis of modern developmental psychology. There exist many descriptions of childhood in working-class communities[1] and accounts of working-class family life.[2] These are interesting and important, but only of limited use here because they say so little about the felt experience of female childhood. It is knowledge of that experience that we need if we are to assess the life that Lindie, Melissa and Carla describe in 'The Tidy House' and their assimilation of its myths and beliefs.

There are two sets of historical material used in this chapter. The first of these consists of the transcribed words of some mid-nineteenth-century little working-class girls. This material is used in the selective manner indicated in Chapter 1, and at the beginning of Part Two of this book, as a way of mapping out a history of attitude and feeling. The other historical material, used at the end of this chapter, is based on the considerable amount of work that has been done on the history of working-class housing. It is briefly presented as a way of setting the experience of Melissa, Lindie and Carla within a more general historical narrative than can be provided by the fragmentary transcriptions of a few Victorian children's words. The house was the groundwork of Carla's, Melissa's and Lindie's metaphors and a history of housing allows us to see them as inheritors of certain social beliefs articulated in the tidy houses – the council houses – they occupied. However, the history of housing takes second place to the narratives of the working-class children who are the subject of this chapter.

We need the evidence of all who can give it of having grown up female under conditions of poverty; and in its turn the insights that conventional child psychology provides are of immense use in interpreting children's words from the past. For to enter the experience of working-class little girlhood into the normative accounts that are usually only used to describe it will not alter the basic structure of those accounts – we will not find in the Victorian children considered here an altered sequence of grammatical acquisition or strange and exotic ideas about the nature of the physical universe.[3] What will be altered is a sense of what children *do* in the course of development and the particular inquiry here is to find a sharper outline of the processes by which working-class girl children take part in their own socialisation.

In the mid-nineteenth-century narratives that are considered in this chapter, it was womanhood, or rather motherhood, that the children dwelt on. These little girls, mothered by women and early in life presented with the idea that they too would one day be mothers, had a vital and personal relationship with the idea of parenting that boys – at least on the evidence available – do not seem to have possessed.[4] The girls whose transcribed evidence is used here had an understanding of the organisation of their households and the ties of money and responsibility that held particular family members together. Their understanding was linked not only to what they, as girl children, apprehended was going to happen to them, but to what they also saw as *already* happening. Like the evidence of 'The Tidy House', then, their words offer insight into a pattern of life that they perceived was to be their fate.

The story of the working-class mother's domestic power is available from many literary and sociological sources. Few women have modified this male portraiture, which provides a basic formulation within the sociology of the working-class family: 'mother raises the children, father provides the werewithal'.[5] All the children interviewed in the 1850s and 1860s, boys and girls, were clear about their mother's domestic power and importance and spontaneously mentioned their mothers far more than they mentioned their fathers. It is not always clear whether or not their fathers were living with them and certainly, given the conventional arrangements of family life, mothers are perceived by young children as the vital providers of food and comfort, whilst the father's role often remains a mystery.[6] This is a pattern of relationship very clearly evidenced by Melissa, Carla and Lindie in their discussion of 'The Tidy House' (TH tapes: pp. 179, 180) and is represented in much of their writing: we never find out what the fictional Mark and Jason, or the sacked Jack (of

111

'Jack Got the Sack') actually do for a living.

But most of the Victorian children interviewed had a very clear and sophisticated notion of the economic basis of family life; some of them knew exactly how much came into the household each week and what was spent. Knowing about their fathers' role as wage earners and some-times knowing exactly what it was he did in order to earn money (many of these children grew up in homes where the family trade was still prac-tised), some of them still characterised their fathers as quiet, unimportant figures on the domestic scene: 'he's very good to me . . . he never hardly speaks'; 'he's a very quiet man'.[7] Fathers were particularly characterised in this way when the child was able to present some information about her mother's role in making economic decisions within the household. In fact this role, in her daughter's eyes, was her central one. In the evidence of all these children, but particularly that of little girls, it was mothers who decided when children should leave school and start working, it was mothers to whom, almost without exception, these children turned over their wages.[8] The children often aligned this economic supervision with a more powerful physical role. One little girl described her mother berating a school master for hitting her and, when girls mentioned physical punishment, they told of mothers administering it: 'She don't often beat me,' said an eight-year-old watercress seller, 'but when she do, she don't play with me.'[9]

The power and importance of mothers was a perception of their children and we must see their presentation of this perception in the same way as we see the created figures of Jo and Jamie in 'The Tidy House', as an interpretation by children of what is both a reality of their social world and an outline, for us as readers of their words, of the limited and confined nature of the power their mothers represented. What all these children chose to represent was an affective relationship that defined both who they were and what they might become; their interest in, and under-standing of, the wider arena of economic and sexual relationships, that made their mother the most significant of their parents, was limited. In fact, these Victorian children's emotional account of their mothers' authority and importance is also a historical description of severe curtail-ment and restriction in the life of working-class women and girls.

The children may have described family relationships that differed radically and, at many points, from those that form the bedrock of current descriptive child psychology, but out of them it was still recog-nisably little girls that were made. Quiet, docile, willing to please, employers preferred them because 'they attend so much more to what is said to them'.[10] In poverty-stricken homes, where a mother's primary role was understood by her children to be breadwinner, not housewife, little girls still developed the characteristic 'felt need to do housework'.[11] The eight-year-old watercress seller said that she cleaned up her family's two rooms because she wanted to and, with a pleasure that has been more recently noted,[12] described how she went about her task:

> mother doesn't make me do it, I does it myself. I cleans the chairs though there's only two to clean. I takes a tub and scrubbing brush and flannel and scrubs the floor – that's what I do three or four times a week.[13]

The common domestic economy that many nineteenth-century girls described, that of their mothers laying aside part of their earnings to pay for their clothes,[14] was presented by their children as the most significant feature of their mother's domestic power; but it was in fact a means of circumventing a severe social restriction in the lives of women and girl children. Their access to any public place was severely curtailed if they lacked the outward show of decent clothing[15] and a regular system of saving up for clothes ensured them some kind of social life. All these points are considered again later in this chapter, the theme of which is, in fact, the restrictive nature of the closed system of identification between mother and little girl.

In the matter of dress and appearance, the subject on which they dwelt most consistently, the mid-nineteenth-century children had some fairly reliable measure of the way in which they were seen by other people. Their understanding of how they were perceived was a dominant feature of the growth of their sense of self, just as, out of very different circumstances, Carla's, Lindie's and Melissa's understanding of how parents saw their children propelled self-perception. Throughout the two-hundred-year history of child psychology that was outlined in the last chapter, it was the mirror that provided the most potent image for an adult understanding of children's growth of the idea of selfhood. As long as parents have made records of child development they have held their infants up to the glass, and shown them pictures of human faces in order to measure their understanding of their own identity.[16] So powerful is this picture, so revelatory an image of development does the baby smiling at itself in the glass offer, that it has come to be used as the very mark of our humanity.[17] The metaphor of the reflection of the child in others, and the child's recognition of this, has been extended into many accounts of growth[18] and the image haunts the transcriptions of the conversations with mid-nineteenth-century girl children that are used in this chapter. Before the words of these little girls are used to outline a history of affective relationships that Carla, Melissa and Lindie inherited, the value of linguistic evidence as historical evidence has to be discussed, as must the relationship between interviewed and interviewer, for what was most striking to the middle-class gentlemen who collected these children's words was the absence from their faces of the image of childhood.

The historical material used in this chapter is derived mainly from the six reports compiled by the Children's Employment Commission of 1862 (published between 1863 and 1866), the report of the commission appointed to inquire into the employment of women and children in agriculture (published in 1867) and, from some fifteen years before, the interviews collected by Henry Mayhew between 1849 and 1852 when he compiled most of the material for what eventually became *London Labour and the London Poor*. These two sets of sources represent children from widely differing working-class backgrounds.[19] Mayhew only reported on conversations with a handful of London children, whilst the children's employment commissioners interviewed several hundred from around the country. The two investigations represented differing sets of family and economic circumstances as well. Mayhew's interviewees were all street traders, either the children of street traders themselves, or with partially employed craft workers as parents, and they generally worked alone. The Children's Employment Commission (1862) was appointed to investigate the situation of child workers not already regulated by law (that is, working at jobs not controlled by the existing factories and mines acts), and they represented a very wide range of trades.[20] Many of the children questioned worked with their parents, or other family members and friends. Some parents clearly saw the child's work as a preliminary to factory employment (for which there was an age restriction), or as a means of supervision and discipline while they themselves were away from home at work.

Extracting the words of a few hundred working-class children from the 1850s and 1860s in this way removes their testimony from a coherent historical narrative, says nothing about the history of child labour in the earlier stages of industrialisation,[21] nor about the development of protective legislation. It does not take into account the removal of children from the work-force and their wholesale entry into the school system by the beginning of this century.[22] It is the quality and availability of the evidence that has led to this particular selection of sources, not the demands of historical narration. For instance, the main reason for using the reports of the Children's Employment Commission of 1862, and not the earlier, much more extensive reports of the commission of 1842, is that the later collection offers much more insight into the beliefs about the world held by the children interviewed. In both sets of reports, those of 1842 and of 1862, the evidence of the children was usually transcribed rather than summarised; but in the reports of the commission of 1862 a much greater attention was paid by the interviewers both to the child's state of mind and its expression in spoken language.

The restrictive legislation that followed on the inquiries of the 1842 commission left the children who still laboured in workshop and manu- factury, or in domestic industry, an exception to a general trend. The adult sense of these children as being left behind, as particularly deprived, coupled with a clear and forceful theory about physical and cognitive development in childhood, with which the commissioners were armed before they set out on their investigations,[23] made them particularly sensi- tive to the emotional state of the children they spoke with. In most cases these male interviewers seem to have established a warm relationship with the children they questioned and to have inspired, often, confidence and revelation. There are enough pitfalls in modern test or interview situations with young children, where even jean-clad, familiar and friendly adults provoke confusion and wrong answers, to make us marvel that in such an unfamiliar relationship, with the interviewers speaking quite differently from the way in which the children had probably heard adults speak before, taller than those they knew, dressed in unfamiliar clothing, such confidence was created.

One of the reasons for the rapid establishment of a relationship that inspired confidence in some of the children was the deep interest in their own reactions to them felt by these middle-class men. 'I did not know how to speak with her,' mused Mayhew of the little watercress seller,[24] and the children's employment commissioners recorded how their gentle request for a sad, depressed little girl to read aloud to them made her burst into tears.[25] They watched and recorded their own reactions to the smiles that enlivened impassive faces, and occasionally, across the wastes of class and disgust, saw briefly that things might be quite different from the way they were and movingly recorded that perception.[26] The evidence of these men was, then, the product of emotionally heightened and brief contacts and all the more revelatory for that.

It is the assumption of this chapter that it is possible to link the written words of eight- and nine-year-old girls in late twentieth-century Britain with the transcribed words of working-class girls of the same age from the mid-nineteenth century. We are enabled to do this by considering child language development as a historically continuous system. The child's acquisition of the basic structure of English by the age of four or five and the continued, though much slower, acquisition that is a feature of the years between five and adolescence, marks out a stage of development that can be relied upon across class barriers and across history. Indeed, nineteenth-century diary studies of child language development provide not only the bedrock of modern developmental linguistics,[27] but also demonstrate that the order in which linguistic structures have been learned by children speaking modern English as their first language have remained consistent within our recent history.

It is of immense importance to be reminded that the seven- eight- and nine-year-olds, whose evidence from the mid-nineteenth century is used here, were at a recognisable stage of language development, found the same occasional difficulties in tense usage and their use of pronouns as Melissa, Lindie and Carla did and, like them, often confused paired verbs ('learn' and 'teach', 'lend' and 'borrow', 'ask' and 'tell'). Usages like these, to be found in modern children of the same age, allow us to assume that the children of a century ago were parallel in other areas of development.[28] In this way it is possible to use a modern understanding of child language, and development in general, as a device of historical interpretation.

None of this is to deny that the experience of poverty, the individual manner of parenting experienced by children, lack of food and security, anxiety and depression in childhood, may all make a difference to children's ability to use the structures they have acquired. There were theories about working-class children's language deprivation in the nineteenth century, just as there are today and as in most of such theories blame for working-class parents hovered beneath the civilised sympathy of the argument. Here is an upper-middle-class family at breakfast in a Bedfordshire village in 1833:

> The conversation . . . turned on the education of poor children for
> mamma happened to be reading an article on the subject . . . It mentioned
> that poor children of about 7 or 8 had more vacancy and stupidity of mind
> than those of the higher ranks . . . Papa (said) 'I do not think that it is a
> natural want of intelligence, but because they are not drawn out by

questions; they are not in the habit of being taught to apply what they know. Now, see how much more handy they are in some things than other children; a boy takes care of his younger brother . . . or . . . a horse . . . But as to intellect, if a child asks any questions, he is told to do something or other and if he does not understand, then comes a great thump on the head and the child is knocked down[29]

The consistency of the language system, the basic order of its development in young children and a historical continuity of attitude towards the language of working-class children offer great scope for historical inquiry. But major difficulties do stand in the way of using their linguistic evidence. The conventions of transcription, the dictates of shorthand recording, a style of speaking imposed by the interrogator when writing down the children's words, can all stand in the way of actually hearing the children's voices.

But there are ways through this difficulty. Mayhew, for instance, perfected a technique of rendering all his subjects' fragmentary answers into a continuous and connected monologue. Knowing this, we can, on a careful reading, hear the place where he put his questions to the children and where, in the monologue that he structured out of their answers, he ascribed repetition of his question to their narrative. What is more, Mayhew used the technique of suggesting accent and dialect by the use of certain phonetic markers, as in the extract from the crossing sweeper, repeated below, where the words in italics serve the function of *indicating* to the reader what the child sounded like:[30]

When I *fust* went they said 'here's another fresh *'un.*' They *come* up to me and *says* 'Are you going to sweep here?' and I *says* 'Yes' and they *says* 'You mustn't come here, there's too many;' and I *says* 'They're different ones every day' . . . It's a capital crossing but there's so many of us, it *spiles* it'[31]

This method of using phonetic and dialect markers is not an attempt to render the child's language phonetically and it therefore does not erect barriers between the reader and the narrative as does this more phonetic transcription, recorded some thirty years later on the streets of London by a different investigator:

I dunno who my father was: mother's dead. I live at aunt's . . . O' course aunt can't keep me, she's got a lot o' kids of her own an' sometimes they can't git anythink to eat . . . Now and agin she'll give me a bit o' bread, and she'll ollus let me sleep at her place . . . If I'm

117

stumped now Aunt'll lend me a brown or two when she's 'em, but I
don't know hanybody else as would[32]

The resolute stage cockney of this transcript distances the child into a
curiosity, an abstract figure of pity and amusement.

Styles of transcription different from the one Mayhew employed are of
equal historical use: one of the assistants to the Children's Employment
Commission (1862) had a considerable knowledge of dialect and folklore.[33] Not only was he scrupulous about only using inverted commas for
the actual utterances of the children he spoke with, but his interest in
dialect meant that he had a finely tuned ear for children's speech errors as
well as specific dialect use and these were much more consistently
reported by him than by the other two assistant commissioners who did
not share his interests.

The images of perception and reflection were at the base of much
comment by these male middle-class investigators of working-class
childhood. Mayhew, for instance, saw quite clearly that his own image of
childhood was not mirrored in the faces of the street traders he spoke
with:

> the little watercress girl . . . although only eight years of age, had already
> lost all childish ways, and was indeed, in thoughts and manner, a
> woman . . . her little face, pale and thin with privation, was wrinkled
> where the dimples ought to have been[34]

Often, confronted with such unfamiliar manifestations of childhood, he
was unable to avoid the expression of repulsion from physically altered
features, passive countenances, shuffling gait, broken boots – and the
hair, in little girls, always the hair, its smoothness the very badge of
appealing and docile femininity, in his description of the street traders
nearly always rusty and wild, 'foul and matted', standing out roughly
from the children's heads.[35] Like other investigators of his time, he was
gratified when a pretty frown, the rounded cheek of babyhood, showed
through the dirt and the adult's conception of how she ought to be was
reflected in the child's face. 'She frowned,' he said of one pleasingly clean
little crossing sweeper, 'like a baby in its sleep when thinking of the
answer.'[36] The same sudden vision of a face that matched the image lit up
a Birmingham button manufactury for one member of the Children's
Employment Commission in 1864: he saw 'a girl of six . . . one of three
sisters working here . . . She was a beautiful child with a bright,
innocent face, but looking lost and bewildered.' Her two sisters provided

a facial allegory of her inevitable fall from grace: 'her eldest sister, 12, had a sullen hardened look and manner; the middle sister seemed in the intermediate stage'.[37] 'Their eyes glisten so,' an employer told the assistant commissioner later that day, speaking of the children who beseeched him for employment. 'Some's skin's as beautiful as a lady's.'[38]

However, far more revelatory than the blank absence of childhood from the faces of these children in their interviewers' accounts was their own account of their fragmentary, incomplete sense of selfhood. The next part of this chapter explores the means by which some children came, in the 1850s and 1860s, to understand who they were.

Some time during the winter of 1849–50, when Henry Mayhew was collecting material for his *Morning Chronicle* series of articles on London poverty and London employment,[39] he was pursued by a little girl who tried to sell him some bootlaces. She 'offered them to me most perseveringly. She was turned nine, she said, and had sold things in the streets for two years past'.[40] The social investigator questioned the child and, with the warmth and gentleness that seems to have characterised all his dealings with children, he obtained from her not only an account of her family's economic circumstances, but also a recital – hesitant at first, at best fragmentary – of her own feelings about herself.

What seems to have particularly struck Mayhew about her narrative was her relationship with, and understanding of, the world of adult intention and motivation that surrounded her. He, like her parents, was concerned about the sexual danger that the child ran by stopping strangers in the street: considerable efforts had been made to provide her with chaperonage, as was the case with all but one of the little girls that Mayhew reported interviewing:[41] 'I could do better,' said the laces seller, 'if I went into public houses, but I'm only let go to Mr Smith's, because he knows father and Mrs Smith and him recommends me and wouldn't let anyone mislest [molest] me.' As Mayhew pursued the question, she told him of selling nuts and oranges to soldiers – 'they never say anything rude to me, never' – and then suddenly, vividly, recalled (in a passage quoted earlier), an incident that she could not explain:

> I was once in a great crowd getting crushed and there was a very tall soldier close by me and he lifted me, basket and all, right up to his shoulder and carried me clean out of the crowd. He had stripes on his arm. 'I shouldn't like you to be in such a trade,' says he 'if you were my

child.' He didn't say why he wouldn't like it. Perhaps because it was beginning to rain[42]

What Mayhew noticed, and what a reading of his transcription of the child's narrative offers, is that she could not in this instance see herself as others did, did not know that she could be pitied for the poverty of her dress, her frail stature, the economic necessity that sent her on to the streets at seven to earn a few pennies. This is not to say that this unarticulated insight on the interviewer's part could have been characterised in this way in the mid-nineteenth century. 'Innocence' perhaps, the presentation of a naive dislocation between the child's view and the adult's view, the vehicle for sentimentality in many Victorian novels where children figure large,[43] would have been ascribed to the laces seller's uncertainty about the soldier's meaning.

The peculiar sadness of the laces seller's account lies in the fact that the child could not see herself through the soldier's eyes. Yet out of many equally miserable sets of circumstances, children did wrest the sense of selfhood, not in spite of hunger, physical ill-health and great burdens of worry and responsibility, but using such disadvantages as aids to self-description. Mayhew's interviewees saw themselves reflected in the common and distasteful reaction to their appearance and the way in which they were spoken to and treated.[44] Some of the children were provided with the measure of their parents' words and family memory by which to assess their own growth and development. Sarah Wedge, steel-pen worker of Birmingham, knew that she and her sisters had been sent to school 'ever since mother could see us reach the top of the stool when we was little children'.[45] Ellen Pearl, farm labourer's wife of Monk Soham, Suffolk, turned to her daughter in the course of her interview with an assistant commissioner in 1867, remarking that:

My girl Alice went dropping beans with her father up beyond Kenton . . . when she was 4 years old. We particularly marked that because he had to carry her when she first began to learn . . . You remember when you were a little dawdy . . . child, don't you?[46]

This sense of physical growth, of knowing that one was once smaller, seems an important dimension of childhood development. It is to be seen in 'The Tidy House' in the children's description of the language and behaviour of children much younger than they.[47]

In some cases, self-identity was articulated through well-learned adult formulation: 'I hope I never shall get tired of work,' said Ann Powell, a twelve-year-old who laboured in a Staffordshire brickyard. 'My mother always brought me up to be a good worker.'[47] Many of the girls, interviewed in the 1860s, displayed an obsession with work and would not rest. They had learned their self-definition as workers very well.[48] The sense of self derived from adult prescription could be obtained from religious teaching as well and some little girls knew from what impossible standards they fell short: Mary Ann Taylor, nine-year-old worker in the firearms industry knew that if she was 'a good girl He [would] send me into heaven'.[49] 'An angel is very pretty. I wished I was an angel,' said Ann Powell. 'I hope I shall be one day and sit in Jesus' lap.'[50] For some other children, a very limited idea of choice, for instance having been out to service and knowing that match making was preferred, formulated two possible courses of action and further defined the self.[51]

But all of this only shows the tenacity of human growth and the possibilities that can be wrought out of the most threadbare material. Many of these children, in fact, showed themselves to be uncertain about their public and social identity. The watercress seller, for example, knew that she was a worker and formulated this identity as it must have been formulated for her by the adults around her in many ways – in her detailed discussion of the profit to be made out of an armful of cresses, in the pattern of her working day, in the description of her strictly economic relations with the market people she encountered and of her going to bed early so that she could get up in time the next morning. The relationship she described in the greatest detail (apart from the one with her mother) was yet another work relationship, one she had with a Jewish couple, for whom, as a weekend job, she did the necessary household work on the Sabbath. She knew that she was not a child, for children were those who played in the streets and bought sweets, and she was certain that she did neither of these things. 'I asked her about her toys and games with her companions,' reported Mayhew; 'but the look of amazement that answered me soon put an end to any attempt of fun on my part'. 'No; I never has no sweet stuff; I never buy none – I don't like it . . . I never had no doll'. Yet in the course of her long conversation with Mayhew, the child revealed another self that lay beneath the public formulation: 'Oh yes; I've got some toys at home. I've got a fireplace, and a box of toys, and a knife and a fork and two little chairs'. She said too that she knew 'a good many games' though she was too tired to play them: 'Sometimes we has a game of "honeypots" with the girls in the court . . . We plays too at "kiss-in-the-ring".'[52]

The evidence here of the watercress seller's movement between the images of herself as worker and herself as child is of extraordinary value. It is certain that under the conditions of distress and poverty that her family endured she received the most praise and encouragement from the adults closest to her when she made one shilling out of three pence worth of cresses. Yet she personally strove, as children do in play, to be 'big and grown up', and at every turn overtly denied her childish pursuits. The work she did demanded of her what in more favourable circumstances children evince spontaneously in imaginative play, that is, a striving at the edge of their competence to both make sense of, and be part of, an adult world. But, in play, children can control the adult world they represent to themselves; the watercress seller, on the other hand, was not able to do this, for she had already become part of that world.

Though the watercress seller (and other children) did give evidence of playing, particularly of taking part in organised street games,[53] they also demonstrated that the desires and wishes that they might have shown in imaginative play were, in fact, channelled into work. The obsessive manner of some little girls' working, their pushing of themselves to the very edge of their capacities, which was the result of deflecting development in this way, was frequently noted by adults at the time.[54] Whether children earned money by organising time and space, by buying goods and selling them at a profit, or finding a patch of road, laying claim to it and sweeping it for pedestrians, or whether they worked long hours at repetitive, unchanging tasks, such as dropping seals into percussion caps or plaiting straw for bonnets,[55] they were all characterised for the adults who made contact with them by a fixed and impassive countenance and a burden of worry and responsibility.[56] These effects of work in childhood are extensively documented across many societies.[57]

The sources used here supply evidence from both boys and girls, but it was the girls who were particularly aware of the precise economic terms on which they were sent out to work and the way in which their earnings were laid out. The primary parental motive was certainly the need for every coin that could be brought home – 'If it's only 1 penny you make,' said the laces seller's mother to her when she was seven, 'it's a good piece of bread' – but many little girls described in some detail a domestic economy which has already been mentioned, whereby part of their earnings were laid aside by their mothers to pay for the girls' clothes.

There is a long tradition of comment on the tendency of working-class parents to dress up their little girls as if for display.[58] Some recent comments echo a Nottingham lace mistress who in 1863 condemned the parents of the children who worked for her for decking them out 'in a large crinoline and smart summer frock without hardly any bonnet, cloak or shoes'.[59] It is clear, however, that the children themselves saw finery and the work arrangements that procured it as a matter of the utmost necessity: 'Some of the young children would work all manner of hours – would go through fire and water – sooner than miss a chance [of going to a Band of Hope fête] . . . One was laying by 5 or 6 weeks for a bonnet and frock.'[60] Decent clothing as the essential passport to any kind of social life has already been mentioned; the children's awareness of this and their presentation of the way in which, under the supervision of their mother, they kept themselves clothed gives the clearest access to the significance of this practice.

The children interviewed by Mayhew and the children's employment commissioners seemed often to describe their families as economic units that operated at two levels of organisation, where the mother was deemed responsible for feeding and clothing her children, whether she lived with a man or not and whether he or she brought in the major part of the household income. Some of the little girls who described a direct economic relationship with their mother and not with their father were at pains to point out that those quiet background figures were not their real fathers[61] and certainly many working-class men interviewed by Mayhew at the same time held to a thesis that ascribed the greater power of love, responsibility and care to mothers, whatever their marital circumstances.[62] The assumption that women and children should provide for their own keep is an old, pre-industrial notion;[63] the important point here is that the emotional and sexual relationships that arose from it were a dominant feature in the little girl's growth of self-identity.

Making money, getting clothes, being good workers, were responsibilities that the children clearly articulated. Yet they rarely mentioned as burdensome another responsibility that many of them had carried some time in their short lives: that of child-care. The watercress seller had the toys of little girlhood, the miniature chairs, the pretend fireplace with hob, the toy cutlery; but, significantly, she had no doll. She did not need to play at being a mother in order to assimilate that role, for, in fact, to all intents and purposes she and other girls like her *were* mothers, did not play *at* having babies, but played with them:[64]

On and off, I've been very near a twelvemonth on the streets. Before that I had to take care of a baby for my aunt. No; it wasn't heavy – it was only two months old; but I minded it for ever such a long time – till it could walk. It was a very nice little baby, not a very pretty one, but if I touched it under the chin it would laugh. Before I had a baby I used to help mother . . . Sometimes we has a game . . . in the court . . . Me and Carrie H—— carries the little ones . . . I misses little sister – she's only two years old . . . father and mother sleeps with little sister . . . and me and brother and other sister sleeps in the top room.

I hadn't to do any work, only just clean the room and nuss the child. It was a nice little thing.

She had to mind 'her sisters till she came to work one and a half years ago.'

I had to mind my baby while mother was away.[65]

To be left in sole charge of younger children is not as common an experience for working-class girls as it was,[66] though Carla's poem, quoted in Chapter 1 (p. 39), shows that it is still a felt experience. There is a still more significant difference than this across the years: for children like the watercress seller, child-care generally represented *paid* employment. Even when starting work was delayed for little girls because they looked after younger siblings for a working mother, their labour represented what would have had to be paid for if they hadn't existed.

From the words of these little girls, a common pattern of childhood employment emerges and the watercress seller's narrative outlines a general experience most clearly. Her first experience of work was in helping her mother. This may have included housework, but the child did not mention it: her mother 'was in the fur trade; and if there was any slits in the fur I'd sew them up. My mother learned me to needlework and to knit when I was about five'.[67] Then, for about eighteen months, when she was six and seven, she worked as a baby minder, and started street trading when she was about seven and a half. This pattern of helping at a family trade followed by a period child-care, with regular shop, manufactury or street work starting at about eight, varied widely from area to area and from trade to trade and depended ultimately upon a family's particular economic circumstances. But the girls themselves reckoned that five was the age at which children could start becoming useful: 'when I goes a-crossing sweeping I takes them along with me,' said a twelve-year-old to Mayhew, 'and they sits on the steps close by

. . . sister's three and a half years old, and brother's five years, so he's just beginning to help me'.[68]

These children represented a set of economic circumstances and house-hold economies that were not long to endure. But there is evidence that the two major economic factors they outlined, that of their own financial relationships with their families, and of their household operated and controlled by their mothers, survived long after children were removed from the labour market in the late nineteenth century. Joy Parr in *Labouring Children* describes a common assumption in working-class households, right into this century, that children must work in order to pay their parents back for all the kept years of childhood. The period of nurturance and dependence was assumed to last until about the age of five or six, when children, even though at school, could start to make a con-tribution to the household, by running errands, street trading, doing housework and minding younger children. When the period of real wage earning began in the early teens, children were meant to hand their wages over to their mother, so that paying back the debt of childhood could begin in earnest. It is noted that girls were let out of this financial obliga-tion earlier than boys, perhaps because they had paid off more during the helping years.[69]

The words of little girls from the 1850s and 1860s contain a good deal of evidence as to the economic basis of their feelings and affections. The children knew their homes not only as places where they slept and where they were fed, but as financial entities, places of work and of earning. What they mentioned of babies was not only learned in their home (though much of it must have been), but also as workers, substitute mothers receiving payment for mothering. All the children in the two surveys used in this chapter who mentioned babies mentioned them with fondness and affection, often using the possessive pronoun to describe their relationship with them ('my baby', 'I had the baby'). They remembered playing with them, the smiles of infancy, their laughter, the warmth of a small body at night.[70] The fondness of their memories and their unproblematic relationship with the babies they minded derived from two sources: the baby as a source of play and affection and the baby as a source of income and adult praise for earning that income.

In contemporary Western society, and within the recent history of it that is being dealt with here, nearly all children are and have been mothered by women and for small children a mother's role is more com-prehensible than that of an absent father, simply because it is visible and produces concrete results – gets the food on the table.[71] For little girls, learning to be a woman is at once an easier and less conscious task than learning to be a man is for little boys. In the asymmetrical family where women mother and fathers are largely absent boys have to be *taught* how to be men in a way that girls do not have to be taught how to be women.[72] This account of the psychological processes by which girls retain strong emotional links with their mothers[73] can be particularised and modified through the accounts of these working-class girls from the mid-nineteenth century. The particularity lies in the fact that the water-cress seller's relationship with her mother was based on a set of mutually understood *economic* circumstances. The financial basis of this tie was fiercely reckoned and a reconstruction of the feelings it engendered can, in its turn, throw light on the words of other working-class girls living at different stages of the history of working-class girlhood. In this way, through a continuity of certain beliefs and attitudes, the experiences of little girls who were workers and those who were schoolchildren can be bridged.

The first element of the relationship to be defined was a sense of obliga-tion and reciprocation, not in the manner of metaphor, but in terms of hard cash, handed over: 'I always gives mother my money, she's so good to me,' said the watercress seller.[74] The sense of obligation was strength-ened by the girl child's *knowing* what it was like to be a woman and a worker, partly because many of the skills women took on to the market-place were those they practised daily on the domestic front.[75] This iden-tification and obligation shades sometimes into the more traditional picture of the working-class girl acting out a family role that is almost hers. Lilian Westall remembered waiting with her mother in the 1890s for her father to come home: 'as the second eldest I would often keep her company, sitting on the edge of the bed, until late at night, as she nursed the baby and waited'.[76] But this kind of portraiture misses the angry sense of debt and payment due that earlier economic relationships between mothers and daughters in working-class households left as a legacy of metaphor and feeling. Kathleen Woodward, remembering her childhood in Bermondsey at the turn of the century, insisted that what she felt for her mother had absolutely nothing to do with love and nothing to do with affection. So different is her account from the story of 'our mam', and accounts of a wellspring of love and affection within the working-class family, that it is worth entering it on the records. In the past, when other working-class women have tried to speak of feelings like these, their testimony has been treated with puzzlement or simply not believed.[77] In *Jipping Street* Kathleen Woodward makes it quite clear that her attachment and identification was due payment, an angry and hateful reckoning of what she owed. Her mother often told the child of an earlier miscarriage: 'Pulled this way and that with that dead child I was,' said the adult to the little girl,

> pulled inside out; everybody in the room bobbing up and down: For the sake of God Almighty, let me die! They say I tore the doctor's coat in shreds. Fifteen weeks I was in bed after that dead child, had to crawl downstairs on my back when I was better . . .' I used to think of the dead child in bed at night before I went to sleep, and it would fill me with horror and suffocating fear; and in the darkness I would see mother sliding down the stairs on her back, white, trembling, to cut up bread for the children's tea, and stronger than the fear and suffocating horror, there would well up in me a deep surging passion of growth towards her[78]

'I lived close to my mother, held fast by strong ties which existed without love or affection; indissolubly we were bound.'[79] To call this gratitude is to trivialise it. What child can feel gratitude for knowing that it is the likes of her that causes such agony and that, quite simply, it would have been better had she never been born? The essential factor of the relationship defined by payment of what is due is that no one has any choice in the matter, and they hand over their obligation like the children of the 1850s and 1860s laid their wages in their mother's hand.

A great deal more evidence needs to be resurrected to substantiate this pattern of affective relationships in the development of working-class girls. However, the metaphoric echoes of these financial ties are apparently still strong. The mysterious letter that Carla has her character Jason's mother write (TH transcript: p. 47) includes a direct quote from a record that was in the charts for six weeks from May 1976. J.J. Barrie's 'No Charge', a remake of an earlier country and western hit, recounts an incident in a middle-American kitchen, where a small boy approaches his mother whilst she is cooking supper with a list of household tasks accomplished and a request for payment. His mother turns his account over and draws up her own. She mentions buying his clothes, feeding him, nursing him, saving up for him to go to college, praying for him, wiping his nose and gives special prominence to 'the nine months I carried you/Growing inside me'. This nauseating yet riveting ballad, in which the adult's detailing of precisely what motherhood has cost her belies the overt message that 'the full cost of my love/ Is No Charge',[80] obviously transfixed the imagination of Carla. 'No Charge' reflected an economic and affective relationship that she understood very well: 'if you never had no children, you'd be well off, wouldn't you. You'd have plenty of money' (TH tapes p. 168).

What links Carla, Lindie, Melissa and the watercress seller across the years is their manipulation of the symbol of the baby; what divides them is their attitude towards the baby as an emblem of selfhood and, by implication, of their future. To Mayhew, at least, the little girls he spoke with mentioned quite spontaneously the babies and toddlers they had spent long days with. Their recitals were, of course, in response to questions about their history as workers, but they moved from simple narration to fond descriptions of the little bodies they had held. Within the space afforded them by their interviewer, they could have mentioned the burden of those small bodies, but, even when prompted, they denied the burden: 'No; it wasn't heavy'.[81] To the watercress seller, the niece or nephew and the little sister she had cared for were important representations of what she knew herself to be: a female child, a worker, a good and helpful girl. In other circumstances she might have played at having babies, but her job of work was child-care and it became part of her apprehension of what she already was and not a means of exploring a relationship nor a way of abstracting from reality the meaning of the relationship with the baby. Imaginative play can help young children to take notice of relationships and examine them in a way that they cannot be examined in real life.[82] But the circumstances forced upon the watercress seller did not allow her to distance herself from her social and emotional reality and she was only permitted to take on the real role of her future: 'Never had no doll'.

For Lindie, Carla and Melissa, growing up under vastly different conditions of poverty, the babies in their story operated as symbols of ambivalence, conflict and resistance. It is at this point that the analogies between their fictional narrative and play are most useful, for 'The Tidy House' enabled them to play at reality and to notice things about that reality that might otherwise have escaped them. The story operated as an abstraction of meaning from circumstances and it allowed the children to comprehend new forms of desire by manipulating the desires and wishes of their fictitious characters. The children explored their own feelings about motherhood through the artefacts of Jamie and Jo and in the process created their own highly resentful statement about mothering, child-care and the future that awaited them.

However, 'The Tidy House' was not a piece of imaginative play but a piece of writing. By writing, particularly by their use of dialogue, the children were able to move outside the confines of play-acting, where the rules of the reality that they are exploring dictate investigation of only one viewpoint at a time. In their story, Carla, Lindie and Melissa were able to be male babies and irritated mothers both at the same time. Holding together and synthesising two opposing views in their narrative, they were able to articulate their contradictory feelings about their future in a way impossible for children who cannot use written language. For us, as readers of the watercress seller's narrative, the baby can be seen as the symbol of the severest restriction in her life and the very name of her unproblematic acceptance of her future; yet in 'The Tidy House' the figure of the baby becomes the most ready vehicle of protest against a similar fate. This perception was available to the children who wrote the story as well as to us, the readers of it.

In the past few pages the real, living babies minded and watched by children like the watercress seller have been used as symbols both of their socialisation and their inevitable future as working-class women; but, unconscious of the meaning of the work they did in baby minding, those Victorian children were unable to transform the reality into a revelatory symbol as did Lindie, Carla and Melissa in their use of the character Carl.

In a fashion similar to the way they wrote about their character Carl, the children wrote about a real house in their story – or rather rows and rows of tidy houses stretching up the hillside to the horizon. In doing this, they reworked not just a pile of bricks and mortar, but also a set of ideas about how people should live that was embodied in the houses they occupied. Before the children's transformation of a council house into the symbolic tidy house is dealt with, a history of working-class housing needs to be briefly presented.

A good deal is known about working-class housing over the last century and a half because working-class homes have been (and still are) relentlessly visited by social investigators, social workers (in the past, Poor Law officials), and various kinds of police (social security officers, NSPCC inspectors and so on). With such witnesses we should not expect to find out very much about what it was actually like to live in such homes. Yet through visitors' praise or condemnation for their cooking and sleeping arrangements and the decor of their rooms we can discern, although dimly, through the pattern of domestic arrangements that the visitors took with them as blueprint, the rooms themselves and life within them.[83] Occasionally, as in the watercress seller's words, there is direct evidence of what arrangements in those rooms were like, how a household lived and the attachment and affection that two rooms, two chairs and some well-scrubbed floorboards could promote in a child.[84]

State intervention in housing provision came late in this country compared with the continent, and it was not until after the First World War that subsidies to local authorities were inaugurated in order to increase the supply of working-class housing.[85] In the 1930s, much older ideas about sanitary reform and slum clearance were married to the principle of providing low-cost housing.[86] This meant, in effect, that people displaced by slum clearance also had to be rehoused and Carla, Melissa and Lindie inhabited a council estate on which building had started in the mid-1930s as part of a programme of demolition in the old town.

Long before the state intervention of the 1920s and 1930s, much late nineteenth-century philanthropic social work was directed at the working-class woman in the setting of her home, teaching her how to organise time, space and money, how to cook nourishing meals out of practically nothing and keep her children clean against all odds. Before statutory legislation had provided the ordered rows of council houses that were the legacy of Carla, Melissa and Lindie, mothers had been identified with their homes and the possession of halfway decent housing seen as a possible reward for her keeping the children off the streets and in school and men out of the pub and in work.[87] The role of the working-class mother as a kind of state nurse was elaborated in the period between the Boer War and the First World War, when national defence came to be seen as partly resting on the physical condition of working-class children.

Legislative changes like those indicated above confirmed the power of the working-class mother within her home, though that power no longer derived from her economic role, as it had done in the eyes of some mid-Victorian children like the watercress seller and the laces seller. The identification of mothers and houses, together understood by their children to provide all comfort as well as the threat of homelessness and displacement, was what Melissa, Carla and Lindie elaborated in 'The Tidy House'. Their story was in this way a reflection of real historical circumstances, though the children themselves had no access to that history, nor to the sets of ideas it embodied. They occupied a tiny, tidy house partly out of a refusal on the part of many nineteenth-century working people to live in anything that looked like a barracks – 'the Big House', the workhouse – [88] and partly because divided sleeping quarters, kitchen space, living space and the provision of gardens articulated a set of social theories held by sanitary reformers and town planners about how working people should live and how a family's life should be arranged. Again, this history is represented in the children's story without any knowledge of it on their part. But the history they did articulate, the social theory that they did observe at work and which they attempted to comprehend in 'The Tidy House' was that of the mother in the house. It was through their manipulation of this image that the children, in building their fictitious house, came most clearly to see it as a place of confinement as well as of comfort and security. The task they set themselves of describing and understanding both mothers in the house, and mothers as houses, is the central theme of Part Three of this book.

PART THREE

So with the house empty and the doors locked and the mattresses rolled round, those stray airs, advance guards of great armies, blustered in, brushed bare boards, nibbled and fanned, met nothing in bedroom or drawing-room that wholly resisted them but only hangings that flapped, wood that creaked, the bare legs of tables, saucepans and china already furred, tarnished, cracked. What people had shed and left – a pair of shoes, a shooting cap, some faded skirts and coats in wardrobes – these alone kept the human shape and the emptiness indicated how once they were filled and animated; how once hands were busy with hooks and buttons; how once the looking glass had held a face; had held a world hollowed out in which a figure turned, a hand flashed, the door opened, in came children, rushing and tumbling; and went out again.

[Virginia Woolf, *To the Lighthouse* (1929), Penguin, Harmondsworth, 1975, p. 147]

6

THE TIDY HOUSE OF FICTION:
SEX AND STORIES,
GENDER AND LANGUAGE

Every instinct possessed by those who grew up in the culture that produced 'The Tidy House' insists that it must have been written by little
girls and that it never could have been written by little boys. In the classroom where Lindie, Melissa and Carla worked, little boys did write,
certainly not with the alacrity displayed by the girls, but sometimes at
great length, frequently producing episodic, epic adventures with lone
male heroes moving through time and space. As a group, the boys in this
particular classroom (as in many others) demonstrated far less competence
in reading and writing than did the girls. Several of them were only just
beginning to read at the age of eight and did not have the means to
produce extended pieces of writing.

Primary school classrooms can suggest to little girls a purpose of
activity, a kind of comprehensible system, that they do not always
suggest to little boys: rooms need ordering, things have places to be put
away, the day must be planned around human needs, just as the tidy
houses must be put in order and food got to the table. The activity of girls
within houses makes the working of an institution more comprehensible
than it is to boys; a classroom was a place they understood and they went
about its activities with a calm comprehension.[1] They also spent more
time in it than did the boys (the school had a policy of allowing children to
decide whether or not they stayed in at playtime and dinnertime)[2] and
though lonely, depressed, anxious little boys, feminised by disaster,
stayed within its walls too, the girls who elected to stay there spent a
good deal of time writing.

A great many more children write spontaneously than is commonly
supposed. In the Newson's Nottingham survey they found that 27 per
cent of class IV and 31 per cent of class V seven-year-old girls wrote 'a lot'

for pleasure in their own time at home. The figures for boys are 21 per cent and 5 per cent respectively, and all of them compare with figures of 29 per cent and 17 per cent of the overall population of seven-year-olds.[3] It is not clear, however, how much of this writing was creative, and how much involved copying from books; but the chances are that a good deal of writing produced at home *is* creative. The 400-word story called 'The Magic Cat' which is reproduced in Chapter 4 (p. 105) was written by Donna in bed at night in a tiny five pence notebook and brought to school after the weekend in which it was composed.

When the girls worked together in writing, they operated by a model of social life that demonstrated to them more cohesion and co-operation between women than it did between men. There were pressures on the boys to act aggressively and to display their conflict with each other, though the girls too were usually told to hit back. When Lisa, who joined the three writers of 'The Tidy House' after several days of diplomatic approaches (TH tapes: pp. 164, 182), wrote a portion of the text, she had the character Jamie tell her nine-year-old son Carl to fight back in the playground. This scene echoed many conversations with *all* the children throughout the year in which they would patiently explain to me, yet again, that whilst the school's most stringently enforced rule forbade fighting, they had been *told* by their parents to hit back. Of course, Lisa had not been prepared for physical combat in wrestling games with her father, but, in writing the following scene, she remembered similar conversations with her own mother:

> One day his two friends
> broke friends with him.
> He did not have no friends to play with.
> Now, the boys who was his friends
> got boys and started to fight him.
> When Carl went home he told Jamie
> but Jamie said,
> 'You stick up for yourself.'
> 'But I –'
> 'But what?'
> 'I can't because they are bigger than me.'
> 'You can get Jason on the ground.'
> 'Yes I know . . .
> but you get the blame when it is not you.'
> 'Oh shut up.'

[TH transcript; p. 54]

This passage by Lisa mirrored her own, very recent experience. She had had two close friends, Carla and Melissa. They had gone to nursery school together, walked back and forth together, sat together and played in the streets together through five long years. The arrival of Lindie in the spring had disturbed the balance of this old friendship. Admitted back into the fold towards the end of the week, the constraints of the plot that Lisa was faced with and the gender of the child character she had to write about meant that there was no alternative but to write of herself as Carl, the boy.

Within any symbolic system that is available to children at any one time, they are able to make metaphoric use of those symbols and in this way to invest them with a variety of new meanings, as Lisa did with the character Carl. This capacity belongs of course equally to boys, though they, having been exposed to a literature where the active majority of characters are male, have less need to perform the kind of transforming trick that has just been indicated. In the following story, which was written out of desperation and a modicum of hope by a nine-year-old boy with severely limited writing skills, the symbols available from a folk-tale (Ruth Manning-Sanders' recounting of *Tripple-Trapple*)[4] are used to describe a father's violence, an abused mother and sisters (though the sisters disappear in this account), fear of kidnapping, or something worse and, finally, hope, in the shape of a new man in the house. In the Manning-Sanders version the iron pot is the anti-hero, and there is no devil in the original. He is the child's device, as is the capitalisation of his name. The rabbits come from a gentler source – soft symbols of innocence and frailty.

> Once there was two rabbits. One day they went out down the hill and they saw a little man and he said My name is Devil and I live in a wood. The Devil went home into the wood and took his pot with him and had his tea and went to bed and in the morning he went out of the wood into the home of the rabbit. The rabbit was telling his mum rabbit and the Devil was coming nearer and nearer. Then a man was walking along the road with a gun in his hand and he wanted to kill the Devil with his gun. But he did not see the Devil and the pot so he did not kill him this time, so the Devil looked and looked but he did not see the home of the rabbit and the Devil and the pot went to the wood. The Devil went to the door and saw the two rabbits. He ran to get his pot and ran to the rabbit and the rabbit saw the Devil and a man shot him. The pot blowed him up and the rabbits and the mum rabbit and the man live happily ever after.
> Two Rabbits and a Devil and a Pot. This is a story by Shaun.

[Shaun, story, December 1975]

137

The child who wrote this was in a situation of physical and psychological emergency certainly not experienced by the three girls at the time they wrote 'The Tidy House'. Neither is it the case that distress necessarily calls forth a transformation of symbols. In the account below, Carla merely recounts the death of her much loved grandfather:

> My grandad is dead he's about 60 or 61 he is going to be buried on
> Tuesday at 10 o'clock. It makes you feel funny when a cat dies and two
> grandads dead actually two cats died one cat we had is in the shop it had
> diahorrea so one dog and forty three pigeons. I did have seven dogs. Four
> went to the poodle parlour, my nan had one.
>
> [Carla, diary entry, October 1975]

Written words are used here simply to think by and the dead pigeons, the dogs sold, the cats disappeared were simply other examples of mortality that she had experienced. 'The Tidy House' is important precisely because it shows children manipulating a set of symbols outside a situation of immediate emergency: the children's choice of metaphors was the product of deliberation and reflection and can therefore demonstrate far more their own estimation of themselves than might an arbitrarily used set, taken from a literary model, as was Shaun's example above.

'The Tidy House' is a story written by female children, without reference to literary models, in circumstances that offered ease and time for reflection. It would seem, then, that there are exceptionally good opportunities here for considering little girls' use of written language and their understanding of the social use of language. We know by now what are some of the questions to ask on the border of this huge terrain, though many of the answers that have been given seem often only to confirm old beliefs and prejudices rather than revealing facts about women's use of language. How do women use language? They learn silence and evasion.[5] How do children learn what language is appropriate to the sexes? In some far reaches of our culture, we are told, some six-year-olds listen to 'Oh dear, the TV set broke,' and know that it is a lady who speaks. (Men it seems, say, 'Damn it, the TV set broke.')[6] How do little boys use written language compared with little girls? Little boys prepare lists and guidebooks and write their own encyclopaedias, whilst girls write soft cosy stories and poems about domestic subjects.[7] The trouble with these answers is that none of them quite fit with the language represented by the children who wrote 'The Tidy House'. The dislocation between these theories about female language and the children's representation of what they heard in the social world is examined throughout this chapter. It is certain, though, that *beliefs* about women's language have massively dimmed the real voices of real women. Older prejudices are easier to see: the only published story that I have come across that was written by a girl who did not belong to the middle or upper classes was reproduced in the journal the *Paidologist* in 1903. Nine-year-old Lottie's editor understood that in literature, as in life, the proper concern of poor children was domestic subjects and he smugly indicated that all was well: 'Lottie hurries on telling the story, speaking only of what interests a nine-year-old. To marry, to die, to sleep, to eat, to play, to be ill'.[8] He would probably have made a similar interpretation of 'The Tidy House'.

Some questions about women's language and the learning of it in childhood have received more satisfactory answers than the ones indicated above. What do we do with a language like English that has its pronouns so relentlessly gendered? Ten years ago it was possible to postulate that gendered pronouns were in the nature of the language, unalterable and therefore unimportant, to agree that they were in fact neutral and did not play so large a role in the socialisation of children through the agency of language as did the linguistic signals of powerlessness and lack of confidence that are conveyed by women's *manner* of speaking.[9] We have now a partly written new history that can demonstrate the cumulative effect of always using the male pronoun to stand for the human race, of never, ever, as a wider effect of this usage, finding one's complete image upon the page. What is more, we have discovered that there are ways of writing and speaking that avoid the use of the 'generic "he" '.[10]

The questions above are at once general and specific. They are to do with the socialisation of little girls into womanhood through language used and language understood; and they are about specific language use in working-class England in the mid-1970s. For though the children who wrote 'The Tidy House' revealed themselves to be concerned with a female future that they saw fraught with irritation and confinement – that they had no difficulty in presenting in a bad light – they both understood women's language and used language themselves, as a system of power, capable of the transformation of reality.

The work that has been done on children's acquisition of sexual stereotypes in spoken language is class and culture bound. It may be that in 'white middle-class English-speaking Albuquerque' women really do faintly murmur, 'My goodness, there's the President,' whilst their rugged male companions gruffly ejaculate, 'I'll be damned, there's the President,' and that children really do believe that this is the sex-appropriate way to speak. But in working-class Nottingham, for instance, mothers seem more concerned with stopping all their children from using bad language,[11] rather than in teaching little girls how to talk like ladies, and Carla, Lindie and Melissa certainly presented the adult female characters of their story as more verbally aggressive than the men.

The three girls' most consistent presentation of their own fathers, and their fictional male characters, was as absences and their perception of the immediate and situational structure of power in the home echoes that described by some of the Victorian working-class children of the last chapter. In 'The Tidy House' it is the words of women that make things happen, just as the conversation between Jo and Jamie produced not only twins for Jo, but a new brother for Carl. It took me a very long time and many readings of 'The Tidy House' to understand (so convinced was I by the image of the tidy house protected against invasion) that in the bedroom scene of Carla's first contribution to the story it is Jo who tries to get Mark to impregnate her – 'she wanted a baby from the beginning' (TH tapes: p. 176) – not Jo who tiredly protests against his advances. I could have learned this at the time from Carla if I had not been too eager to preserve classroom propriety by cutting short her words (TH tapes: p. 176).

Evidently then, the children had no difficulty in hearing a man say protestingly, 'I want to get asleep,' and 'Don't let us, really, this time of the night' (TH transcript: p. 43). It is difficult to doubt that the children's presentation of male language here was based on realistic observation. Were we not to believe that they represented what they had heard in the real world, we would have to suggest that they used this language, assigning it a gender in a metaphoric way and bestowed the female qualities of resistance and hesitation on a male character. This seems highly unlikely, given the role of their female characters in the story. 'The Tidy House' was the apotheosis of nine years of very careful listening. The children were not trapped, then, by a gendered language; in fact their text may offer evidence that it is not gendered in the manner commonly supposed.[12]

It would seem that many women, living through the years of the 'sex-neutral "he" ', refused, when they heard or used that pronoun, to image a man. They thought rather of a genderless 'human being' or 'person'. Some of them, with much struggle, actually managed to image themselves – in the category of genderless human being. Men, on the other hand, have all these years been understanding and using 'he' in its *specific*, not its *generic* sense.[13] Quite simply then, within the confines of linguistic usage, women have made their own meanings, in the way that Carla, Lindie and Melissa did when they played about with the dialogue of 'The Tidy House'.

Yet the question asks itself: what is it never to see yourself reflected in the words, never quite to find a woman in the glass, but always struggled for, dimly made out, 'the human being', a 'person'? And what if the symbols used for thought, reflection and the transformation of experience can only be seen through the glass of their official meaning – if the baby, the nest and the house can only be interpreted as avowals of a traditional femininity?

It was only long after I had established the practice of reading folk-fairy-tales to the children that I started to worry about what I was doing. Before doubts began to circulate about the damaging messages encoded in them, Bettleheim's work, published in the mid-1970s, confirmed that the use of the fairy-tale was therapeutic, that the story's description of the small against the great, the weak against the strong, the resolution of conflict through action, all provide children with vehicles of thought and strategies of belief for the exigencies of their daily life.[14] (Even then, though, Bettleheim's examples of this nourishing and therapeutic process at work seemed poor illustrations of the general thesis. *Snow White* is a fine stage for the production by a Freudian analyst of a feminised oedipal conflict; fairly inadequate as a scenario of struggle, consciousness and resolution.[15])

When children do confront daily the problems of poverty, sexual conflict between adults, love and hatred, despair and rejection, then fairy-tales can provide easily assimilable metaphors for children's social and personal feelings, confirming both that pain and the possibility of comfort are real, and that through action there may be resolution. This confirmation and mirroring of the self at many levels of consciousness is indeed the mission of all literature for children. The particular advantage of the fairy-tale is that it provides an *abstract* mirroring of a child's real circumstances. Set out of real time it makes easily manipulable the symbols it presents.

But the classic fairy-tale encodes other meanings. Most simply and

141

clearly it tells the story of women in our culture, and simply states that they must be either innocent and beautiful, so passive that they are almost dead, or profoundly and monstrously evil: good mother, bad mother.[16] The hero of the classic tale is the positive opposite to the negative heroine; the heroine is always she to whom things are done. The classic tales – *Cinderella*, *Sleeping Beauty*, *Snow White*, *Little Red Riding Hood* – have a very wide circulation in our society not only through recounting in nursery and infant school and on children's television, but also through the distribution network of Ladybird Books of Loughborough. Very cheap and very well made, realistically illustrated, their 'Well-Loved Tales' series, which includes nearly all the European classic fairy-stories, sells between 80,000 and 90,000 copies of each title per year.[17] Ladybird Books are often the only children's books on sale in working-class areas. They are sold in paper shops and mini-supermarkets (Carla on her way to the sweet shop (TH tapes: 165) would have found a rack of them there) and they are bought by parents and children. In 1976 they were only 12p each and they were the most familiar non-school books to the children in the class where 'The Tidy House' was written. Most children possessed some Ladybird titles; the girls particularly owned many of their 'Well-Loved Tales'.

The classic fairy-tale conveys the vast and destructive messages outlined above to little girls (and of course to little boys) and does it so effectively because it operates at the mythic level of our common currency of social belief, setting out power and money, glamour and romance, sex and death, good and evil, like pieces on a chessboard ready to be played with. It is of course, as well, a highly articulate rendering of what every little girl knows, that mothers are quite simply monstrous, however good they may be and however much they love, and the real problem, for little girls, is that they too are likely to become mothers.

There is however a body of folk-fairy-tales that has a much smaller circulation than the classic tales and which seems to me to embody far less articulate but perhaps more pervasive social beliefs. What is in Britain embodied in 'Cap o' Rushes', 'Tom-Tit-Tot', 'Kate Crackernuts', 'Clever Oonagh', 'The Secret Room,' 'The Midnight Hunt', 'Well o' the World's End', and in other recently rediscovered and published tales from other countries,[18] did not receive the canonisation that the classic tale did at the hands of their eighteenth- and nineteenth-century male collectors and editors. Our myths are, indeed, official ones.

In the folk-fairy-tale (and the reference here is to Amabel Williams

Ellis's *Fairy Tales from the British Isles*) it is indubitably men who make the world, whose power and intentions dictate circumstances, but within these circumstances it is women who matter, who are true heroines in that being done to, they *do* back, who actively, verbally or physically *make things happen* and draw the plot to its conclusion. There are too, in these tales, clear reflections of historically accurate social circumstances: the majority of households depicted in them are either all-female or fatherless. Circumstances may be dictated by men, but they don't stay around to live through them. We are beginning to learn from sociological investigation at just how many points in a woman's life 'the role of husband/father most of the time, quite marginal',[19] and the folk-fairy-tale provides a kind of fictional reflection of these circumstances. It offers a much more accurate representation of the circumstances of most children's lives than does the kingdom of the bourgeois household that is depicted in the classic tales. It seems to me that the folk-fairy-tale represents a vast and unofficial reckoning of circumstances: once the external and economic dimensions of male domination have been taken into account, men simply do not matter in the way that women do, to children. Their characters are not rounded, they cannot be understood, their motives are inexplicable (though their actions may have far-reaching and terrifying results) and their infrequent presence is tolerated as a puzzling and negative principle on the domestic scene (which is not to say that households do not revolve around their coming home).

Some of our current understanding of patriarchy may be based on the childhood domestic circumstances of the women who have described it and it is important to at least consider that the dimensions of power and sexual relationships that are seen to be descriptive of the working-class family during recent history may be based on an extrapolation from the paternal presence in the bourgeois home.[20] I now see, with hindsight, that I read so many folk-fairy-tales to the children because they embodied a reality for me, and a reckoning of the children's reality, that was not available in the legitimated mythology of *Rapunzel* and *Cinderella*.

An understanding of this view of social and domestic life is essential if we are to explore the symbols that the children appear to use in 'The Tidy House'. Our commonly used set of interpretative symbols is no less official than the mythic order of the classic fairy-tale (Nancy Chodorow has called those of the Freudian psychoanalytic tradition 'our cultural psychology')[21] and we do Carla, Lindie and Melissa a grave disservice if we interpret their words as only embodying the official meaning. We could, for instance, explore the children's written words, their commentary on them and the drawings and painting that accompanied them and find that their narrative rested on four central images: the house, the nest, the heart and the baby. Having done this we could then agree with Freud that (in dreams) 'the one typical . . . representation of the human figure . . . is a house', that 'some symbols have more connection with the uterus . . . thus cupboards . . . and more especially rooms', and that babies represent the genitalia, frequently, for girls, the missing penis.[22] We could then confirm this interpretation by observing that in their play with manipulable objects girls will construct enclosed spaces, whilst boys will build projected structures.[23] Finally, because it is, after all, writing that is being dealt with here, we could note that in their very earliest writing, when they are heavily dependent on adults spelling words for them, little girls will ask for 'mummy' and 'house', whilst little boys demand 'rocket' and 'car'.[24] (There is of course a particular delight in pursuing this symbolism to the edges of its meaning, and seeing Carl of 'The Tidy House' as a penis, a demanding nuisance, a burden to be got through the day – a perception of many children of both sexes, in fact, before they learn that its possession ought to be a matter of pride to one and envy to the other.)[25]

Children however have rarely been asked what the employment of such symbolism means to them, and analysis has rather depended on the theory of the questioner that the child's revelations confirmed. But it is clear from even a casual reading of 'The Tidy House' that the use of this particular set of symbols does not necessarily represent a struggle against, and final acceptance of, a traditional and official femininity. The house is there, but it is invaded and though the invasion is asked for it is bitterly resented. The babies are born, but their presence spells weariness and regret.

Indeed, when considering the spontaneous productions of children, rather than those that result from a test situation or questioning by an adult, it is best to match the investigation as closely as possible to the direction suggested by the child. In this way, as anthropologists have found in the study of some alien cultures,[26] it becomes clear that the notion of symbolism is far too large and cumbersome an analytic device with which to approach 'The Tidy House'. A series of symbols, like those of traditional psychoanalysis indicated above, contain so many highly condensed meanings that it is often impossible to use them to expose an underlying system of conviction and belief on the part of the symbol user.

Fortunately, Carla, Melissa and Lindie made it quite clear that they saw real and *visual* connection between the symbols of their story and their social environment. Their drawings showed the house and detailed the nest of babies. It is more useful to approach the house, the nest, and the baby as metaphors, where the children saw some connection between the entities and ideas they represent and objects in the real world. By making connections between the two, they elucidated their meaning. To do this is to fix their story firmly in the social environment and it is also to explore their investigation of themselves and their feelings as a constant movement between the self and a particular social world.

If we consider this kind of metaphoric use on the children's part, we are able to explore not only the ideas that they made visible (embodied in the house and the nest) but those that were never drawn. There are no pictures of the child characters, though they filled the rooms of the tidy house with their noise and confusion and, in the children's collage picture of the exterior, only one nameless adult female smiles in the garden outside the house. But it is clear that the female characters of their story were used by the children in this way, to represent themselves, just as the baby boys represented another version of selfhood. The children saw, and drew, and often sought to explain real relations between the images of their story and real people and real objects; the idea of metaphorical usage allows us to witness the process of the making of meanings and to understand how real people and real objects came to represent regret, inevitability and compulsion for Carla, Melissa and Lindie.

To the list of the children's images – the house, the heart, the nest, the baby – we need to add the mother. Carla, Lindie and Melissa saw many connections between their female characters, one a mother at the beginning of the story, the other soon to become one, and themselves. In the children's eyes they shared youth with their adult characters and the fictional adults had interests and concerns that were comprehensible to them. Indeed, they shared the same language:

> One day a girl and a boy said/ Is it springtime? Look, Polkadot's had babies./ Can Jamie and Jason have one, Jo?/ Yes, Mark, if they want./ Jason, let's have Ginger./ Jamie's made up a name for him already./

> Down Jo's street/ is a big boy called Fred./ He made fun of Jo,/ he called her big head,/ but Jo got her own back./ She called out,/ Big bully/ big nut/ and big bum.

One day Mark said/ I'll go shopping for you./

[TH transcript: pp. 42, 45]

All of this was, to a large extent, based on direct observation: the mothers the children knew were often very young and Carla's and Melissa's mother had both had their first child at seventeen. The sixteen-year-old bride on their housing estate was quite likely to have to run the verbal gauntlet of wandering teenage gangs if she walked up the street. And the interest in animals shown by the characters in 'The Tidy House' (the rabbits in the opening scene) wasn't simply a projection of childish interests on to their adult characters, for pets were widely kept on the estate and all the children knew that a bed covered with furry toy animals was perfectly acceptable (indeed desirable) bedroom decor (TH tapes: p. 178)

The children presented their female characters as embodying a continuum of their own experience. Yet it is clear at the same time that they found this mirroring of their own experience in that of Jamie and Jo complicated and disturbing, and that at many points they refused identification with the mothers they had created. This is evident in the children's discussion of their own mothers' feelings about them: 'If you never had no children, you'd be well off wouldn't you'; 'Probably hates kids . . . I think all mums do, don't they?'; 'My mum would love us if we didn't want to come home' (TH tapes: pp. 176, 167)

It has been pointed out before, in Chapter 1, that all the child characters created by Lindie, Melissa and Carla were boys. It has been suggested that this was a device that allowed the children in the story to be what the children writing it were often considered to be – noisy, untidy, inconsiderate – without implicating themselves in these accusations. The children did, in fact, have one brief, elliptical discussion about the sex of their proposed characters, the twins Simon and Scott:

Carla: It's about time Jason and Jamie and Thingybob had babies.
            Supposing that we put in the book that they had twins.
Melissa: Yeah.
Carla: Two boys.
Lindie: No, two girls.
Melissa: A boy and a girl.
Lindie: That would make no difference though, would it?

[TH tapes: pp. 167–168]

They seem here to have come to the conclusion that in the face of the double difficulty the twins would present to their mother their gender was pretty irrelevant.

The state of motherhood represented by Melissa, Carla and Lindie in their text is the unofficial version that has only recently come to be described within socialism and feminism. The legitimate version of motherhood in our society trails clouds of glory and fulfilment; the tiredness and hard work of the state have rarely entered into official accounts of it. Yet the children were quite aware of the unofficial view and there was a kind of tautological despair about the tag they chose to demonstrate their understanding with: 'What is the mother without them' (TH tapes: p. 178).[27] Children, struggling to grow up through all those unofficial motherhoods of tiredness, bad temper and hardship, have always known the true story and understood with all the love and affection and the meals got (at what odds) to the table that, quite simply, it would have been better had they never existed.[28]

Yet the children's fiction remains: in their story it was the presence of *boys* that acted as sources of irritation and regret to Jo and Jamie. It was Carl's whining, his tears, the ice cream dropped messily on the carpet, that demonstrated their understanding of the unofficial view of motherhood. And it is boy twins who get born in the story, in spite of the girl child struggling for existence:

> Jamie wanted a baby./ She wanted a girl/ because she had thought up/ a name. The name was Jeannie./ Jamie adored that name/ she thought it was lovely/ and Jo thought it was a good idea/ to have a girl and call it Jeannie/ and Mark agreed./[29]

[TH transcript: p. 54]

It was not just that the children could not create themselves because their fictional mothers did not want them, nor that characterisation as a boy is some kind of compromise between not being alive at all and being a nuisance. It was rather that, within the story they constructed, to be born a girl would inevitably be to become a mother and thus to condemn oneself and find oneself a matter for regret. Girl children are not only the invaders of the tidy house, those who make it untidy, just like boys; at the same time they are the house itself, likely in their turn to be mothers. Lindie, Melissa and Carla avoided writing this thesis down because they understood its implications very well.

The house (and as a simple primitive version of it, the nest) has been, for the male theorists and critics who have outlined its inner spaces and detailed its connection with their first dwelling place of the womb, a place of retreat and safety, 'one of the greatest powers of integration for the thoughts, memories and dreams of mankind'.[30] But as feminist critics have turned to examine this felicitous inner space, they have discovered in the words of the women who have inhabited the dream houses, in particular those of the nineteenth-century women novelists, only empty rooms, a negative space, madness at the head of the stair.[31]

But if Melissa, Lindie and Carla saw the tidy house as themselves, their bodies, then they built this analogy on the images of their own three-up, three-down, semi-detached council houses with gardens. (If they had lived in one of the three blocks of flats on the estate, then it is unlikely that they would have pursued their questions in the form that 'The Tidy House' took.) The children were not dealing with either the architectural or domestic arrangements of people, time and space that have made the houses of the bourgeois patriarch so useful for a re-reading of the nineteenth-century women novelists. Indeed, on many occasions during the writing of their story, the children obviously saw their tidy houses as places of safety and refuge from the hostile streets outside (TH transcript: p. 45). Their characters travel through those streets to reach places of safety, relief from pain, friendship, conviviality, a good time and baby-sitting services. The house itself is presented positively, as a place of warmth and comfort, no madwomen in the attic, no miasma in the cellar. (These particular council houses possessed neither attic nor cellar.)[32]

Yet when objections such as these to the idea of the house as a *consistent* female metaphor have been laid aside the *loss* of the house, the safe and private place, remains the particular image chosen by little girls to describe their growth into womanhood. The overriding theme of 'The Tidy House' is that it becomes 'The Tidy House that is no more a Tidy House' (TH transcript: p. 53). Its state changes and its loss is inevitable. 'The first of all my losses,' wrote Elizabeth Barrett remembering her childhood, 'was the losing of the bower.' The poem 'The Lost Bower' recounts an incident from her girlhood when, playing in the Malvern Hills above her family home at Hope End, she came across a small natural enclosure in the woods. The woman (perhaps remembering the child she had been) furnished the bower in her mind's eye: it was 'finely fixed and fitted', 'carpet smooth with moss and grass'. Playing houses, the poet positively furnished the enclosed space for the child who found it, gave it 'door and window mullion', saw the ground 'paved with glory', the leaves above as 'the ceiling's miracle'. By making the house, the child found peace (though she would scarcely have been able to call it that at the time):

a green elastic cushion
Clasped within the linden root
Took me in a chair of silence
very rare and absolute.[33]

The house is another version of Maggie Tulliver's Red Deeps in *The Mill on the Floss*, and Mary Wollstonecraft's craggy little ravine, that 'landscape of female self-indulgence' that Ellen Moers described in *Literary Women*,[34] and indulgence does seem the precisely appropriate word for the quiet and private places where all these children knew themselves before they were invaded by the precise expectations of a social and sexual role. The difference between the tidy house and the half-houses of the adult poetic imagination is that Carla, Lindie and Melissa were able to explore it at the same time as it presented them with problems. They thus had a sharper vision of its contradictions and could see it as a prison-house as well as a place of safety. (It is perfectly possible of course that Mary Ann Evans, Mary Wollstonecraft and Elizabeth Moulton Barrett dealt with these questions as children and young girls as well as by memory as adult women; but at least in Elizabeth Barrett's childhood writing, an enormous quantity of which is preserved, there is no indication that she ever did.)

If the tidy house, and its loss, is a female image, then we need to understand its particular usefulness for three working-class girls shortly before their ninth birthdays. The children presented the house positively, though never again, after the opening scene, is there achieved the bright clarity of idea and theme involved in setting foot outside the house, into the garden. The sunflowers, the bounding dog, Polkadot the rabbit and her babies, all represent for Jo and Mark, whose tidy house it is, what is soon going to happen within its walls. We are led inevitably, by the children's selection and placing of images, to a consideration of the house as the central vehicle of metaphor. Yet the only places that the children detailed physically were the garden, the exterior of the house, and bedroom. Indeed, for a description of the last we have to rely on Melissa's drawing and the exterior of the tidy house was only detailed so precisely by her because she was describing a collage picture that the children had made of it. By contrast with the rest of the story, Carla's opening scene is crowded with objects. In the rest of the text, no person is detailed. The objects mentioned after the opening scene are: cups of tea, pieces of cake, a candle, ice creams, a birthday card, money, a shirt, a colouring book, pencils, plastic shapes to draw round (these last four are the presents that

Carl receives for his fourth birthday), a toy car, a bottle of lemonade and a bit of bread. These are all (except for the toy car) quite incidental to the plot and none of them are described.

Though the exterior of the house had a solid existence, its interior (with the exception of the bedroom) remained a visual mystery. Nothing is seen there, but the voices echo through its rooms and it is the place where decisions are taken, conflict is played out and life begins. It is not clear what gynaecological information the children actually possessed, nor how detailed was their knowledge of the process of conception and gestation. Out of some accurate teaching and rather more observation and listening they had constructed their own sexual theories and they knew in general what went on in the dark bedrooms. The specific act implied in Lindie's 'Do it, darling', and in Carla's 'What, do the —— harder? (TH transcript: pp. 52, 53) is not really a contradiction of 'they sat up all night, kissing Jo all night' (TH transcript: p. 52). All three descriptions imply that a lot of physical effort goes into making a baby and one of the children evidently believed that the harder the effort, the more children were there made: 'He [the doctor] said I think if you tried harder you will have twins' (TH transcript: p. 53). The 'nest of babies' seems so felicitous an image for the ovaries that it is tempting to interpret it as the children's rendering of adult teaching; but it is far more likely that for children as familiar as they were with domestic animals – coops of pigeons, rabbits in a hutch, cats and kittens all over the place – the nest as a representation of maternal care from before conception until after birth must have seemed obvious enough.

In the picture of the tidy house bedroom, the rug/nest occupies a position opposite to the bed. Within a wide brown border is a collection of tiny red hearts scattered at random, one large red heart and a small ovoid brown blob. The bed in fact is not shown in full, being cut off by the right-hand side of the page; but it was to the bed that the children wished to draw attention:

Teacher:	(Pointing to Melissa's picture): That's the rug, is it?
Melissa:	No, that's a nest of babies.
Teacher:	(Taken aback): Oh. A nest of babies. (Recovering self) Of course, in every bedroom a nest of babies!
Lindie:	Yes of course there is. (Quotes) 'What is the mother without them.'
All:	Mmm.
Teacher:	(to Melissa): But your mum hasn't got a *nest*. She's only got –

Melissa: No, not a nest, but she's got this big bed, and she's got all
these cuddly toys around it. She's got a teddy this big.

[TH tapes: p. 178]

It is difficult to describe the tenor of this conversation. Stunned as I was
by this calm exposition of psychoanalytic theory, I realised that part of
what the children were doing was telling a good joke (widened eyes,
nonchalant voices, followed by giggling).[35] Out of my own particular
repertoire of images I interpreted the nest as 'a houseful of children', 'a lot
of children' ('tha'rt the prettiest bird we han in nest; but tha' shouldn'a
come just when tha' did'). But Melissa was not to be deflected by this
misinterpretation: there may not have actually been a nest of babies, she
agreed, but there was a bed, and it was her mother's bed, and the cuddly
toys, the teddies that decorated it, were like the babies in the nest. The
large, flamboyant red heart on the rug (in the nest) has, in this context of
the child's analogy, to be seen as the mother. The brown blob may be a
blocked-out error (but it is a very carefully executed drawing), or it may
be the father. It is the mother's bed that lies at the heart of the house. The
hearts in this picture are a reworking of the conventional symbol for
romantic love (difficult for anyone listening to fairy-tales, Radio 1,
common discourse and buying birthday cards in late twentieth-century
Britain to avoid hearts as vehicles of an enormously wide range of
meanings). But the children worked this conventional symbol into their
own metaphor for the central power and purpose of the house – their
mother.

Though they may be represented as absences (and perhaps as small
brown blobs) fathers were given their due in the children's story. Their
role in conception was understood; one of the hinges of the plot is the per-
suading of men to become fathers. No matter what hard work and
nuisance follows on the production of children, the women in 'The Tidy
House' are shown as being initially successful in getting their own way.
But they are punished for their desire, in a way that the two fathers are
not, by the presence of the children that they cajoled into life. The
relationship of the character Jason to his child Carl is presented as quite
unproblematic. When he reaches his friend Mark's house after work to
find the child screaming for his dropped ice cream, he simply picks him
up, removes him from the tidy house and deposits him with another
woman – his own mother.

The house is a metaphor for the bodies of mothers and of the children
who will one day be mothers themselves. It represents, in this way, order

151

and safety. The precise arrangement of its appurtenances, the neat symmetry of its rooms were detailed with great enjoyment by Melissa ('I did some windows on a house that auntie copied for me,' noted Mary Elizabeth Coleridge with a similar satisfaction in March 1873[36]). Order and precision made the house comprehensible, containable, a most valuable possession, a place of self-definition (as indeed the possession of a council house actually was, in the children's experience). The voices rang clearly through its rooms, the quarrels, the crying, the singing of happy birthday. All becomes suddenly and startlingly visible, as it did to the children, in the drawing of the bedroom at the heart of the house. It is then possible to see the scenes in the bedrooms as a kind of allegory of the whole story: the tidy house made untidy.

It was the children's title that made the most explicit statement of their meaning and, in fact, before my misreading of Carla's draft gave her story a title in the singular (TH facsimile: p. 184) it is clear that she meant to indicate that *all* houses with children in them were untidy.[37] The disturbance and difficulty that the production of children entailed for women was the disorder wrought in the tidy house (TH transcript: p. 53/TH tapes: p. 175).[38] The only actual mother in the room on the afternoon in question quite inadvertently confirmed the children's convictions about the disordering tendencies of little boys (TH tapes: p. 178). The children knew quite well that their presence spelled untidiness to adults – they were told so frequently, at school and at home – and in the house made untidy by children can be seen the children's understanding of the invasion of the body by conception, pregnancy and motherhood.

The children made their own fictional tidy house out of a history of housing and the life of households that has been already briefly described. We can use their written words to gain insight into the psychological reverberations of a process of which the children were not consciously aware. To do this is to make an interpretative use of the children's words and not to describe the function that writing served the children.

Scrupulous attention has been paid in these pages to the distinction between these two usages; but there comes a point where they must be linked. Carla, Lindie and Melissa were able to use their particular local and personal experiences to construct meanings that have a general cultural validity. Out of their extremely limited experience they were able to draw on, and transform, a powerful set of symbols: 'the poetic depth of the space of the house',[39] mothers, babies, birth. Anyone who writes creatively is after all bound to do this and to demonstrate what Carla, Lindie and Melissa did is after all to say no more than that a little language goes a very long way. That the particular style of spoken language that these children used is still condemned, that the shade of 'linguistic deprivation' still stalks the working-class primary school, in spite of the efforts of researchers like Basil Bernstein in demonstrating that their work is not a description of something that can be called an inferior language, is the exposition of a wider social assumption that this book has attempted to outline. This assumption is that the world that working-class children manipulate in spoken and written language is simply not worth taking seriously.

When Elizabeth Moulton Barrett got lost in the woods as a child and played houses beneath the trees, she did that out of an apprehension of the meaning of the Palladian mansion at the bottom of the hill, a mother whose encouragements to literary production from her children bordered on the fanatic, a powerful and absent patriarch as a father, a family income based on investment and colonial speculation, a social hierarchy mirrored in the domestic arrangements at Hope End.[40] What the child understood of this world is as much or as little as Carla, Melissa and Lindie understood of the historical transformation of the working-class home from the defensive hovel to the hygienic space (as in one recent account of state encroachment into working-class life),[41] the dependance of working-class women on the family wage,[42] the power of the mother and its encouragement by the state and the history of working-class family arrangements. At eight and nine children know very little of these matters, but they grow up in particular adult worlds that each have histories. The difference between the self-socialisation of Elizabeth Moulton Barrett and the children who wrote 'The Tidy House' is that the culture and society to which the first child referred in her writing are seen as belonging to the mainstream of literary and social history, whilst the underlying system of meanings with which Melissa, Carla and Lindie performed exactly the same task, which was to grow up and become women, have scarcely yet been entered into the record books of our society.

7

FLOWER LADY: THE END

And then an event did occur to Emily, of considerable importance. She suddenly realised who she was. There is little reason that one can see why it should not have happened to her five years earlier, or even five years later; and none, why it should have come that particular afternoon. She had been playing houses in a nook, right in the bows, behind the windlass (on which she had hung a devil's claw as a door knocker); and tiring of it was walking rather aimlessly aft, thinking vaguely about some bees and a fairy queen, when it suddenly flashed into her mind that she was *she*.[1]

'The Tidy House' has been presented throughout these pages as a collaborative effort, the production of three children combining memory and conviction to produce one story. This indeed is the most significant aspect of the way in which the narrative was made; but before she was joined by Lindie and Melissa, it was, briefly, Carla's story and as such stood at the apex of a period of extraordinary creativity in her life. Reading in chronological order through the writing she produced during the school year 1975–6, shows her demonstrating, from the beginning of 1976, a spontaneous and objective interest in the alliterative and assonant possibilities of the English language. Before this, at the beginning of the school year, snatches of rhyme, refrains from songs in the charts and jingles often entered into her story and diary writing. But by the end of 1975, she had evolved a method of exploring the sound system of the English language by creating characters whose names and utterances were structured around the poetic possibilities of sounds. This is a very early example from January,1976:

> One day I saw a man, his name was Jim Sithim, who's always drinking gin. He will drink all day and will fade away – but not his big feet. In shoes he took size 40, so he made a pair of thick socks and Jim Sithim lived happily ever after.

This simple and crude technique was refined and elaborated during the next two terms. As 'The Tidy House' was started, Carla was in the process of copying out a series of what she called 'songs' to be bound, with paintings, into a large format book. There were five of these songs and they included the sophisticated and controlled 'Jack Got the Sack' (p. 97) where Carla's interest in rhyme and assonance operated in perfect demonstration of the protagonists she created in Jeannie and Jack. The series of songs also included a very long narrative, called 'Punch and Judy', which allowed her a pure and delighted manipulation of sounds:

> I'm Punch with no hunch; I am Old Punch;
> hu hu hunch, Old Pu Pu Punch
> ta la ta la Old Puhunch;
> ta la ta cra Bom Bom.
> That's what he sang going to the town.
> Then he got to town. He said,
> Can I have some sausages, please,
> in a husky voice.

The narrative, true to tradition, was about quarrelling. The argument between Punch and Judy was light-hearted here, but it foretold the more serious dispute of Jack and Jeannie in 'Jack Got the Sack':

> Judy, don't be silly. No, I am not being silly.
> Plod, Plod, said Punch. You should have been
> down the market. A girl got killed.
> No she never, Punch. Oh yes she did.
> Oh no she never. Oh yes she did . . .
>
> 'Jack, you've got the sack.'
> 'I've got the sack.'
> 'What are we going to do now?'
> 'Don't ask me.'

Three of Carla's songs described quarrels, and 'The Tidy House' itself is the epitome of the children's concern about the arguments of adults and the power of their words to change circumstances. We should expect writing, like play, to allow a child to express this sort of fear and apprehension.[2]

But more revelatory and surprising than this is the depth and sophistication of the cultural referents available to Carla (and indeed, to all the children in her class). These contemporary representatives of poverty and deprivation were highly literate children. They had an enormous range of dramatic styles, both visual and aural, to draw on, a fund of allusion and metaphor to use; they knew, albeit not yet articulately, the ways of rhetoric and the purposes of narrative communication.

In the six weeks from the middle of June 1976, Carla produced more writing than she had in all the other weeks of the school year put together. In a way, it is a mistake to look for obvious causes of this creativity in her domestic circumstances, or in the enabling atmosphere of a classroom. What Carla was doing in those six weeks was developing rapidly her own skills in written language, in something of the way that small children set detachedly about the developmental task of acquiring spoken language.[3] To some extent, this is a good analogy, for it places the credit where it belongs – with the child, and it emphasises the pure intellectual inquiry that is the mark of the baby babbling and the child writing the 'The Tidy House'. But there is a difference between nine months and nine years; it measures out the extent of a life and this book has drawn largely on the child's growing understanding of the social world and her manipulation of its meanings. In fact, through her increased interest in writing, its technical and poetic possibilities, she saw something of her self and her social environment that she might not otherwise have been able to see.

Just as Carla's songs, copied out by her, were about to be bound, she produced the fifth one. It is not clear exactly when the first draft was composed, whether before or after the writing of 'The Tidy House'; but in the argument that has been constructed out of the children's words, it is permissible to see 'Flower Lady' as both a comment on, and a liberation from, the tidy house.

> One day, Flower Lady went for a walk.
> She was sad because she had no friends.
> She sang a sweet song, and it went like this:
> 'No friends, no meat, no food to eat;
> At least I've got to have some wheat.'
> That's what she sang, going along the road.
>
> Flower Lady lived in a den,
> with chairs and tables, happily.
>
> One evening, when it was very dark,
> Flower Lady sang the sweetest song
> she'd ever made. It went like this:
> 'My name is Flower Lady.
> You may like me.

Maybe you like me better than a bee
and I love trees and bumble bees.'
Then she went to bed and had a dream
about songs and laughter.
O, what a night!

It is almost certain that here again Carla remembered her maternal grandfather, who had died the previous autumn (p. 138). He had been banned from tidy houses before his death and his body had been found in a little den that he had constructed on some waste land. If memory of him provided Carla's image of freedom, then she made herself the elegaic self-containment of Flower Lady's song.[4] The tidy house is left behind, the den furnished in imagination, her own place, as the house had never been, the child alone in the dark, rushing night, making her song.

'The Tidy House' and the other writing that provided its context is valuable because it represents a process that we have heard about but can only rarely witness. A few working-class women over the last century have described how, in childhood, they *worked it out*, saw the hollowness of social and sexual expectation and achieved, momentarily, a radical revision of circumstances.[5] But adult then, they could not describe *how* this came about. 'The Tidy House' is a small piece of evidence, an example of how, taking the circumstances of their own life and the materials to hand, people can, without the benefit of theory or the expectations of others, critically confront the way things are and dimly imagine, out of those very circumstances, the way they might be.

APPENDIX 1

THE TIDY HOUSE TAPES

–   speech broken off
. . .   voice tails away/pause/continued speaking
+ + +   taped material undecipherable

TAPE 1/SIDE 1
WEDNESDAY A.M.

[The first part of this tape is taken up with a class lesson, after which the children divided up to pursue group or individual activities. When the tape recorder was first placed on the writers' table it caused a lot of interest among the children in the immediate vicinity. They and the writers spent about ten minutes trying it out, singing into the microphone, watching the volume indicator. There were two boys who were particularly interested in what was going on.]

Teacher   [talking to second teacher]: There's something I want to show you; and the n – they're writing the second volume and talking about it. I would really like to know . . .

[There is a continued discussion of the already completed volume of 'The Tidy House' by the two teachers. Their voices can occasionally be heard above the background noise of the classroom.]

Second
Teacher   [to the three writers]: Can I put this here, on the table. Carry on, take no notice, OK?
Where would it be out of the way? Put it here?
[Commenting on someone's work] That's absolutely beautiful. Decorated sums.

Melissa   [referrring to sums]: I didn't do that.

[Second teacher moves to another part of the room.]

Richard: Have you turned it on?

Carla   [whisper]: Don't know.

Lindie: It is. [Excited] It is on!

159

Carla:	Oh gawd.
Melissa	[looking at counter]: It's number nine now.
Carla	[about the volume indicator]: It tells you how loud you talk.
Lindie:	Doiley! Doiley![1]

[This word is repeated at intervals during the next few minutes by various children, in order to make the needle move.]

Carla:	Hellooo! Oooo!
Melissa:	One hundred and forty-two.
Lindie:	Hello! Hello! Mummy!
Melissa:	They're going to tape you on this now.
Carla:	I'm getting one of these.
Lindie:	Are you?
Carla:	Yeah . . .
Richard	[to second teacher who has returned]: What's that . . . pointing there?
Second Teacher:	What, this? It shows you how loud the sound is. If you make a loud sound here, like this [Claps], look, it'll jump. Oh, didn't seem to work then. You need a different kind of sound. [The children start to clap.] I shouldn't do that too much, you're distracting the other children. But . . . if that never moves it means it's not turned up high enough and you have to alter the setting. You know, just carry on, don't take any notice.
Lindie	[talking about a tape recorder at home]: . . . It's the same size but things go up that end and that's down here, see.
Richard:	I thought it was a tape recorder.
Lindie:	It is.
Second Teacher:	It is a tape recorder, yes. You can hear a bit later on if you carry on . . .
Melissa:	It's moving now.
Richard:	Doiley! Doiley!
	I thought it was one so I just sung doiley.
Lindie:	Oh doiley! [They all laugh.]
Richard:	Doiley! [Blows raspberry] Doiley!
Melissa:	Don't!
Carla:	Look. Listen! [Blows raspberry]
Richard:	Oi! Look at this. [Bangs table] Doiley!
Melissa:	Richard, go and sit down in your own place.
Teacher:	Richard, I want you to go and see what you've got to do next on the chart.
Richard:	I want to do *Stig of the Dump*.[2] [Pause] Doiley!
Lindie	[sings]: Gina, you're not allowed on this table because you're . . .

Teacher	[to Richard]: What have you got to do?
Carla:	Barry!
Barry:	Hello!
Lindie	[warning]: It is on.
Barry:	Is it?
Teacher:	Look, Melissa, I don't want you to wander around the room.
Barry:	Is it off or is it on?
Lindie:	On.
Carla	[reading text of new portion of 'Tidy House']: Lissa, what's it say?
Lindie:	Well, do you want to rub it out for Melissa?
Melissa:	No, I'll put it straight.
Carla:	Don't make sense.
Melissa:	Anyway, it's all going to be typed out properly again, anyway.
Carla:	It must be 'he was four' . . . 'he was four and' . . .
Melissa:	'August . . . due' . . .
Lindie	[whispers to another child]: Go away.
Second Teacher:	What is it you're doing here? Is it . . . ?
Melissa:	It's 'The Tidy House'. In our next exercise they get married. We've just done some pictures and we're writing a story about it.
Second Teacher:	People in that story seem . . . [To Richard] Do you think you could just go and sit down and leave that alone.
Teacher:	And you too, Barry.
Richard:	Only watching.
Second Teacher:	No. I think you've got some work to do. You'd better go and sit down. You'd better go and sit down.
Richard:	I haven't got no work to do.
Teacher:	Barry! I'm going to be cross in a moment. [Indicates some activity]
Barry:	Don't want to do that.
Teacher:	Well, pack up then.[3]
Nicola	[who has been on a search for ball bearings to do a science experiment with returns to the classroom]: Said he didn't have no ball bearings but he gave us a magnet.
Teacher:	That won't do at all. Go and say thank you very much and say they're no good.
[For the first time, the writers are left alone.]	
Carla:	[whispers]: Write the phone numbers down.[4]
Melissa:	Do you think I should start again?
Lindie:	Go *away*, Barry.
Melissa:	Go away, you're distracting us from our work. Shall I start again? . . . Oh, miss . . . I don't know if it's all right.

Carla:	It's all got to be typed out. You're only doing it roughly anyway, aren't you?
Melissa:	Shall I write 'a special day' . . . ?

[Long pause whilst the children write.]

	I writ so far, 'It was a special day today because it was Carl's birthday. He was four. He opened his cards, he got one' . . .
Carla:	Shall I read what I've put and you read what you've put? This is episode two of 'The Tidy House'. 'One day on a Monday, August the 21st, it was Carl's birthday. He was four. Jamie was quite pleased to get him off to school. She went up Jo's house. Jo gave Paul a card. He wanted a present so he started to cry. Stop it now! Boys don't cry on their birthday, do they. That minute the ice-cream man came round. Jo gave Carl 15 pence to get an ice cream. Jamie said, Don't spend too much. Give me the ten pence, there's a good boy. So he did. He got a five-pence ice cream.
Lindie:	Do you want me to write about at school? What happens at school?
Carla:	Yeah.
Lindie:	Shall I just put 'This is the beginning of episode two' down there?
Carla:	Yeah.
Lindie:	Shall I just put 'At School'? Put he was scared and sort of crying . . .
Melissa:	I writ, 'It was a special day today. He was four. He opened his cards. He got a card from Jamie and Jason and one from Jo and Mark' . . . Who else can he get one from?
Lindie:	Nan and grandad.
Melissa:	'Nan and grandad' . . . [Writes] 'And his auntie in Australia' . . . [Pause] Hang on. I've got to check where she is. Australia or . . . [Pause] What's the little boy's name? Jamie?
Carla:	Carl. Jamie's his mum and Jason's his dad.
Melissa:	Oh. And what's the other two?
Carla:	Jo and Mark. And they haven't had a family . . . His mum isn't in the USA.
Melissa:	No, this is about his nan and grandad. [Pause] What's his mum's name?
Carla:	Jamie. His dad's Jason.
	[Pause.]
Lindie:	Carla, I've put, 'At school Carl cried all the time. When Jamie left the school Carl was a bit better. He stopped crying and played with the other children.' That all right?
Carla:	Yeah. Look, shall I read mine all over again?
Lindie:	Yeah.
Carla:	'One day on a Monday, August 7th, it was Carl's birthday. He was four. Jamie was quite pleased to get him off to school. She went up Jo's house. Jo gave Carl a card. He wanted a present so he

started to cry. Stop it now! Boys don't cry on their birthday, do they? That minute the ice-cream man came round. Jo gave Carl fifteen pence to get an ice cream. Jamie said, Don't spend too much. Give me the ten pence, there's a good boy. So he did. He got a five-pence ice cream. While Carl was getting his ice cream Jamie said to Jo, Tonight me and Jason are taking Carl out and Mark and you can come too. Thank you. I've got a present upstairs for Carl.'

Melissa: Ah, I ain't. I've writ so far: 'It was a special day today because it was Carl's birthday. He opened his cards. He got a card from Jamie and Jason and one from Jo and Mark and he got one from his nan and grandad. He got ten pence with that. He got one from the USA. His aunt sent it with an American pound. He thought it was a neat little car.' That's it.

Carla: That all you writ?
[Tape ends.]

TAPE 1/SIDE 2
WEDNESDAY A.M.

Lindie: When Jamie came he didn't want to go home, because he got so used to playing at school, you know. How you spell 'Jamie'? G-A-M-I-E, isn't it?
[Pause whilst the children write.]
Carla: We're going round here, we're going . . . [5]
Lindie: Who?
Carla: We are. I keep going for my leg, you're going for your elbow and I'm going for my leg.
Melissa [reaching out towards the tape recorder]: See if I touch this . . . you push it, don't you. No, I can't.
Lindie: You push it, don't you?
Melissa: No – look.
Lindie: See if I can touch this tape. No I can't.
Melissa: I know what you do. You go, you go like that, then you go . . . Shorter than your arm.
Lindie [reaching towards the pencil pot]: See can I touch this tin. No I can't.
Melissa: Yeah.
Lindie: Go like that.
Carla: Look, one of my hand's shorter than the other.
Melissa: Everybody's got one thing that's different, because if they didn't . . .
Lindie: Yeah, my clogs. One of them fits and one of them don't . . .
[The children continue to compare reach and grasp.]
Carla [about another child who has come over to their table for some

163

pencil crayons, in an American accent]: Who's nicking our pencils, Lissa?

[Pause whilst the children write.]

That tape recorder's taped everything we've said . . .

Lindie: I've got 'At School'.

Carla: I can't hear.

Lindie: Look, shall I carry on writing something?

Carla: Give something to Miss. Because, you see, got to have five pages of it. Each thing. Here you are. Look.

Lindie: Hang on. Who's episode two? Yours is episode one.

Melissa: Two.

Lindie: Melissa's can be episode one.

Carla: It can't. [Indicating bound volume hanging on wall] Episode one's on there, isn't it?

Lindie: Do you want me to do an episode one?

Melissa: No, we've got one.

Carla: Look, mine should be before Lissa's. Shouldn't it. Look, I'm picking it up . . . [Picks up her writing with exaggeratedly slow movement] It goes like this . . .

[Carla reads her portion of the text up to the words 'he started to laugh and said thank you' (TH transcripts: p. 48) She then reads Lindie's text out loud up to the words, 'No, Mummy' (TH transcript: p. 49). The children all laugh at these words.[6]]

Melissa [handing her writing over to Carla]: And that's the surprise.

[Carla now reads Melissa's text up to the words, 'because he didn't want to go. But Jamie said' (TH transcripts: p. 50). Melissa helps her read the text.]

Melissa [commenting on the abrupt ending to her text]: I ain't got to that bit yet.

Carla [mocking]: She ain't got to that bit yet.

[Pause whilst the children continue to write.]

Lindie: Shall I go and get some more paper?

Carla: After this I'm on my second piece, second and a half.

Lindie [returning with paper]: I don't think this lot should go as quick as the other lot.[7]

Lisa [approaching the table where the three children are writing]: Could I have my times table square back?[8]

Melissa [to Carla]: You didn't take it in the end, did you?

Carla: I did. I remember putting it on the top . . . And I remember you telling me to hold on to it till we got to the path.

Melissa: Don't suppose you dropped it on your way home? You went to learn your nine times table.

Carla: That was two weeks ago..

Melissa: Carla lent yours because she couldn't find hers.[9]

Carla [having looked in her tray]: Oh, there it is. I don't use it. You + + + me and Lissa, don't you?

[Pause. The children write.]

	[To herself] Page . . . one and a half . . .
	[A child from another class enters the room, which prompts the next conversation.]
Carla:	When I was going to the shop to get Sally's birthday card, that Suzanne Williams come and she started hitting me. So I goes . . . wait till you get up school, I'll soon get you.
Melissa:	What she do?
Carla:	She goes . . .
Lindie:	This morning she walked past with that other girl –
Carla:	Rosa Menco. Rosa. Something like Rosa Delmenico.
Melissa:	We call her from Mexico.
Lindie:	This girl – they knew she was behind us – behind them – and she goes, 'Oh, what's the matter? Oh, Alison, what's the matter with you?' and they started cuddling her.
Melissa:	And they knew she was crying.
Carla:	Once me and Rosa had a fight. You should have seen Rosa's face –
Lindie:	And then – what was her name? – the one that was going to beat you up?
Carla:	Suzanne.
Lindie:	Suzanne. She was going, 'Ah, what's the matter?'
Carla:	Who to?
Lindie:	To this, er, Alison, the one that was crying.
Melissa:	You know that girl that's got lovely shoes?
Lindie:	Yeah, lovely shoes. Well, she was crying. Suzanne came up, they was walking up like this, facing the alley and Alison was crying her eyes out. Suzanne goes, 'What's the matter?' They turned round and Suzanne says, 'You're crying. What's the matter, Alison?' She went all . . . she just stood there + + +

(The rest of the story is repeated but the noise level in the classroom makes the tape undecipherable. Having repeated the story of the fight, the children start to make fighting noises in order to make the volume indicator move.)

Carla:	I'm going to take this up to Miss now.
Lindie:	Three and a half pages I got to do. How many pages you done, Lissa?
Melissa:	'Hello, Jo.'
Lindie:	Who said that?
Melissa:	Me.

[One of the children now whispers something obviously naughty to the other.]

Lindie:	Oh! It's going to be taped!
Teacher	[approaching the children's table and sitting down]: Oh, now, episode two of 'The Tidy House'.
Lindie:	Don't think it is a tidy house any more. Not with all those presents around.
Teacher	[looking at children's text]: She seems quite glad to get him off to school.

The Tidy House

Carla: So was my mum. She still wants to get rid of Sarah and Jeannie, but . . . one of them are at school.

Teacher: Who's still at home?

Carla: Jeannie.

Teacher: How old's she?

Carla: Three.

Teacher: What will your mum do when she's off to school?

Carla: Go out, I suppose.

Teacher: What does she *want* to do when she's got them off?

Carla: Go out and get rid of us. That's what she says she's gonna do. And she's not going to come back and she's going to leave my dad, do all the work and he's got to go up and down to school. And she said and if she does come back she's going to come back on one condition, my dad's got to buy her a new car.

Teacher: Has she got a car at the moment?

[Carla shakes her head.]

    Can she drive?

Carla: She's got to go into driving tests. She gets them free. My mum gets her driving tests free.[10]

Lindie: Does she?

Carla: Not going to tell you where . . . She can get it for 10p. A day. 10p a day.

[A pause. Teacher distracted by demands of other children. Classroom administration.]

Teacher   [returning to seat]: So she's just going to drive around in her big car, when you've gone?

Carla: Yep. And she said she's going to go all over the town.

Lindie: Mmm.

Carla: And when my dad's at work Saturdays and Sundays, she can take us out, can't she?

Teacher   [reading text to self]: Is that 'Baby, stop it now'?

Carla: No, 'Boy'.

    Oh, 'Boy'. [Reads out text] Oh, '*boys* don't cry on their birthday' . . . It's always the ice-cream man who rescues him.

Carla: }   Yes.
Melissa: }

Teacher: He's always appearing.

[Pause whilst teacher silently reads the text, distracted occasionally by the demands of classroom administration.]

    Oh, I don't like the sound of Carl, actually. I really don't.

Melissa: He's babyish, isn't he.

Teacher: He really needs to get to school.

Melissa: He is at school.

Teacher: Oh yes, he is at school. But I thought in the first part that he really needed to get to school.

166

Lindie:	Yes, well, you see, he's getting a bit grown up now.
Carla:	Now he goes to school, he won't come home.
Melissa:	See, he goes to school and he doesn't want to come home. First day, he cried all the time and then Jamie went, his mum went, he stopped crying a bit and played with all the other children. When Jamie come to fetch him he wouldn't come, he . . .
Teacher:	How did he get on with his teacher?
Melissa:	All right.
Teacher:	What's she like?
Melissa:	Don't know, really.
Carla:	My mum would love us if we didn't want to come home. From school.
Teacher:	Do you think Carl wants to stay at school because he knows his mum doesn't really want him to come home?
Carla:	Don't know really. Lindie's doing the school bit.
Teacher:	You're doing the bit in school? Do you think he suspects his mum's glad to get rid of him?
Lindie:	Well, in the story she said she's quite glad to get rid of him.
Teacher:	Yes, I know, she says it there, doesn't she?
Carla:	She probably *is*.
Teacher:	Well, he sounds awful.
Lindie:	His dad pampered him.
All:	Yeah.
Lindie:	He's spoiled. By his nan and grandad . . .
Teacher:	I thought his nan did.
Carla:	Because they sent him ten pence and all that, and his aunt sent him an American pound.
Teacher:	Dollar?
Carla: ⎫ Melissa: ⎭	Yeah.

[Teacher is distracted. Classroom administration.]

Teacher:	I'll be back. I want to ask you if she's going to have any more. Carl is the last one? Carl is the last child? The youngest?
Carla:	She ain't got any more.
Teacher:	She's not going to have any?

[Teacher moves to another part of the room.]

Melissa:	Do you think she is going to have any more? She might, in this book, mightn't she?
Carla:	Well, in the fourth book that we make she might, mightn't she?[11]
Lindie:	Yeah.
Carla:	It's about time Jason and Jamie and Jo and Thingybob had babies. Supposing that we put in the book that they had twins?
Melissa:	Yeah.
Carla:	Two boys.
Lindie:	No, two girls.

167

Melissa:	A boy and a girl.
Lindie:	That would make no difference though, would it?
Carla:	We tell Miss now, we don't really know, right, we might. Well, in the third book that we do, we'll put Jo's going to have twins.
Lindie:	Something like that.
Melissa:	Yeah.
Carla:	I think she might have one, might she. [Pause. Then Carla calls out to the teacher] Miss, the other two might have one.
Lindie:	Jo and Mark might have one.
Teacher	[returning and sitting down]: Do you think . . . they seem very happy without one? Don't they? How long have they been married, Jo and Mark?
Carla:	Two years.
Melissa:	And they're like Jason. They pamper Carl as well.
Teacher:	Yes, I think . . .
Carla:	Yes, because she did give him 15p. And I'm not even allowed to have that much.
Lindie:	And she gave him some . . . She gave Carl a big present for his birthday.
Teacher:	She hasn't got any children of her own to spend it on.
Carla:	But if you never had no children you'd be well off, wouldn't you? You'd have plenty of money.
Teacher:	I've got plenty of money.
Carla:	I haven't.

[It is the end of morning school. The next thing that is heard after Carla's laconic remark about poverty is me telling the class to get ready for dinner: 'Everyone, stop talking and listen. Stop, Barry. Switch off. (This refers to the headphone set on which the child was listening to a taped story.) Just *stop*, Simon. Time for you to go downstairs to wash your hands for dinner. Now, if you're in the middle of a piece of work that you're going to finish this afternoon, put your folder in your tray. If you've finished, put your folder in *my* tray, and when you come back, tidy your table.' At the beginning of this, Lindie is heard: 'Carla, shall I ask Miss if we can come in at dinner-time?'

When the children return I read to them a couple of fables from a book that Georgina brought to school that morning. There is discussion of the characteristics of animals in the stories and talk of a recent visit to a farm. During the reading I remove one child from the room for interrupting. I tell the children that no one is to come into the room at dinner-time, though presumably the three writers did ask their question and I did say yes, for a good deal of writing goes on in the next hour. The children leave the room. Richard asks about the library reorganisation that is going on outside the room. I explain the Dewey system to him. The second teacher recognises a woman she knows working on the library books. We all go out to lunch.]

[Tape ends.]

[It is afternoon. The silent reading session is over. Carla, Melissa and Lindie are drawing. The rest of the class is organising afternoon activities. The class is temporarily smaller, as seven children have gone swimming. All interruptions this afternoon of our conversation with the three girls are to do with the activity of painting. The children sing and hum as they draw. They seem very aware of me, commenting on what I'm doing. It turns out that they are making goodbye cards for me.]

Carla   [commenting on own drawing]: Look, here's the sun.

[The children start to sing softly, 'You'll Never Get to Heaven'. This changes rapidly to a chant involving the name of a child in the class: 'Darren Deane, Darren Deane'.]

Lindie   [to teacher]: Can we keep the books?[12]

Teacher   [passing rapidly]: I don't know.

Lindie   [sings]: ' . . . 'cos Darren Deane is a washing machine . . . Darren Deane is a washing machine . . . ain't gonna leave my love no more, ain't gonna leave my love . . . '

Carla: Lindie. Just because the tape recorder's on, you don't have to show off.

Melissa: Have you read *The Secret Garden* out Mr Kent's library?[13]

Lindie: No. I used to have it at home but I didn't like it, so I tore it up.

Melissa: Boring, isn't it?

Lindie: The programme was quite good, it wasn't so – boring – but . . . the book – ooh.

Melissa: You doing that as a birthday card?

Lindie: No. [reads the card she is working on] 'Sad that you're going.' They'll think I mean that they're dying.

Carla   [showing the others her card]: That's their gran – her mum, she's having babies, that's her husband and that's her brother.[14]

[Pause, during which the topic of conversation somehow established is their infant school.]

Carla: Yes, Miss Down was the nicest teacher there.

Melissa: I liked Miss Thompson. She was the nicest teacher there.

Lindie: ⎫
Carla: ⎭   Oh, ooh!

Carla: Was you in the play?

Melissa: Yes, she made me be a dancing girl.

Lindie: What was you, Carla?

Melissa: No, she weren't in it. [Referring to last year of infants school] We were all in together until we had to be split up in the new block. Didn't we?

Carla: We might be split up in the third year.

Lindie: On Monday we're going to know what class we're going to be in.

Melissa:	My brother's finding out what class he's going to be in today. He's going into the new block, he don't even know how to read a book, he don't even know how to write 'the'.
Carla	[to teacher]: Miss, what class am I going in to?
Lindie:	Miss, when do we find out what class we're going into?
Teacher	[passing rapidly]: The last day of term. I really don't know.
Carla	[looking in her tray for something]: Ow. Got me finger stuck.

[Long pause. Preparations for painting by the rest of the class are quite audible.]

Carla	[about Melissa's picture of the tidy house bedroom]: Oh, it's lovely. Aah.

[Long pause. Carla finds a pencil or a felt-tip pen with the price label still on it.]

Here you are. 'I couldn't be bothered to take the price off.' [Sings] ' . . . suppose I never went to heaven' . . .

Lindie	[observing the teacher lifting an easel into place]: Don't strain yourself, Miss.

[The children make heaving noises.]

Melissa	[about her drawing of the tidy house bedroom]: I'm going to do a nice cuddly – I'm going to do a nice cuddly armchair.
Carla:	That's the bedroom?
Melissa:	Yes. And I'm going to do – the front room here.
Carla	[squinting and crossing her eyes]: If you go like this and you want to look down on your nose, it don't half hurt.
Lindie:	Yes it does, doesn't it?
Melissa:	Yes it does, doesn't it? Irritates your nose.
Lindie:	Your *eyes*.
Carla:	Irritates your eyes. They go lopsided, don't they?

[Some papers are dropped on the tape recorder.]

[Reads printing on tape recorder] ' ''Automatic'' – that's my baby.'[15]

[Someone rattles the coloured pencil tray.]

[Sings] 'Shaka-maker, shaka-maker' . . . [16]

Melissa:	What shall I do in the front room . . . make it a –
Lindie:	Chairs, settee.
Melissa:	Make it of a heart, a heart . . . I could do it like that, then a little heart family in the space. Or I could do a lttle picture of a heart family here. I don't know what to do in here. Oh yeah. Heart light. [To Carla] Can you draw me one of your heart lights, please?
Carla:	What colour?
Melissa:	Red. [Watching] Those heart lights you do are good. I like them. They're lovely.
Carla:	Look. That all right?
Melissa:	I'm going to do a picture of them getting married.
Carla:	Oh yeah.
	[One of them softly hums the Wedding March] Look, I've done it orange and red.

Appendix 1

Melissa:	Oh, look . . .
Carla:	What?
Melissa	[commenting on Carla's goodbye card which shows a formal arrangement of wedding photographs on a wall]: Oh, ain't that cute?
Lindie:	Who's that one?
Carla:	The one that got married.
Lindie:	He hasn't got his moustache there, has he? Oh yes he has. Who's that?
Carla:	Her sister and they asked someone to paint it and they left the price on it.[17]
Lindie:	It's lovely.

[Pause. A sharp noise is made which causes the tape-recorder needle to flicker.]

	Oh, Carla. You know you just went like that and it went right to the red thing and back again. Look, it went up again.
Teacher	[stopping by the children's table]: I think you'd better stop now, don't you? Put those away. You can do them last thing when we're having a story. Then you can finish. You need to help Lindie, don't you? You've finished? You've all finished? Well, get them out, let's have a look at them. Because I'll have to take them home and type them tonight. [Addressing whole class] There are only fifteen people in the room and you're making enough noise for twenty-five. Whisper to each other, don't shout.
	Right, give me the first bit . . .
Carla:	My bit.
Melissa:	Episode two.
Carla:	I know . . . here it is, Miss.
Teacher:	Now I got to the bit where he got all those things for his birthday . . . [Reads text] Is that 'gladly'? [TH transcript: p. 49]
Carla:	Yeah.
Teacher:	Oh no: 'if you're glad'. Well, you don't need that 'e' on the end. You make it . . . 'glade' . . .
Carla:	Um, now . . .
Teacher	[reaching for Lindie's portion]: Right. 'At School'. This is the bit I haven't read. [Pause. Reads text] Did he have anything to play with at home, Lindie?
Lindie:	Ye . . . es . . . [Consideringly] He should have.
Teacher:	But he thought the cars at school were better?
Lindie:	He had a lot of cars at home.
Teacher:	No sand?
Lindie:	He didn't have no sand at home.
Carla:	But, er, he did.
Lindie:	Did he?

The Tidy House

Teacher:	What?
Carla:	No, I'm just . . .
Lindie:	He wanted a sandpit, but his mum and dad wouldn't let him have one.
Teacher:	Why not?
Lindie:	They decided it would take up too much room.
Teacher:	Where did they live, in a flat? No, they lived in a house. Was it the bungalow they lived in?
Lindie:	They lived in . . . Oh no, that was Jo and Mark.
Teacher:	Oh yes. I lose track.
Carla:	No. They lived in flat.[18]
Teacher:	They live in a flat . . . well there won't be much room, will there? [Reads]
Melissa:	Do we need all this spare paper?

[Teacher talks to another child and to the other teacher for a few minutes.]

Carla	[looking through the loose sheets of paper on the table]: There's a bit missing, Lissa.
Melissa:	Oh, hang on, hang on. There's none here.
Carla:	Have a look through my lot.
Teacher	[reading text out loud]: 'Hel*lo*, Jo.' [Laughs] Carl's getting on her nerves already? Why? What's he done? Lindie?
Lindie:	Um . . .
Teacher:	She's just collected him from school? [Reading] . . . ' really fed up with him' . . .
Melissa:	He probably kept pulling all the things down at home.
Teacher:	But they haven't been home. Have they?
Lindie:	Yeah. If he collected them . . .
Teacher:	Oh, I see.
Lindie:	She collected him.
Teacher:	I'm not reading it very carefully. What's that word? 'he's so . . . '?
All:	'Spoiled'.
Teacher:	'Sp', 'sp'.
Lindie:	Yeah, I know.
Teacher:	'Oil' with 'sp' at the beginning. Well, I'm going to have to type it all out.

[Pause whilst teacher completes reading of Lindie's section.]

	Right. That's the bit at school. Where's Melissa's piece?
Melissa:	That one's it, Miss. That one's meant to be 'special'. But I couldn't work it out you see.
Teacher:	Ah . . . you couldn't . . . [Reads out loud] 'It was special today, it was Carl's birthday. He was four.'
Carla:	'It *was* a special day,' she's supposed to put.
Teacher:	Well, when you're writing fast you lose – you leave things like that out. [Reads aloud] 'He was four. He opened his cards. He got

172

a card from Jamie and Jason and one from Jo and Mark and he got one from his nan and grandad. He got 10p with that.' What, the one from his nan and grandad?

All: Yeah.

Teacher: But they give him 10p on just an ordinary day, don't they?

Melissa: Well, ye . . . ah . . .

Teacher: Oh, he got one from the USA. What's his aunt's . . . ?

Melissa: Dot.[19]

Teacher: 'An American pound.'

Melissa: American dollar it's meant to be.

Teacher: Shall I put in 'dollar' when I type it? Just one dollar?

Carla: That's only about 35p.

Melissa: He deserves it.

Teacher   [reads aloud]: ' . . . a little car. He thought it was – neat? – a neat little car.' That's a very American thing to say. They always say things are neat, real neat. 'He was playing with it till it was school time. He got so – used? – used . . . '

Carla   [commenting on Melissa's text, which she is looking at]: 'Us', it says.

[Tape ends.]

TAPE 2/SIDE 2
WEDNESDAY P.M.

Teacher   [reading aloud]: ' . . . crying, and got ready – ' [To other child] Yes, Nicola? The paper's under the table. David, I can hear your voice all the way over here. Don't use that big brush, Sharon. It's for spreading glue. You can't paint a decent picture with that.

Carla: . . . my mum says if you cry on my birthday you'll get bad luck –

Melissa: Don't believe . . .

Carla: I took my mum home, so she hit me and I goes . . . [Sniffs]

Teacher   [reads aloud]: 'Don't cry on your birthday. You get bad luck, don't you. Yes, mummy. So he stopped crying and got ready and they went. Carl had a good time at school and when it was time to come home he didn't want to go home.'

Melissa: He never wants to go home.

Teacher: 'So Jamie had to carry him out.'

Lindie: Big lump.

Teacher: ' . . . until he got to the gates' – you put 'and til' – 'then he got to the gates and walked home, when he got home he played with his car and till' – look, you've done it again. 'Until' is one word. Look [Writes word and shows it to child] – 'until it was dinner-time. After dinner they went up Jo and Mark's house and had a cup of tea there and a sandwich and a bit of cake and they sang

173

	happy birthday to him and he got all shy and covered his eyes up and hid behind the chair and when it was over, Jo put a candle in Carl's bit of cake and he blew the candle out and they had a good time up Jo's house. When they had to go, Jo gave him a present. It was a big car. It was as big as . . . as a toy dog'? 'Carl was over-joyed. He fell in love with it . . . '
Melissa:	Miss, it were meant to be a small one.
Carla:	It weren't a car anyway.
Second Teacher	[who has joined the group]: Difficult when you're all writing together to agree together. I think you're doing very well – it all fits together very well.
Melissa:	Change it in a minute, Miss.
Teacher:	What do you want it to be?
Melissa:	It was a little car . . .
Lindie:	Little car like . . .
Melissa:	Was a car, but it was only one of those matchbox cars.
Teacher:	What are you going to say? 'It was as small as a . . . '? Instead of 'as big as a toy dog'?
Melissa:	Matchbox.
Carla:	Yeah. Matchbox.
Teacher:	That's what you want? 'Carl was overjoyed. He fell in love with it. Jamie had trouble in getting him to school because he would not go. So she had to let him take it with him.'
Lindie:	Huh!
Teacher:	That's it, is it?
All:	Yes.
Teacher:	What's going to happen to all these people?
Melissa:	We're going to have another book. We're going to have four books.
Teacher:	Four books?
Lindie:	We're gonna try four books. So, at playtime, can just we three stay in and do the next one?
Teacher:	Yes, I think so.
Lindie:	Thank you.
	[Teacher now turns her attention to getting the class to clear up for playtime.]
Melissa	[trying to gain attention]: Miss!
Lindie:	Miss! [Indicating goodbye card] That's for you, Miss.
Teacher	[talking to other child]: What did you say, Richard?
Carla	[in accented voice]: Don't go all sentimental.
Lindie	[for benefit of second teacher]: Leaving at the end of the week, in't you, Miss?
Teacher:	End of next week. [Reads card] 'Sad that you going.'
Lindie:	'*You're* going'!
Teacher:	'Please don't go. Have a good time you and your husband' . . .

Carla:	Guess what she put on my mum's birthday card.
Teacher:	What?
Carla:	'You're twenty-five today.'
Teacher:	How old was she?
Carla:	Twenty-five. She put it in great big kisses.
Teacher:	And your mum didn't want anyone to know.
	[Pause] Have you got any idea what's going to happen to all these people in the end?
Lindie:	Oh yes, Miss. We was thinking that Jo and . . .
Carla:	They move.
Melissa:	Jo and Mark have twins.
Teacher:	And their tidy house won't be a tidy house any more.
Lindie:	No, it'll be a dirty house.
Melissa:	And we thought, um, that, er, Jamie would have a boy and Carl and the boy, the little boy, always used to have fights. And then, and then . . .
Teacher:	Why do all these people have these babies?
Melissa:	And then Carl won't be pampered, will he?
Carla:	They can't help it, can they?
Teacher:	Can't they?
Carla:	No.
Teacher:	But they've gone two years without having a baby. Why haven't they had one so far?
Lindie:	Because if . . . you read mine . . .
Carla:	She never forgot to take her pill.
Teacher:	So she can help it? Carla? Can't she? She's going to decide to have a baby? Is she deciding . . . if she knows how mad Carl drives her. What it's like.
Carla:	Who? Jamie?
Teacher:	No, not Jamie. Jo. Why is Jo going to have . . .
Lindie:	Yeah, well, did you read my end bit? Jamie had a little row with her, and she told her that they, that her and . . .
Teacher:	Oh. 'I don't like children being spoiled.' So she criticised the way Jamie brought up Carl.[20]
Lindie:	No! Jamie criticised the way Jo spoiled Carl.
Teacher:	And that made Jo think that she ought to have one to show that she could do it?
Carla:	And she has twins.
Teacher:	She has twins. [Laughing] Gets her just deserts for thinking such a silly thing.

[Pause. Teacher turns again to the task of clearing up painting equipment and directing the children to other activities.]

Carla:	Lindie! [Shows Lindie the card she has made.]
Lindie	[reads]: 'Please don't go. We really like you. Happy times from Carla and Melissa.'

[Teacher returns to the children's table.]

Melissa:	We got another book to do, and in the fifth book . . . the fourth book's going to be the longest out of the lot.
Teacher:	And what's the book going to be about? Having babies?
Lindie:	Yeah. The baby year.
Teacher:	The baby year, did you say? You know, I think they could . . . Do you think that Jo and Mark are unhappy? Together? They don't seem unhappy?
Carla:	When Mark woke up they didn't –
Teacher:	They had a quarrel, didn't they, but they made it up. Did Mark want a baby or is it all Jo's idea?
Carla:	Really, it's all Jo's.
Lindie:	Yeah.
Carla:	She's up in competition.
Teacher:	Does Jo go to work?
Carla:	No.
Teacher:	So she's just at home all day by herself?
Second Teacher:	Probably all she's got to think of, isn't it?
Teacher:	What did she do before she got married?
Carla:	Dunno.
Lindie:	She's a typist.
Teacher:	Boring?
Lindie:	My aunt used to be a typist.
Carla:	Then she met Mark. And they decided to get married. And she wanted a baby from the beginning.
Lindie:	But he wouldn't let her.
Carla:	And then he sort of liked the idea.
Second Teacher:	Why didn't he want one?
Carla:	Probably hates kids.
Lindie:	I think all mums do, don't they?
Second Teacher:	No, I don't hate kids.
Lindie:	My mum's got six.
Second Teacher:	I've only got two.
Melissa:	My nan's got ten. My other nan's got eleven.
Second Teacher	[to Carla]: Your mum's got four?
Carla:	Yes.
Melissa:	Got a lot of uncles and aunties, haven't you?
Second Teacher:	Are you the oldest, Carla? The oldest?
Carla:	Yes. My birthday's on the 23rd.

Second Teacher:	Oh, mine's on the 22nd.
Lindie:	My mum's on the 22nd.
Carla:	Hers is on the 24th.
Second Teacher:	All July birthdays.
Lindie:	Mine is on Boxing Day.
Carla:	No one comes to your parties, do they?
Second Teacher:	That's very difficult. I suppose nobody gives you . . .
Lindie:	No. I'm having my party early this year.
Carla:	She does have presents. Her mum and dad spoils her when it's her birthday.
Lindie:	Yeah, I know. I get, I get . . .
Carla:	She gets gold chain necklaces.
Lindie:	Last Easter that is – last Easter me and my brother got – not Easter gone, Easter before – me and my brother got two whole bags of Easter eggs.
Melissa:	I got three last Easter. One from my nan, one from my Aunty Marie, one from my mum.
Lindie:	We got five Easter eggs this year, that's all we got.
Carla:	We got eight, plus one I won. I won a contest. Down the Parade.
Teacher:	When – ?
Carla:	That Easter contest.
Teacher:	Easter bonnet? How'd you make yours?
Carla:	My dad bought a chicken – I had this great big chicken on top, all these feathers, and I came first.
Teacher:	What was the prize?
Carla:	An Easter egg. I got the biggest Easter egg out of the ladies and the men and the other girls. Didn't I?
Lindie:	Yeah.
Melissa:	And you got 10p.
Carla:	No, I got that out of the other contest.
Teacher:	In the same hat? You could have cleaned up the district, couldn't you, in that hat? You could have gone to every Easter bonnet competition there was.
[Pause, whilst teacher deals with other children and looks through the story.]	
	Now, what order is this in?
Lindie:	Carla's first, mine second, and Lissa's last.
Teacher:	OK. You want it in a book [Indicates first volume on wall] – like that?
Melissa	[to second teacher about her drawing]: No, just doing . . . a nest . . .
Second Teacher:	Very pretty, it is, isn't it? Very pretty.

Carla	[commenting on Melissa's drawing of the bedroom of the tidy house]: Miss, never seen heart flowers.
Teacher:	Have you finished? Is that a patchwork quilt?
Melissa:	Yes.
Second Teacher:	Beautiful.
Carla:	My nan done one of them. It took her a year.
Second Teacher:	Did she?
Teacher:	Mine took me four years. I didn't do it very often. I used hexagons, not squares.
Second Teacher:	I crocheted a shawl with hexagons and it was supposed to be for my little boy when he was a baby, but it took me two years to make it and when I gave it to him to put in his cot he started shredding it . . .
Lindie:	To knit a cardigan it only takes my mum about two weeks. She isn't half fast[21] – my dad goes 'Can you stop clicking those blooming needles?'
Teacher	[pointing to Melissa's picture]: That's the rug, is it?
Melissa:	No, that's a nest of babies.
Teacher:	Oh. A nest of babies! Of course, in every bedroom, a nest of babies!
Lindie:	Yes, of course there is. [Quotes] 'What is the mother without them.'[22]
All:	Mmm.
Teacher:	But your mum hasn't got a nest. She's only got –
Melissa:	No, not a nest, but she's got a big bed, and she's got all these cuddly toys around it. She's got a teddy that big.
Second Teacher:	How many children has she got?
Carla:	Two.
Melissa:	Two.
Teacher:	How many has yours got, Carla?
Carla:	Four.
Melissa	[about Lindie]: Her mum's got six.
Teacher:	They're grown up, four of yours, aren't they?
Lindie:	Yeah.
Teacher:	Lindie's the youngest.
Lindie:	Yeah, don't remind me.
Teacher:	Yes, I know.
Lindie:	But four of them aren't my real brothers and sisters.
Teacher:	What do you mean, they're not your real brothers and sisters?
Melissa:	Because her dad died.
Teacher:	Who died?

Lindie:	My mum's first husband, he died.
Teacher:	Then she married again?
Lindie:	And my mum married again. My dad got married and he had two children and my dad's first wife got a divorce.
Teacher:	Do you ever see them?
Lindie:	What?
Teacher:	The children of your –
Lindie:	Yes, of course I do.
Carla:	She runs up their house.
Teacher:	Oh, I see. [Referring to an incident of the previous week] Is that where you got the wild oats from?
Lindie	[nods]: I've only got one real brother.
Teacher:	That's John? In Mrs Martin's class? [In response to a face pulled by Lindie] Mrs Martin thinks he's nice.
Lindie:	I don't.
Teacher:	Well, you see more of him than she does really. No, I suppose she sees more of him.
Lindie:	Yeah, she can have him if she wants him. [To second teacher] He's a fourth year.
Second Teacher:	Two years older than you?
Lindie:	My dad . . . We have fights. My mum and dad break it up. My brother gets sent up the stairs.
Second Teacher:	Not very fair.
Teacher:	What happens to you, madam?
Lindie:	My daddee! . . .
Melissa:	It's me upstairs.
Carla:	Yeah, my dad always goes out, never see him.
Melissa:	My mum –
Carla:	Comes in at eleven, goes out again.
Teacher:	Where does he go?
Carla:	Down the Labour Club. He's got pigeons. He's lost . . . he had seventy-one . . .
Lindie:	My mum and dad don't go out a lot. My dad because my dad don't –
Carla:	He lost them. One flew out the basket. Ted his partner forgot to put the brick on it and it was found out in the shed and he opened the door and it flew away. He had seventy. He put them in a race and now he won't send any more for racing. And he's not a nobbler.[23]
Lindie:	Do your mum and dad go out a lot?
Carla:	Nope.
Lindie:	Do you and your husband go out a lot?

The Tidy House

Second Teacher:	About twice a week.
Lindie:	My mum and dad don't go out a lot.
Melissa:	My mum goes out every Saturday.
Lindie:	Because my dad's – because my dad was in the war, and he got shot in the leg, and while he was lying there, he got shot in the foot and he can't . . . can't walk properly. He has to limp.
Carla:	My grandad died. One died last year, one died when I was five. Never saw much of him.
Melissa:	Jeannie didn't know him, did she?
Carla:	Every time you mention it to my dad he goes . . . . My mum . . . her dad died last year.
Second Teacher:	She's still very upset about it?
Carla:	She had to go all in blue, she never had no black shoes. Don't wear black anyway, do you?
Second Teacher:	No, I went to a funeral the other day and there was nobody in black.
Melissa:	What kind did you wear?
Second Teacher:	I wore a dark blue.
Carla:	Dark blue's next to black, because my mum bought a dark blue skirt and a dark blue top and it came to twenty quid. And my dad went mad – just over a funeral.
Second Teacher:	She could always wear the coat again.
Lindie:	She could've borrowed Miss's socks and Miss's jumper and just bought the skirt.[24]
Second Teacher:	She couldn't very well on her own father's funeral.
Carla:	My mum wants to buy four pairs of shoes.
Second Teacher:	Very nice sandals you've got.
Carla:	Every time, my dad wants me to wear flat sandals.
Lindie:	Eugh!
Carla:	Eugh!
Melissa:	Oh, I can't wear flat things.[25]
Carla:	I got a pair.
Lindie:	You know I got a pair of flip-flops? I had my mum's on –
Second Teacher:	Are you supposed to be doing anything?
Lindie: Melissa: }	Naah. Just talking.

180

Appendix 1

Second Teacher	[about Melissa's drawing]: I think that's quite lovely, what you've drawn.
Melissa:	I don't.
Carla:	I'm wearing my blue and white T-shirt, alright, and I was looking for my velvet top and I couldn't find it, right, and it was underneath this one. I saw this one, but I went past it and my mum went up there and *she* went past it, so I had to wear this one.
Melissa	[discussing her drawing]: She done that heart, which I thought was the best part of it.
Lindie:	What's that?
Carla:	The light.

[Pause. Background clatter from classroom. Melissa takes off her sock to look at a cut on her toe.]

Lindie:	Ask Miss . . . because it's got all dry blood on it.

[Carla has been to fetch the first-aid box.]

Carla:	There you are. Wet a bit of cotton wool and put that on. I'm a nurse to my sisters, you see.
Melissa:	Wonder what I done to my toe. [Pause] You know that time I tripped up the stairs. That's what I done to it.
Carla	[to second teacher]: It's the first-aid box.
Melissa:	What's that? Dettol.
Second Teacher	[to Lindie, who is bathing Melissa's toe]: You'd make a good nurse.
Lindie:	Don't want to be a nurse. Want to be a doctor.
Carla:	Don't want to. Takes a long time.
Lindie:	Well, as long as I could sleep at home, I wouldn't mind that. I can't even sleep at my sisters without crying.
Second Teacher:	Is your mum – sorry? Oh, you get used to it.
Lindie:	I started to get used to it, actually. I've just started to get used to it, but –
Second Teacher:	Have you ever been away with the school? I bet you will one day.
Lindie:	I bet I won't. Because I think something'll happen to my mum whilst I'm away and why they's letting me go. Gives me a horrible feeling.
Melissa:	She's a good nurse, isn't she, Miss.
Second Teacher:	Yes. Whose first-aid book – Mrs Steedman's? – a useful thing to have around. Does every class have a first-aid kit like that?
Lindie:	Don't know.
Carla:	Other teachers might. Nothing we know of.

181

Second Teacher:	You don't have to go bothering people I suppose.
Lindie:	You don't have to go down to the office.
Melissa:	What are you going to do when you grow up, Carla?
Carla:	Dunno.
Second Teacher [to Melissa]:	What are you going to be?
Carla:	Remember what you wanted to be?
Melissa:	One of those + + +

[The class is sent out to play. Lindie, Carla and Melissa remain.]

Lisa [on her way past the children's table]:	You going out to play? See you after play.[26]
Second Teacher:	What time does playtime go on for?
Melissa:	It starts at twenty-five past two till twenty to three.
Second Teacher:	What time does school finish?
Melissa:	Half past three.
Second Teacher:	What time do you start in the morning?
Melissa:	Nine o'clock. On Friday we have assembly. Like they do in churches, don't they?

[Tape ends]

[The children continued to write that afternoon, and on Thursday, when they were joined by Lisa who had been watching them and making approaches to them throughout Wednesday. The ribald bedroom scene constructed by Lindie and Carla (TH transcripts: pp. 52–53) was completed that afternoon, but not shown to me until the next day. Neither this nor the following pages were typed out. By Friday morning the children were bored with the story. It was never concluded. It simply petered out and was abandoned.]

APPENDIX 2

A FACSIMILE OF *THE TIDY HOUSE*

The tidy houses

One day a girl and a boy
said is it Sping-time. Yes
I think so, ~~why~~. ~~be~~
we've got vister. Who!
Jamie and Jason, here thay
come. Hollow! our toby.
I havont seen you for a long

time. Pock adots out side,
and the sun flowers are bigger
than us, mark lets go and
see. ok. Look Rockadots
had babys, can Jamie and
~~Jamson~~ have one Jo. yes
mark if thay whant.
Jason lets have Jinger
Jamies made a name up
for himill Pedy,

It was a louly tea
thank-you, come again
please. give my love.
to mum and dad, We
will. buge see you

soon. What time is
its 11 o)clock at night oh no
lets get to bed ok
right sweet hart.

see you in the monning.

turn the light of mark

iam going to sory alRight

I whant to get aslepe dont

wary. you will get a sleep

in time. dont lets os

rele this time of the

night. Shalle I whaat till

the monning. oh stop it.

monning. dont speek.

no you no why dont you.

look its all over.

thank-you mark. mark

kissed Jo, Jo kissed

mark.

end of Part

(1)

Part two of the tidy house

In the Back garden there is
Lots of Sunflowers. They bigger
than Jo and mark they also
hade rose bush they got a dog
called Toby he is btach with
a white chunst and they got
a rabbit name Poheadot it is
white and blackh. Now
out side there hause it is
brown on the walls and
has Blue cartens on the
right side and brown cord
on the Left and on the

189

the top right hand is Flag
Colvan cuntens and on the top
Left hand Cornen is brown
Cord. The ~~Shlanb~~ Jo and mark
live in is called fletching
and they Number is 60 ~~8b~~
has no Fremnd so her Ffeinds
from ~~Boltgl~~ come up.
Down ~~hleo~~ Stwee is a
big boy called Firdd be
made Fun of Jo he called
her big head but Jo gob her
onw back She called out
big billy big nut and big bum

when she got in she used
to tell mark and mark had

a good go at him he
did not want to see his
wife unhappy . one day mark

said " I" go shopping for
you " ah think-you I
so please any-way I got
a icea . a bad headace "
" I tell you what said do
I go up sasen and asy
her if she got some
tablits for headace all-right
I" go shopping now by

So mark went shopping and do
went up sansen for a talbit
Now sasen live is a

Diffence house she lived

in a bongdong and Jo

lived in a house and

they had they bedroom

up stairs not Down stairs

like sasen bedroom Whice

had a Bedroom Down stairs

Jo got the talbel and

mark got the shopping

and they had tea and
went to bed they all of
a sudden they was a howh
on the door do ausyed
it mark its ~~thai~~ Jamie
and ~~dosto~~ Joson all right ,
come Down Jo Lets all
hove cup of tea alright
Dg you went a cahe
yes Please thanhyou by ,,,
gob to go

the end of Part 2

Part 3 of
the tidy house

Jamie came over to Jos
house. Hollow. Happy

anquesty. oh you silly thing

hang on the door bell is

ringing. aboy said is

my mummy here yes.

Jamie here is (ar).

go home i want bea a

Minnister, no I want to

Stay here, alright.

Stand still and Shuzup,

Jamie smacked Carl

Carl stared to cry,

then mark and Jason

came home. Jason said

wate thes than Carl

ran up and Jason pited him

oP. and Stoped him from crying. he caue Carl 10P to get a ice-cream Whean the ice-cream man came Toonghd. thank-yoo daddy. Carl was ~~theey~~ 3 and a ½ years obl- Jo said lets have some tea, Carl sad can c haue a cup of tea. Please. Please anontty Jo no. so (ar) started to cry.

Shut up. Jason took Carl over his nans, he said mum

will look forder Carl why me and Jamie gose over to Mark a Jos house please.

Yes dear go and injoy youer she,

thanks mum. See you latter Jason, oh and Jason

he Right a letter to Jane Please mum.

this is what she said in
the letter.

Dear Jane   are you still
loving arman that you
Homw,   is there sull no
charch.   dor dor dor dor
do you love Jason and
do and   mum and dad
do you come back to me
from mume   dad   a kids
                    X nocharch

he stared to cry. Stop
it now Boy. dont cry an
there birthday do thay. that
minite the ice-cream man
game loonghd. Jo gave Carl
15p to get an ice-cream.
Jamie said dont speend to
much. gue me the 10p.
thats agood boy. So he did
he got a 5p ice-cream.

While Carl was getting his
ice-cream Jamie said to Jo
tonight me and Jason are
tacking Carl out mark
and you can come to
thank-you, leu got a
Present up stairs for
Carl. Carle game in with
no ice-cream and he was
crying. whats the

Appendix 2

mater carle he droped his
ice-cream. never mind!
Carl anutys got you.

a preson look he stared
to lathe and said

thank-you tomorrow he
gose to school thank god
for that Carls preson
was thre pound a shird
and

201

M.   had a good time at school
and when it was time
to come home he didnt
want to go home he started
to cry so Jamie had to
carry him out and tell he
got to the gates then he
got Down and walked
home and when ~~she~~ got
home he Played with his
car . ~~and till~~ t was Dinner
ime afet Dinner they went
up Jos and Marks house
and . had a sip of tea

up   there   and   a   sandwich and
a   bit   off   cake   and   they

Song   happy   birthday   to   him   he

got   all   shy   and   coved   his

eyes   up   and   hide   behade.

the   chair   and   when   it   M.

was   over   do   put   a   candle

in   Carls   bit   of   cake   and

he   blew   the   candle   out

they   had   a   good   time   if

Jo s   house   then   whod   they   had to

go   Jo   gave   him   a   present.

it was a big car it was
as Big as a toy dog

Carl was overJoyed he
fell in love with t he
was Playing every day
with it Jamie had trouble
gettinga him ta School
because he would not go
So she had to let
him take it with him.
as p

Patt 3 of the tidy
house

at night Jameiy and
Jason went to bed
Jameiy said do it Darling it
in the morning

Jameiy took Carl
to school and
went to see the
dockter when it
was her turn
the docker had
a look at her

Stomek and he
Said come back
tomorow
and I will tell
you tomorow
whats goin to happ
That night in bed
Jameiy said. I dont
no if I m Pregne
I have to see
rhe Dogter again
tomorow good-nigh
thay both went to

sleep in the
morning Jameiy
took Carl to school,
and went back
to the ~~table~~
docter and he
said your Prenent

Epesod 3 of the tidy
hause!

at the night Jo emark
waned ababbie mark agread
abthis. thay sat up all
night kisedg Jo all
night Jo said i have
you. mark said i love you
to thay went asleep
happie.

in the monnig Jo went
to the docters he said
I think if you trid harder
you will have twins. What
do the _____ harder, yes
dear, thank-you docter,
bye. See you soon
iv come up to morrow.

The tidy house that
is know more
a tidy house

Jamewy was soon
Pregnet and soon

she was in the
hospitle she soon had
a baby anuther boy
it was whbe what can
we call it Jason
I dont nowo dear
what about Daron
all right The baby
was called darah

and he was lovley
when he was 4
he and carl were
always fighting but
Daron never got the
blam and Card aways
got ~~sant~~ ~~to bed~~
Card hated him and
mot-led becouse ~~I~~
he was not spoilld
eneymore, and netter
was daran ~~to~~
daran was luckey

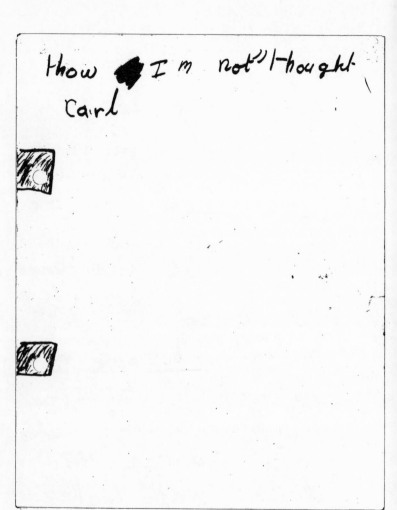

The tidy house
            that is no more
      as tidy house,

When Carl was nine
he was in the middle
School, He only had two
Firends. and one day his
two Firends ~~broak~~ Firends
With him, he did not
have no Firends to play
with. Dow the boys Who
Was his Firends got boys
and started to Fight
ham. When Caril went
home he told Jamie but

Jamiem said "Just stick
up for your self"
"but I" "but what" "I cant
because they are bigger
than me" "you can get
Jason on the ground?
"yes I know but your
get the blam when it
is not yours" oh shutt up"

epesod ④

Jamie wanted a baby she wanted a girl becaus she had frought up a name the name was Julye Jamie ADor that name she thought i⅀ was lovly and ~~Jason~~ do thougth that it was a good iDear to have a girl and call it Julie. and mark gqreead so when Jamie had her

Carl brother was 4 and Carl
Dio not get so much money
as beford whike got Carl into
tempers and went in his
Bedroom and cry so he was
quicte nanteay one day
When Jamie was Down the twa
Jamie brouth Darren a little botile
of Leoman and only got Carl a
cake and that made Carl get in
to a temper and he scarted

Shouted ~~m~~ ~~a~~ and Jamie gave him
a hard smake whice made Carl
cry all the way home when
(
they got home they gave Darren a
bit of breadd and Carl they
~~they~~ went up Jos and mark
(
they saw Sam and scot they
were 1 2 but Darren hetp on
Pushing they twins over and

made them cry so Jamie
had to set him on her lap
and tell it was time for the

twins to go to bed they
she would put him Down
So it went on like that
Soon they went home and

had tea and went to bed

and

NOTES

INTRODUCTION

1. Nearly all of the children's draft appears in facsimile in Appendix 2. The typed classroom edition of 1976 forms the basis of the complete transcript of the story which will be found between pages 42 and 55 of this book. Illustrations that accompanied the story were kept as well, as were other drawings by the children that they produced at the same time and which have some bearing on their narrative.

2. It had been arranged several weeks before that a friend, a lecturer at a local training college, who wanted to collect material for a course she was preparing on child language, would bring her tape recorder in on that particular day.

3. Taping in a class of more than twenty eight- and nine-year-olds meant that some dialogue was lost, but on the occasions when the adults in the room talked to the three girls, and where they talked to each other about their work, there is a remarkable clarity. However, for most of the day in question, Carla, Lindie and Melissa were left pretty much alone and the recordings include a great deal of talk between them. Later these tapes were transcribed and a full account of them can be found in Appendix 1.

4. Margaret Drabble, *Jerusalem the Golden*, Penguin, Harmondsworth, 1969, p. 36: 'she always wore a purple and blue flowered pinny, a garment more in keeping with an aunt or a cleaner than a lover of science. She handled her apparatus with the efficient familiarity with which other women handle their baking boards and rolling pins.'

5. Angie McRobbie, Editorial, *Screen Education*, 38 (Spring 1981), pp. 1–3. For a classic rendering of the unchallengable view of 'real life' by a teacher, see Janetta Bowie, *Penny Buff*, Arrow, London, 1978.

6. Jonathan Kozol, *Death at an Early Age*, Houghton Mifflin, Boston, 1967. James Herndon, *The Way It Spozed To Be*, Simon and Schuster, New York, 1968. John Holt, *How Children Fail*, Penguin, Harmondsworth, 1967; *The Underachieving School*, Penguin, Harmondsworth, 1971. Jules Henry, *Essays on Education*, Penguin, Harmondsworth, 1971.

7. 'Black children are a section of the working class in Britain, and whatever is true of the working class generally, it is also true of West Indian children'; 'The use of social psychological theories to "explain" lower class and/or black low achievement in schools I regard as an unwillingness to relate social psychological theories

219

to the wider historical, sociological and economic factors operating in society, both in terms of working class children generally and of black children in particular.' Maureen Stone, *The Education of the Black Child in Britain: The Myth of Multiracial Education*, Fontana, 1981, pp. 60–61; p. 35. See also p. 69.

8. Boris Ford, 'The Emancipation of Teacher Training', *Universities Quarterly*, 29 (Winter 1974), p. 7. Asher Tropp, *The Schoolteachers*, Heinemann, London, 1957. Frances Widdowson, *Going Up Into the Next Class: Women and Elementary Teacher Training, 1840–1914*, Women's Research and Resources Publications, London, 1980. Robert Roberts, *The Classic Slum*, Manchester University Press, 1971, pp. 104–5.

9. Ann Lee, 'Together We Learn to Read and Write: Sexism and Literacy', in (eds.) Dale Spender and Elizabeth Sarah, *Learning to Lose: Sexism and Education*, The Women's Press, London, 1980, pp. 121–7.

10. Valerie Walkerdine, 'Sex, Power and Pedagogy', *Screen Education*, 38 (Spring 1981), pp. 22–3.

11. Andrea Dworkin, *Woman Hating*, E.P. Dutton, New York, 1974, p. 23.

12. Edward Zigler and Jeanette Valentine, *Project Headstart*, The Free Press, New York, 1979, pp. 405–66.

13. Brian Evans and Bernard Waites, *IQ and Mental Testing*, Macmillan, London, 1981. See also George A. Miller, *Psychology: The Science of Mental Life*, Harper and Row, New York, 1962, pp. 129–46. Leon J. Kamin, *The Science and Politics of IQ*, Penguin, Harmondsworth, 1977. L.S. Hearnshaw, *Cyril Burt: Psychologist*, Random House, New York, 1981, especially chapters 3 and 4. Brian Simon, *Intelligence, Psychology and Education*, Lawrence and Wishart, London, 1971. James Kerr, *The Fundamentals of School Health*, George Allen and Unwin, London, 1926, p. 332. Margaret McMillan, *The Child and the State*, National Labour Press, Manchester, 1911, pp. 17–47.

14. William Labov, 'Finding Out About Children's Language', paper based on a talk given to the Hawaiian Council of the Teachers of English, July 1970.

15. Hearnshaw, *Cyril Burt*, p. 28.

16. E.G. Boring (ed.), *A History of Psychology in Autobiography*, (6 vols.), Clark University Press, Worcester, Massachusetts, vol. 4, pp. 237–56. Hearnshaw, *Cyril Burt*, p. 53.

17. Margaret A. Boden, *Jean Piaget*, Penguin, Harmondsworth, 1979, pp. 43–63.

18. Elena Gianini Belotti, *Little Girls*, Writers and Readers, London, 1975, pp. 108–11.

19. Sylvia Ashton Warner, *Spinster*, Virago, London, 1980; *Teacher*, Virago, London, 1980. Sybil Marshall, *Experiment in Education*, Cambridge University Press, Cambridge, 1963.

20. John and Elizabeth Newson, *Perspectives on School at Seven Years*, George Allen and Unwin, London, 1977, pp. 161–91. Mia Kelmer Pringle, *The Needs of Children*, Hutchinson, London, 1975, pp. 114–15. Harriet Wilson and G.W. Herbert, *Parents and Children in the Inner City*, Routledge and Kegan Paul, London, 1978, pp. 180–98.

21. A.H. Halsey (ed.), *Educational Priority*, (5 vols.), HMSO, London, 1972–4. Miriam E. David, *The State, the Family and Education*, Routledge and Kegan Paul, London, 1980, pp. 89–90.

22. The Department of Education and Science does not separate the total of primary and secondary Social Priority schools.

23. Herb Kohl, *Thirty-Six Children*, Penguin, Harmondsworth, 1971, p. 232. George

Dennison, *The Lives of Children*, Penguin, Harmondsworth, 1972. Morris Fraser, *Children in Conflict*, Penguin, Harmondsworth, 1974, pp. 11–25. Eleanor Craig, *PS Your (sic) Not Listening*, New American Library, New York, 1973, pp. 127–8.

24. Marion Bowley, *Housing and the State*, George Allen and Unwin, London, 1947, pp. 94–131.

25. For a description of such a housing estate, see John and Elizabeth Newson, *Four Years Old in an Urban Community*, George Allen and Unwin, London, 1968, pp. 30–31; pp. 36–9.

26. Mary Brown and Norman Precious, *The Integrated Day in the Primary School*, Ward Lock Educational, London, 1968, describes the organisation of time and space in this way in the context of the child-centred movement of the Plowden era. In fact my influences derived from a much older source of ideas about putting children in charge of the environment of their learning, that of the Dalton Plan, which was adopted by many elementary and secondary schools in the 1920s and 1930s. By the 1950s it was (as far as I know) followed in only one state school in this country, the one I attended between the age of eleven and eighteen. Helen Parkhurst, *Education on the Dalton Plan*, G. Bell and Sons, London, 1922.

27. In Philip Jackson, *Life in Classrooms*, Holt, Rinehart and Winston, New York, 1968, the general experience of the majority of children is described as 'waiting' – to have their work marked, to speak, for the loan of a rubber, for a pencil to be sharpened.

28. Joseph Jacobs, *English Fairy Tales*, Bodley Head, London, 1968. Amabel Williams Ellis, *Fairy Tales from the British Isles*, Blackie and Sons, Glasgow, 1960.

1 AT THE DOOR OF THE TIDY HOUSE

1. The scenes that particularly interested the children were: the birthday scene (TH transcript: pp. 48–49, 50); the scene that involves the character Carl's first day at school (TH transcript: pp. 41, 51); and the second bedroom scene (TH transcript: p. 52).

2. Glenda L. Bissex, *Gnys at Wrk: A Child Learns to Read and Write*, Harvard University Press, Cambridge, Massachusetts, 1980, pp. 106–7.

3. The interrelation of names in 'The Tidy House' must make it initially as difficult to read a commentary on it as it was for us to work out the plot at the time it was written (TH tapes: p. 175). But it is important that the child character Carl is the male version of his creator, Carla, and that Jeannie, the longed-for girl child of the story who never gets born (TH transcripts: p. 54) is at once the name of Carla's own younger sister (TH Tapes: p. 166) and the independent heroine of *Jack Got the Sack*, p. 97. Fashion also dictated the naming of characters: 1976 saw the first summer of Jamie Somers, the Bionic Woman. Clive James, *Visions Before Midnight*, Picador, London, 1981, p. 169.

4. This remark by Lindie in inverted commas here is in the nature of a well-known consolatory phrase or saying. For other examples see John and Elizabeth Newson, *Patterns of Infant Care*, Penguin, Harmondsworth, 1976, p. 18 and Ann Oakley, *The Sociology of Housework*, Martin Robertson, London, 1974, pp. 167–8.

5. The unsayable, unwritable word is of course 'fuck' or 'fucking'. A tug at the sleeve, an affronted child: 'Miss, Darren just said the ef word to me . . .'

6. In the mid-1970s, nursery places were often available to all parents who wanted them in Social Priority Areas. Oakley, *Sociology of Housework*, p. 177; 'when he turns three he's off [to nursery school] . . . They're irritating . . .'

The Tidy House

7. Marion Glastonbury, 'The Best Kept Secret: How Working Class Women Live, and What They Know', in *Women's Studies International Quarterly*, 2 (1979), p. 26, quoting Winifred Foley, *A Child in the Forest*, BBC, London, 1973, p. 101.

8. The narrative structure of 'The Tidy House' bears obvious relation to the loose, episodic structure of television soap operas, such as 'Crossroads'. Most of the children did in fact watch 'Crossroads' relentlessly; but, given the visual insubstantiality of their story, it is not likely that television serials like this were used as a model for their story, though the emphasis on people talking to each other that is their feature may have confirmed the children's pre-existing notions about the role and power of dialogue in social life. See also Courtney B. Cazden, 'The Neglected Situation in Child Language Research and Education', in (ed.) F. Williams, *Language and Poverty*, Markham, Chicago, 1976, pp. 81–101, where she suggests that the presence of visual images actually constrains children's ability to direct narrative and draw on their own observation and knowledge of the language when writing.

9. On this last point see David Vincent (ed.), James Dawson Burn, *Autobiography of a Beggar Boy*, Europa, London, 1978, pp. 5–6; pp. 12–16; pp. 39–80. Fred Reid, *Keir Hardy: The Making of a Socialist*, Croom Helm, London, 1978, pp. 13–30. Thea Thompson, *Edwardian Childhoods*, Routledge and Kegan Paul, London, 1980.

10. Jack Goody (ed.), *Literacy in Traditional Societies*, Cambridge University Press, Cambridge, 1968, pp. 1–63. Jack Goody, *The Domestication of the Savage Mind*, Cambridge University Press, Cambridge, 1977. Paulo Freire, *Pedagogy of the Oppressed*, Penguin, Harmondsworth, 1972. Robert Roberts, *Imprisoned Tongues*, Manchester University Press, Manchester, 1971. Jonathan Kozol, *Children of the Revolution*, DelaCourte Press, New York, 1978, pp. 11–42. David Olson, 'From Utterance to Text: The Bias of Language in Speech and Writing', *Harvard Educational Review*, 47:3 (August 1977), pp. 257–81. Jonathan Culler, *The Pursuit of Signs*, Routledge and Kegan Paul, London, 1981, p. 6; pp. 14–15. Constructing psychological theory in a period of enormous social upheaval, L.S. Vygotsky *did* address this question: L.S. Vygotsky, 'The Prehistory of Written Language', *Mind in Society*, Harvard University Press, Cambridge, Massachusetts, 1978, pp. 105–19.

11. Catherine Garvey, *Play*, Harvard University Press, Cambridge, Massachusetts, 1977, pp. 99–100. John and Elizabeth Newson, *Seven Years Old in the Home Environment*, George Allen and Unwin, London, 1976, pp. 163–4. L.S. Vygotsky, 'Play in Its Role in the Mental Development of the Child', in *Mind in Society*, pp. 92–104.

12. Nora Goddard, *Literacy: Language Experience Approaches*, Macmillan, London, 1974.

13. John Berger, *Permanent Red: Essays in Seeing*, Writers and Readers, London, 1979, p. 65.

14. Berger, *Permanent Red*, p. 65.

15. Aaron V. Cicourel, *Language Use and School Performance*, Academic Press, New York, 1974, pp. 301–2. Matthew Speier, 'The Everyday World of the Child', in Jack Douglas (ed.), *Understanding Everyday Life*, University of California Press, San Diego, 1970, pp. 136–68.

16. Peter L. Berger and Thomas Luckman, *The Social Construction of Reality*, Doubleday and Co., New York, 1966, pp. 121–35.

17. John and Elizabeth Newson, *Patterns of Infant Care*, Penguin, Harmondsworth,

1976. John and Elizabeth Newson, *Four Years Old in an Urban Community*, George Allen and Unwin, London, 1968. John and Elizabeth Newson, *Seven Years Old in the Home Environment*, George Allen and Unwin, London, 1976.

18. Newson, *Infant Care*, pp. 80–101, particularly pp. 80–82.

19. Newson, *Four Years Old*, pp. 67–103, particularly pp. 70–72.

20. Newson, *Infant Care*, pp. 80–81, p. 97. *Four Years Old*, pp. 447–53. Oakley, *Sociology of Housework*, p. 173.

21. Newson, *Seven Years Old*, pp. 225–36. Carla, Lindie and Melissa seemed more aware of economic circumstances than Nottingham mothers presented their seven-year-olds as being.

22. Newson, *Four Years Old*, p. 138.

23. Newson, *Infant Care*, p. 136; *Four Years Old*, p. 486; pp. 514–15. Oakley, *Sociology of Housework*, pp. 179–80.

24. Newson, *Infant Care*, pp. 70–71. Oakley, *Sociology of Housework*, p. 176: 'I can't stand a lot of whining, this sort of thing . . . '

25. Newson, *Four Years*, pp. 153–62; p. 212; pp. 390–91; pp. 397–9; p. 400.

26. Newson, *Four Years Old*, pp. 407–8; *Seven Years*, pp. 328–9.

27. Newson, *Four Years*, pp. 231–2; pp. 308–9; p. 407.

28. Newson, *Four Years*, p. 57.

29. Newson, *Four Years*, p. 474; *Seven Years*, pp. 351–63.

30. Newson, *Infant Care*, p. 111; Oakley, *Sociology of Housework*, pp. 166–80.

31. Oakley, *Sociology of Housework*, p. 116.

32. Newson, *Four Years*, pp. 108–9; pp. 114–35. *Seven Years*, pp. 50–51; pp. 195–7; pp. 199–206.

33. Ann Oakley, *Housewife*, Penguin, Harmondsworth, 1976, pp. 80–90; pp. 186–221. L. Rainwater, R.P Coleman, Gerald Handel, *Workingman's Wife*, Oceana Publications, New York, 1959, p. 88.

34. Francis Place, *The Autobiography of Francis Place, 1771–1854*, (ed.) Mary Thale, Cambridge University Press, Cambridge, 1972, p. 21. Robert Roberts, *The Classic Slum*, Manchester University Press, Manchester, 1971. D.H. Lawrence, *Sons and Lovers* (1913), Penguin, Harmondsworth 1980, Book 1, Chapters 2,3 and 4. Richard Hoggart, *The Uses of Literacy*, Chatto and Windus, London, 1957. A.S Jasper, *A Hoxton Childhood*, Barrie and Rockliff, London, 1969. For a revealingly contradictory statement about 'our mam' from a woman, see May Hobbs, *Born to Struggle*, Quartet Books, London, 1973, Foreword and p. 29 f.

35. Oakley, *Sociology of Housework*, p. 166. Nancy Chodorow, *The Reproduction of Mothering: Psychoanalysis and the Sociology of Gender*, University of California Press, Berkeley and Los Angeles, 1978, pp. 4–6, on the role of mother and housewife.

36. Oakley, *Housewife*, p. 193. Michele Barrett, *Women's Oppression Today*, Verso, London, 1980, p. 73: 'we cling desperately to that wonderful discovery of Margaret Mead – the Tchambuli, where the women manage and the men are coquettish'.

37. *History Workshop: A Journal of Socialist Historians*, vol. 1 (Spring 1976).

38. James Walvin, *A Child's World: A Social History of English Childhood, 1800–1914*, Penguin, Harmondsworth, 1982, pp. 11–12.

39. See Beatrice Webb, *My Apprenticeship*, Penguin, London, 1971, pp. 192–3; Elinor S. Ouvry (ed.), *Extracts from Octavia Hill's Letters to Fellow Workers 1864–1911*, Adelphi Bookshop, London, 1933, pp. 6–7. I am grateful to Standish Meacham for these references and for pointing out that both *North and South* and 'Janet's Repentance' express the notion that contemplating the misery of others will do

good to oneself. Elizabeth Gaskell, *North and South*, Penguin, Harmondsworth, 1970; George Eliot, *Scenes of Clerical Life*, Penguin, Harmondsworth, 1973, pp. 400–402.

40. For other discussion by the children of clothes, see (TH tapes: pp. 165, 180).
41. Henry Mayhew, *London Labour and the London Poor* (4 vols.), vol. 1, George Woodfall and Son, London, 1851, p. 152. Mayhew, however, was a deeply sensitive interviewer and it is instructive to read his interview with the watercress seller, and watch his attitude change from that of conventionally sorrowful observer to interested and reflexive interlocutor.
42. Mayhew, *London Labour*, vol. 1, p. 151.
43. Adrienne Rich, *On Lies, Secrets and Silence*, Virago Press, London, 1979, p. 43.

3 DOMESTIC EDUCATION AND THE READING PUBLIC: THE HISTORICAL USES OF CHILDREN'S WRITING

1. Graham Ovenden and Robert Melville, *Victorian Children*, Academy Editions, London, 1972. Jean Gattégno, *Lewis Carroll*, Crowell, New York, 1976.
2. Eve V. Clark, 'What's in a Word? On the Child's Acquisition of Semantics in His First Language', in (ed.) T.E. Moore, *Cognitive Development and the Acquisition of Language*, Academic Press, New York, 1973, p. 65.
3. Susan Ervin-Tripp and Claudia Mitchell Kernan, *Child Discourse*, Academic Press, New York, 1977, p. 7. Mina P. Shaughnessy, *Errors and Expectations*, Oxford University Press, New York, 1977, p. 87.
4. Jean Piaget, *The Child's Conception of the World*, Kegan Paul, Trench and Trubner, London, 1929, pp. 10–23.
5. Peter Coveney, *Poor Monkey: The Child in Literature*, Rockcliff, London, 1957, pp. 30–45; pp. 192–4.
6. Florence Rush, *The Best Kept Secret: The Sexual Abuse of Children*, Prentice Hall, New Jersey, 1980, pp. 56–73.
7. The literary cult of the little girl is still alive and well, as a glance at the number of impressions that *Mr God, This Is Anna* has gone through since 1974 will reveal. 'Fynn', *Mr God, This Is Anna*, Collins, London, 1974. It achieved its twelfth impression in 1981.
8. At the age when the girls whose diaries form the subject of this chapter composed them, their brothers were generally at school. Very young boys not yet at boarding school and instructed by their mothers did produce diaries. W.R. Clark, *Little Charlie's Life: By Himself*, Saunder, Otley and Co., London, 1868. Richard Barrett, Holograph Diary 310188B, Berg Collection, New York Public Library, 7pp., probable date, December 1820.
9. Earl Barnes, 'Methods of Studying Children', *The Paidologist*, 1 (April 1899), pp. 9–17. Sara E. Wiltse, 'Children's Autobiographies', *The Paidologist*, 1:3 (November 1899), pp. 155–7. Earl Barnes, 'Young Children's Stories', *The Paidologist*, 2:1 (April 1900), pp. 17–21. S. Levinstein, 'Children's Stories', *The Paidologist*, 5:1 (February 1903), pp. 14–20.
10. James Sully, *Studies of Childhood*, Longman's, Green and Co., London, 1896, p. 9; pp. 22–3.
11. Sully, *Studies*, pp. 2–4.
12. Paul Roazen, *Freud and His Followers*, Alfred A. Knopf, New York, 1975, pp. 442–3. Rush, *Best Kept Secret*, pp. 97–8.

Notes

13. Eden and Cedar Paul (eds.), *A Young Girl's Diary*, prefaced with a letter by Sigmund Freud, George Allen and Unwin, London, 1921, pp. 5–6. This document is still reproduced as an authentic piece of writing, though the story of its fakery is well known. See Betsy Dinesen, *Rediscovery*, The Women's Press, London, 1981, pp. 31–6.

14. Coveney, *Poor Monkey*, pp. 192–228. John Brown, *Marjorie Fleming: A Sketch*, Edinburgh, 1863. Margaret Emily Shore, *Journal of Emily Shore*, Routledge and Kegan Paul, London, 1891. Anna Green Winslow, *Diary of Anna Green Winslow* (ed. Alice Morse Earle), Houghton Mifflin, Cambridge, Massachusetts, 1894.

15. Shore, *Journal*, Introduction. Frank Sidgwick, *The Complete Marjory Fleming*, Sidgwick and Jackson, London, 1934, pp. xvi–xvii.

16. Sidgwick, *Marjory Fleming*, p. xvi, p. xix.
    John Brown, *Marjory Fleming: A Sketch*, Edinburgh, 1863. H.B. Farnie, *A Story of Child Life Fifty Years Ago* (2nd edn), Edinburgh, 1863. John Brown, *Marjory Fleming: A Sketch. Being the paper entitled 'Pet Marjorie: A Story of Child Life Fifty Years Ago'*, Edinburgh, 1863.

17. Clark, *Little Charlie*, p. 10, p. 15.

18. Ovenden and Melville, *Victorian Children*; Rush, *Best Kept Secret*, p. 60.

19. Opal Whiteley, *The Story of Opal: The Journal of an Understanding Heart*, Atlantic Monthly Press, Boston, 1920. Published in the UK and edited by Grey of Fallodon as *The Diary of Opal Whiteley*, Putnam, London, 1920. There was a family interest here in the messages of children: Pamela Grey (Lady Grey of Fallodon), *The Sayings of the Children, Written Down by Their Mother*, Stokes and Co., New York, 1924.

20. Elisabeth Bradburne, *Opal Whiteley: The Unsolved Mystery*, Putnam, London, 1962. Joseph and Elizabeth Berger, *Small Voices*, Paul S. Eriksson, New York, 1966. Jane Boulton, *Opal*, Macmillan, New York, 1976.

21. Not all contemporary reviewers were enthusiastic. There were several comments made about the intentional humour of the child's arch innocence of the reproductive process. *Athenaeum*, 17 September 1920, p. 372; *Spectator*, 16 October 1920, p. 504.

22. Elbert Bede, *Fabulous Opal Whiteley*, Binfords and Mort, Portland, Oregon, 1954, pp. 102–32.

23. Sigmund Freud, 'Family Romances' (1909), *Standard Edition of the Collected Works*, Hogarth Press, London, 1959, vol. ix, pp. 237–41.

24. John and Elizabeth Berger, *Small Voices*, Paul S. Eriksson, New York, 1966, p. 31.

25. Anais Nin, *Lintotte: The Early Diary of Anais Nin, 1914–1920*, Harcourt Brace Jovanovitch, New York, 1978. Laurel Holliday, *Heart Songs: The Intimate Diaries of Young Girls*, Bluestocking Press, Berkeley, California, 1978.

26. Karen Horney, *The Adolescent Diaries of Karen Horney*, Basic Books, New York, 1980, p. 3.

27. Betty Boyd Bell, *Circus: A Girl's Own Story* (ed. Janet Mabie), Brewer, Warren and Putnam, New York, 1931. Hilda Conklin, *Poems by a Little Girl*, Stokes, New York, 1920.

28. Margaret O'Brien, *My Diary*, J.B. Lippincott, New York, 1947. This book had a profound effect on some contemporary children. See Phyllis Theroux, *California and Other States of Grace*, Fawcett Crest, New York, 1980, pp. 80–88.

29. Elizabeth Luling, *Do Not Disturb*, with an Introduction and Notes by Sylvia Thompson (Her Mother), Oxford University Press, New York, 1937. Sylvia McNeely, *Diary of Sylvia McNeely*, Longmans Green and Co., New York, 1931.

Kathie Gray, *Kathie's Diary: Leaves from an Old, Old Diary*, (ed.) Margaret W. Eggleston, New York, 1926.

30. O'Brien, *My Diary*, p. 1: 'Mama always seems to know when I get into mischief. Sometimes she is strict with me but in the end I always find out that she is right and I love her very much.'

31. O'Brien, *My Diary*, Introduction by Lionel Barrymore. Conklin, *Poems*, Introduction by Amy Lowell. Mary Virginia Harriss, *Blue Beads and Amber*, Norman Remington Co., Baltimore, 1923, Introduction by William Kavanagh Doty. Mimpsy Rhys, *Mr Hermit Crab: A Tale for Children by a Child*, Macmillan, New York, 1929, Introduction by Mary Elizabeth Barnacle, Department of English, New York University. Julia Rosa Newberry, *Julia Newberry's Diary*, W.W. Norton and Co., New York, 1933, Introduction by Margaret Ayer Barns and Janet Ayer Fairbank. Mary Paxson, *Her Book, 1880–1884*, Doubleday Doran and Co., New York, 1936, Introduction by Agnes Sligh Turnbull. Winslow, *Diary*, Introduction by Alice Morse Earle. Helen Douglas Adam, *The Elfin Pedlar and Other Tales Told by Pixie Pool*, Putnams, New York, Introduction by the Reverend John A. Hutton.

32. Newberry, *Diary*, p. 173. 'A member of the family found it one rainy Sunday, stored away in a chest'.

33. Rhys, *Hermit Crab*, Introduction, p. vii.

34. Rhys, *Hermit Crab*, p. vi.

35. Rhys, *Hermit Crab*, p. v.

36. Paxson, *Her Book*, Introduction.

37. Ann Thwaite, *Waiting for the Party: The Life of Frances Hodgson Burnett*, Secker and Warburg, London, 1974, pp. 92–4.

38. Paxson, *Her Book*, p. 3.

39. Shore, *Journal*.

40. Berger and Berger, *Small Voices*, p. 289.

41. Shore, *Journal*.

42. Berger and Berger, *Small Voices*, p. 289.

43. Boulton, *Opal*, Introduction; Berger and Berger, *Small Voices*, p. vii; Paxon, *Her Book*, Introduction.

44. Douglas Adam, *Elfin Pedlar*, p. ix.

45. Douglas Adam, *Elfin Pedlar*, p. 43.

46. R.D. Laing, *Conversations with Children*, Allen Lane, London, 1978, p. vii.

47. Clarke, *Little Charlie*, p. 8.

48. Winslow, *Diary*; A. Aspinwall, *Lady Bessborough and Her Family Circle*, John Murray, London, 1940, pp. 18–30. Sidgwick, *Marjory Fleming*; Shore, *Journal*; Ednah D. Cheney, *Louisa May Alcott: Her Life, Letters and Journals*, Roberts Bros, Boston, 1899.

49. Daisy Ashford, *The Young Visiters, or Mr Salteener's Plan*, with a Preface by J.M. Barrie, Chatto and Windus, London, 1919.

50. Tuli Kupferberg and Sylvia Topp, *A Big Bibliography: Children as Writers*, Birth Press, New York, 1959, p. 3.

51. Elizabeth Barrett Browning, *Hitherto Unpublished Poems and Stories* (2 vols.), The Bibliophile Society, Boston, 1914. Nin, *Lintotte*.

52. Sidgwick, *Marjory Fleming*, p. xv.

53. Susanna Arethusa Cullam, Diaries, 1822–4, West Suffolk Record Office, MSS E2/44. Constance Emily Primrose, Diary, 1856, West Sussex County Record Office, Petworth House Archives, MSS 1680.

54. Mary Georgiana Wilkinson, Journal, 11 September – 12 October 1819, Nottinghamshire Record Office, MSS DDW 170.

55. The transcription of Marjory Fleming's writing in Sidgwick, *Marjory Fleming*, shows her cousin and tutor Isa's underlinings and corrections to be quite unsystematic.

56. E.P. Peabody, *Record of a School*, Roberts Bros, Boston, 1874, pp. 274–5; pp. 291–2.

57. Anna Alcott, Journal, Alcott Papers, Family Letters, 1837–1850, vol. i, Domestic, 59M 305(24), Houghton Library, Cambridge, Massachusetts. Entries dated 11,20 September 1839.

58. Peabody, *Record of a School*, pp. 274–5.

59. Elizabeth Sewell Alcott, 'Elizabeth's Diary, 1846', Alcott Papers, Family Letters, 1837–1850, Domestic, 59M–305(24), entries for 3, 4, 14 May 1846. Anna Alcott, Journal, Alcott Papers, Family Letters, 1837–1850, Domestic, 59M–305 (24), entry for 30 September 1839. Bronson Alcott's mother had kept a journal, Madelon Bedell; *The Alcotts: Portrait of a Family*, Clarkson N. Potter, New York, 1980, pp. 8–9.

60. Paul, *Young Girl's Diary*, p. 6. For a recent account of this idea within reading theory, see Bruno Bettelheim and Karen Zelan, *On Learning to Read: The Child's Fascination with Meaning*, Knopf, New York, 1982.

61. Charles Read, 'Pre-School Children's Knowledge of English Phonology', *Harvard Educational Review*, 41:1 (February 1971), pp. 1–34.

62. Glenda L. Bissex, *Gnys at Wrk: A Child Learns to Read and Write*, Harvard University Press, Cambridge, Massachusetts, 1980, pp. 43–4. Margaret L. Peters, *Spelling: Caught or Taught?*, Routledge and Kegan Paul, London, 1967, pp. 18–35.

63. Boulton, *Opal*, p. 3; Paxson, *Her Book*, p. 89. The most complete representation of an adult notion of how children spell is to be found in one of the tiny handful of boy children's writing to be published. Henry Shute, *The Real Diary of a Real Boy*, Reilly and Britton Co., Chicago, 1917. Written in the style of *1066 And All That*, 'it was an immediate best seller – the best thing that ever happened to Judge Shute.' Berger and Berger, *Small Voices*, p. 261.

64. Florence Lind Coleridge, Diary, September 1874, Coleridge Collection, Humanities Research Center, University of Texas at Austin; entry dated 1 September 1874.

65. Constance Primrose, Diary, 1856, West Sussex County Record Office, Petworth House Archives, MSS 1680; entry for 12 November 1856.

66. Florence Lind Coleridge, Diary, MS in notebook, 54pp.; Mary Elizabeth Coleridge, Diaries, MS in six notebooks, 670pp., Coleridge Collection, Humanities Research Center, University of Texas at Austin.

67. Writing immediately after an incident has taken place frequently makes children produce brief and formal summaries of what has happened. For a discussion of this question, and of the effect of time and reflection on children's writing, see Michael Armstrong, *Closely Observed Children: The Diary of a Primary Classroom*, Chameleon Books in association with Writers and Readers, London, 1980, pp. 10–11; p. 19; p. 160. Mary Georgiana Wilkinson, Journal, 11 September – 12 October 1819, Nottinghamshire Record Office, MSS DDW, 170–71, pp. 5–6.

68. Susanna Arethusa Cullam, Diary, 1822–4, West Suffolk Record Office, MSS E2/44.

69. Clara Endicott Sears, *Bronson Alcott's Fruitlands*, Houghton Mifflin, Cambridge, Massachusetts, 1915, pp. 103–4.

70. Mary Elizabeth Coleridge, Diary, vol. 1, Humanities Research Center, University of Texas at Austin, entries for 31 August 1870; vol. 2, entry for 12 October 1870, 3 February 1871.

71. Published examples of the tagged-on incident are to be found in Ellen R.C. Creighton, *Ellen Buxton's Journal*, Geoffrey Bles, London, 1967, p. 17: 'I forgot to say that a few days before Christmas Miss Smith went out for her holiday'; and in Shore, *Journal*, p. 4: 'I had forgot to mention in the proper place that after I came home from Ramsgate I made a pasteboard model of the steam packet in which we went to Broadstairs.'

72. Mary Elizabeth Coleridge, Diary, Coleridge Collection, Humanities Research Center, University of Texas at Austin, vol. 1, entries for 24 August, 3,18 September 1870.

73. Coleridge, Diary, vol. 2, entry for 16 March 1871.

74. Theresa Whistler (ed.), *The Collected Poems of Mary Elizabeth Coleridge*, Rupert Hart Davis, London, 1954, p. 31.

75. Peter L. Berger and Thomas Luckman, *The Social Construction of Reality*, Doubleday and Co., New York, 1966, p. 37.

76. Elinor Ochs, 'What Child Language Can Contribute to Pragmatics', in Elinor Ochs and Bambi Shieffelin, *Developmental Pragmatics*, Academic Press, New York, 1979, pp. 1–6.

77. Elizabeth Barrett Browning Papers, Berg Collection, New York Public Library, 'Sebastian; Or Virtue Rewarded', Holograph MS, 65B2763; 'The Way to Humble Pride', Holograph MS 65B2779. These scribbled, badly spelled (that is, spelled in a manner typical of an eight-year-old acquiring written language) manuscripts are to be found punctuated and transcribed in an elegant hand in the Armstrong Browning Library, Baylor University, Waco, Texas; Elizabeth Barrett Browning Papers, M2–39, M2–50, M2–4.

78. Barrett Browning, *Poems and Stories*, vol. 1, p. 27. See also Ellen Moers, *Literary Women*, The Women's Press, London, 1978, pp. 5–8.

79. Barrett Browning, *Poems and Stories*, p. 5. 'When we came home one day after having written a page of poetry which I considered models of beauty I ran downstairs to the library to seek Pope's *Homer* in order to compare them that I might enjoy my own SUPERIORITY'; p. 12.

80. Cheney, *Louisa May Alcott*, p. 38.

81. The Moulton Barrett family collection in the Berg Collection, New York Public Library, contains a large amount of material showing the serious game of literary education that Mary Moulton Barrett set all her children. They were encouraged to communicate with her and each other by letter, the house had a family post-box, they were expected to compose odes in honour of family birthdays and to construct books. 65B2406; 65B2407; 65B2409; 65B2411; 65B2401; 65B7734; 65B2735. 65b210, ALS to Mary Graham Clarke Moulton Barrett (n.d.) signed Elizabeth and Henrietta: 'To our kind/mama an answer/to the nursery/My dearest and kind Mama/As I know you will not refuse/request that is reasonable I venture/to address you remember that we have/a great many things to do tomorrow/to alter my poetry and get flowers and/write my verbs and so has Hen so/Pray dear Mama do excuse us our/haste tomorrow and believe us you affect. children Elizth. & Henrietta'. Elizabeth Moulton Barrett also received a great deal of encouragement to write from her paternal grandmother: Pierpont Morgan Library, New York, Elizabeth Barrett Browning Collection, Birthday Odes and Various Correspondence, letter from Mrs Moulton to Elizabeth Moulton Barrett, dated 18 July 1809

or 1810, 6 March 1810 or 1811, two undated letters, 1817–18.

82. Armstrong Browning Library, Baylor University, Waco, Texas, Elizabeth Barrett Browning papers, L3–1; L3–2.

83. A humorous family magazine that provided for hilarious contact between family members is to be found in 'Lewis Carroll', *The Rectory Magazine*, University of Texas Press, Austin, Texas, 1975.

84. Houghton Library, Cambridge, Massachusetts, Alcott Papers, Family Letters, 1837–56, vol. 1, Domestic, 59M–305 (24), Anna Alcott, Journal, entry dated 8 August 1839.

85. Frank Sidgwick, *The Complete Marjory Fleming*, Sidgwick and Jackson, London, 1934, p. 28; pp. 40–42.

86. Sidgwick, *Marjory Fleming*, p. 166, letter from Marjory Fleming to Isabella Keith, dated 1 September 1811.

87. Ellen Moers, *Literary Women*, The Women's Press, London, 1978, pp. 211–42. 'Isabella teaches me everything I know/and I am much indebted to her/she is learn/en witty & sensible' was Marjory Fleming's comment on her own educating heroine. Sidgwick, *Marjory Fleming*, p. 3.

88. Sidgwick, *Marjory Fleming*, p. 33; p. 41; pp. 43–4; p. 45.

89. Sidgwick, *Marjory Fleming*, Introduction, pp. xvi–xxii for a history of this publication. His account omits the many American editions published.

90. James Sully, *Studies*, p. 4.

91. Mark Twain, 'The Wonder Child', *Harper's Bazaar* (December 1909).

92. Samuel Clemens, *Mark Twain's Autobiography* (2 vols.), P.F. Collier and Sons, New York, 1925, vol. 2, p. 43; pp. 64–6; pp. 66–147.

93. Walter de la Mare, *Early One Morning in the Spring*, Macmillan, New York, 1935, p. 419.

94. Sidgwick, *Marjory Fleming*, p. 179, letter from Isabella Keith to Marjory's mother, Isabella Fleming, dated 1 April 1811; p. 12.

95. Sidgwick, *Marjory Fleming*, p. 179.

96. Sidgwick, *Marjory Fleming*, pp. 3–4; pp. 113–14.

97. Sidgwick, *Marjory Fleming*, Preface, p. v.

98. Moers, *Literary Women*, p. 197.

99. Among the books they read were *The Arabian Nights*; Maria Edgeworth, *Tales of Fashionable Life* (6 vols.), J. Johnson and Co., London, 1809–12; Ann Radcliffe, *Mysteries of Udolpho* (4 vols.), London, 1794; Sarah Trimmer, *Fabulous Histories*, T. Longman and Co., London, 1786.

100. Sidgwick, *Marjory Fleming*, p. 103.

101. Sidgwick, *Marjory Fleming*, pp. 37–8; p. 49; p. 77; p. 101.

102. Sidgwick, *Marjory Fleming*, p. 103; p. 108; p. 49.

103. Sidgwick, *Marjory Fleming*, p. 49; p. 108.

104. Sidgwick, *Marjory Fleming*, p. 109.

105. Sidgwick, *Marjory Fleming*, p. 102; pp. 67–8; p. 109.

106. Sidgwick, *Marjory Fleming*, p. 20. Lillian Faderman, *Surpassing the Love of Men*, William Morrow and Co., New York, 1981, p. 75.

107. Sidgwick, *Marjory Fleming*, p. 8, p. 23, p. 24.

108. Frances Hodgson Burnett, *The One I Knew Best of All*, Frederick Warne and Co., London, 1893. Her first stories were written on her slate 'and in old account books'; pp. 186–7; p. 190; pp. 208–9.

109. Armstrong Browning Library, Baylor University, Waco, Texas, Elizabeth Barrett

Browning Papers, three stories, 'Sebastian, or the Lost Child', 'Disobedience', 'The Way to Humble Pride'. M2–39; M2–50; M2–4.

110.   This may still be a desire on the part of a certain readership. *A Young Girl's Diary* has recently been reissued, even though it is known to be a literary fake. See above p. 64, and note 13, p. 225.

111.   Maria Montessori, *The Formation of Man*, Theosophical Publishing House, Adyar, India, 1969, p. 107: 'The education of the masses . . . proclaimed a task requiring mental effort from every individual; and the task was entrusted to children'. Carlo M. Chipolla, *Literacy and Development in the West*, Penguin, Harmondsworth, 1969, pp. 62–99.

4 LEARNING THE SOCIAL WORLD: CHILDREN'S USE OF WRITING

1.   Coleridge Papers, Humanities Research Center, University of Texas at Austin; Sara Coleridge, 'Diary of Her Children's Early Years', 1830–38, p. 2.

2.   Philippe Aries, *Centuries of Childhood*, Vintage, New York, 1965, pp. 62f. Ellen Moers, *Literary Women*, The Women's Press, London, 1978, p. 14. David Hunt, *Parents and Children in History*, Basic Books, New York, 1970.

3.   Cheshire Record Office, DSA 75, Catherine Stanley of Alderley, 'Journal of Her Four Children'; quotation from Thomas Read, *Works*, (ed.) G.N. Wright (4 vols.), Edinburgh, 1843, 1846.

4.   Catherine Stanley, 'Journal of Her Five Children', entry for March 1812, Cheshire Record Office, DSA, 75.

5.   Charles Darwin, 'A Biographical Sketch of an Infant', *Mind*, 2:7 (July 1877), pp. 285–94. 'Darwin legitimised the baby journal'; William Kessen, *The Child*, John Wiley and Sons, New York, 1965, p. 117. Darwin, however, operated not only within a long domestic tradition, but within a family one too. In 1953 Darwin's granddaughter noted that her great-grandfather, Josiah Wedgewood II had kept a developmental journal of his son in the years 1797–9. 'Some of the children's conversations are recorded . . . talking in bed at night . . . one can feel quite certain that Josiah wrote down the actual words they used, as he stood listening behind the door'. Gwen Raverat, *Period Piece*, W.W. Norton and Co., New York, 1953, pp. 154–5. For a fairly full list of developmental diaries written by fathers, see the Bibliography for Robin Campbell and Roger Wales, 'The Study of Language Acquisition', in (ed.) John Lyons, *New Horizons in Linguistics*, Penguin, Harmondsworth, 1970, pp. 242–60; and the Bibliography for Eve V. Clark, 'What's in a Word? On the Child's Acquisition of Semantics in the First Language', in (ed.) T.E. Moore, *Cognitive Development and the Acquisition of Language*, Academic Press, New York, 1973, pp. 65–110. See Vilhelm Rasmussen, *Diary of a Child's Life*, Gyldendal, London, 1931. There are also useful references in J.H. Muirhead, 'The Founders of Child Study in England', *Paidologist*, 2:2 (July 1900), pp. 114–24, and in H. Holman, 'Rev. Henry Wolton: A Pioneer in Child Study', *Child Study*, 8:7 (November 1915), pp. 127–33; 8:8 (December 1915), pp. 143–56; 9:1 (February 1916), pp. 13–17; 9:2 (March 1916), pp. 29–32.

6.   James Sully, *Studies of Childhood*, Longmans, Green and Co., London, 1896, pp. 20–23. 'Editorial', *The Paidologist*, 1 (April 1899).

7.   James Mark Baldwin, *Mental Development in the Child and the Race*, Macmillan, New York, 1894. Hippolyte Taine, *On Intelligence* (2 vols.), London, 1871.

8.   The mothers' developmental journals that have been consulted for this chapter are:

Cheshire County Record Office, DSA 75, Catherine Stanley of Alderley, 'Journal of Her Four Children, 1811–19'. Coleridge Papers, Humanities Research Center, University of Texas at Austin, Sara Coleridge, 'Diary of Her Children's Early Years', 1830–38; 'Diary of Bertha Fanny's Death'. City of Bristol Museum and Art Gallery, Diaries of Ellen Sharples, 1803–32 (the early entries are concerned with the education and development of her daughter Rolinda). Elizabeth Cleghorn Gaskell, *My Diary*, (ed.) Clement Shorter, privately printed, 1923. Margaret Isabella Stevenson, *Stevenson's Baby Book*, printed for John Howell by John Henry Nash, San Francisco, 1922. See also Joseph Estlin Carpenter, *The Life and Work of Mary Carpenter*, McMillan, London, 1881, which describes and uses a developmental journal kept by her mother, Anna Penn Carpenter, now lost. See Dale Spender, *Man Made Language*, Routledge and Kegan Paul, London, 1980, p. 192, on the elaboration of the 'private sphere' of women's writing, which, added to the factors that prevented mothers' developmental journals being published, may account for the ease with which they have been lost and the indifference with which they are catalogued in libraries and record offices.

9.   Gaskell, *Diary*, pp. 6–7, 'she shouts and murmurs and talks in her way, just like conversation'; p. 19, 'scarcely attempting to walk with two hands, though nearly sixteen months'; p. 8, 'sometimes she will cry a little, and when I turn her over in her cot she fancies she is going to be taken up and is still in a moment, making the peculiar little triumphing noise she always does when she is pleased'.

10.   The *Stevenson Baby Book* had the form of a diary, with space for recording physical growth.

11.   Roger Brown, *A First Language*, Penguin, Harmondsworth, 1976, Introduction.

12.   M.K. Halliday, *Learning How to Mean*, Edward Arnold, London, 1975. Susan K. Braunwald and Richard W. Brislin, 'The Diary Method Updated', in Elinor Ochs and Bambi Shieffelin, *Developmental Pragmatics*, Academic Press, New York, 1979, pp. 21–42. Roger Brown, *Psycholinguistics*, The Free Press, New York, 1970, p. 77.

13.   Sigmund Freud, 'Little Hans' (1909), *Standard Edition of the Collected Works*, 1959, vol. x, pp. 101–3.

14.   Jean Piaget, *The Language and Thought of the Child*, Kegan Paul, Trench and Trubner, London, 1926, p. 5: 'activities take place in complete freedom . . . no intervention takes place unless it is asked for . . . the groups are formed and then break up again without any interference on the part of the adult'. Vygotsky commented on this arrangement: 'the developmental uniformities established by Piaget apply to the given milieu . . . They are not laws of nature but historically and socially determined . . . Piaget observed children at play together in a particular kindergarten . . . Stern points out that in a . . . kindergarten in which there was more group activity . . . and . . . in the home children's speech tends to be predominantly social at a very early age'. L.S. Vygotsky, *Thought and Language*, MIT Press, Cambridge, Massachusetts, 1962.

15.   See Spender, *Man Made Language*, pp. 148–51, for a history of the grammatical artefact of 'man' used to represent the human race. See also Wendy Martyna, 'What Does "He" Mean? Use of the Generic Masculine', *Journal of Communications*, 28:1 (Winter 1978), pp. 131–8.

16.   Girls did not have to have brothers for them to be weighed against a masculine norm; but occasionally in developmental diaries written by mothers of only daughters there is the sense that the children were being taught to be women within an exclusively feminine sphere. For a classic comparison between brother and sister see Darwin, 'Biographical Sketch', pp. 289–90.

The Tidy House

17. Spender, *Man Made Language*, pp. 171–81. Nancy Chodorow, *Mothering: Psychoanalysis and the Reproduction of Gender*, University of California Press, Berkeley and Los Angeles, 1978, pp. 115–17; pp. 125–9.

18. Jean Piaget, *Language and Thought*, p. 5.

19. There are new and notable exceptions. See Margaret Boden, *Jean Piaget*, Penguin, Harmondsworth, 1979, in which the child is referred to as 'she'. For evidence of the real struggle of conscience that has led to this point, see Margaret Donaldson, *Children's Minds*, Fontana, 1978, p. 10, and Mina P. Shaughnessy, *Errors and Expectations*, Oxford University Press, New York, 1977, p. 4, note 1.

20. There are exceptions to this general organising principle. See William Labov, *Language in the Inner City*, University of Pennsylvania Press, 1972, p. 393. Carol Chomsky, *The Acquisition of Syntax in Children from 5–10*, MIT Press, Cambridge, Massachusetts, 1969. See also D. McNeill, *The Acquisition of Language*, Harper and Row, New York, 1970. But however much such work can tell us about the linguistic development of older children, it has to be explicitly rejected as evidence of a process that is *defined* as belonging to early development. See Clark, 'What's in a Word', pp. 67–8.

21. Chomsky, *Acquisition of Syntax*, pp. 102–11; p. 121.

22. C. Bereiter and S. Engelman, *Teaching Disadvantaged Children in the Pre-School*, Prentice Hall, New York, 1966. A. Jensen, 'Social Class and Verbal Learning', in Deutch *et al.* (eds.), *Social Class Race and Psychological Development*, Holt, Rhinehart and Winston, 1968. See W. Labov, 'The Logic of Non-Standard English', in *Language in Education*, Routledge and Kegan Paul for the Open University, London, 1972.

23. Marion Glastonbury, 'The Best Kept Secret: How Working Class Women Live and What They Know', *Women's Studies International Quarterly*, 2:2 (1979), pp. 171–83. Spender, *Man Made Language*, pp. 225–6.

24. Charles Read, 'Pre-School Children's Knowledge of English Phonology', *Harvard Educational Review*, 41:1 (February 1971), pp. 1–34. Carol Chomsky, 'Write Now, Read Later', *Childhood Education* (47), 1971, pp. 296–9. L.S. Vygotsky, 'The Prehistory of Written Language', *Mind in Society*, Harvard University Press, Cambridge, Massachusetts, 1978, pp. 105–19. There have been efforts made to categorise the errors children make when they write. Lester S. Golub, *Linguistic Structures and Deviations in Children's Written Sentences*, Center for Cognitive Learning, University of Wisconsin, 1970.

25. Harold and Connie Rosen, *The Language of Primary School Children*, Penguin, Harmondsworth, 1973, pp. 85–155; pp. 267–9. Carol Burgess *et al.*, *Understanding Children Writing*, Penguin, Harmondsworth, 1973.

26. Peter L. Berger and Thomas Luckmann, *The Social Construction of Reality*, Doubleday and Co., New York, 1966, pp. 121–35.

27. To be non-judgemental is the modern expression of the nineteenth-century spirit of naturalistic observation. See pp. 85–87.

28. Jessie Reid, *Breakthrough in Action*, Longmans, London, 1974, pp. 70–89. M.K. Halliday, ' "Breakthrough to Literacy": Foreward to the American edition,' in *Language as Social Semiotic*, Edward Arnold, London, 1978, pp. 205–10.

29. Glenda L. Bissex, *Gnys at Wrk: A Child Learns to Read and Write*, Harvard University Press, Cambridge, Massachusetts, pp. 43–4.

30. Many children in the school system between 1870 and the period when ideas about writing creatively became common currency in schools can never have seen 'I' upon the page. It would be impossible to discover if this made any difference to their

Notes

perception of themselves in relation to social reality, but it is likely that it did. For brief descriptions of the limited range of writing styles still encountered by children in schools, see *Times Educational Supplement*, 2 May 1980. See also Michael Armstrong (ed.), *The Monday Report: A Child's Eye View of School*, Chameleon Books in association with Writers and Readers, London, 1981. Douglas Barnes *et al.*, *Language, the Learner and the School*, Penguin, Harmondsworth, 1969, pp. 164–6.

31. Berger and Luckmann, *Social Construction of Reality*, p. 36.

32. Jack Goody, *Literacy in Traditional Societies*, Cambridge University Press, Cambridge, 1968, p. 62.

33. Maria Montessori, *The Formation of Man*, Theosophical Publishing House, Adyar, India, 1969, pp. 112–15; p. 118. Vygotsky, 'Prehistory of Written Language', pp. 105–6, p. 117. Writing should be taught so that it is 'necessary for something', said Vygotsky, commenting directly on Montessori's methods. 'If [it is] used only to write official greetings to the staff or whatever the teacher thinks up (and clearly suggests to them) then the exercise will be purely mechanical.' M.K. Halliday, Foreword, in David Mackay *et al.* (eds.), *Breakthrough to Literacy*, Longmans, London, 1978.

34. Vygotsky, 'Prehistory of Written Language', pp. 105–6.

35. Donaldson, *Children's Minds*, pp. 97–100.

36. Vygotsky, 'Prehistory of Written Language', p. 106.

37. Bissex, *Gnys at Wrk*, pp. 3–33; pp. 40–73.

38. That is, they offer a clear example of children using their own knowledge of spoken language in order to decide how to spell a word. Read 'Pre-School Children's Knowledge of English Phonology', pp. 6–21.

39. Vygotsky, *Thought and Language*, p. 98.

40. Vygotsky, *Thought and Language*, p. 99.

41. Vygotsky, *Thought and Language*, pp. 98–101.

42. Shaughnessy, *Errors and Expectations*, p. 79, p. 82.

43. Glastonbury, *The Best Kept Secret*.

44. Mary Sanchez and Barbara Kirshenblatt-Gimblett, 'Children's Traditional Speech Play and Child Language', in Barabara Kirshenblatt-Gimblett, *Speech Play*, University of Pennsylvania Press, 1976, p. 85, p. 91, pp. 102f.

45. Sanchez and Kirshenblatt-Gimblett, 'Children's Traditional Speech Play.' Karen Ann Watson Gegeo and Stephen T. Boggs, 'From Verbal Play to Talk Story: The Role of Routines in Speech Events among Hawaiian Children', in (eds.) Susan Ervin-Tripp and Claudia Mitchell Kernan, *Child Discourse*, Academic Press, New York, 1977, pp. 67f. Catherine Garvey, *Play*, Harvard University Press, Cambridge Massachusetts, 1977, pp. 59–76. Catherine Garvey, 'Play with Language and Speech', in (eds.) Susan Ervin Tripp and Claudia Mitchell Kernan, *Child Discourse*, pp. 27f.

46. L.S. Vygotsky, 'Play and Its Role in the Mental Development of the Child', *Mind in Society*, pp. 92–104. Garvey, *Play*, p. 91. Sigmund Freud, 'Creative Writers and Day Dreaming' (1908), *Standard Edition of the Collected Works*, Hogarth Press, London, 1959, vol. ix, p. 146. Elizabeth Barrett Browning, 'Glimpses into My Own Life and Literary Character', in *Hitherto Unpublished Poems and Stories* (2 vols.), The Bibliophile Society, Boston, 1914, vol. i, pp. 3–28. She describes her reading habits as a six-and seven-year-old, p. 8: 'it is worthy of remark that in a novel I carefully passed over all the passages which described CHILDREN'.

47. Edward Zigler *et al.*, 'Cognitive Challenge as a Factor in Children's Humour

The Tidy House

Appreciation', *Journal of Personality and Social Psychology*, 6:3, 1967, pp. 332–6. Thomas R. Schultz, 'Development of the Appreciation of Riddles', *Child Development*, 45 (1974), pp. 100–105. Norman M. Prentice and Robert E. Fatham, 'Joking Riddles', *Development Psychology*, 11 (1975), pp. 210–16. J. Kenneth Whitt and Norman M. Prentice, 'Cognitive Processes in the Development of Children's Enjoyment and Comprehension of Joking Riddles', *Development Psychology*, 13:1, pp. 29–136. I am grateful to Danielle M. Roemer and the extremely useful Bibliography to her thesis, for drawing my attention to these references. Danielle Marie Roemer, *A Social Interactional Analysis of Anglo Children's Folklore*, unpublished Ph.D thesis, University of Texas at Austin, 1977.

48. M.K. Halliday, 'The Significance of Bernstein's Work for Sociolinguistic Theory', *Language as Social Semiotic*, pp. 101–7, discusses Bernstein's work as an exception to this general trend.

49. Jonathan Culler, *The Pursuit of Signs*, Routledge and Kegan Paul, London, 1981, pp. 169–87.

50. Tiny Tears is the trade name of a doll that both weeps real tears and wets it knickers. It is manufactured by Pali Toys of Leicester.

51. Labov, *Language in the Inner City*, p. 359.

52. Henry Mayhew, *London Labour and the London Poor*, vol. 1, George Woodfall and Sons, London, 1851, p. 480.

53. Labov, *Language in the Inner City*, p. 364, p. 376, pp. 390–93.

54. It is not clear whether or not Carla's father had lost more than one pigeon and what precisely it was that had stopped him from competing with them. The transcripts show that whilst no one was particularly interested in her narrative, neither was Carla particularly concerned with forcing them to listen to her. She told a story that operated halfway between thinking aloud and recounting. Discussions of verbal narrative rarely take into account the moment by moment service that telling performs for the teller.

55. Labov, *Language in the Inner City*. Watson, Gegeo and Boggs, 'Verbal Play'. Louise Bates Ames, 'Children's Stories', *Genetic Psychological Monographs*, 73:2 (1966), pp. 337–96. E.G. Pitcher and Ernest Prelinger, *Children Tell Stories: An Analysis of Fantasy*, International Universities Press, New York, 1963.

56. Henry Mayhew, *London Labour and the London Poor*, vol. 2, Griffin Bohn and Co., London, 1861, p. 507.

57. Harvey Sacks, 'On the Analyzability of Stories by Children', in John J. Gumpertz and Dell Hymes, *Directions in Sociolinguistics*, Holt, Rhinehart and Winston, New York, 1972, p. 345.

58. Labov, *Language in the Inner City*, pp. 370–71. *The Pursuit of Signs*, pp. 184–7.

59. Sacks, 'Stories by Children', p. 345.

60. Jonathan Culler, *Structuralist Poetics*, Routledge and Kegan Paul, London, 1975, pp. 199–200.

61. The factors that prevent this particular manipulation of the text equally prevent the story from being recast in the future tense.

62. Garvey, *Play*, p. 92, for a description of children's lack of overt planning before starting imaginative play and their use of 'a repertoire of action sequences that can be indicated quite economically' so that play can commence without discussion.

63. Piaget, *Language and Thought of the Child*. Boden, *Jean Piaget*, pp. 55–9.

64. Vygotsky, *Thought and Language*, pp. 44–51, p. 149.

65. Vygotsky, *Thought and Language*, pp. 97–101.

66. And to some illiterate children. It is illuminating to read Mayhew's transcription of

his conversation with a twelve-year-old streetseller of ballads. This child had a perfect understanding of the function of written language and of the motivations of readers: 'I used to sing "The Red White and Blue", and "Mother Is the Battle Over" . . . At last the songs grew so stale people wouldn't listen to them, and as I can't read, I couldn't learn anymore, sir. My big brother and father used to learn me some, but I never could get enough of them for the streets'. Mayhew, *London Labour*, vol. 2, pp. 505–6. It would have been very easy to teach this child to read: she had the essential equipment – she knew what the process was all about. Jessie M. Reid, 'Learning to Think About Reading', *Educational Research* (9), 1966, pp. 56–62; Margaret M. Clark, *Young Fluent Readers*, Heinemann, London, 1976, pp. 105–6.

67. Gunther Kress, *Learning to Write*, Routledge and Kegan Paul, London, 1982.

5 SELF AND SOCIALISATION : THE LOST HISTORY OF WORKING-CLASS CHILDHOOD

(Throughout the notes to this chapter, the abbreviation PP stands for Parliamentary Papers Series.)

1. See Jean McCrindle and Sheila Rowbotham, *Dutiful Daughters*, Penguin, Harmondsworth, 1970, pp. 10–19; pp. 113–38; pp. 187–215. Winifred Foley, *A Child in the Forest*, BBC, London, 1973. Catherine Cookson, *Our Kate*, Macdonald, London, 1969. See Henry James, 'The Consciousness of Self', in *Principles of Psychology*, (2 vols.) Henry Holt and Co., New York, 1890, vol. i, pp. 291–401, especially p. 335 where he describes the child remembered by the adult as 'a foreign creature'.

2. Michael Anderson, *Family Structure in Nineteenth Century Lancashire*, Cambridge University Press, Cambridge, 1971.

3. The nineteenth-century children dealt with here were not considered by their interviewers to have strange ideas about the physical world, only a lack of knowledge about it: 'With regard to the ignorance of common objects of nature or things or places a little removed from their own narrow limit found in many, it is true that their hard working life has given them but little chance of enjoying or seeing such objects and places themselves; but that will perhaps be thought the more reason why they should be taught something about them.' PP 1864, xxii, p. 62.

4. Nancy Chodorow, *The Reproduction of Mothering: Psychoanalysis and the Sociology of Gender*, University of California Press, Berkeley and Los Angeles, 1978. Ann Oakley, *Housewife*, Penguin, Harmondsworth, 1974, pp. 95–96.

5. M.L. Kohn, 'Social Class and Parent–Child Relationships', in (ed.) Michael Anderson, *Sociology of the Family*, Penguin, Harmondsworth, 1971, pp. 323–38.

6. Chodorow, *Reproduction of Mothering*, pp. 179–80.

7. Mayhew, *London Labour and the London Poor*, George Woodfall and Son, London, 1851, vol. 1, p. 151; p. 481.

8. Mayhew, *London Labour*, vol. 1, p. 152, p. 480. PP 1863, xvii, p. 63, evidence of Sara Ann Davis; pp. 66–9, evidence of Esther Caroline Dutton, Ellen Ednay, Amelia Littlemore; p. 275, evidence of Jane White. PP 1864, xxii, p. 9, evidence of Martha Jane Slater; p. 88, evidence of Sarah Ann Wedge. PP 1867–8, xvii, p. 35, evidence of Sarah Wright. However, if a child worked in the same place as her father, her wages were handed over to him. PP 1863, xvii, p. 63.

9. Mayhew, *London Labour*, vol. 1, pp. 151–2. 'I used to go to school . . . mother took me away because the master whacked me . . . I didn't like him at all. What do

you think? He hit me three times, ever so hard across the face with his cane and made me go dancing downstairs, and when mother saw the marks on my cheek,she went to blow him up, but she couldn't see him – he was afraid. That's why I left school.'

10.   PP 1863, xviii, p. 113.

11.   Oakley, *Sociology of Housework*, p. 196.

12.   Oakley, *Sociology of Housework*, pp. 100–112.

13.   Mayhew, *London Labour*, vol. 1, p. 152.

14.   Mayhew, *London Labour*, vol. 1, p. 152, 'All my money I puts it in a club and draws it out to buy clothes with.' PP 1863, xviii, p. 66, 'we likes to have it in our clothes'; PP 1867–8 xvii, p. 351.

15.   Eileen Yeo and E.P. Thompson, *The Unknown Mayhew*, Penguin, Harmondsworth, 1973, p. 200, p. 213; PP 1863, xviii, p. 223; PP 1864, xxii, pp. 104–5; Mayhew, *London Labour*, vol. i, p. 151.

16.   Charles Darwin, 'A Biographical Sketch of an Infant', *Mind*, 2:7 (July 1977), pp. 285–94. Hippolyte Taine, 'The Acquisition of Language in Children', *Mind*, 2:6 (April 1877), pp. 252–9. James Mark Baldwin, *Mental Development in the Child and the Race*, Macmillan, New York, 1894, pp. 114–20; pp. 319–21. Jean Piaget, *The Child's Conception of the World*, Kegan Paul, Trench and Trubner, London, 1929, p. 130.

17.   Jacques Lacan, 'The Mirror Phase as Formative of the Function of the "I" ', *New Left Review*, 51, 1968, pp. 63–7. Roger Shattuck, *The Forbidden Experiment*, Farrar Straus and Giroux, New York, 1980, pp. 16–17.

18.   In some accounts of language development an adult formulation of children's activity and the accompanying imputation of intention to their utterances are described as providing them with a model of the conventional interpretation of their words that can be used like a mirror. In children's own invented formulations about the world – in play – they mirror the adult society; they imitate with the realistic distortions that the looking glass makes: transformations may take place the lines drawn by generation (children play at being older than they are), but rarely across sex boundaries. See, for example, John Dore, 'Conversational Acts and the Acquisition of Language', in Elinor Ochs and Bambi Shieffelin (eds.), *Developmental Pragmatics*, Academic Press, New York, 1979, pp. 339–72, especially p. 345. William A. Corsaro, 'Sociolinguistic Patterns in Adult Child Interaction', Ochs and Shieffelen, *Developmental Pragmatics*, pp. 373–89, especially pp. 338–9. Catherine Garvey, *Play*, Harvard University Press, Cambridge, Massachusetts, 1977, pp. 89–90.

19.   Children's Employment Commission (1862), First Report, PP 1863, xviii; Second Report, PP 1864, xxii; Third Report, PP 1864, xxii; Fourth Report, PP 1865, xx; Fifth Report, PP 1866, xxiv; Sixth Report, PP 1867, xvi. Commission on the Employment of Women and Children in Agriculture (1867), First Report, PP 1867–8, xvii. Henry Mayhew, *London Labour and the London Poor* (4 vols.), vol. 1, George Woodfall and Son, London, 1851; vol. 2, Griffin, Bohn and Co., London, 1861.

20.   Most of the mid-nineteenth-century children whose evidence is used in this chapter worked in what have been characterised as 'the smaller domestic industries'. Ivy Pinchbeck, *Women Workers and the Industrial Revolution*, Virago Press, London, 1981, pp. 202–39.

21.   For a historical narrative, see James Walvin, *A Child's World: A Social History of English Childhood 1800–1914*, Penguin, Harmondsworth, 1982, and for an account

of protective legislation, see Ivy Pinchbeck and Margaret Hewitt, *Children in English Society* (2 vols.), Routledge and Kegan Paul, London, 1973, vol. 2.

22. Brian Simon, *Studies in the History of Education*, Lawrence and Wishart, London, 1960, pp. 337–68. J.S. Hurt, *Elementary Schools and the Working Classes, 1860–1918*, Routledge and Kegan Paul, London, 1979.

23. PP 1863, xviii, pp. 337–8. Instructions from the Children's Employment Commissioners to the Assistant Commissioners, 10 April 1862: 'Throughout the whole of this inquiry you cannot too constantly bear in mind . . . that childhood is essentially the period of activity of the nutritive processes necessary to the growth and maturity of the body; that if at this period the kind and quantity of food necessary . . . be not supplied . . . if the comparatively tender and feeble frame be taxed til beyond its strength . . . if the day be consumed in labour . . . the whole system will sustain an injury which cannot be repaired at any subsequent stage of human life; and that above all, that childhood is no less essentially the period of the development of the mental faculties, on the culture and direction of which at this tender age the intellectual, moral and religious qualities and habits of the future almost wholly depend'.

24. Mayhew, *London Labour*, vol. 1, p. 151.

25. PP 1863, xviii, p. 259, evidence of Lucy Reed, seven years.

26. PP 1863, xviii, p. 71. 'This is a pale and at first sight rather wretched looking boy, partly no doubt from the marks of the small pox and poor clothing, with several of his teeth decayed . . . His manner however, though timid, is very winning, and he is only one of the many I have seen who, though wretchedly ignorant and uncared for, seem to want nothing but the opportunity of a better atmosphere, physical and social to grow up good and gentle hearted men and women.'

27. See note 5, p. 230, especially, Eve V. Clark, 'What's in a Word?' where diary studies dating from 1877 are cited to establish evidence for a particular notion within the area of semantic acquisition, pp. 77–8.

28. Cognitive and linguistic development is a much more accessible historical measure of a child's growth than is physical maturity – for in considering spoken language, the evidence lies trapped in the child's words on the page. For other measures of childhood, see Walvin, *Child's World*, pp. 12–13.

29. Margaret Emily Shore, *Journal of Emily Shore*, Kegan Paul, London, 1891, p. 40, entry for 30 March 1833. Mayhew, vol. i, p. 475: 'As to the opinions of the street children, I can say little. For the most part they have formed no opinions of anything beyond what affects their struggles for bread'; pp. 477–478: 'They often sell . . . little necklaces composed of red berries strung together upon thick thread, for dolls and children, but although I have asked several of them, I have never yet found one who collected the berries and made the necklaces themselves; neither have I met with a single instance in which the girl vendors knew the name of the berries thus used, nor indeed that they *were* berries. The invariable reply to my questions upon the subject has been that they ''are called necklaces''; that ''they are just as they sells 'em to us''; that they ''don't know whether they are made or whether they grow'' '.

30. Eileen Yeo and E.P. Thompson, *The Unknown Mayhew*, Penguin, Harmondsworth, 1973, p. 71. Elinor Ochs, 'Transcription as Theory', in Elinor Ochs and Bambi Schieffelin, *Developmental Pragmatics*, Academic Press, New York, 1979, pp. 43–72, especially p. 61: 'Strictly standard orthography should be avoided . . . a modified orthography (gonna/wanna, etc.) captures roughly the way in which a lexical item is pronounced'.

31. Mayhew, *London Labour*, vol. 2, p. 507.

32. Richard Rowe, *Life in the London Streets*, Nimmo and Bain, London, 1881, pp. 118–19.

33. This was J.E. White of New College, Oxford, Barrister at Law. See, for instance, PP 1867, xvi, pp. 115–16 on the occasion of his interviewing Ellen Pearl, labourer's wife of Monks Soham, Suffolk. Ellen Pearl remarked to White that 'my girl Alice went dropping beans with her father . . . when she was 4 years old. We particularly marked that because he had to carry her when she first began to learn.' She then turned to Alice and said, 'You remember when you were a little dawdy child, don't you?' [Alice said no.] White offered 'dotty' to replace dawdy and also suggested 'or like Scotch "dawtit", i.e. fondled?' He had a fine ear for the nuances of dialect.

34. Mayhew, *London Labour*, vol. 1, p. 151. Mayhew *started* his interview with this conventional reaction; he ended up seeing and hearing a quite different child to the abject, ageless, figure of pity he at first contemplated. See also Jacob Bronowski, *The Ascent of Man*, BBC, London, 1974, pp. 425.

35. Mayhew, *London Labour*, vol. 1, p. 477; vol. 2, p. 505, 'her hair was tidily dressed'; vol. 2, p. 506, 'her head with the hair as rough as tow'. This mid-Victorian preoccupation was used by George Eliot as the device by which Maggie Tulliver's parents were able to discuss her femininity in *The Mill on the Floss*. George Eliot, *The Mill on the Floss*, Penguin, Harmondsworth, 1979, Book 1, chapter 2. See also PP 1861, viii, Report of the Select Committee on the Education of Destitute Children, p. 10.

36. Mayhew, *London Labour*, vol. 2, p. 506.

37. PP 1864, xxii, p. 94.

38. PP 1864, xxii, pp. 104–5.

39. The material he published in the *Morning Chronicle* is nearly all reproduced in Yeo and Thompson, *Unknown Mayhew*.

40. Mayhew, *London Labour*, vol. 1, p. 480.

41. Chaperonage consisted of knowing where the child was; expecting her back at certain times; sending her out in the company of an older girl or younger siblings; having her work near home; not allowing her to go out of her immediate neighbourhood; not allowing her out except when working; expecting her to stay at home on non-working days. See Mayhew, *London Labour*, vol. 1, p. 152; vol. 2, pp. 505–6; p. 507. See Harriet Wilson and G.W. Herbert, *Parents and Children in the Inner City*, Routledge and Kegan Paul, London, 1978, pp. 168–79 for a general description of chaperonage provided by modern working-class parents. See also John and Elizabeth Newson, *Seven Years Old in the Home Environment*, George Allen and Unwin, London, 1976, pp. 100–101 on the chaperonage of female children: 'children who are kept under constant surveillance must inevitably come under consistently greater pressure towards conformity with adult standards and values'.

42. Mayhew, *London Labour*, vol. 1, p. 480.

43. Peter Coveney, *Poor Monkey: The Child in Literature*, Rockcliff, London, 1957, pp. 150–68.

44. Mayhew, *London Labour*, vol. 1, p. 151, p. 480; vol. 2, p. 506.

45. PP 1864, xxii, p. 88.

46. PP 1867, xvi, pp. 115–16; PP 1863, xvii, p. 110. See Newson, *Seven Years Old*, pp. 404–5: 'One of the means by which the ordinary child achieves a sense of personal identity is through his store of memories going back into his own past

Notes

. . . the child . . . has them repaired, added to and embroidered upon in everyday conversation with his family.'

47. Much recently written history of childhood has been designed to demonstrate that, in mid-twentieth-century terms, the idea of childhood did not exist until very recently and that it is, in fact, a social construct. Philippe Ariès, *Centuries of Childhood*, Penguin, Harmondsworth, 1979. Lloyd de Mause, *The History of Childhood*, Psychohistory Press, New York, 1974. Shulamith Firestone, *The Dialectic of Sex*, The Women's Press, London, 1979, pp. 73–90. Michele Barrett, *Women's Oppression Today*, Verso, London, 1980. The popularised version of this history, which implies that somehow in the recent past people just did not recognise childhood as a state either of body or of mind, is argued against cogently by Peter Fuller, 'Pictorial Essay: Uncovering Childhood', in (ed.) Martin Hoyles, *Changing Childhood*, Writers and Readers, London, 1979, pp. 71–108, and is flatly contradicted by working-class children like these, who partly *knew* themselves through an observation of their own physical growth.

48. PP 1864, xxii, p. 139.

49. PP 1863, xviii, p. 186; PP 1864, xxii, p. 175.

50. PP 1863, xviii, pp. 93–4.

51. PP 1863, xvii, p. 70; Mayhew, *London Labour*, vol. 1, p. 481.

52. For a description of 'honeypots', and 'kiss-in-the-ring', see Iona and Peter Opie, *Children's Games in Street and Playground*, Oxford University Press, London, 1969, pp. 243–5; pp. 201–2.

53. PP 1863, xvii, p. 94, p. 200; PP 1867, p. 132, p. 86.

54. PP 1864, xxii, p. 8; p. 175; pp. 104–5, p. 139.

55. Many adults working with the latter group of children spontaneously mentioned their need for movement and play. PP 1863, xviii, p. 244: 'As the days go on the girls seem to want a bit of play.' See also PP 1864, xxii, p. 99; p. 205.

56. Many parents noted the premature look of old age of their working children: 'they don't look like children'. PP 1863, xviii, p. 186; p. 168. PP 1867–8, xvii, pp. 317–19: 'lads that do go to work every day often get to look like old men before their time'. PP 1864, xxii, p. 136: 'I should not like my little boy there, now five to begin before 9 . . . he is but a little mossel'.

57. Elias Mendelievich, *Children at Work*, International Labour Office, Geneva, 1979, pp. 44–9.

58. Ann Oakley, *Sociology of Housework*, Martin Robertson, London, 1974, p. 173. L. Rainwater, R.P. Coleman, Gerald Handel, *Workingman's Wife*, Oceana Publications, New York, 1959, p. 89, p. 98. John and Elizabeth Newson, *Seven Years Old in the Home Environment*, George Allen and Unwin, 1976, p. 259.

59. PP 1867–8, xvii, pp. 226–7.

60. PP 1864, xxii, pp. 104–5.

61. Mayhew, *London Labour*, vol. 1, p. 152: 'I ain't got no father, he's a father in law. No; mother ain't married again – he's a father in law.'

62. Yeo and Thompson, *Unknown Mayhew*, p. 209; p. 262.

63. Pinchbeck, *Women Workers*, pp. 1–2, p. 202. Ann Oakley, *Housewife*, p. 39: 'that women and children should, in any case, support themselves through their labour was the general working class view at the time' – in the period 1750–1841.

64. Oakley, *Housewife*, pp. 192–3.

65. Mayhew, *London Labour*, vol. 1, p. 151; p. 506. PP 1863, xvii, p. 113; p. 9.

66. Newson, *Seven Years Old*, pp. 248–9, Evelyn Sharp, *The London Child*, John Lane at the Bodley Head, London, 1927, pp. 22–3. Report of the Select Committee on

the Education of Destitute Children, PP 1861, vii, p. 166, where the care of small children by girls 'hired for the purpose' is spoken of as extremely common in working-class areas.

67. Mayhew, *London Labour*, vol. 1, p. 151. One child spontaneously mentioned helping her mother with housework: 'When I go home now I am not tired. I help mother wash up.' PP 1864, xxii, p. 9, evidence of Martha Jane Slater.

68. Mayhew, *London Labour*, vol. 2, p. 505.

69. Joy Parr, *Labouring Children*, Croom Helm, London, 1980, pp. 14–26. Alexander Paterson, *Across the Bridges*, Edward Arnold, London, 1914, p. 22.

70. Mayhew, *London Labour*, vol. 1, p. 151, p. 152; vol. 2, p. 506.

71. Chodorow, *Reproduction of Mothering*, pp. 174. Newson, *Seven Years Old*, pp. 143–6.

72. Chodorow, *Reproduction of Mothering*, p. 176.

73. Chodorow, *Reproduction of Mothering*, pp. 111–29.

74. Mayhew, *London Labour*, vol. 1, p. 152.

75. A group of Plymouth children were observed watching prostitutes being taken to an examination centre under the operation of the Contagious Diseases Act. One little girl was heard to remark that prostitutes got more money than her mother 'who went out washing. My mother is out now . . . and will be tired to death'. Judith Walkowitz, 'The Making of an Outcast Group: Prostitutes and Working Women in Nineteenth Century Plymouth and Southampton', in Martha Vicinus (ed.), *A Widening Sphere*, Methuen, 1977, pp. 72–93, especially p. 88.

76. John Burnett, *Useful Toil*, Penguin, Harmondsworth, 1977, p. 217.

77. McCrindle and Rowbotham, *Dutiful Daughters*, p. 4. ' "I hate my mother" . . . Maggie Fuller is expressing a bitterness about her mother which is shared by most of the older women . . . We were surprised by this hostility'. Marion Glastonbury, 'The Best Kept Secret: How Working Class Women Live and What They Know', *Women's Studies International Quarterly*, 2:2 (1979), pp. 171–83. On p. 177 she comments thus on the quotation from *Dutiful Daughters* above: 'In contrast to women whose recollections have been recorded in interviews, those who set out to write at length about their lives usually do so in a spirit of homage to their mothers. Autobiography may be undertaken in a payment of a debt of gratitude'.

78. Kathleen Woodward, *Jipping Street*, Virago Press, London, 1983, p. 6.

79. Woodward, *Jipping Street*, p. 18.

80. Harlen Howard, '*No Charge*', recorded by Melba Montgomery on Elektra, New York, 1974; by Shirley Caesar on Pye, London, 1975; by J.J. Barrie, on the Chopper Label © FMI Music Publishing Co., London, 1976. I am grateful to Simon Frith for finding me all these versions and for originally pointing out what the phrase 'no charge' in Carla's text referred to.

81. Mayhew, *London Labour*, vol. 1, p. 151.

82. L.S. Vygotsky, 'Play and Its Role in the Mental Development of the Child', *Mind in Society*, Harvard University Press, Cambridge, Massachusetts, 1978, pp. 92–104, especially pp. 94–5: 'what passes unnoticed by the child in real life becomes a rule of behaviour in play'.

83. David Rubinstein, *Victorian Homes*, David and Charles, Newton Abbot, 1974, pp. 110–55. Octavia Hill, *Homes of the London Poor*, Macmillan, London, 1875.

84. Ann Oakley, *Housewife*, Penguin, Harmondsworth, 1974, p. 54: 'Only from . . . [the second half of the nineteenth century] did the working class family acquire the idea of a dwelling place as a home, composed of different rooms with different

functions.' The watercress seller's evidence (see p. 113) suggests either that the process took place earlier than this (she was interviewed in the winter of 1849–50) or that the idea of a home did not depend on its material arrangements. See also Yeo and Thompson, *The Unknown Mayhew*, pp. 259–61; p. 314.

85. Marion Bowley, *Housing and the State*, George Allen and Unwin, London, 1947, pp. 94–131. John Burnett, *A Social History of Housing*, Methuen, London, 1980, pp. 215–43.

86. Bowley, *Housing and the State*, pp. 1–10. Rubinstein, *Victorian Homes*, pp. 109–87.

87. Jacques Donzelot, *The Policing of Families*, Random House, New York, 1979, pp. 40–45. Margaret Leonora Eyles, *The Woman in the Little House*, Grant Richards, London, 1922. Anna Davin, 'Imperialism and Motherhood', *History Workshop Journal*, 5 (Spring 1978), pp. 9–65.

88. Gauldie, *Cruel Habitations*, p. 223.

6 THE TIDY HOUSE OF FICTION : SEX AND STORIES, GENDER AND LANGUAGE

1. Valerie Walkerdine, 'Sex, Power and Pedagogics', *Screen Education*, 38 (Spring 1981), pp. 14–24. 'It is the relation between the domestic and the pedagogic and the way in which women signify as mothers and teachers, taking positions of power within those practices which provides the space for the early success of girls' (p. 23).

2. On the day the tape recordings represent, I did not allow all the children to exercise this choice.

3. John and Elizabeth Newson, *Seven Years Old in the Home Environment*, George Allen and Unwin, London, 1976, pp. 113–15.

4. Ruth Manning-Sanders, *Tripple-Trapple*, BBC, London, 1973.

5. Robin Lakoff, *Language and Women's Place*, Harper and Row, New York, 1975, pp. 3–19.

6. Carol Edelsky, 'Acquisition of an Aspect of Communicative Competence: Learning What It Means to Talk Like a Lady', in Susan Ervin-Tripp and Claudia Mitchell Kernan, *Child Discourse*, Academic Press, New York, 1977, pp. 225f.

7. Glenda L. Bissex, *Gnys at Wrk: A Child Learns to Read and Write*, Harvard University Press, Cambridge, Massachusetts, 1980, pp. 110–11.

8. Lottie wrote her story in collaboration with her thirteen-year-old cousin, though the original idea was hers. She was the adopted child of a small village shopkeeping family that consisted of a mother and an aunt. S. Levinstein, 'Children's Stories', *Paidologist*, 5:1 (February 1903), pp. 14–20.

9. Lakoff, *Language and Women's Place*, pp. 43–50.

10. Dale Spender, *Man Made Language*, Routledge and Kegan Paul, London, 1980, pp. 8–12, pp. 145–56. Wendy Martyna, 'Beyond the "He/Man" Approach: The Case for Non-Sexist Language', *Signs*, 5:3 (Spring 1980), pp. 482–93.

11. Edelsky, 'Talking Like a Lady', p. 228. See Spender, *Man Made Language*, p. 34. Newson, *Seven Years Old*, pp. 366–70. This is not to deny that in many circumstances little girls are subject to overt teaching on this matter: 'To Day I bronunced a/ word which should never/ come out of a ladys lips it was/ that I caled John a Impu-/dent Bitch and afterwards told/me that I should never say/ it even in a joke'. Frank Sidgwick, *The Complete Marjory Fleming*, Sidgwick and Jackson, London, 1934, pp. 50–51; it is rather that we need to know what children observe in the real world, not what they believe the contents of adult intentions are.

12. Spender, *Man Made Language*, pp. 8–12.

13. Martyna, 'Beyond the "He/Man" Approach', p. 489.

14. Bruno Bettelheim, *The Uses of Enchantment*, Penguin, Harmondsworth, 1978, pp. 6–11.

15. Sandra M. Gilbert and Susan Gubar, *The Madwoman in the Attic*, Yale University Press, New Haven and London, 1979, pp. 37–41.

16. Andrea Dworkin, *Woman Hating*, E.P. Dutton, New York, 1974, pp. 34–49.

17. Private communication from Ladybird Books of Loughborough, Leicestershire. I would like to express my thanks to Mr Vernon Mills, the editorial director, for providing me with these sales figures.

18. Alison Lurie, *Clever Gretchen and Other Forgotten Folktales*, Thomas Y. Crowell, New York, 1980. Ethel Johnson Phelps, *The Maid of the North: Feminist Folktales from Around the World*, Holt Rhinehart and Winston, New York, 1981.

19. Ann Oakley, *From Here to Maternity: Becoming a Mother*, Penguin, Harmondsworth, 1981, p. 6.

20. Michele Barrett, *Women's Oppression Today*, Verso, London, 1980, pp. 202–4 for the conceptualisation of the 'family' within recent history.

21. Nancy Chodorow, *The Reproduction of Mothering: Psychoanalysis and the Sociology of Gender*, University of California Press, Berkeley, 1978, p. 142. Ann Oakley, *Women Confined: Towards a Sociology of Childbirth*, Martin Robertson, London, 1980, p. 289.

22. Sigmund Freud, 'Symbolism in Dreams' (1916), *Standard Edition of the Collected Works*, Hogarth Press, London, 1963, vol. xv, pp. 149–69.

23. Erik H. Erikson, *Childhood and Society*, W.W. Norton and Co., New York, 1963, pp. 97–108. See also Kate Millett, *Sexual Politics*, Virago Press, London, 1977, pp. 210–20; and also Mark Poster, *Critical Theory of the Family*, Seabury Press, New York, 1978, p. 76.

24. Sylvia Ashton Warner, *Teacher*, Virago, London, 1980, pp. 36–38.

25. Spender, *Man Made Language*, pp. 181–182. Florence Rush, *The Best Kept Secret: The Sexual Abuse of Children*, Prentice Hall, New Jersey, 1980, p. 143.

26. James W. Fernandez, 'The Mission of Metaphor in Expressive Culture', *Current Anthropology*, 15:2 (June 1974), pp. 119–33. I am grateful to Elizabeth Warnock Fernea and Sabra Weber for drawing my attention to the distinctions made between symbol and metaphor in some anthropological inquiry.

27. Spender, *Man Made Language*, pp. 54–8. Adrienne Rich, *Of Woman Born*, Virago Press, London, 1977. Ann Oakley, *The Sociology of Housework*, Martin Robertson, London, 1974, pp. 166–80. See page 221 note 4.

28. Marion Glastonbury, 'The Best Kept Secret: How Working Class Women Live and What They Know', *Women's Studies International Quarterly*, 2:2 (1979), p. 178. Kathleen Woodward, *Jipping Street*, Virago Press, London, 1983, p. 7.

29. This portion of the text was written on Thursday when there was no tape recorder running on the children's table. It is possible that there was a now missing page that explains the sudden transition from 'So when Jamie had her – ' to 'Carl's brother was called Darren'.

30. Gaston Bachelard, *The Poetics of Space*, Orion Press, New York, 1964.

31. Gilbert and Gubar, *Madwoman*.

32. On the terrifying poetics of the cellar, see Kate Millett, *The Basement: Meditations on a Human Sacrifice*, Simon and Schuster, New York, 1979, pp. 19–21.

Notes

33. Elizabeth Barrett Browning, 'The Lost Bower', *The Poetical Works of Elizabeth Barrett Browing*, Houghton Mifflin Co., Boston, 1974, pp. 149–55.

34. George Eliot, *The Mill on the Floss*, Penguin, Harmondsworth, 1979, Book v, Chapter i, 'Red Deeps'. Mary Wollstonecraft, *Mary: A Fiction, and the Wrongs of Woman*, Oxford University Press, London, 1976, pp. 9–11. Ellen Moers, *Literary Women*, The Women's Press, London, 1978, pp. 254–7.

35. It should be pointed out here that a great deal of the children's interaction with us that day was in the half-serious form of joking play. They were receiving rather more adult attention than was usual in the normal course of things and on several occasions were clearly practising the formulae of adult interchange. At the basis of this reaction was their unspoken acknowledgement of the fact that we took their story seriously. They also attempted the style when they were on their own, as in their dismissal of *The Secret Garden* as 'boring' (TH tapes: p. 169). What I think they were doing here is playing at television book programmes.

36. Coleridge Papers, Humanities Research Center, University of Texas at Austin; Mary Elizabeth Coleridge, Journal, vol. 2, entry for 29 March 1873.

37. Transcribing Carla's first contribution, I typed 'House' for 'Houses' and labelled the cover of the book I made for her 'The Tidy House'. She did not comment on this and, from the Tuesday morning of the week in question, that is how the story was always referred to, by the children and by me.

38. Oakley, *Sociology of Housework*, pp. 166–180.

39. Bachelard, *Poetics of Space*, p. 6.

40. Gardner B. Taplin, *The Life of Elizabeth Barrett Browning*, Yale University Press, New Haven, 1957, pp. 1–43.

41. Jacques Donzelot, *The Policing of Families*, Random House, New York, 1979, pp. 40–45.

42. Ivy Pinchbeck, *Women Workers in the Industrial Revolution*, Virago Press, London, 1981, pp. 306–316. Oakley, *Housewife*, pp. 43–59. Wanda Fraiken Neff, *Victorian Working Women*, Columbia University Press, New York, 1929, pp. 83–4; pp. 247–52.

7 FLOWER LADY : THE END

1. Richard Hughes, *A High Wind in Jamaica* (1929), Triad Granada, London, 1977, p. 85.

2. Richard M. Jones, *Fantasy and Feeling in Education*, Penguin, Harmondsworth, London, 1972, pp. 192–219.

3. Ruth H. Weir, *Language in the Crib*, Mouton, The Hague, 1962. Courtney B. Cazden, 'Play with Language and Meta-linguistic Awareness: One Dimension of Language Experience', in (ed.) Jerome Bruner, *Play: Its Role in Development and Evolution*, Basic Books, New York, 1976, pp. 603–8.

4. The translation of Carla's diary entry of September 1975 into Flower Lady (June/July 1976) is an extremely clear example of the way in which time affects the use children make of reality in their writing. See Michael Armstrong, *Closely Observed Children: The Diary of a Primary Classroom*, Chameleon Books in association with Writers and Readers, London, 1980, p. 11, p. 19.

5. Glastonbury, 'Best Kept Secret', p. 178. Jean McCrindle and Sheila Rowbotham, *Dutiful Daughters*, p. 363. Jane Humphries, 'Class Struggle and the Persistence of the Working-Class Family,' *Cambridge Journal of Economics*, 1 (1977), pp. 255–6.

The Tidy House

APPENDIX 1

1. I have been unable to find out what this word – or sound – means – if anything.
2. That is, Richard wanted to listen to a pre-recorded story on the headphone set and as he knew it was already being used was actually telling me that he wanted to hang around the table where the girls were working. Clive King, *Stig of the Dump*, Puffin Books, Penguin, Harmondsworth, 1963.
3. This was not a rude rejoinder on my part. As it was quite close to dinner-time I was telling him to pack away the things he had been using that morning.
4. This obviously refers to a conversation the children were having before the tape recorder was placed on their table.
5. Carla must have been watching one of the others absent-mindedly scratching her leg, or something like that. The oblique reference at the end of this piece of dialogue is to the fact that human bodies are asymmetrical.
6. The children laughed because they thought this accurately funny as a representation of infantile language.
7. This is an imitation of adult language and attitude. In fact they did want to have the paper go as fast as possible because they enjoyed the idea of writing in quantity.
8. This is Lisa's first diplomatic approach of the day. She obviously found a real reason for approaching the others, for Carla had borrowed the square of card on which the children computed their tables. But Melissa quite effectively excluded Lisa by discussing the matter with Carla before Carla could reply to her.
9. That is, the tables square.
10. Carla meant driving lessons.
11. The idea of *intention* in the construction of children's written plots retreats even further when it is considered that but for this casual question on my part 'The Tidy House' may have taken a quite different direction.
12. That is, the bound volumes of 'The Tidy House'.
13. The headmaster of this school ran a fiction library that operated separately from class fiction libraries and the library collection of non-fiction books.
14. The card shows a formal arrangement of wedding photographs hanging on a wall.
15. Hits that contain the phrase 'automatic that's my baby' have only come out in the last couple of years, so it is not clear what the source of this quotation is. I am indebted to Simon Frith for this information.
16. *Shaker-Maker*, Ideal Toys of Reading, was a manufactured activity – very popular at the time – that consisted of a series of moulds in which plaster of paris could be shaken to produce figures of animals, etc. The phrase could also have a source in Mud's 'Shake it Down', a hit that summer.
17. On Carla's drawing of the wedding photograph (which she calls a painting here – most of the children in the room were painting) there is a tiny drawing of a price tag. The children evidently believed that a full luxuriant moustache was as much male equipment for a wedding as a new suit. She took Lindie's criticism seriously and improved the appearance of the one on the face of her bridegroom.
18. In some places the children were as unclear about the details of their plot as we, the readers, were.
19. That is, his aunt in America is called Dot.
20. This very confused recounting on my part can only be put down to the white heat of the classroom day – and the constant attention that needs to bestowed on all members of it, all the time.
21. The word Lindie omitted here was 'knitter' – 'a fast knitter'.

22. The children obviously all knew this consolatory saying. See p. 221, note 4.
23. 'Nobbler': one who tampers with a racing animal in order to impede its performance.
24. I must have been wearing a lot of navy blue that day.
25. This was the high summer of the platform sole. No little girl would be willingly caught dead in a pair of flat-heeled sandals.
26. Lisa's second diplomatic approach (though there may have been others at dinner-time). Whatever happened after school, the difference was made up by Thursday morning, when Lisa wrote her first and only portion of the text.

BIBLIOGRAPHY

1 BOOKS AND ARTICLES

Adam, Helen Douglas, *The Elfin Pedlar and Tales Told by Pixie Pool*, with a foreword by the Rev. John A. Hutton, D.D. Putnams, New York, 1924.

Ames, Louise Bates, 'Children's Stories', *Genetic Psychological Monographs*, 73:2 (1966), pp. 337–96.

Anderson, Michael, *Family Structure in Nineteenth Century Lancashire*, Cambridge University Press, Cambridge, 1971.

Anderson, Michael (ed.), *Sociology of the Family*, Penguin, Harmondsworth, 1971.

Aries, Philippe, *Centuries of Childhood*, Penguin, Harmondsworth, 1979.

Armstrong, Michael, *Closely Observed Children: The Diary of a Primary Classroom*, Chameleon Books in association with Writers and Readers, London, 1980.

Armstrong Michael (ed.), *The Monday Report: A Child's Eye View of School*, Chameleon Books in association with Writers and Readers, London, 1981.

Ashford, Daisy, *The Young Visiters, or Mr Salteena's Plan*, with a preface by J.M. Barrie, Chatto and Windus, London, 1919.

Aspinwall, A., *Lady Bessborough and Her Family Circle*, John Murray, London, 1940.

Bachelard, Gaston, *The Poetics of Space*, Orion Press, New York, 1964.

Baldwin, James Mark, *Mental Development in the Child and the Race*, the Macmillan Company, New York, 1894.

Barnes, Douglas et al., *Language, the Learner and the School*, Penguin, Harmondsworth, 1969.

Barnes, Earl, 'Methods of Studying Children', *The Paidologist*, 1 (April 1899), pp. 9–17.

Barnes, Earl, 'Young Children's Stories', *The Paidologist*, 5:1 (February 1903), pp. 17–21.

Barrett, Michèle, *Women's Oppression Today*, Verso, London, 1980.

Bede, Elbert, *Fabulous Opal Whiteley*, Binfords and Mort, Portland, Oregon, 1954.

Bedell, Madelon, *The Alcotts: Portrait of a Family*, Clarkson N. Potter, New York, 1980.

Bell, Betty Boyd, *Circus: A Girl's Own Story*, (ed.) Janet Mabie, Brewer Warren and Putnam, New York, 1931.

Belotti, Elena Gianini, *Little Girls*, Writers and Readers, London, 1975.

Bereiter C. and Engelman S., *Teaching Disadvantaged Children in the Pre-School*, Prentice Hall, New York, 1966.

Berger, John, *Permanent Red: Essays in Seeing*, Writers and Readers, London, 1979.

Berger, Joseph and Elizabeth, *Small Voices*, Paul S. Eriksson, New York, 1966.

247

Berger Peter L. and Luckmann, Thomas, *The Social Construction of Reality*, Doubleday and Co., New York, 1966.

Bernstein, Basil, 'Education Cannot Compensate for Society', in *Language in Education*, Routledge and Kegan Paul, London, 1972.

Bettelheim, Bruno, *The Uses of Enchantment*, Penguin, Harmondsworth, 1978.

Bettelheim, Bruno and Zelan, Karen, *On Learning to Read: The Child's Fascination with Meaning*, Knopf, New York, 1982.

Bissex, Glenda L., *Gnys at Wrk: A Child Learns to Read and Write*, Harvard University Press, Cambridge, Massachusetts, 1980.

Boden, Margaret A., *Jean Piaget*, Fontana, London, 1979.

Boulton, Jane, *Opal*, Macmillan, New York, 1976.

Bowie, Janetta, *Penny Buff*, Arrow, London, 1978.

Bowley, Marion, *Housing and the State*, George Allen and Unwin, London, 1947.

Bradburne, Elisabeth, *Opal Whiteley: The Unsolved Mystery*, Putnam, London, 1962.

Braunwald Susan R. and Breslin, Richard W., 'The Diary Method Updated', in Elinor Ochs and Bambi S. Schieffelin, *Development Pragmatics*, Academic Press, New York, 1979, pp. 21–42.

Bronowski, Jacob, *The Ascent of Man*, BBC, London, 1973.

Brown, John, *Marjorie Fleming: A Sketch*, Edinburgh, 1863.

Brown, John, *Marjorie Fleming: A Sketch, Being the Paper Entitled 'Pet Marjorie: A Story of Child Life Fifty Years Ago'*, Edinburgh, 1863.

Brown, Mary, and Precious, Norman, *The Integrated Day in the Primary School,*, Ward Lock Educational, London, 1968.

Brown, Roger, *Psycholinguistics*, The Free Press, New York, 1970.

Brown, Roger, *A First Language*, Penguin, Harmondsworth, 1976.

Browning, Elizabeth Barrett, *The Poetical Works*, Houghton Mifflin Co., Boston, 1974.

Browning, Elizabeth Barrett, 'Glimpses into My Own Life and Literary Character', in *Hitherto Unpublished Poems and Stories* (2 vols.), The Bibliophile Society, Boston, 1914, vol. I, pp. 3–28.

Burgess, Carol, *et al.*, *Understanding Children Writing*, Penguin, Harmondsworth, 1973.

Burnett, Frances Hodgson, *The One I Knew Best of All*, Frederick Warne and Co., London, 1893.

Burnett, John, *Useful Toil*, Penguin, Harmondsworth, London, 1977.

Burnett, John, *A Social History of Housing, 1815–1970*, Methuen, London, 1980.

Campbell, Robin, and Wales, Roger, 'The Study of Language Acquisition', in (ed.), John Lyons *New Horizons in Linguistics*, Penguin, London, 1970.

Carpenter, Joseph Estlin, *The Life and Work of Mary Carpenter*, Macmillan, London, 1881.

'Carroll, Lewis', *The Rectory Magazine*, University of Texas Press, Austin, 1975.

Cazden, Courtney B., 'The Neglected Situation in Child Language Research and Education', in (ed.) Frederick Williams, *Language and Poverty*, Markham, Chicago, 1970, pp. 80–101.

Cazden, Courtney B., 'Play with Language and Meta-linguistic Awareness: One Dimension of Language Experience', in (ed.) Jerome Bruner, *Play: Its Role in Development and Evolution*, Basic Books, New York, 1976, pp. 603–608.

Cheney, Ednah D., *Louisa May Alcott: Her Life, Letters and Journals*, Roberts Brothers, Boston, 1889.

Chipolla, Carlo M., *Literacy and Development in the West*, Penguin, Harmondsworth, 1969.

Chodorow, Nancy, *The Reproduction of Mothering: Psychoanalysis and the Sociology of Gender*, University of California Press, Berkeley and Los Angeles, 1978.

Bibliography

Chomsky, Carol, *The Acquisition of Syntax in Children from 5-10*, MIT Press, Cambridge, Massachusetts, 1969.

Cicourel, Aaron V., *Language Use and School Performance*, Academic Press, New York, 1974.

Clark, Eve V., 'What's in a Word? On the Child's Acquisition of Semantics in the First Language', in (ed.) Moore, T.E., *Cognitive Development and the Acquisition of Language*, Academic Press, New York, 1973, pp. 65–110.

Margaret M. Clark, *Young Fluent Readers*, Heinemann, London, 1976.

Clark, W.R., *Little Charlie's Life: By Himself*, Saunders, Otley and Co., London, 1868.

Clemens, Samuel, *Mark Twain's Autobiography*, P.F. Collier and Son, New York, 1925.

Conklin, Hilda, *Poems by a Little Girl*, Stokes, New York, 1920.

Cookson, Catherine, *Our Kate*, Macdonald, London, 1969.

Cosaro, William A., 'Sociolinguistic Patterns in Adult Child Interaction', in (eds.) Elinor Ochs and Bambi S. Shieffelin, *Developmental Pragmatics*, Academic Press, New York, 1979, pp. 373–89.

Coveney, Peter, *Poor Monkey: The Child in Literature*, Rockliff, London, 1957.

Craig, Eleanor, *P.S. Your Not Listening*, New American Library, New York, 1973.

Creighton, Ellen R.C., *Ellen Buxton's Journal, 1860–1864*, Geoffrey Bles, London, 1967.

Creighton, Ellen R.C., *A Family Sketch Book a Hundred Years Ago*, Geoffrey Bles, London, 1964.

Culler, Jonathan, *Structuralist Poetics*, Routledge and Kegan Paul, London, 1975.

Culler, Jonathan, *The Pursuit of Signs*, Routledge and Kegan Paul, London, 1981.

Darwin, Charles, 'A Biographical Sketch of an Infant', *Mind*, 2:7 (July 1877), pp. 285–94.

David, Miriam E., *The State, the Family and Education*, Routledge and Kegan Paul, London, 1980.

Davin, Anna, 'Imperialism and Motherhood', *History Workshop Journal*, 5 (Spring 1978), pp. 9–65.

de la Mare, Walter, *Early One Morning in the Spring*, Macmillan, New York, 1935.

Dennison, George, *The Lives of Children*, Penguin, Harmondsworth, 1972.

Dinesen, Betsy, *Rediscovery*, The Women's Press, London, 1981, pp. 31–6.

Donaldson, Margaret, *Children's Minds*, Fontana, 1978.

Donzelot, Jacques, *The Policing of Families*, Random House, New York, 1979.

Dore, John, 'Conversational Acts and the Acquisition of Language', in (eds.) Elinor Ochs and Bambi S. Shieffelin, *Developmental Pragmatics*, Academic Press, New York, 1979, pp. 339–72.

Drabble, Margaret, *Jerusalem the Golden*, Penguin, Harmondsworth, 1969.

Dworkin, Andrea, *Woman Hating*, E.P. Dutton, New York, 1974.

Edelsky, Carol, 'Acquisition of an Aspect of Communicative Competence: Learning What It Means to Talk Like a Lady', in (eds.) Susan Ervin Tripp and Claudia Mitchell Kernan, *Child Discourse*, Academic Press, New York, 1977.

Edgeworth, Maria, *Tales of Fashionable Life* (6 vols.), J. Johnson and Co., London, 1809–12.

Ellis, Amabel Williams, *Fairy Tales from the British Isles*, Blackie and Sons, Glasgow, 1960.

Eliot, George, 'Janet's Repentance', *Scenes of Clerical Life*, Penguin, Harmondsworth, 1973.

Eliot, George, *The Mill on the Floss*, Penguin, Harmondsworth, 1979.

Eyles, Margaret Leonora, *The Woman in the Little House*, Grant Richards Ltd, London, 1922.

Erikson, Erik H., *Childhood and Society*, W.W. Norton and Co., New York, 1963.

Faderman, Lillian, *Surpassing the Love of Men*, William Morrow and Co., New York, 1981.

Farnie, H.B., *A Story of Child Life Fifty Years Ago* (2nd ed.), Edinburgh, 1863.

Fernandez, James W., 'The Mission of Metaphor in Expressive Culture', *Current Anthropology*, 15:2 (June 1974), pp. 119–33.

Fernandez, James W., 'Persuasions and Performances: of the Best in Every Body . . . and the Metaphors of Everyman', in (ed.) *Myth, Symbol and Culture*, W.W. Norton and Co., New York 1971.

Firestone, Shulamith, *The Dialectic of Sex*, The Women's Press, London, 1979.

Foley, Winifred, *A Child in the Forest*, BBC, London, 1973.

Ford, Boris, 'The Emancipation of Teacher Training', Universities Quarterly, 29 (Winter 1974), pp. 7–43.

Fraser, Morris, *Children in Conflict*, Penguin, Harmondsworth, 1974.

Freire, Paulo, *Pedagogy of the Oppressed*, Penguin, Harmondsworth, 1972.

Freud, Sigmund, 'Creative Writers and Daydreaming' (1908), *Standard Edition of the Complete Works*, Hogarth Press, London, 1959, vol. ix, pp. 143–53.

Freud, Sigmund, 'On the Sexual Theories of Children' (1908), *Standard Edition*, Hogarth Press, London, 1959, vol. ix, pp. 209–26.

Freud, Sigmund, 'Family Romances' (1909), *Standard Edition*, Hogarth Press, London, 1959, vol. ix, pp. 237–41.

Freud, Sigmund, 'Little Hans' (1909), *Standard Edition*, Hogarth Press, London, 1959, vol. x, pp. 5–147.

Freud, Sigmund, 'Symbolism in Dreams' (1916), *Standard Edition*, Hogarth Press, London, 1963, vol. xv, pp. 149–69.

Fuller, Peter, 'Pictorial Essay: Uncovering Childhood' in (ed.) Martin Hoyles, *Changing Childhood*, Writers and Readers, London, 1979.

Garvey, Catherine, 'Play with Language and Speech', in (eds.) Susan Ervin Tripp and Claudia Mitchell Kernan, *Child Discourse*, Academic Press, New York, 1977.

Garvey, Catherine, *Play*, Harvard University Press, Cambridge, Massachusetts, 1977.

Gaskell, Elizabeth Cleghorn, *My Diary*, (ed.) Clement Shorter, privately printed, 1923.

Gaskell, Elizabeth Cleghorn, *North and South*, Penguin, Harmondsworth, 1970.

Gattegno, Jean, *Lewis Carroll*, Crowell, New York, 1976.

Gauldie, Enid, *Cruel Habitations*, George Allen and Unwin, London, 1974.

Gegeo, Karen Ann Watson and Boggs, Stephen T., 'From Verbal Play to Talk Story: The Role Routines in Speech Events among Hawaiian Children', in (ed.) Susan Ervin-Tripp and Claudia Mitchell Kernan, *Child Discourse*, Academic Press, New York, 1977.

Gilbert, Sandra M. and Gubar, Susan, *The Madwoman in the Attic*, Yale University Press, New Haven and London, 1979.

Gimblett, Barbara Kirshenblatt, *Speech Play*, University of Pennsylvania Press, 1976.

Glastonbury, Marion, 'The Best Kept Secret: How Working Class Women Live and What They Know', *Women's Studies International Quarterly*, 2 (1979), pp. 171–81.

Goddard, Nora, *Literacy: Language Experience Approaches*, Macmillan, London, 1974.

Golub, Lester S., *Linguistic Structures and Deviations in Children's Written Sentences*, Center for Cognitive Learning, University of Wisconsin, 1970.

Goody, Jack, (ed.), *Literacy in Traditional Societies*, Cambridge University Press, Cambridge, 1968.

Goody, Jack, *Domestication of the Savage Mind*, Cambridge University Press, Cambridge, 1977.

Gray, Kathie, *Kathie's Diary: Leaves from an Old Old Diary*, Doran, New York, 1926.

Grey, Pamela, (Lady Grey of Fallodon), *The Sayings of the Children, Written Down by Their Mother*, Stokes and Co., New York, 1924.

Halliday, M.K., *Learning How to Mean*, Edward Arnold, London, 1975.

Bibliography

Halliday, M.K., ' "Breakthrough to Literacy": Foreward to the American Edition' in *Language as Social Semiotic*, Edward Arnold, London, 1978.

Halliday, M.K., 'The Significance of Bernstein's Work for Sociolinguistic Theory', in *Language as Social Semiotic*, Edward Arnold, London, 1978.

Halsey, A.H. (ed.), *Educational Priority* (5 vols.), HMSO, London, 1972–4.

Handel, Gerald *et al.*, *Workingman's Wife*, Oceana Publications, New York, 1959.

Harriss, Mary Virginia, *Blue Beads and Amber*, with an Introduction by William Kavanagh Doty, The Norman Remington Co., Baltimore, 1923.

Hearnshaw, L.S., *Cyril Burt, Psychologist*, Random House, New York, 1981.

Henry, Jules, *Essays on Education*, Penguin, Harmondsworth, 1971.

Herndon, James, *The Way Things Spozed to Be*, Simon and Shuster, New York, 1968.

Hill, Octavia, *Homes of the London Poor*, Macmillan, London, 1875.

Hobbs, May, *Born to Struggle*, Quartet Books, London, 1973.

Hoggart, Richard, *The Uses of Literacy*, Chatto and Windus, London, 1957.

Holliday, Laurel, *Heart Songs: The Intimate Diaries of Young Girls*, Bluestocking Press, Berkeley, California, 1978.

Holman, H., 'The Rev. Henry Wolton: A Pioneer in Child Study', *Child Study*, 8:7 (November 1915), pp. 127–33; 8:8 (December 1915), pp. 143–56); 9:1 (February 1916), pp. 13–17; 9:2 (March 1916) pp. 29–32.

Holt, John, *How Children Fail*, Penguin, Harmondsworth, 1967.

Holt, John, *The Underachieving School*, Penguin, Harmondsworth, 1971.

Horney, Karen, *The Adolescent Diaries of Karen Horney*, Basic Books, New York, 1980.

Hughes, Richard, *A High Wind in Jamaica*, Triad Granada, London, 1977.

Humphries, Jane, 'Class struggle and the Persistence of the Working Class Family', *Cambridge Journal of Economics*, 1 (1977), pp. 255–6.

Hunt, David, *Parents and Children in History*, Basic Books, New York, 1970.

Hurt, J.S., *Elementary Schooling and the Working Classes, 1860–1918*, Routledge and Kegan Paul, London, 1979.

Jackson, Philip, *Life in Classrooms*, Holt Rinehart and Winston, New York, 1968.

Jacobs, Joseph, *English Fairy Tales*, The Bodley Head, London, 1968.

James, Clive, *Visions Before Midnight*, Picador, London, 1981.

James, William, 'The Consciousness of Self', in *Principles of Psychology*, Henry Holt and Co., New York, 1890, vol. i.

Jensen, Arthur, 'Social Class and Verbal Learning', in Deutch *et al.* (eds.) *Social Class and Psychological Development*, Holt, Rhinehart and Winston, New York, 1968.

Jasper, A.L., *A Hoxton Childhood*, Barrie and Rockliff, London, 1969.

Jones, Richard M., *Fantasy and Feeling in Education*, Penguin, Harmondsworth, 1972.

Kamin, Leon J., *The Science and Politics of IQ*, Penguin, Harmondsworth, 1977.

Kerr, James, *The Fundamentals of School Health*, George Allen and Unwin, London, 1926.

Kessen, William, *The Child*, John Wiley and Sons, New York, 1965.

King, Clive, *Stig of the Dump*, Penguin, Harmondsworth, 1963.

Kohl, Herb, *Thirty-Six Children*, Penguin, Harmondsworth, 1971.

Kohn, M.L., 'Social Class and Parent–Child Relationships', in (ed.) Michael Anderson, *Sociology of the Family*, Penguin, Harmondsworth, 1971, pp. 323–38.

Kozol, Jonathan, *Death at an Early Age*, Houghton Mifflin, Boston, 1967.

Kozol, Jonathan, *Children of the Revolution*, Delacorte Press, New York, 1978.

Kupferberg, Tuli and Topp, Sylvia, *A Big Bibliography: Children as Authors*, Birth Press, New York, 1959.

Labov, William, 'The Logic of Non-Standard English', in *Language in Education*, Routledge and Kegan Paul, London, 1972.

Labov, William, *Language in the Inner City*, University of Pennsylvania Press, Philadelphia, 1972.

Lacan, Jacques, 'The Mirror Phase as Formation of the Function of the "I" ', *New Left Review* 51, (1968) pp. 63–7.

Laing, R.D., *Conversations with Children*, Allen Lane, London, 1978.

Lakoff, Robin, *Language and Women's Place*, Harper and Row, New York, 1975.

Lawrence, D.H., *Sons and Lovers*, Penguin, Harmondsworth, 1980.

Lee, Ann, 'Together We Learn to Read and Write: Sexism and Literacy', in (eds.) Dale Spender and Elizabeth Sarah, *Learning to Lose: Sexism and Education*, The Women's Press, London, 1980, pp. 121–7.

Levinstein, S., 'Children's Stories', *The Paidologist*, 5:1 (February 1903), pp. 14–20.

Luling, Elizabeth, *Do Not Disturb*, with an Introduction by Sylvia Thompson, Oxford University Press, New York, 1937.

Lurie, Alison, *Clever Gretchen and Other Forgotten Folktales*, Thomas Y. Crowell, New York, 1980.

McMillan, Margaret, *The Child and the State*, National Labour Press, Manchester, 1911.

McNeill, David, *The Acquisition of Language*, Harper and Row, New York, 1970.

McNeely, Sylvia, *Diary of Sylvia McNeely*, Longmans, Green and Co., New York, 1931.

Marshall, Sybil, *Experiment in Education*, Cambridge University Press, Cambridge, 1963.

Martyna, Wendy, 'Beyond the "He/Man" Approach: the Case for Nonsexist Language', *Signs*, 5:3 (Spring 1980), pp. 482–93.

Mayhew, Henry, *London Labour and the London Poor* (4 vols.), vol. i, George Woodfall and Son, London, 1851; vol. 2, Griffin Bohn and Co., London, 1861.

McCrindle, Jean and Rowbotham, Sheila, *Dutiful Daughters*, Penguin, Harmondsworth, 1970.

Medelievich, Elias, *Children at Work*, International Labour Office, Geneva, 1979.

Miller, George A., *Psychology: The Science of Mental Life*, Harper and Row, New York, 1962.

Millett, Kate, *Sexual Politics*, Virago Press, London, 1977.

Millett, Kate, *The Basement: Meditations on a Human Sacrifice*, Simon and Shuster, New York, 1979.

Moers, Ellen, *Literary Women*, The Women's Press, London, 1978.

Montessori, Maria, *The Formation of Man*, Theosophical Publishing House, Adyar, India, 1969.

Muirhead, J.H., 'The Founders of Child Study in England', *Paidologist*, 2:2 (July 1900), pp. 114–24.

Neff, Wanda Fraiken, *Victorian Working Women*, Columbia University Press, New York, 1929.

Newberry, Julia Rose, *Julia Newberry's Diary*, with an Introduction by Margaret Ayer Barns and Janet Ayer Fairbank, W.W. Norton and Co., New York, 1933.

Newson, John and Elizabeth, *Patterns of Infant Care*, Penguin, Harmondsworth, 1976.

Newson, John and Elizabeth, *Four Years Old in an Urban Community*, George Allen and Unwin, London, 1968.

Newson, John and Elizabeth, *Seven Years Old in the Home Environment*, George Allen and Unwin, London, 1976.

Newson, John and Elizabeth, *Perspectives on School at Seven Years*, George Allen and Unwin, London, 1977.

Nin, Anaïs, *Lintotte: The Early Diary of Anaïs Nin, 1914–1920*, Harcourt Brace Jovanovich, New York, 1978.

Oakley, Ann, *Housewife*, Allen Lane, Penguin, London, 1974.

Bibliography

Oakley, Ann, *The Sociology of Housework*, Martin Robertson, London, 1974.

Oakley, Ann, *Women Confined: Towards a Sociology of Childbirth,* Martin Robertson, London, 1980.

Oakley, Ann, *From Here to Maternity: Becoming a Mother*, Penguin, Harmondsworth, 1981.

O'Brien, Margaret, *My Diary*, with a Foreword by Lionel Barrymore, J.B. Lippincott, New York, 1947.

Ochs, Elinor and Schieffelin, Bambi S., *Development Pragmatics*, Academic Press, New York, 1979.

Ochs, Elinor, 'Transcription as Theory' in Ochs and Schieffelin, *Developmental Pragmatics*.

Ochs, Elinor, 'What Child Language Can Contribute to Pragmatics', in Ochs and Schieffelin, *Developmental Pragmatics*.

Olson, David R., 'From Utterance to Text: The Bias of Language in Speech and Writing', *Harvard Educational Review*, 47:3 (August 1977), pp. 257–81.

Opie, Iona and Peter, *Children's Games in Street and Playground*, Oxford University Press, London, 1969.

Ouvry, Elinor S. (ed.), *Extracts from Octavia Hill's Letters to Fellow Workers, 1864–1911*, Adelphi Bookshop, London, 1933.

Ovenden, Graham and Melville, Robert, *Victorian Children*, Academy Editions, London, 1972.

Parkhurst, Helen, *Education on the Dalton Plan*, G. Bell and Sons, London, 1922.

Parr, Joy, *Labouring Children*, Croom Helm, London, 1980.

Paul, Eden and Cedar (eds.), *A Young Girl's Diary*, prefaced with a letter by Sigmund Freud, George Allen and Unwin, London, 1921.

Paterson, Alexander, *Across the Bridges*, Edward Arnold, London, 1914.

Paxon, Mary, *Her Book, 1880–1884*, with an Introduction by Agnes Sligh Turnbull, Doubleday Doran and Co., New York, 1936.

Peabody, E.P., *Record of a School*, Roberts Bros, Boston, 1874.

Phelps, Ethel Johnson, *The Maid of the North: Feminist Folktales from Around the World*, Holt, Rhinehart and Winston, New York, 1981.

Piaget, Jean, *The Language and Thought of the Child*, Kegan Paul, Trench and Trubner, London, 1926.

Piaget, Jean, *The Child's Conception of the World*, Kegan Paul, Trench and Trubner, London, 1929.

Piaget, Jean, 'Jean Piaget', in (ed.) E.G. Boring, *A History of Psychology in Autobiography*, Clark University Press, Worcester, Massachusetts, 1952, vol. iv, pp. 237–56.

Pinchbeck, Ivy, and Hewitt, Margaret, *Children in English Society* (2 vols.), Routledge and Kegan Paul, London, 1969, 1973.

Pinchbeck, Ivy, *Women Workers and the Industrial Revolution*, Virago Press, London, 1981.

Pitcher, E.G. and Prelinger, Ernest, *Children Tell Stories: An Analysis of Fantasy*, International Universities Press, New York, 1963.

Place, Francis, *The Autobiography of Francis Place, 1771–1854*, (ed.) Mary Thale, Cambridge University Press, Cambridge, 1972.

Poster, Mark, *Critical Theory of the Family*, The Seabury Press, New York, 1978.

Pringle, Mia Kelmer, *The Needs of Children*, Hutchinson, London, 1975.

Radcliffe, Ann, *Mysteries of Udolpho* (4 vols.), London, 1794.

Rasmussen, Vilhelm, *Diary of a Child's Life*, Gyldedal, London, 1931.

Raverat, Gwen, *Period Piece*, W.W. Norton and Co., New York, 1953.

Read, Charles, 'Pre-School Children's Knowledge of English Phonology', *Harvard Educational Review*, 41:1 (February 1971), pp. 1–34.

Read, Thomas, *Works* (ed. G.N Wright) (4 vols.), Edinburgh, 1843, 1846.

Reid, Fred, *Keir Hardy: The Making of a Socialist*, Croom Helm, London, 1978.

Reid, Jessie, 'Learning to Think About Reading', *Educational Research*, 9 (1966), pp. 56–62.

Reid, Jessie, *Breakthrough in Action*, Longmans, London, 1974.

Rhys, Mimsy, *Mr Hermit Crab: A Tale for Children by a Child*, Macmillan, New York, 1929.

Rich, Adrienne, *Of Woman Born*, Virago Press, London, 1977.

Rich, Adrienne, *On Lies, Secrets and Silence*, Virago Press, London, 1979.

Roazen, Paul, *Freud and His Followers*, Alfred A. Knopf, New York, 1975.

Roberts, Robert, *Imprisoned Tongues*, Manchester University Press, Manchester, 1968.

Roberts, Robert, *The Classic Slum*, Manchester University Press, Manchester, 1971.

Rosen, Harold and Connie, *The Language of Primary School Children*, Penguin, Harmondsworth, 1973.

Rowe, Richard, *Life in the London Streets*, Nimmo and Bain, London, 1881.

Rubinstein, David, *Victorian Homes*, David and Charles, Newton Abbot, 1974.

Rush, Florence, *The Best Kept Secret*, Prentice Hall, New Jersey, 1980.

Sacks, Harvey, 'On the Analyzability of Stories by Children', in (eds.) John J. Gumpertz and Dell Hymes, *Directions in Sociolinguistics*, Holt, Rhinehart and Winston, New York, 1972.

Sanchez, Mary and Kirshenblatt-Gimblett, Barbara, 'Children's Traditional Speech Play and Child Language', in (ed.) Kirshenblatt-Gimblett, *Speech Play*, University of Pennsylvania Press, 1976.

Sanders, Ruth Manning, *Tripple-Trapple*, BBC, London, 1973.

Schultz, Thomas R., 'Development of the Acquisition of Riddles', *Child Development*, 45 (1974), pp. 100–5.

Sears, Clara Endicott, *Bronson Alcott's Fruitlands*, Houghton Mifflin, Cambridge, Massachusetts, 1915.

Sharp, Evelyn, *The London Child*, John Lane at the Bodley Head, London, 1927.

Shattuck, Roger, *The Forbidden Experiment*, Farrar Straus and Giroux, New York, 1980.

Shaughnessy, Mina P., *Errors and Expectations*, Oxford University Press, New York, 1977.

Shore, Margaret Emily, *Journal of Emily Shore*, Kegan Paul, London, 1891.

Shute, Henry, *The Real Diary of a Real Boy*, The Reilly and Britton Co., Chicago, 1917.

Sidgwick, Frank, *The Complete Marjory Fleming*, Sidgwick and Jackson, London, 1934.

Simon, Brian, *Intelligence, Psychology and Education*, Lawrence and Wishart, London, 1971.

Studies in the History of Education, Lawrence and Wishart, London, 1960, pp. 337–368.

Smith, Brian Sutton, 'The Importance of the Story Taker', *Urban Review*, 8:2 (Summer 1975), pp. 82–95.

Speier, Matthew, 'The Everyday World of the Child', in (ed.), Jack D. Douglas *Understanding Everyday Life*, University of California Press, San Diego, 1970, pp. 136–68.

Spender, Dale, *Man Made Language*, Routledge and Kegan Paul, London, 1980.

Stevenson, Margaret Isabella, *Stevenson's Baby Book*, printed for John Howell for John Henry Nash, San Francisco, 1922.

Stone, Maureen, *The Education of the Black Child in Britain: The Myth of Multi-racial Education*, Fontana, London, 1981.

Sully, James, *Studies of Childhood*, Longmans, Green and Co., London, 1896.

Taine, Hippolyte, *On Intelligence* (2 vols.), London, 1871.

Taine, Hippolyte, 'The Acquisition of Language in Children', *Mind*, 2:6 (April 1877), pp. 252–9.

Bibliography

Taplin, Gardner B., *The Life of Elizabeth Barrett Browning*, Yale University Press, New Haven, 1957.

Theroux, Phyllis, *California and Other States of Grace*, Fawcett Crest, New York, 1980.

Thompson, Thea, *Edwardian Childhoods*, Routledge and Kegan Paul, London, 1980.

Thwaite, Ann, *Waiting for the Party: The Life of Frances Hodgson Burnett*, Secker and Warburg, London, 1974.

Trimmer, Sarah, *Fabulous Histories*, T. Longman and Co., London, 1786.

Tripp, Susan Ervin and Kernan, Claudia Mitchell, *Child Discourse*, Academic Press, New York, 1977.

Tripp, Susan Ervin, 'Children's Sociolinguistic Competence', in Susan Ervin Tripp, *Language Acquisition and Communicative Choice*, Stanford University Press, Stanford, 1973, pp. 262–91.

Tropp, Asher, *The Schoolteachers*, Heinemann, London, 1957.

Twain, Mark, 'The Wonder Child', *Harper's Bazaar*, December 1909.

Vincent David (ed.), James Dawson Burns, *Autobiography of a Beggar Boy*, Europa, London, 1978.

Vygotsky, L.S., *Thought and Language*, MIT Press, Cambridge, Massachusetts, 1962.

Vygotsky, L.S., 'Play in Its Role in the Mental Development of the Child' and 'The Prehistory of Written Language', in *Mind in Society*, Harvard University Press, Cambridge, Massachusetts, 1978.

Walkerdine, Valerie, 'Sex, Power and Pedagogics', *Screen Education*, 38 (Spring 1981), pp. 14–24.

Walvin, James, *A Child's World: A Social History of English Childhood, 1800–1914*, Penguin, Harmondsworth, 1982.

Warner, Sylvia Ashton, *Spinster*, Virago, London, 1980.

Warner, Sylvia Ashton, *Teacher*, Virago, London, 1980.

Webb, Beatrice, *My Apprenticeship*, Penguin, London, 1971.

Weir, Ruth H., *Language in the Crib*, Mouton, The Hague, 1962.

Whistler, Theresa (ed.), *The Collected Poems of Mary Elizabeth Coleridge*, Rupert Hart Davis, London, 1954.

Whiteley, Opal, *The Diary of Opal Whiteley* (ed. Grey of Fallodon), Putnam, London, 1920.

Whiteley, Opal, *The Story of Opal: The Journal of an Understanding Heart*, Atlantic Monthly Press, Boston, 1920.

Whitt, J. Kenneth and Prentice, Norman M., 'Cognitive Processes in the Development of Children's Enjoyment and Comprehension of Joking Riddles', *Developmental Psychology*, 13:1, pp. 29–136.

Widdowson, Frances, *Going Up Into the Next Class: Women and Elementary Teacher Training, 1840–1914*, Women's Research and Resources Publications, London, 1980.

Wilson, Harriet and Herbert, G.W., *Parents and Children in the Inner City*, Routledge and Kegan Paul, London, 1978.

Wiltse, Sara E., 'Children's Autobiographies', *The Paidologist*, 1:3 (November 1899).

Winslow, Anna Green, *Diary of Anna Green Winslow*, (ed.) Alice Morse Earle, Houghton Mifflin, Cambridge, Massachusetts, 1894.

Wollstonecraft, Mary, *Mary: A Fiction and The Wrongs of Woman*, Oxford University Press, London, 1976.

Woodward, Kathleen, *Jipping Street*, Virago Press, London, 1983.

Woolf, Virginia, *To the Lighthouse*, Penguin, Harmondsworth, 1975.

Yeo, Eileen and Thompson, E.P., *The Unknown Mayhew*, Penguin, Harmondsworth, 1973.

Zigler, Edward *et al.*, 'Cognitive Challenge as a Factor in Children's Humour Appreciation', *Journal of Personality and Social Psychology*, 6:3 (1967), pp. 332–6.
Zigler, Edward and Valentine, Jeanette, *Project Headstart*, The Free Press, New York, 1979.

2 PRIMARY SOURCES

Armstrong Browning Library, Baylor University, Waco, Texas:
Elizabeth Barrett Browning Papers; three stories, M2–39, M2–50, M2–4; two letters, L3–1, L3–2.

Henry W. and Albert A. Berg Collection, New York Public Library, Astor, Lennox and Tilden Foundation:
Elizabeth Barrett Browning Collection; 'Sebastian, Or Virtue Rewarded', Holograph MS, 62B2763; 'The Way to Humble Pride', Holograph MS 65B2779.
Moulton Barrett Family Collection: 65B2406; 65B2407; 65B2411; 65B2401; 65B7734; 65B2735; ALS to Mary Graham Clarke Moulton Barrett, 65B10.

Cheshire Record Office:
Catherine Stanley of Alderley, 'Journal of Her Five Children, 1811–1819', DSA 75.

City of Bristol Museum and Art Gallery:
Ellen Sharples, Diaries, 1803–32.

Houghton Library, Harvard University, Cambridge, Massachusetts:
Alcott Papers; Anna Alcott, Journal, Family Letters, 1937–1856, vol. i, Domestic; 59M–305 (24).
Alcott Papers; Elizabeth Sewell Alcott, 'Elizabeth's Diary, 1846', Family Letters, 1837–50, Domestic; 59M305 (24).

Humanities Research Center, University of Texas at Austin:
Coleridge Collection; Florence Lind Coleridge, Diary, September 1874, MS in 1 notebook, 54pp.
Coleridge Collection, Diaries, 1870–79, MSS in 6 notebooks, 670pp.
Coleridge Collection, Sara Coleridge, 'Diary of Her Children's Early Years', 1830–38.

Pierpont Morgan Library, New York:
Elizabeth Barrett Browning Collection, Birthday Odes and Various Correspondence; Letters from Mrs Moulton to Elizabeth Barrett, 18 July 1809 or 1810; 6 March 1810 or 1811; four undated letters, 1817–18.

Nottinghamshire Record Office:
Mary Georgiana Wilkinson, Journal. 11 September – 12 October 1819, MSS DDW 170.

West Suffolk County Record Office:
Susanna Arethusa Cullam, Diaries, 1822–4, MSS E2/44.

West Sussex County Record Office:
Constance Emily Primrose, Diary, 1856, Petworth House Archives, MSS 1680.

Bibliography

Parliamentary Papers Series:

Children's Employment Commission (1862). First Report, PP 1863, xviii; Second Report, PP 1864, xxii; Third Report, PP 1864, xxii; Fourth Report, PP 1865, xx; Fifth Report, PP 1866, xxiv; Sixth Report, PP 1867, xvi.

Commission of Inquiry into the Employment of Women and Children in Agriculture (1867). First Report, PP 1867-8, xvii.

Report of the Select Committee on the Education of Destitute Children, PP 1861, vii.

INDEX

Adam, Helen Douglas, 68
Alcott, Abigail, 77
Alcott, Amos Bronson, 70, 73
Alcott, Anna, 73
Alcott, Louisa May, 77
Ashford, Daisy, 69, 82

Barrett, Elizabeth, 69, 76–7, 82, 148, 149, 153
Barrett, Mary Moulton, 77
Berger, John, 30
Bernstein, Basil, 153
Bettleheim, Bruno, 141
Buxton, Ellen, 69

children: characteristics of central child figure Carl, 32–4; child labour in nineteenth century, 114–15, 120–25; child psychology and interpretation of children's works, 111; cross-cultural comparisons of growth and development in childhood, 35; economic basis of feelings and affections of nineteenth century children, 125; foundations of child psychology, 87–8; nineteenth century cult of the child, 62; nineteenth century observation of child development, 85–7; two theories of child-rearing presented in 'The Tidy House', 32; work on children's acquisition of sexual stereotypes in spoken language, 139–40; *see also* girls; language, children's; writing, children's
Children's Employment Commission 1862, 114, 115, 118
Chodorow, Nancy, 143
Chomsky, Carol, 89
class attitudes: differences underlined by mental testing, 5–6; in primary schools, 3, 5; *see also* working-class
Coleridge, Florence Lind, 72, 74, 76
Coleridge, Mary Elizabeth, 72, 73–5, 76, 152
Coleridge, Sara, 85, 86–7
Conversations with Children (Laing), 68
Cullam, Arethusa, 73

Darwin, Charles, 86
de la Mare, Walter, 79
Diary of Anna Green Winslow, 69
diary-writing, 69–70, 72–5
Drabble, Margaret, 2
Dworkin, Andrea, 4

education, domestic: evidence of provided by girls' diaries, 69, 78; story-writing rarely encouraged,

259

difficulties in written language, 27; assessment of information provided by outside world, 74–5; cannot be equated with adult writing, 30; children's use of their narrative in 'The Tidy House', 37–40; content of nineteenth century little girls' writing, 72–5; as demonstration of children's involvement in their own socialization, 12; diary-writing, 69–70, 72–5, 99–100; editing of children's work, 28–9; folk-fairy-tale as model for, 104–6; girls and boys and, 135–7; influence of literature on, 11; influence of reading methods on, 91–2; as insight into pattern of life, 111; invented spelling strategies, 70–71; manipulation and re-ordering of social and emotional experiences in written language, 76, 83–4; as method of dealing with systems of social meanings, 98–9; modern reactions to, 82–4; pattern of presentation of children's texts to the public, 67; as product of social circumstances, 61–2; relation to imaginative play, 28; tension between form and content, 93–4; three waves in publication of, 63–4; use of children's texts to adults, 67–9; *see also* 'Tidy House, The'

Young Girl's Diary, A (Hug-Hellmuth), 63–4, 70

Young Visiters, The (Ashford), 69, 82

If you would like to know more about Virago books, write to us at Ely House, 37 Dover Street, London W1X 4HS for a full catalogue.

Please send a stamped addressed envelope

Book Tokens

Give them
the pleasure of choosing
Book Tokens can be bought
and exchanged at most
bookshops.